BOOKS BY TRUMAN CAPOTE

Three by Truman Capote

Three by Truman Capote

Other Voices, Other Rooms
Breakfast at Tiffany's
Music for Chameleons

Truman Capote

Random House   New York

Library of Congress Cataloging in Publication Data

Capote, Truman, 1924–1984
Three by Truman Capote.

Contents: Other voices, other rooms—Breakfast at
Tiffany's—Music for chameleons.
I. Title.
PS3505.A59A6   1985   813'.54   84–42999
ISBN 0-394-54513-3

Contents

Other Voices, Other Rooms

*The heart is deceitful
above all things, and
desperately wicked.
Who can know it?*

JEREMIAH 17:9

For Newton Arvin

Preface

Other Voices, Other Rooms (my own title: it is not a quotation) was published in January 1948. It took two years to write and was not my first novel, but the second. The first, a manuscript never submitted and now lost, was called *Summer Crossing*—a spare, objective story with a New York setting. Not bad, as I remember: technically accomplished, an interesting enough tale, but without intensity or pain, without the qualities of a private vision, the anxieties that then had control of my emotions and imagination. *Other Voices, Other Rooms* was an attempt to exorcise demons: an unconscious, altogether intuitive attempt, for I was not aware, except for a few incidents and descriptions, of its being in any serious degree autobiographical. Rereading it now, I find such self-deception unpardonable.

Surely there were reasons for this adamant ignorance, no doubt protective ones: a fire curtain between the writer and the true source of his material. As I have lost contact with the troubled youth who wrote this book, since only a faded shadow of him is any longer contained inside myself, it is difficult to reconstruct his state of mind. However, I shall try.

At the time of the appearance of *Other Voices, Other Rooms*, critics, ranging from the warmest to the most hostile, remarked that obviously I was much influenced by such Southern literary artists as Faulkner and Welty and McCullers, three writers whose work I knew well and admired. Nevertheless, the gentlemen were mistaken, though understandably. The American writers who had been most valuable to me were, in no particular order, James, Twain,

Poe, Cather, Hawthorne, Sarah Orne Jewett; and, overseas, Flaubert, Jane Austen, Dickens, Proust, Chekhov, Katherine Mansfield, E. M. Forster, Turgenev, De Maupassant and Emily Brontë. A collection more or less irrelevant to *Other Voices, Other Rooms;* for clearly no one of these writers, with the conceivable exception of Poe (who was by then a blurred childhood enthusiasm, like Dickens and Twain), was a necessary antecedent to this particular work. Rather, they *all* were, in the sense that each of them had contributed to my literary intelligence, such as it was. But the real progenitor was my difficult, subterranean self. The result was both a revelation and an escape: the book set me free, and, as in its prophetic final sentence, I stood there and looked back at the boy I had left behind.

I was born in New Orleans, an only child; my parents were divorced when I was four years old. It was a complicated divorce with much bitterness on either side, which is the main reason why I spent most of my childhood wandering among the homes of relatives in Louisiana, Mississippi and rural Alabama (off and on, I attended schools in New York City and Connecticut). The reading I did on my own was of greater importance than my official education, which was a waste and ended when I was seventeen, the age at which I applied for and received a job at *The New Yorker* magazine. Not a very grand job, for all it really involved was sorting cartoons and clipping newspapers. Still, I was fortunate to have it, especially since I was determined never to set a studious foot inside a college classroom. I felt that either one was or wasn't a writer, and no combination of professors could influence the outcome. I still think I was correct, at least in my own case; however, I now realize that most young writers have more to gain than not by attending college, if only because their teachers and classroom comrades provide a captive audience for their work; nothing is lonelier than to be an aspiring artist without some semblance of a sounding board.

I stayed two years at *The New Yorker,* and during this period published a number of short stories in small literary magazines. (Several of them were submitted to my employers, and none accepted, though once one was returned with the following comment: "Very good. But romantic in a way this magazine is not.") Also, I wrote *Summer Crossing.* Actually, it was in order to complete the book that I took courage, quit my job, left New York and settled with relatives, a cotton-growing family who lived in a remote part of Alabama: cotton fields, cattle pastures, pinewoods, dirt roads, creeks and slow little rivers, jaybirds, owls, buzzards circling in empty skies, distant train whistles —and, five miles away, a small country town: the Noon City of the present volume.

It was early winter when I arrived there, and the atmosphere of the roomy farmhouse, entirely heated by stoves and fireplaces, was well suited to a fledgling novelist wanting quiet isolation. The household rose at four-thirty, breakfasted by electric light, and was off about its business as the sun ascended—leaving me alone and, increasingly, in a panic. For, more and more, *Summer Crossing* seemed to me thin, clever, unfelt. Another language, a secret spiritual geography, was burgeoning inside me, taking hold of my night-dream hours as well as my wakeful daydreams.

One frosty December afternoon I was far from home, walking in a forest along the bank of a mysterious, deep, very clear creek, a route that led eventually to a place called Hatter's Mill. The mill, which straddled the creek, had been abandoned long ago; it was a place where farmers had brought their corn to be ground into cornmeal. As a child, I'd often gone there with cousins to fish and swim; it was while exploring under the mill that I'd been bitten in the knee by a cotton-mouth moccasin—precisely as happens to Joel Knox. And now as I came upon the forlorn mill with its sagging silver-grey timbers, the remembered shock of the snakebite returned; and other memories too—of Idabel, or rather the girl who was the counterpart of Idabel, and how we used to wade and swim in the pure waters, where fat speckled fish lolled in sunlit pools; Idabel was always trying to reach out and grab one.

Excitement—a variety of creative coma—overcame me. Walking home, I lost my way and moved in circles round the woods, for my mind was reeling with the whole book. Usually when a story comes to me, it arrives, or seems to, *in toto:* a long sustained streak of lightning that darkens the tangible, so-called real world, and leaves illuminated only this suddenly seen pseudo-imaginary landscape, a terrain alive with figures, voices, rooms, atmospheres, weather. And all of it, at birth, is like an angry, wrathful tiger cub; one must soothe and tame it. Which, of course, is an artist's principal task: to tame and shape the raw creative vision.

It was dark when I got home, and cold, but I didn't feel the cold because of the fire inside me. My Aunt Lucille said she had been worried about me, and was disappointed because I didn't want any supper. She wanted to know if I was sick; I said no. She said, "Well, you *look* sick. You're white as a ghost." I said good night, locked myself in my room, tossed the manuscript of *Summer Crossing* into a bottom bureau drawer, collected several sharp pencils and a fresh pad of yellow lined paper, got into bed fully clothed, and with pathetic optimism, wrote: "*Other Voices, Other Rooms*—a novel by Truman Capote." Then: "Now a traveller must make his way to Noon City by the best means he can . . ."

It is unusual, but occasionally it happens to almost every writer that the writing of some particular story seems outer-willed and effortless; it is as though one were a secretary transcribing the words of a voice from a cloud. The difficulty is maintaining contact with this spectral dictator. Eventually it developed that communication ran highest at night, as fevers are known to do after dusk. So I took to working all night and sleeping all day, a routine that distressed the household and caused constant disapproving comment: "But you've got everything turned upside down. You're ruining your health." That is why, in the spring of the year, I thanked my exasperated relatives for their generosity, their burdened patience, and bought a ticket on a Greyhound bus to New Orleans.

There I rented a bedroom in the crowded apartment of a Creole family who lived in the French Quarter on Royal Street. It was a small hot bedroom almost entirely occupied by a brass bed, and it was noisy as a steel mill. Streetcars racketed under the window, and the carousings of sightseers touring the Quarter, the boisterous whiskey brawlings of soldiers and sailors made for continuous pandemonium. Still, sticking to my night schedule, I progressed; by late autumn the book was half finished.

I need not have been as lonely as I was. New Orleans was my hometown and I had many friends there, but because I did not desire that familiar world and preferred to remain sealed off in the self-created universe of Zoo and Jesus Fever and the Cloud Hotel, I called none of my acquaintances. My only company was the Creole family, who were kindly working-class people (the father was a dock hand and his wife a seamstress), or encounters with drugstore clerks and café folk. Curiously, for New Orleans is not that sizable a town, I never saw a soul I knew. Except, by accident, my father. Which was ironic, considering that though I was unaware of it at the time, the central theme of *Other Voices, Other Rooms* was my search for the existence of this essentially imaginary person.

I seldom ate more than once a day, usually when I finished work. At that dawn hour I would walk through the humid, balconied streets, past St. Louis Cathedral and on to the French Market, a square crammed in the murky early morning with the trucks of vegetable farmers, Gulf Coast fishermen, meat vendors and flower growers. It smelled of earth, of herbs and exotic, gingery scents, and it rang, clanged, clogged the ears with the sounds of vivacious trading. I loved it.

The market's chief gathering place was a café that served only bitter-black chicory coffee and the crustiest, most delicious fresh-fried doughnuts. I had discovered the place when I was fifteen, and had become addicted. The proprietor of the café gave all its habitués a nickname; he called me the Jockey, a reference to my height and build. Every morning as I plowed into the coffee and the doughnuts, he would warn me with a sinister chuckle, "Better watch it, Jockey. You'll never make your weight."

It was in this café that five years earlier I'd met the prototype of Cousin Randolph. Actually, Cousin Randolph was suggested by two people. Once, when I was a very young child, I had spent a few summer weeks in an old house in Pass Christian, Mississippi. I don't remember much about it, except that there was an elderly man who lived there, an asthmatic invalid who smoked medicinal cigarettes and made remarkable scrapquilts. He had been the captain of a fishing trawler, but illness had forced him to retire to a darkened room. His sister had taught him to sew; in consequence, he had found in himself a beautiful gift for designing cloth pictures. I often used to visit his room, where he would spread his tapestry-like quilts on the floor for me to admire: rose bouquets, ships in full sail, a bowl of apples.

The other Randolph, the character's spiritual ancestor, was the man I met in the café, a plump blond fellow who was said to be dying of leukemia. The proprietor called him the Sketcher, for he always sat alone in a corner drawing pictures of the clientele, the truckers and cattlemen, in a large loose-leaf notebook. One night it was obvious that I was his subject; after sketching for a while, he moseyed over to the counter where I was sitting and said, "You're a *Wunderkind,* aren't you? I can tell by your hands." I didn't know what it meant—*Wunderkind;* I thought that either he was joking or making a dubious overture. But then he defined the word, and I was pleased: it coincided with my own private opinion. We became friends; afterwards I saw him not only at the café, but we also took lazy strolls along the levee. We did not have much conversation, for he was a monologist obsessed with death, betrayed passions and unfulfilled talent.

All this transpired during one summer. That autumn I went to school in the East, and when I returned in June and asked the proprietor about the Sketcher, he said, "Oh, he died. Saw it in the *Picayune.* Did you know he was rich? Uh huh. Said so in the paper. Turned out his family owned half the land around Lake Pontchartrain. Imagine that. Well, you never know."

The book was completed in a setting far removed from the one in which it was begun. I wandered and worked in North Carolina, Saratoga Springs, New York City and, ultimately, in a rented cottage on Nantucket. It was there, at a desk by a window with a view of sky and sand and arriving surf, that I wrote the last pages, finishing them with disbelief that the moment had come, a wonder simultaneously regretful and exhilarated.

I am not a keen rereader of my own books: what's done is done. Moreover, I am always afraid of finding that my harsher detractors are correct and that the work is not as good as I choose to think it. Until the subject of the present reissue arose, I never again really examined *Other Voices, Other Rooms.* Last week I read it straight through.

And? And, as I have already indicated, I was startled by its symbolic subterfuges. Also, while there are passages that seem to me accomplishments, others arouse uneasiness. On the whole, though, it was as if I were reading the fresh-minted manuscript of a total stranger. I was impressed by him. For what he had done has the enigmatic shine of a strangely colored prism held to the light—that, and a certain anguished, pleading intensity like the message of a shipwrecked sailor stuffed into a bottle and thrown into the sea.

T.C.

One

One

Now a traveler must make his way to Noon City by the best means he can, for there are no buses or trains heading in that direction, though six days a week a truck from the Chuberry Turpentine Company collects mail and supplies in the next-door town of Paradise Chapel: occasionally a person bound for Noon City can catch a ride with the driver of the truck, Sam Radclif. It's a rough trip no matter how you come, for these washboard roads will loosen up even brandnew cars pretty fast; and hitchhikers always find the going bad. Also, this is lonesome country; and here in the swamplike hollows where tiger lilies bloom the size of a man's head, there are luminous green logs that shine under the dark marsh water like drowned corpses; often the only movement on the landscape is winter smoke winding out the chimney of some sorry-looking farmhouse, or a wing-stiffened bird, silent and arrow-eyed, circling over the black deserted pinewoods.

Two roads pass over the hinterlands into Noon City; one from the north, another from the south; the latter, known as the Paradise Chapel Highway, is the better of the pair, though both are much the same: desolate miles of swamp and field and forest stretch along either route, unbroken except for scattered signs advertising Red Dot 5¢ Cigars, Dr. Pepper, NEHI, Grove's Chill Tonic, and 666. Wooden bridges spanning brackish creeks named for long-gone Indian tribes rumble like far-off thunder under a passing wheel; herds of hogs and cows roam the roads at will; now and then a farm-family pauses from work to wave as an auto whizzes by, and watch sadly till it disappears in red dust.

One sizzling day in early June the Turpentine Company's driver, Sam Radclif, a big balding six-footer with a rough, manly face, was gulping a beer at the Morning Star Café in Paradise Chapel when the proprietor came over with his arm around this stranger-boy.

"Hiya, Sam," said the proprietor, a fellow called Sydney Katz. "Got a kid here that'd be obliged if you could give him a ride to Noon City. Been trying to get there since yesterday. Think you can help?"

Radclif eyed the boy over the rim of his beer glass, not caring much for the looks of him. He had his notions of what a "real" boy should look like, and this kid somehow offended them. He was too pretty, too delicate and fair-skinned; each of his features was shaped with a sensitive accuracy, and a girlish tenderness softened his eyes, which were brown and very large. His brown hair, cut short, was streaked with pure yellow strands. A kind of tired, imploring expression masked his thin face, and there was an unyouthful sag about his shoulders. He wore long, wrinkled white linen breeches, a limp blue shirt, the collar of which was open at the throat, and rather scuffed tan shoes.

Wiping a mustache of foam off his upper lips, Radclif said: "What's you name, son?"

"Joel. Jo-el Har-ri-son Knox." He separated the syllables explicitly, as though he thought the driver deaf, but his voice was uncommonly soft.

"That so?" drawled Radclif, placing his dry beer glass on the counter. "A mighty fancy name, Mister Knox."

The boy blushed and turned to the proprietor, who promptly intervened: "This is a fine boy, Sam. Smart as a whip. Knows words you and me never heard of."

Radclif was annoyed. "Here, Katz," he ordered, "fillerup." After the proprietor trundled away to fetch a second beer, Sam said kindly, "Didn't mean to tease you, son. Where bouts you from?"

"New Orleans," he said. "I left there Thursday and got here Friday . . . and that was as far as I could go; no one come to meet me."

"Oh, yeah," said Radclif. "Visiting folks in Noon City?"

The boy nodded. "My father. I'm going to live with him."

Radclif raised his eyes ceilingward, mumbled "Knox" several times, then shook his head in a baffled manner. "Nope, don't think I know anybody by that name. Sure you're in the right place?"

"Oh, yes," said the boy without alarm. "Ask Mister Katz, he's heard about my father, and I showed him the letters and . . . wait." He hurried back among the tables of the gloomy café, and returned toting a huge tin suitcase that, judging by his grimace, was extremely heavy. The suitcase was colorful with faded souvenir stickers from remote parts of the globe: Paris, Cairo, Venice, Vienna, Naples, Hamburg, Bombay, and so forth. It was an odd thing to see on a hot day in a town the size of Paradise Chapel.

"You been all them places?" asked Radclif.

"No-o-o," said the boy, struggling to undo a wornout leather strap which held the suitcase together. "It belonged to my grandfather; that was Major Knox: you've read about him in history books, I guess. He was a prominent figure in the Civil War. Anyway, this is the valise he used on his wedding trip around the world."

"Round the world, eh?" said Radclif, impressed. "Musta been a mighty rich man."

"Well, that was a long time ago." He rummaged through his neatly packed possessions till he found a slim package of letters. "Here it is," he said, selecting one in a watergreen envelope.

Radclif fingered the letter a moment before opening it; but presently, with clumsy care, he extracted a green sheet of tissue-like paper and, moving his lips, read:

> Edw. R. Sansom, Esq.
> Skully's Landing
> May 18, 19–

My dear Ellen Kendall,
  I am in your debt for answering my letter so quickly; indeed, by return post. Yes, hearing from me after twelve years must have seemed strange, but I can assure you sufficient reason prompted this long silence. However, reading in the *Times-Picayune,* to the Sunday issue of which we subscribe, of my late wife's passing, may God the Almighty rest her gentle soul, I at once reasoned the honorable thing could only be to again assume my paternal duties, forsaken, lo, these many years. Both the present Mrs Sansom and myself are happy (nay, overjoyed!) to learn you are willing to concede our desire, though, as you remark, your heart will break in doing so. Ah, how well I sympathize with the sorrow such a sacrifice may bring, having experienced similar emotions when, after that final dreadful affair, I was forced to take leave of my only child, whom I treasured, while he was still no more than an infant. But that is all of the lost past. Rest assured, good lady, we here at the Landing have a beautiful home, healthful food, and a cultured atmosphere with which to provide my son.
  As to the journey: we are anxious Joel reach here no later than June First. Now when he leaves New Orleans he should travel via train to Biloxi, at which point he must disembark and purchase a bus ticket for Paradise Chapel, a town some twenty miles south of Noon City. We have at present no mechanical vehicle; therefore, I suggest he remain overnight in P.C. where rooms are let above the Morning Star Café, until appropriate arrangements can be made. Enclosed please find a cheque covering such expenses as all this may incur.

> Yrs. Respct.
> Edw. R. Sansom

The proprietor arrived with the beer just as Radclif, frowning puzzledly, sighed and tucked the paper back in its envelope. There were two things about this letter that bothered him; first of all, the handwriting: penned in ink the rusty color of dried blood, it was a maze of curlicues and dainty i's dotted with daintier o's. What the hell kind of a man would write like that? And secondly: "If your Pa's named Sansom, how come you call yourself Knox?"

The boy stared at the floor embarrassedly. "Well," he said, and shot Radclif a swift, accusing look, as if the driver was robbing him of something, "they were divorced, and mother always called me Joel Knox."

"Aw, say, son," said Radclif, "you oughtn't to have let her done that! Remember, your Pa's your Pa no matter what."

The proprietor avoided a yearning glance for help which the boy now cast in his direction by having wandered off to attend another customer. "But I've never seen him," said Joel, dropping the letters into his suitcase and buckling up the strap. "Do you know where this place is? Skully's Landing?"

"The Landing?" Radclif said. "Sure, sure I know all about it." He took a deep swallow of beer, let forth a mighty belch, and grinned. "Yessir, if I was your Pa I'd take down your britches and muss you up a bit." Then, draining the glass, he slapped a half-dollar on the counter, and stood meditatively scratching his hairy chin till a wall clock sounded the hour four: "O.K., son' let's shove," he said, starting briskly towards the door.

After a moment's hesitation the boy lifted his suitcase and followed.

"Come see us again," called the proprietor automatically.

The truck was a Ford of the pick-up type. Its interior smelled strongly of sun-warmed leather and gasoline fumes. The broken speedometer registered a petrified twenty. Rainstreaks and crushed insects blurred the windshield, of which one section was shattered in a bursting-star pattern. A toy skull ornamented the gear shift. The wheels bump-bumped over the rising, dipping, curving Paradise Chapel Highway.

Joel sat scrunched in a corner of the seat, elbow propped on windowframe, chin cupped in hand, trying hard to keep awake. He hadn't had a proper hour's rest since leaving New Orleans, for when he closed his eyes, as now, certain sickening memories slid through his mind. Of these, one in particular stood out: he was at a grocery counter, his mother waiting next him, and outside in the street January rain was making icicles on the naked tree limbs. Together they left the store and walked silently along the wet pavement, he holding a calico umbrella above his mother, who carried a sack of tangerines. They passed a house where a piano was playing, and the music sounded sad in the grey afternoon, but his mother remarked what a pretty song. And when they reached home she was humming it, but she felt cold and went to bed, and the doctor came, and for over a month he came everyday, but she was always cold, and Aunt Ellen was there, always smiling, and the doctor, always smiling, and the uneaten tangerines shriveled up in the icebox; and when it was over he went with Ellen to live in a dingy two-family house near Pontchartrain.

Ellen was a kind, rather gentle woman, and she did the best she knew how. She had five school-aged children, and her husband clerked in a shoe store, so there was not a great deal of money; but Joel wasn't dependent, his mother having left a small legacy. Ellen and her family were good to him, still he resented them, and often felt compelled to do hateful things, such as tease the older cousin, a dumb-looking girl named Louise, because she was a little deaf: he'd cup his ear and cry "Aye? Aye?" and couldn't stop till she broke into tears. He would not joke or join in the rousing after-supper games his uncle inaugurated nightly, and he took odd pleasure in bringing to attention a slip of grammar on anyone's part, but why this was true puzzled him as much as the Kendalls. It was as if he lived those months wearing a pair of spectacles with green, cracked lenses, and had wax-plugging in his ears, for everything seemed to be something it wasn't, and the days melted in a constant dream. Now Ellen liked to read Sir Walter Scott and Dickens and Hans Andersen to the children before sending them upstairs, and one chilly March evening she read "The Snow Queen." Listening to it, it came to Joel that he had a lot in common with Little Kay, whose outlook was twisted when a splinter from the Sprite's evil mirror infected his eye, changing his heart into a lump of bitter ice: suppose, he thought, hearing Ellen's gentle voice and watching the firelight warm his cousins' faces, suppose, like Little Kay, he also were spirited off to the Snow Queen's frozen palace? What living soul would then brave robber barons for his rescue? And there was no one, really no one.

During the last weeks before the letter came he skipped school three days out of five to loaf around the Canal Street docks. He got into a habit of sharing the box-lunch Ellen fixed for him with a giant Negro stevedore who, as they talked together, spun exotic sea-life legends that Joel knew to be lies even as he listened; but this man was a grown-up, and grown-ups were suddenly the only friends he wanted. And he spent solitary hours watching the loading and unloading of banana boats that shipped to Central America, plotting of course a stowaway voyage, for he was certain in some foreign city he could land a good-paying job. However, on his thirteenth birthday, as it happened, the first letter from Skully's Landing arrived.

Ellen had not shown him this letter for several days. It was peculiar, the way she'd behaved, and whenever her eyes had met his there was a look in them he'd never seen before: a frightened, guilty expression. In answering the letter she'd asked assurance that, should Joel find himself discontented, he would be at once allowed to return; a guarantee his education would be cared for; a promise he could spend Christmas holidays with her. But Joel could sense how relieved she was when, following a long correspondence, Major Knox's old honeymoon suitcase was dragged down from the attic.

He was glad to go. He could not think why, nor did he bother wondering, but his father's more or less incredible appearance on a scene strangely deserted twelve years before didn't strike him as in the least extraordinary, inasmuch as he'd counted on some such happening all along. The miracle he'd planned, however, was in the nature of a kind old rich lady who, having glimpsed him on a street-corner, immediately dispatched an envelope stuffed with thousand-dollar bills; or a similar Godlike action on the part of some goodhearted stranger. And this stranger, as it turned out, was his father, which to his mind was simply a wonderful piece of luck.

But afterwards, as he lay in a scaling iron bed above the Morning Star Café, dizzy with heat and loss and despair, a different picture of his father and of his situation asserted itself: he did not know what to expect, and he was afraid, for already there were so many disappointments. A panama hat, newly bought in New Orleans and worn with dashing pride, had been stolen in the train depot in Biloxi; then the Paradise Chapel bus had run three hot, sweaty hours behind schedule; and finally, topping everything, there had been no word from Skully's Landing waiting at the café. All Thursday night he'd left the electric light burning in the strange room, and read a movie magazine till he knew the latest doings of the Hollywood stars by heart, for if he let his attention turn inward even a second he would begin to tremble, and the mean tears would not stay back. Toward dawn he'd taken the magazine and torn it to shreds and burned the pieces in an ashtray one by one till it was time to go downstairs.

"Reach behind and hand me a match, will you, boy?" said Radclif. "Back there on the shelf, see?"

Joel opened his eyes and looked about him dazedly. A perfect tear of sweat was balanced on the tip of his nose. "You certainly have a lot of junk," he said, probing around the shelf, which was littered with a collection of yellowed newspapers, a slashed inner tube, greasy tools, an air pump, a flashlight and . . . a pistol. Alongside the pistol was an open carton of ammunition; bullets the bright copper of fresh pennies. He was tempted to take a whole handful, but ended by artfully dropping just one into his breast pocket. "Here they are."

Radclif popped a cigarette between his lips, and Joel, without being asked, struck a match for him.

"Thanks," said Radclif, a huge drag of smoke creeping out his nostrils. "Say, ever been in this part of the country before?"

"Not exactly, but my mother took me to Gulfport once, and that was nice because of the sea. We passed through there yesterday on the train."

"Like it round here?"

Joel imagined a queerness in the driver's tone. He studied Radclif's blunt profile, wondering if perhaps the theft had been noticed. If so, Radclif gave no sign. "Well, it's . . . you know, different."

"Course I don't see any difference. Lived hereabouts all my life, and it looks like everywhere else to me, ha ha!"

The truck hit suddenly a stretch of wide, hard road, unbordered by tree-shade, though a black skirt of distant pines darkened the rim of a great field that lay to the left. A far-off figure, whether man or woman you could not tell, rested from hoeing to wave, and Joel waved back. Farther on, two little white-haired boys astride a scrawny mule shouted their delight when the truck

passed, burying them in a screen of dust. Radclif honked and honked the horn
at a tribe of hogs that took their time in getting off the road. He could swear
like nobody Joel had ever heard, except maybe the Negro dockhand.

A while later, scowling thoughtfully, Joel said: "I'd like to ask you something, o.k.?" He waited till Radclif nodded consent. "Well, what I wanted to
ask was, do you know my . . . Mister Sansom?"

"Yeah, I know who he is, sure," said Radclif, and swabbed his forehead with
a filthy handkerchief. "You threw me off the track with those two names,
Sansom and Knox. Oh sure, he's the guy that married Amy Skully." There
was an instant's pause before he added: "But the real fact is, I never laid eyes
on him."

Joel chewed his lip, and was silent a moment. He was crazy with questions
he wanted answered, but the idea of asking them embarrassed him, for to be
so ignorant of one's own blood-kin seemed shameful. Therefore he said what
he had to in a very bold voice: "What about this Skully's Landing? I mean,
who all lives there?"

Radclif squinted his eyes while he considered. "Well," he said at last,
"they've got a coupla niggers out there, and I know them. Then your daddy's
wife, know her: my old lady does dressmaking for her now and again; used
to, anyway." He sucked in cigarette smoke, and flipped the butt out the
window. "And the cousin . . . yes, by God, the cousin!"

"Oh?" said Joel casually, though never once in all the letters had such a
person been mentioned, and his eyes begged the driver to amplify. But Radclif
merely smiled a curious smile, as if amused by a private joke too secret for
sharing.

And that was as far as the matter went.

"Look sharp now," said Radclif presently, "we're coming into town."

A house. A grey clump of Negro cabins. An unpainted clapboard church
with a rain-rod steeple, and three Holy panes of ruby glass. A sign: The Lord
Jesus Is Coming! Are You Ready? A little black child wearing a big straw hat
and clutching tight a pail of blackberries. Over all the sun's stinging glaze.
Soon there was a short, unpaved and nameless street, lined with similar one-
floored houses, some nicer-looking than others; each had a front porch and a
yard, and in some yards grew scraggly rose bushes and crepe myrtle and China
trees, from a branch of which very likely dangled a child's play swing made
of rope and an old rubber tire. There were Japonica trees with waxy blackgreen
polished leaves. And he saw a fat pink girl skipping rope, and an elderly lady
ensconced on a sagging porch cooling herself with a palmetto fan. Then a
red-barn livery stable: horses, wagons, buggies, mules, men. An abrupt bend
in the road: Noon City.

Radclif braked the truck to a halt. He reached across and opened the door
next to Joel. "Too bad I can't ride you out to the Landing, son," he said
hurriedly. "The company'd raise hell. But you'll make it fine; it's Saturday,
lotsa folks living out thataway come into town on Saturday."

Joel was standing alone now, and his blue shirt, damp with sweat, was pasted to his back. Toting the sticker-covered suitcase, he cautiously commenced his first walk in the town.

Noon City is not much to look at. There is only one street, and on it are located a General Merchandise store, a repair shop, a small building which contains two offices, one lodging a lawyer, the other a doctor; a combination barber-shop-beautyparlor that is run by a one-armed man and his wife; and a curious, indefinable establishment known as R. V. Lacey's Princely Place where a Texaco gasoline pump stands under the portico. These buildings are grouped so closely together they seem to form a ramshackle palace haphazardly thrown together overnight by a half-wit carpenter. Now across the road in isolation stand two other structures: a jail, and a tall queer tottering ginger-colored house. The jail has not housed a white criminal in over four years, and there is seldom a prisoner of any kind, the Sheriff being a lazy no-good, prone to take his ease with a bottle of liquor, and let trouble-makers and thieves, even the most dangerous type of cutthroats, run free and wild. As to the freakish old house, no one has lived there for God knows how long, and it is said that once three exquisite sisters were raped and murdered here in a gruesome manner by a fiendish Yankee bandit who rode a silver-grey horse and wore a velvet cloak stained scarlet with the blood of Southern womanhood; when told by antiquated ladies claiming one-time acquaintance with the beautiful victims, it is a tale of Gothic splendor. The windows of the house are cracked and shattered, hollow as eyeless sockets; a rotted balcony leans perilously forward, and yellow sunflower birds hide their nests in its secret places; the scaling outer walls are ragged with torn, weather-faded posters that flutter when there is a wind. Among the town kids it is a sign of great valor to enter these black rooms after dark and signal with a matchflame from a window on the topmost floor. However, the porch of this house is in pretty fair condition, and on Saturdays the visiting farm-families make it their headquarters.

New people rarely settle in Noon City or its outlying parts; after all, jobs are scarce here. On the other hand, seldom do you hear of a person leaving, unless it's to wend his lonesome way up onto the dark ledge above the Baptist church where forsaken tombstones gleam like stone flowers among the weeds.

Saturday is of course the big day. Shortly after daylight a procession of mule-drawn wagons, broken-down flivvers, and buggies begins wheeling in from the countryside, and towards midmorning a considerable congregation is gathered. The men sport their finest shirts and store-bought breeches; the women scent themselves with vanilla flavoring or dime-store perfume, of which the most popular brand is called Love Divine; the girls wear dodads in their cropped hair, inflame their cheeks with a lot of rouge, and carry five-cent paper fans that have pretty pictures painted on them. Though barefoot and probably half-naked, each little child is washed clean and given a few pennies to spend on something like a prize-inside box of molasses popcorn. Finished poking around in the various stores, the womenfolk assemble on the porch of the old house, while their men mosey on over to the livery stable. Swift and eager, saying the same things over and over, their voices hum and weave through the long day. Sickness and weddings and courting and funerals and God are the favorite topics on the porch. Over at the stable the men joke and drink whiskey, talk crops and play jackknife: once in a while there are terrible fights, for many of these men are hot-tempered, and if they hold a grudge against somebody they like to wrestle it out.

When twilight shadows the sky it is as if a soft bell were tolling dismissal, for a gloomy hush stills all, and the busy voices fall silent like birds at sunset. The families in their vehicles roll out of town like a sad, funeral caravan, and the only trace they leave is the fierce quiet that follows. The proprietors of the different Noon City establishments remain open an hour longer before bolting their doors and going home to bed; but after eight o'clock not a decent soul is to be seen wandering in this town except, maybe, a pitiful drunk or a young swain promenading with his ladylove.

"Hey, there! You with the suitcase!"

Joel whirled round to find a bandy-legged, little one-armed man glowering at him from the doorway of a barbershop; he seemed too sickly to be the owner of such a hard, deep voice. "Come here, kid," he commanded, jerking a thumb at his aproned chest.

When Joel reached him, the man held out his hand and in the open palm shone a nickel. "See this?" he said. Joel nodded dumbly. "O.K.," said the man, "now look up the road yonder. See that little gal with the red hair?"

Joel saw whom he meant all right. It was a girl with fiery dutchboy hair. She was about his height, and wore a pair of brown shorts and a yellow polo shirt. She was prancing back and forth in front of the tall, curious old house, thumbing her nose at the barber and twisting her face into evil shapes. "Listen," said the barber, "you go collar that nasty youngun for me and this nickel's yours for keeps. Oh-oh! Watch out, here she comes again. . . ."

Whooping like a wildwest Indian, the redhead whipped down the road, a yelling throng of young admirers racing in her wake. She chunked a great fistful of rocks when she came opposite the spot where Joel was standing. The rocks landed with a maddening clatter on the barbershop's tin roof, and the one-armed man, his face an apoplectic color, hollered: "I'll getcha, Idabel! I'll getcha sure as shooting; you just wait!" A flourish of female laughter floated through the screen door behind him, and a waspish-voiced woman shrilled: "Sugar, you quit actin the fool, and hie yourself in here outa that heat." Then, apparently addressing a third party: "I declare but what he ain't no better'n that Idabel; ain't neither one got the sense God gave 'em. Oh shoot, I says to Miz Potter (she was in for a shampoo a week ago today and I'd give a pretty penny to know how she gets that mop so filthy dirty), well, I says: 'Miz Potter, you teach that Idabel at the school,' I says, 'now how come she's so confounded mean?' I says: 'It do seem to me a mystery, and her with that sweet ol sister—speakin of Florabel—and them two twins, and noways alike.' Well-sir, Miz Potter answers me: 'Oh, Miz Caulfield, that Idabel sure do give me a peck of trouble and it's my opinion she oughta be in the penitentiary.' Uh huh, that's just what she said. Well, it wasn't no revelation to me cause I always knew she was a freak, no ma'am, never saw that Idabel Thompkins in a dress yet. *Sugar, you come on in here outa that heat. . . .*"

The man made a yoke with his fingers and spit fatly through it. He gave Joel a nasty look, and snapped, "Are you standing there wanting my money for doing nothing whatsoever, is that it, eh?"

"*Sugar, you hear me?*"

"Hush your mouth, woman," and the screen door whined shut.

Joel shook his head and went on his way. The redheaded girl and her loud gang were gone from sight, and the white afternoon was ripening towards the quiet time of day when the summer sky spills soft color over the drawn land. He smiled with chilly insolence at the interested stares of passers-by, and when he reached the establishment known as R. V. Lacey's Princely Place, he stopped to read a list that was chalked on a tiny, battered blackboard which stood outside the entrance: Miss Roberta V. Lacey Invites You to Come in and Try Our Tasty Fried Catfish and Chicken—Yummy Dixie Ice Cream—Good Delicious Barbecue—Sweet Drinks & Cold Beer.

"Sweet drinks," he said half-aloud, and it seemed as if frosty Coca-Cola was washing down his dry throat. "Cold beer." Yes, a cold beer. He felt the lumpy outline of the change purse in his pocket, then pushed the swinging screen door open and stepped inside.

In the box-shaped room that was R. V. Lacey's Princely Place there were about a dozen people standing around, mostly overalled boys with rawboned, sun-browned faces, and a few young girls. A hubbub of talk faded to nothing when Joel entered and self-consciously sat himself down at a wooden counter which ran the length of the room.

"Why, hello, little one," boomed a muscular woman who immediately strode forward and propped her elbows on the counter before him. She had long ape-like arms that were covered with dark fuzz, and there was a wart on her chin, and decorating this wart was a single antenna-like hair. A peach silk blouse sagged under the weight of her enormous breasts; a zany light sparkled in the red-rimmed eyes she focused on him. "Welcome to Miss Roberta's." Two of her dirty-nailed fingers reached out to give his cheek a painful pinch. "Say now, what can Miss Roberta do for this cute-lookin fella?"

Joel was overwhelmed. "A cold beer," he blurted, deafly ignoring the titter of giggles and guffaws that sounded in the background.

"Can't serve no beer to minors, babylove, even if you are a mighty cute-lookin fella. Now what you want is a nice NEHI grapepop," said the woman, lumbering away.

The giggles swelled to honest laughter, and Joel's ears turned a humiliated pink. He wondered if the woman was a lunatic. And his eyes scanned the sour-smelling room as if it were a madhouse. There were calendar portraits of toothy bathing beauties on the walls, and a framed certificate which said: This is to certify that Roberta Velma Lacey won Grand Prize in Lying at the annual Double Branches Dog Days Frolic. Hanging from the low ceiling were several poisonous streamers of strategically arranged flypaper, and a couple of naked lightbulbs that were ornamented with shredded ribbons of green-and-red crepe paper. A water pitcher filled with branches of towering pink dogwood sat on the counter.

"Here y'are," said the woman, plunking down a dripping wet bottle of purple sodapop. "I declare, little one, you sure are hot and dusty-lookin." She gave his head a merry pat. "Know somethin, you must be the boy Sam Radclif brung to town, say?"

Joel admitted this with a nod. He took a swallow of the drink, and it was lukewarm. "I want . . . that is, do you know how far it is from here to Skully's Landing?" he said, realizing every ear in the place was tuned to him.

"Ummn," the woman tinkered with her wart, and walled her eyes up into her head till they all but disappeared. "Hey, Romeo, how far you spec it is out to The Skulls," she said, and grinned crazily. "I call it The Skulls on accounta . . ." but she did not finish, for at that moment the Negro boy of whom she'd asked the information, answered: "Two miles, more like three, maybe, ma'am."

"Three miles," she parroted. "But if I was you, babylove, I wouldn't go traipsin over there."

"Me neither," whined a yellow-haired girl.

"Is there anyway I could get a ride out?"

Somebody said, "Ain't Jesus Fever in town?"

Yeah, I saw Jesus—Jesus, he parked round by the Livery—What? Y'all mean old Jesus Fever? Christamighty, I thought he was way gone and buried! —Nah, man. He's past a hundred but alive as you are.—Sure, I seen Jesus— Yeah, Jesus is here . . .

The woman grabbed a flyswatter and slammed it down with savage force. "Shut up that gab. I can't hear a thing this boy says."

Joel felt a little surge of pride, tinged with fright, at being the center of such a commotion. The woman fixed her zany eyes on a point somewhere above his head, and said: "What business you got with The Skulls, babylove?"

Now this again! He sketched the story briefly, omitting all except the simplest events, even to excluding a mention of the letters. He was trying to locate his father, that was the long and short of it. Could she help him?

Well, she didn't know. She stood silent for some time, toying with her wart and staring off into space. "Hey, Romeo," she said finally, "you say Jesus Fever's in town?"

"Yes'm." The boy she called Romeo was colored, and wore a puffy, stained chef's cap. He was stacking dishes in a sink behind the counter.

"Come here, Romeo," she said, beckoning, "I got something to discuss." Romeo joined her promptly in a rear corner. She began whispering excitedly, glancing over her shoulder now and then at Joel, who could not hear what they were saying. It was quiet in the room, and everyone was looking at him. He took out the bullet thefted from Sam Radclif and rolled it nervously in his hands.

Suddenly the door swung open. The skinny girl with fiery, chopped-off red hair swaggered inside, and stopped dead still, her hands cocked on her hips. Her face was flat, and rather impertinent; a network of big ugly freckles spanned her nose. Her eyes, squinty and bright green, moved swiftly from face to face, but showed none a sign of recognition; they paused a cool instant on Joel, then traveled elsewhere.

Hi, Idabel—Whatchasay, Idabel?

"I'm hunting sister," she said. "Anybody seen her?" Her voice was boy-husky, sounding as though strained through some rough material: it made Joel clear his throat.

"Seen her sitting on the porch a while back," said a chinless young man.

The redhead leaned against the wall, and crossed her pencil-thin, bony-kneed legs. A ragged bandage stained with mercurochrome covered her left knee. She pulled out a blue yo-yo and let it unwind slowly to the floor and spin back. "Who's that?" she asked, jerking her head towards Joel. When nobody answered, she loopty-looped the yo-yo, shrugged and said: "Who cares, pray tell?" But she continued to watch him cagily from the corners of her eyes. "Hey, hows about a dope on credit, Roberta?" she called.

"*Miss* Roberta," said the woman, momentarily interrupting her confab with Romeo. "I don't need to tell you you have a right smart tongue, Idabel Thompkins, and always did have. And till such time as you learn a few ladylike manners, I'd be obliged if you'd keep outa my place, hear? Besides, since when have you got all this big credit? Ha! March now . . . and don't come back till you put on some decent female clothes."

"You know what you can do," sassed the girl, stomping out the door. "This old dive'll have a mighty long wait before I bring my trade here again, you betcha." Once outside, her silhouette darkened the screen as she paused to peer in at Joel.

And now dusk was coming on. A sea of deepening green spread the sky like some queer wine, and across this vast green, shadowed clouds were pushed sluggishly by a mild breeze. Presently the trek homeward would commence, and afterwards the stillness of Noon City would be almost a sound itself: the sound a footfall might make among the mossy tombs on the dark ledge. Miss Roberta had lent Romeo as Joel's guide. The two kept duplicate pace; the Negro boy carried Joel's bag; wordlessly they turned the corner by the jail, and there was the stable, a barnlike structure of faded red which Joel had noticed earlier that day. A number of men who looked like a gang of desperadoes in a Western picture-show were congregated near the hitching post, passing a whiskey bottle from hand to hand; a second group, less boisterous, played a game with a jackknife under the dark area of an oak tree. Swarms of dragon-flies quivered above a slime-coated watertrough; and a scabby hound dog padded back and forth, sniffing the bellies of tied-up mules. One of the whiskey drinkers, an old man with long white hair and a long white beard, was feeling pretty good evidently, for he was clapping his hands and doing a little shuffle-dance to a tune that was probably singing in his head.

The colored boy escorted Joel round the side of the stable to a backlot where wagons and saddled horses were packed so close a swinging tail was certain to strike something. "That's him," said Romeo, pointing his finger, "there's Jesus Fever."

But Joel had seen at once the pygmy figure huddled atop the seatplank of a grey wagon parked on the lot's further rim: a kind of gnomish little Negro whose primitive face was sharp against the drowning green sky. "Don't less us be fraid," said Romeo, leading Joel through the maze of wagons and animals with timid caution. "You best hold tight to my hand, white boy: Jesus Fever, he the oldest ol buzzard you ever put eyes on."

Joel said, "But I'm not afraid," and this was true.

"Shhh!"

As the boys approached, the little pygmy cocked his head at a wary angle; then slowly, with the staccato movements of a mechanical doll, he turned sideways till his eyes, yellow feeble eyes dotted with milky specks, looked down on them with dreamy detachment. He had a funny derby hat perched rakishly on his head, and in the candy-striped ribbon-band was jabbed a speckled turkey feather.

Romeo stood hesitantly waiting, as if expecting Joel to take the lead; but when the white child kept still, he said: "You lucky you come to town, Mister Fever. This here little gentman's Skully kin, and he going out to the Landing for to live."

"I'm Mister Sansom's son," said Joel, though suddenly, gazing up at the dark and fragile face, this didn't seem to mean much. Mr. Sansom. And who was he? A nothing, a nobody. A name that did not appear even to have particular significance for the old man whose sunken, blind-looking eyes studied him without expression.

Then Jesus Fever raised the derby a respectful inch. "Say I should find him here: Miss Amy say," he whispered hoarsely. His face was like a black with-ered apple, and almost destroyed; his polished forehead shone as though a purple light gleamed under the skin; his sickle-curved posture made him look as though his back were broken: a sad little brokeback dwarf crippled with age. Yet, and this impressed Joel's imagination, there was a touch of the wizard in his yellow, spotted eyes: it was a tricky quality that suggested, well, magic and things read in books. "I here yestiday, day fore, cause Miss Amy, she say wait," and he trembled under the impact of a deep breath. "Now I can't talk no whole lot: ain't got the strenth. So up, child. Gettin towards night, and night's misery on my bones."

"Right with you, Mister Jesus," said Joel without enthusiasm. Romeo gave him a boost into the wagon, and handed up the suitcase. It was an old wagon, wobbly and rather like an oversized peddler's cart; the floor was strewn with dry cornhusks and croquer sacks which smelled sweetly sour.

"Git, John Brown," urged Jesus Fever, gently slapping the reins against a tan mule's back. "Lift them feet, John Brown, lift them feet. . . ."

Slowly the wagon pulled from the lot and groaned up a path onto the road. Romeo ran ahead, gave the mule's rump a mighty whack and darted off; Joel felt a quick impulse to call him back, for it came to him all at once that he did not want to reach Skully's Landing alone. But there was nothing to be done about it now. Out in front of the stable the bearded drunk had quit dancing, and the hound dog was squatting under the water trough scratching fleas. The wagon's rickety wheels made dust clouds that hung in the green air like powdered bronze. A bend in the road: Noon City was gone.

It was night, and the wagon crept over an abandoned country road where the wheels ground softly through deep fine sand, muting John Brown's forlorn hoofclops. Jesus Fever had so far spoken only twice, each time to threaten the mule with some outlandish torture: he was going to skin him raw or split his head with an axe, possibly both. Finally he'd given up and, still hunched upright on the seatplank, fallen asleep. "Much further?" Joel asked once, and there was no answer. The reins lay limply entwined round the old man's wrists, but the mule skillfully guided the wagon unaided.

Relaxed as a rag doll, Joel was stretched on a croquer-sack mattress, his legs dangling over the wagon's end. A vine-like latticework of stars frosted the southern sky, and with his eyes he interlinked these spangled vines till he could trace many ice-white resemblances: a steeple, fantastic flowers, a springing cat, the outline of a human head, and other curious designs like those made by snowflakes. There was a vivid, slightly red three-quarter moon; the evening wind eerily stirred shawls of Spanish moss which draped the branches of passing trees. Here and there in the mellow dark fireflies signaled one another as though messaging in code. He listened contented and untroubled to the remote, singing-saw noise of night insects.

Then presently the music of a childish duet came carrying over the sounds of the lonesome countryside: "What does the robin do then, poor thing . . ." Like specters he saw them hurrying in the moonshine along the road's weedy edge. Two girls. One walked with easy grace, but the other moved as jerky and quick as a boy, and it was she that Joel recognized.

"Hello, there," he said boldly when the wagon overtook them.

Both girls had watched the wagon's approach, and slowed their step perceptibly; but the one who was unfamiliar, as if startled, cried, "Gee Jemima!" She had long, long hair that fell past her hips, and her face, the little he could see of it, smudged as it was in shadow, seemed very friendly, very pretty. "Why, isn't it just grand of you to come along this way and want to give us a ride?"

"Help yourself," he said, and slid over to make a seat.

"I'm Miss Florabel Thompkins," she announced, after she'd hopped agilely up beside him, and pulled her dress-hem below her knees. "This is the Skullys' wagon? Sure, that's Jesus Fever . . . is he asleep? Well, don't that beat everything." She talked rapidly in a flighty, too birdlike manner, as if mimicking a certain type of old lady. "Come on, sister, there's oodles of room."

The sister trudged on behind the wagon. "I've got two feet and I reckon I'm not such a flirt I can't find the willpower to put one in front of the other, thanks all the same," she said, and gave her shorts an emphatic hitch.

"You're welcome to ride," said Joel weakly, not knowing what else to do; for she was a funny kid, no doubt about it.

"Oh, folderol," said Florabel Thompkins, "don't you pay her no mind. That's just what Mama calls Idabel Foolishness. Let her walk herself knock-kneed for what it means to the great wide world. No use trying to reason with her: she's got willful ways, Idabel has. Ask anybody."

"Huh," was all Idabel said in her defense.

Joel looked from one to the other, and concluded he liked Florabel the best; she was so pretty, at least he imagined her to be, though he could not see her face well enough to judge fairly. Anyway, her sister was a tomboy, and he'd had a special hatred of tomboys ever since the days of Eileen Otis. This Eileen Otis was a beefy little roughneck who had lived on the same block in New Orleans, and she used to have a habit of waylaying him, stripping off his pants, and tossing them high into a tree. That was years gone by, but the memory of her could infuriate him still. He pictured Florabel's redheaded sister as a regular Eileen Otis.

"We've got us a lovely car, you know," said Florabel. "It's a green Chevrolet that six persons can ride in without anybody sitting on anybody's lap, and there are real windowshades you can pull up or down with darling toy babies. Papa won this lovely Chevrolet from a man at a cock-fight, which I think was real smart of him, only Mama says different. Mama's as honest as the day is long, and she don't hold with the cock-fights. But what I'm trying to say is: we don't usually have to hitch rides, and with strangers, too . . . course we do know Jesus Fever . . . kinda. But what's your name? Joel? Joel what? Knox . . . well, Joel Knox, what I'm trying to say is my Papa usually drives ut to town in our lovely car. . . ." She jabbered on and on, and he was content to listen till, turning his head, he saw her sister, and thought she was looking at him peculiarly. As this exchange of stares continued, a smileless but amused look that passed between them was lighted by the moon; it was as if each were saying: *I don't think so much of you, either.* ". . . but one time I just happened to slam the door on Idabel's hand," Florabel was still talking of the car, "and now her thumbnail won't grow the least bit: it's all lumpy and black. But she didn't cry or take on, which was very brave on her part; now me, I couldn't stand to have such a nasty old . . . show him your hand, sister."

"You let me alone or I'll show it to you o.k.: in a place you're not expecting."

Florabel sniffed, and glanced peevishly at Joel because he laughed. "It don't pay to treat Idabel like she was a human being," she said ominously. "Ask anybody. The tough way she acts you'd never suppose she came from a well-to-do family like mine, would you?"

Joel held his peace, knowing no matter what he said it would be the wrong thing.

"That's just what I mean," said Florabel, turning the silence to her own advantage, "you'd never suppose. Naturally she is as we're twins: born the same day, me ten minutes first, so I'm elder; both of us twelve, going on thirteen. Florabel and Idabel. Isn't it tacky the way those names kinda rhyme? Only Mama thinks it's real cute, but . . ."

Joel didn't hear the rest, for he suddenly noticed Idabel had stopped trailing the wagon. She was far back and running, running like a pale animal through the lake of weeds lining the wayside towards a flowering island of dogwood that bloomed lividly some distance off like seashore foam on a black beach. But before he could point this out to Florabel, her twin was gone and lost between the shining trees. "Isn't she afraid to be out there all alone in the dark?" he interrupted, and with a gesture indicated where Idabel had disappeared.

"That child is afraid of nothing," stated Florabel flatly. "Don't you fret none over her; she'll catch up when she gets to feeling like it."

"But out in those woods . . ."

"Oh, sister takes her notions and there's no sense in asking why. We were born twins, like I told you, but Mama says the Lord always sends something bad with the good." Florabel yawned and leaned back, the long hair sprawling about her shoulders. "Idabel will take any kind of a dare; even when we were real little she'd go up and poke around the Skullys' and peek in all the windows. One time she even got a good look at Cousin Randolph." Lazily she reached up and seized a firefly that was pulsing goldenly in the air above her head, then: "Do you like living at that place?"

"What place?"

"The Landing, silly."

Joel said: "I may, but I haven't seen it yet." Her face was close to his, and he could tell she was disappointed with the answer. "And you, where's your house?"

She waved an airy hand. "Just a little ways up yonder. It's not far from the Landing, so maybe you could come visit sometime." She tossed the firefly into the air where it hung suspended like a small moon. "Naturally I didn't know whether to think you lived at the Landing or not. Nobody ever sees any of them Skullys. Why, the Lord himself could be living there with none the wiser. Are you kin to . . ." but this was cut short by a terrible, paralyzing wail, and wild crashing in the all-around darkness.

Idabel bounded into the road from the underbrush. She was flailing her arms and howling loud and fierce.

"You darn fool!" her sister screamed, but Joel did nothing, for his heart was lodged somewhere in his throat. Then he turned to check Jesus Fever's reaction, but the old man still snoozed; and strangely the mule had not bolted with fright.

"That was pretty good, eh?" said Idabel. "I'll bet you thought the devil was hot on your trail."

Florabel said: "Not the devil, sister . . . he's inside you." And to Joel: "She'll catch it when I tell Papa, cause she couldn't have got up here without us seeing unless she cut through the hollow, and Papa's told her and told her about that. She's all the time snooping around in there hunting sweetgum: some day a big old moccasin is going to chew off her leg right at the hip, mark my word."

Idabel had returned carrying a spray of dogwood, and now she smelled the blooms exultantly. "I've already been snakebit," she said.

"Yes, that's the truth," her sister admitted. "You should've seen her leg, Joel Knox. It swelled up like a watermelon; all her hair fell out; oh, she was dogsick for two months, and Mama and me had to wait on her hand and foot."

"It's lucky she didn't die," said Joel.

"I would've if I was you and didn't know how to take care of myself," said Idabel.

"She was smart, all right," conceded Florabel. "She just went smack in the chicken yard and snatched up this rooster and ripped him wide open; never heard such squawking. Hot chicken blood draws the poison."

"You ever been snakebit, boy?" Idabel wanted to know.

"No," he said, feeling somehow in the wrong, "but I was nearly run over by a car once."

Idabel seemed to consider this. "Run over by a car," she said, her woolly voice tinged with envy.

"Now you oughtn't to have told her that," snapped Florabel. "She's liable to run straight off and throw herself in the middle of the highway."

Below the road and in the shallow woods a close-by creek's sliding, pebble-tinkling rush underlined the bellowed comments of hidden frogs. The slow-rolling wagon cleared a slope and started down again. Idabel picked the petals from the dogwood spray, dripping them in her path, and tossed the rind aside; she tilted her head and faced the sky and began to hum; then she sang: "When the northwind doth blow, and we shall have snow, what does the robin do then, poor thing?" Florabel took up the tune: "He got to the barn, to keep he-self warm, and hide he-self under he wing, poor thing!" It was a lively song and they sang it over and over till Joel joined to make a trio; their voices pealed clear and sweet, for all three were sopranos, and Florabel vivaciously strummed a mythical banjo. Then a cloud crossed the moon and in the black the singing ended.

Florabel jumped off the wagon. "Our house is over in there," she said, pointing toward what looked to Joel like an empty wilderness. "Don't forget . . . come to visit."

"I will," he called, but already the tide of darkness had washed the twins from sight.

Sometime later a thought of them echoed, receded, left him suspecting they were perhaps what he'd first imagined: apparitions. He touched his cheek, the cornhusks, glanced at the sleeping Jesus—the old man was trancelike but for his body's rubbery response to the wagon's jolting—and was reassured. The guide reins jangled, the hoofbeats of the mule made a sound as drowsy as a fly's bzzz on a summer afternoon. A jungle of stars rained down to cover him in blaze, to blind and close his eyes. Arms akimbo, legs crumpled, lips vaguely parted—he looked as if sleep had struck him with a blow.

Fence posts suddenly loomed; the mule came alive, began to trot, almost to gallop down a graveled lane over which the wheels spit stone; and Jesus Fever, jarred conscious, tugged at the reins: "Whoa, John Brown, whoa!" And the wagon presently came to a spiritless standstill.

A woman slipped down the steps leading from a great porch; delirious white wings sucked round the yellow globe of a kerosene lantern that she carried high. But Joel, scowling at a dream demon, was unaware when the woman bent so intently towards him and peered into his face by the lamp's smoky light.

Two

falling . . . Falling . . . FALLING! a knifelike shaft, an underground corridor, and he was spinning like a fan blade through metal spirals; at the bottom a yawning-jawed crocodile followed his downward whirl with hooded eyes: as always, rescue came with wakefulness. The crocodile exploded in sunshine. Joel blinked and tasted his bitter tongue and did not move; the bed, an immense four-poster with different rosewood fruits carved crudely on its high headboard, was suffocatingly soft and his body had sunk deep in its feathery center. Although he'd slept naked, the light sheet covering him felt like a wool blanket.

The whisper of a dress warned him that someone was in the room. And another sound, dry and wind-rushed, very much like the beat of bird wings; it was this sound, he realized while rolling over, which had wakened him.

An expanse of pale yellow wall separated two harshly sunlit windows which faced the bed. Between these windows stood the woman. She did not notice Joel, for she was staring across the room at an ancient bureau: there, on top a lacquered box, was a bird, a bluejay perched so motionless it looked like a trophy. The woman turned and closed the only open window; then, with prissy little sidling steps, she started forward.

Joel was wide awake, but for an instant it seemed as if the bluejay and its pursuer were a curious fragment of his dream. His stomach muscles tightened as he watched her near the bureau and the bird's innocent agitation: it hopped around bobbing its blue-brilliant head; suddenly, just as she came within striking distance, it fluttered its wings and flew across the bed and lighted on a chair where Joel had flung his clothes the night before. And remembrance of the night flooded over him: the wagon, the twins, and the little Negro in the derby hat. And the woman, his father's wife: Miss Amy, as she was called. He remembered entering the house, and stumbling through an odd chamber of a hall where the walls were alive with the tossing shadows of candleflames; and Miss Amy, her finger pressed against her lips, leading him with robber stealth up a curving, carpeted stairway and along a second corridor to the door of this room; all a sleepwalker's pattern of jigsaw incidents; and so, as Miss Amy stood by the bureau regarding the bluejay on its new perch, it was more or less the same as seeing her for the first time. Her dress was of an almost transparent grey material; on her left hand, for no clear reason, she wore a matching grey silk glove, and she kept the hand cupped daintily, as if it were crippled. A wispy streak of white zigzagged through the dowdy plaits of her brownish, rather colorless hair. She was slight, and fragile-boned, and her eyes were like two raisins embedded in the softness of her narrow face.

Instead of following the bird directly, as before, she tiptoed over to a fireplace at the opposite end of the huge room, and, artfully twisting her hand, seized hold of an iron poker. The bluejay hopped down the arm of the chair, pecking at Joel's discarded shirt. Miss Amy pursed her lips, and took five rapid, lilting, ladylike steps. . . .

The poker caught the bird across the back, and pinioned it for the fraction of a moment; breaking loose, it flew wildly to the window and cawed and flapped against the pane, at last dropping to the floor where it scrambled along dazedly, scraping the rug with its outspread wings.

Miss Amy trapped it in a corner, and scooped it up against her breast.

Joel pressed his face into the pillow, knowing that she would look in his direction, if only to see how the racket had affected him. He listened to her footsteps cross the room, and the gentle closing of the door.

He dressed in the same clothes he'd worn the previous day: a blue shirt, and bedraggled linen trousers. He could not find his suitcase anywhere, and wondered whether he'd left it in the wagon. He combed his hair, and doused his face with water from a washbasin that sat on a marble-topped table beside the rosewood four-poster. The rug, which was bald in spots and of an intricately oriental design, felt grimy and rough under his bare feet. The stifling room was musty; it smelled of old furniture and the burned-out fires of wintertime; gnat-like motes of dust circulated in the sunny air, and Joel left a dusty imprint on whatever he touched: the bureau, the chiffonier, the washstand. This room had not been used in many years certainly; the only fresh things here were the bedsheets, and even these had a yellowed look.

He was lacing up his shoes when he spied the bluejay feather. It was floating above his head, as if held by a spider's thread. He plucked it out of the air, carried it to the bureau, and deposited it in the lacquered box, which was lined with red plush; it also occurred to him that this would be a good place to store Sam Radclif's bullet. Joel loved any kind of souvenir, and it was his nature to keep and catalogue trifles. He'd had many grand collections, and it pained him sorely that Ellen persuaded him to leave them in New Orleans. There had been magazine photos and foreign coins, books and no-two-alike rocks, and a wonderful conglomeration he'd labeled simply Miscellany: the feather and bullet would've made good items for that. But maybe Ellen would mail his stuff on, or maybe he could start all over again, maybe . . .

There was a rap at the door.

It was his father, of that he was sure. It must be. And what should he say: hello, Dad, Father, Mr Sansom? Howdyado, hello? Hug, or shake hands, or kiss? oh why hadn't he brushed his teeth, why couldn't he find the Major's suitcase and a clean shirt? He whipped a bow into his shoelace, called, "Yeah?" and straightened up erect, prepared to make the best, most manly impression possible.

The door opened. Miss Amy, her gloved hand cradled, waited on the threshold; she nodded sweetly, and, as she advanced, Joel noticed the vague suggestion of a mustache fuzzing her upper lip.

"Good morning," he said, and, smiling, held out his hand. He was of course disappointed, but somehow relieved, too.

She stared at his outstretched hand, a puzzled look contracting her puny face. She shook her head, and skirted past him to a window where she stood with her back turned. "It's after twelve," she said.

Joel's smile felt suddenly stiff and awkward. He hid his hands in his pockets.

"Such a pity you arrived last night at so late an hour: Randolph had planned a merrier welcome." Her voice had a weary, simpering tone; it struck the ear like the deflating whoosh of a toy balloon. "But it's just as well, the poor child suffers with asthma, you know: had a wretched attack yesterday. He'll be ever so peeved I haven't let him know you're here, but I think it best he stay in his room, at least till supper."

Joel rummaged around for something to say. He recalled Sam Radclif having spoken of a cousin, and one of the twins, Florabel, of a Cousin Randolph. At any rate, from the way she talked, he supposed this person to be a kid near his own age.

"Randolph is our first cousin, and a great admirer of yours," she said, turning to face him. The hard sunshine emphasized the pallor of her skin, and her tiny eyes, now fixing him shrewdly, were alert. There was lack of focus in her face, as though, beneath the uningratiating veneer of fatuous refinement, another personality, quite different, was demanding attention; the lack of focus gave her, at unguarded moments, a panicky, dismayed expression, and when she spoke it was as if she were never precisely certain what every word signified. "Have you money left from the check my husband sent Mrs. Kendall?"

"About a dollar, I guess," he said, and reluctantly offered his change purse. "It cost a good bit to stay at that café."

"Please, it's yours," she said. "I was merely interested in whether you are a wise, thrifty boy." She appeared suddenly irritated. "Why are you so fidgety? Must you use the bathroom?"

"Oh, no." He felt all at once as though he'd wet his pants in public. "Oh, no."

"Unfortunately, we haven't modern plumbing facilities. Randolph is opposed to contrivances of that sort. However," and she nodded toward the washstand, "you'll find a chamber pot in there . . . in the compartment below."

"Yes'm," said Joel, mortified.

"And of course the house has never been wired for electricity. We have candles and lamps; they both draw bugs, but which would you prefer?"

"Whichever you've got the most of," he said, really wanting candles, for they brought to mind the St. Deval Street Secret Nine, a neighborhood detective club of which he'd been both treasurer and Official Historian. And he recalled club get-togethers where tall candles, snitched from the five 'n' dime, flamed in Coca-Cola bottles, and how Exalted Operative Number One, Sammy Silverstein, had used for a gavel an old cow bone.

She glanced at the firepoker which had rolled halfway under a wing chair. "Would you mind picking that up and putting it over by the hearth? I was in here earlier," she explained, while he carried out her order, "and a bird flew in the window; such a nuisance: you weren't disturbed?"

Joel hesitated. "I thought I heard something," he said. "It woke me up."

"Well, twelve hours sleep should be sufficient." She lowered herself into the chair, and crossed her toothpick legs; her shoes were low-heeled and white, like those worn by nurses. "Yes, the morning's gone and everything's all hot again. Summer is so unpleasant." Now despite her impersonal manner, Joel was not antagonized, just a little uncomfortable. Females in Miss Amy's age bracket, somewhere between forty-five and fifty, generally displayed a certain tenderness toward him, and he took their sympathy for granted; if, as had infrequently happened, this affection was withheld, he knew with what ease it could be guaranteed: a smile, a wistful glance, a courtly compliment: "I want to say how pretty I think your hair is: a *nice* color."

The bribe received no clear-cut appreciation, therefore: "And how much I like my room."

And this time he hit his mark. "I've always considered it the finest room in the house. Cousin Randolph was born here: in that very bed. And Angela Lee . . . Randolph's mother: a beautiful woman, originally from Memphis . . . died here, oh, not many years ago. We've never used it since." She perked her head suddenly, as if to hear some distant sound; her eyes squinted, then closed altogether. But presently she relaxed and eased back into the chair. "I suppose you've noticed the view?"

Joel confessed that no, he hadn't, and went obligingly to a window. Below, under a fiery surface of sun waves, a garden, a jumbled wreckage of zebrawood and lilac, elephant-ear plant and weeping willow, the lace-leafed limp branches shimmering delicately, and dwarfed cherry trees, like those in oriental prints, sprawled raw and green in the noon heat. It was not a result of simple neglect, this tangled oblong area, but rather the outcome, it appeared, of someone having, in a riotous moment, scattered about it a wild assortment of seed. Grass and bush and vine and flower were all crushed together. Massive china- berry and waterbay formed a rigidly enclosing wall. Now at the far end, opposite the house, was an unusual sight: like a set of fingers, a row of five white fluted columns lent the garden the primitive, haunted look of a lost ruin: Judas vine snaked up their toppling slenderness, and a yellow tabby cat was sharpening its claws against the middle column.

Miss Amy, having risen, now stood beside him. She was an inch or so shorter than Joel.

"In ancient history class at school, we had to draw pictures of some pillars like those. Miss Kadinsky said mine were the best, and she put them on the bulletin board," he bragged.

"The pillars . . . Randolph adores them, too; they were once part of the old side porch," she told him in a reminiscing voice. "Angela Lee was a young bride, just down from Memphis, and I was a child younger than you. In the evening we would sit on the side porch, sipping cherryade and listen to the crickets and wait for the moonrise. Angela Lee crocheted a shawl for me: you must see it sometime, Randolph uses it in his room as a tablescarf: a waste and a shame." She spoke so quietly it was as though she intended only herself to hear.

"Did the porch just blow away?" asked Joel.

"Burned," she said, rubbing a clear circle on the dusty glass with her gloved hand. "It was in December, the week before Christmas, and at a time when there was no man on the place but Jesus Fever, and he was even then very old. No one knows how the fire started or ended; it simply rose out of nothing, burned away the dining room, the music room, the library. . . . and went out. No one knows."

"And this garden is where the part that burned up was?" said Joel. "Gee, it must've been an awful big house."

She said: "There, by the willows and goldenrod . . . that is the site of the music room where the dances were held; small dances, to be sure, for there were few around here Angela Lee cared to entertain. . . . And they are all dead now, those who came to her little evenings; Mr. Casey, I understand, passed on last year, and he was the last."

Joel gazed down on the jumbled green, trying to picture the music room and the dancers ("Angela Lee played the harp," Miss Amy was saying, "and Mr. Casey the piano, and Jesus Fever, though he'd never studied, the violin, and Randolph the Elder sang; had the finest male voice in the state, everyone said so"), but the willows were willows and the goldenrod goldenrod and the dancers dead and lost. The yellow tabby slunk through the lilac into tall, concealing grass, and the garden was glazed and secret and still.

Miss Amy sighed as she slipped back into the shade of the room. "Your suitcase is in the kitchen," she said. "If you'll come downstairs, we'll see what Missouri has to feed you."

A dormer window of frost glass illuminated the long top-floor hall with the kind of pearly light that drenches a room when rain is falling. The wallpaper had once, you could tell, been blood red, but now was faded to a mural of crimson blisters and maplike stains. Including Joel's, there were four doors in the hall, impressive oak doors with massive brass knobs, and Joel wondered which of them, if opened, might lead to his father.

"Miss Amy," he said, as they started down the stairs, "where is my dad? I mean, couldn't I see him, please, ma'am?"

She did not answer. She walked a few steps below him, her gloved hand sliding along the dark, curving bannister, and each stairstep remarked the delicacy of her footfall. The strand of grey winding in her mousy hair was like a streak of lightning.

"Miss Amy, about my father . . ."

What in hell was the matter with her? Was she a little deaf, like his cousin Louise? The stairs sloped down to the circular chamber he remembered from the night, and here a full-length mirror caught his reflection bluely; it was like the comedy mirrors in carnival houses; he swayed shapelessly in its distorted depth. Except for a cedar chest supporting a kerosene lantern, the chamber was bleak and unfurnished. At the left was an archway, and a large crowded parlor yawned dimly beyond; to the right hung a curtain of lavender velvet that gleamed in various rubbed places like frozen dew on winter grass. She pushed through the parted folds. Another hall, another door.

The kitchen was empty. Joel sat down in a cane-bottom chair at a large table spread with checkered oilcloth, while Miss Amy went out on the backsteps and stood there calling, "Yoo hoo, Missouri, yoo hoo," like an old screech owl.

A rusty alarm clock, lying face over on the table, ticktucked, ticktucked. The kitchen was fair-sized, but shadowed, for there was a single window, and by it the furry leaves of a fig tree met darkly; also, the planked walls were the somber bluegray of an overcast sky, and the stove, a woodburning relic with a fire pulsing in it now, was black with a black chimney flute rising to the low ceiling. Worn linoleum covered the floor, as it had in Ellen's kitchen, but this was all that reminded Joel of home.

And then, sitting alone in the quiet kitchen, he was taken with a terrible idea: what if his father had seen him already? Indeed, had been spying on him ever since he arrived, was, in fact, watching him at this very moment? An old house like this would most likely be riddled with hidden passages, and picture-eyes that were not eyes at all, but peepholes. And his father thought: that runt is an impostor; my son would be taller and stronger and handsomer and smarter-looking. Suppose he'd told Miss Amy: give the little faker something to eat and send him on his way. And dear sweet Lord, where would he go? Off to foreign lands where he'd set himself up as an organ grinder with a little doll-clothed monkey, or a blind-boy street singer, or a beggar selling pencils.

"Confound it, Missouri, why can't you learn to light in one place longer than five seconds?"

"I gotta chop the wood. Ain't I gotta chop the wood?"

"Don't sass me."

"I ain't sassin nobody, Miss Amy."

"If that isn't sass, what is it?"

"Whew!"

Up the steps they came, and through the back screen door, Miss Amy, vexation souring her white face, and a graceful Negro girl toting a load of kindling which she dropped in a crib next to the stove. The Major's suitcase, Joel saw, was jammed behind this crib.

Smoothing the fingers of her silk glove, Miss Amy said: "Missouri belongs to Jesus Fever; she's his grandchild."

"Delighted to make your acquaintance," said Joel, in his very best dancing-class style.

"Me, too," rejoined the colored girl, going about her business. "Welcome to," she dropped a frying pan, "the Landin."

"If we aren't more careful," stage-whispered Miss Amy, "we're liable to find ourselves in serious difficulty. All this racket: Randolph will have a conniption."

"Sometime I get so tired," mumbled Missouri.

"She's a good cook . . . when she feels like it," said Miss Amy. "You'll be taken care of. But don't stuff, we have early supper on Sundays."

Missouri said: "You comin to Service, Ma'am?"

"Not today," Miss Amy replied distractedly. "He's worse, much worse."

Missouri placed the pan on a rack and nodded knowingly. Then, looking square at Joel: "We countin on you, young fella."

It was like the exasperating code-dialogue which, for the benefit and bewilderment of outsiders, had often passed between members of the St. Deval Street Secret Nine.

"Missouri and Jesus hold their own prayer meeting Sunday afternoons," explained Miss Amy.

"I plays the accordion and us sings," said Missouri. "It's a whole lota fun."

But Joel, seeing Miss Amy was preparing to depart, ignored the colored girl, for there were certain urgent matters he wanted settled. "About my father . . ."

"Yes?" Miss Amy paused in the doorway.

Joel felt tongue-tied. "Well, I'd like to . . . to see him," he finished lamely.

She fiddled with the doorknob. "He isn't well, you know," she said. "I don't think it advisable he see you just yet; it's so hard for him to talk." She made a helpless gesture. "But if you want, I'll ask."

With a cut of cornbread, Joel mopped bone-dry the steaming plate of fried eggs and grits, sopping rich with sausage gravy, that Missouri had set before him.

"It sure do gimme pleasure to see a boy relish his vittels," she said. "Only don't spec no refills cause I gotta pain lickin my back like to kill me: didn't sleep a blessed wink last night; been sufferin with this pain off and on since I'm a wee child, and done took enough medicine to float the whole entire United States Navy: ain't nona it done me a bita good nohow. There was a witch woman lived a piece down the road (Miz Gus Hulie) usta make a fine magic brew, and that helped some. Poor white lady. Miz Gus Hulie. Met a terrible accident: fell into an ol Injun grave and was too feeble for to climb out." Tall, powerful, barefoot, graceful, soundless, Missouri Fever was like a supple black cat as she paraded serenely about the kitchen, the casual flow of her walk beautifully sensuous and haughty. She was slant-eyed, and darker than the charred stove; her crooked hair stood straight on end, as if she'd seen a ghost, and her lips were thick and purple. The length of her neck was something to ponder upon, for she was almost a freak, a human giraffe, and Joel recalled photos, which he'd scissored once from the pages of a *National Geographic,* of curious African ladies with countless silver chokers stretching their necks to improbable heights. Though she wore no silver bands, naturally, there was a sweat-stained blue polka-dot bandanna wrapped round the middle of her soaring neck. "Papadaddy and me's countin on you for our Service," she said, after filling two coffee cups and mannishly straddling a chair at the table. "We got our own little place backa the garden, so you scoot over later on, and we'll have us a real good ol time."

"I'll come if I can, but this being my first day and all, Dad will most likely expect me to visit with him," said Joel hopefully.

Missouri emptied her coffee into a saucer, blew on it, dumped it back into the cup, sucked up a swallow, and smacked her lips. "This here's the Lord's day," she announced. "You believe in Him? You got faith in His healin power?"

Joel said: "I go to church."

"Now that ain't what I'm speakin of. Take for instance, when you thinks bout the Lord, what is it passes in your mind?"

"Oh, stuff," he said, though actually, whenever he had occasion to remember that a God in heaven supposedly kept his record, one thing he thought of was money: quarters his mother had given him for each Bible stanza memorized, dimes diverted from the Sunday School collection plate to Gabaldoni's Soda Fountain, the tinkling rain of coins as the cashiers of the church solicited among the congregation. But Joel didn't much like God, for He had betrayed him too many times. "Just stuff like saying my prayers."

"When I thinks bout Him, I thinks bout what I'm gonna do when Papa-daddy goes to his rest," said Missouri, and rinsed her mouth with a big swallow of coffee. "Well, I'm gonna spread my wings and fly way to some swell city up north like Washington, D.C."

"Aren't you happy here?"

"Honey, there's things you too young to unnerstand."

"I'm thirteen," he declared. "And you'd be surprised how much I know."

"Shoot, boy, the country's just fulla folks what knows everythin, and don't unnerstand nothin, just fullofem," she said, and began to prod her upper teeth: she had a flashy gold tooth, and it occurred to Joel that the prodding was designed for attracting his attention to it. "Now one reason is, I get lonesome: what I all the time say is, you ain't got no notion what lonesome is till you stayed a spell at the Landin. And there ain't no mens round here I'm innersted in, leastwise not at the present: one time there was this mean buzzard name of Keg, but he did a crime to me and landed hisself on the chain gang, which is sweet justice considerin the lowdown kinda trash he was. I'm only a girl of fourteen when he did this bad thing to me." A fist-like knot of flies, hovering over a sugar jar, dispersed every whichaway as she swung an irritated hand. "Yessir, Keg Brown, that's the name he go by." With a fingertip she shined her gold tooth to a brighter luster while her slanted eyes scrutinized Joel; these eyes were like wild foxgrapes, or two discs of black porcelain, and they looked out intelligently from their almond slits. "I gotta longin for city life poisonin my blood cause I was brung up in St. Louis till Papadaddy fetched me here for to nurse him in his dyin days. Papadaddy was past ninety then, and they say he ain't long for this world, so I come. That be thirteen year ago, and now it look to me like Papadaddy gonna outlive Methusaleh. Make no mistake, I love Papadaddy, but when he gone I sure aimin to light out for Washington, D.C., or Boston, Coneckikut. And that's what I thinks bout when I thinks bout God."

"Why not New Orleans?" said Joel. "There are all kinds of good-looking fellows in New Orleans."

"Aw, I ain't studyin no New Orleans. It ain't only the mens, honey: I wants to be where they got snow, and not all this sunshine. I wants to walk around in snow up to my hips: watch it come outa the sky in gret big globs. Oh, pretty . . . pretty. You ever see the snow?"

Rather breathlessly, Joel lied and claimed that he most certainly had; it was a pardonable deception, for he had a great yearning to see bona fide snow: next to owning the Koh-i-noor diamond, that was his ultimate secret wish. Some-times, on flat boring afternoons, he'd squatted on the curb of St. Deval Street and daydreamed silent pearly snowclouds into sifting coldly through the boughs of the dry, dirty trees. Snow falling in August and silvering the glassy pavement, the ghostly flakes icing his hair, coating rooftops, changing the grimy old neighborhood into a hushed frozen white wasteland uninhabited except for himself and a menagerie of wonder-beasts: albino antelopes, and ivory-breasted snowbirds; and occasionally there were humans, such fantastic folk as Mr. Mystery, the vaudeville hypnotist, and Lucky Rogers, the movie star, and Madame Veronica, who read fortunes in a Vieux Carré tearoom. "It was one stormy night in Canada that I saw the snow," he said, though the farthest north he'd ever set foot was Richmond, Virginia. "We were lost in the mountains, Mother and me, and snow, tons and tons of it, was piling up all around us. And we lived in an ice-cold cave for a solid week, and we kept slapping each other to stay awake: if you fall asleep in snow, chances are you'll never see the light of day again."

"Then what happened?" said Missouri, disbelief subtly narrowing her eyes.

"Well, things got worse and worse. Mama cried, and the tears froze on her face like little BB bullets, and she was always cold. . . ." Nothing had warmed her, not the fine wool blankets, not the mugs of hot toddy Ellen fixed. "Each night hungry wolves howled in the mountains, and I prayed. . . ." In the darkness of the garage he'd prayed, and in the lavatory at school, and in the first row of the Nemo Theatre while duelling gangsters went unnoticed on the magic screen. "The snow kept falling, and heavy drifts blocked the entrance to the cave, but uh . . ." Stuck. It was the end of a Saturday serial that leaves the hero locked in a slowly filling gas chamber.

"*And?*"

"And a man in a red coat, a Canadian mountie, rescued us. . . . only me, really: Mama had already frozen to death."

Missouri denounced him with considerable disgust. "You is a gret big story."

"Honest, cross my heart," and he x-ed his chest.

"Uh uh. You Mama die in the sick bed. Mister Randolph say so."

Somehow, spinning the tale, Joel had believed every word; the cave, the howling wolves, these had seemed more real than Missouri and her long neck, or Miss Amy, or the shadowy kitchen. "You won't tattle, will you, Missouri? About what a liar I am."

She patted his arm gently. "Course not, honey. Come to think, I wish I had me a two-bit piece for every story I done told. Sides, you tell good lies, the kind I likes to hear. We gonna get along just elegant: me, I ain't but eight years older'n you, and you been to the school." Her voice, which was like melted chocolate, was warm and tender. "Les us be friends."

"O.K.," said Joel, toasting her with his coffee cup, "friends."

"And somethin else is, you call me Zoo. Zoo's my rightful name, and I always been called by that till Papadaddy let on it stood for Missouri, which is the state where is located the city of St. Louis. *Them,* Miss Amy 'n Mister Randolph, they so proper: Missouri this 'n Missouri t'other, day in, day out. Huh! You call me Zoo."

Joel saw an opening. "Does my father call you Zoo?"

She dipped down into the blouse of her gingham dress, and withdrew a silver compact. Opening it, she took a pinch of snuff, and sniffed it up her wide nose. "Happy Dip, that's the bestest brand."

"Is he awful sick—Mister Sansom?" Joel persisted.

"Take a pinch," she said, extending her compact.

And he accepted, anxious not to offend her. The ginger-colored powder had a scalding, miserable taste, like devil's pepper; he sneezed, and when water sprang up in his eyes he covered his face ashamedly with his hands.

"You laughin or cryin, boy?"

"Crying," he whimpered, and this came close to truth. "Everybody in the house is stone deaf."

"I ain't deaf, honey," said Zoo, sounding sincerely concerned. "Have the backache and stomach jitters, but I ain't deaf."

"Then why does everybody act so queer? Gee whiz, every time I mention Mister Sansom you'd think . . . you'd think . . . and in the town . . ." He rubbed his eyes and peeked at Zoo. "Like just now, when I asked if he was really ill . . ."

Zoo glanced worriedly at the window where fig leaves pressed against the glass like green listening ears. "Miss Amy done tol you he ain't the healthiest man."

The flies buzzed back to the sugar jar, and the ticktuck of the defective clock was loud. "Is he going to die?" said Joel.

The scrape of a chair. Zoo was up and rinsing pans in a tub with water from a well-bucket. "We friends, that's fine," she said, talking over her shoulder. "Only don't never ax me nothin bout Mister Sansom. Miss Amy the one take care of him. Ax her. Ax Mister Randolph. I ain't in noways messed up with Mister Sansom; don't even fix him his vittels. Me and Papadaddy, us got our own troubles."

Joel snapped shut the snuff compact, and revolved it in his hands, examining the unique design. It was round and the silver was cut like a turtle's shell; a real butterfly, arranged under a film of lime glass, figured the lid; the butterfly wings were the luminously misty orange of a full moon. So elegant a case, he reasoned, was never meant for ordinary snuff, but rare golden powders, precious witch potions, love sand.

"Yessir, us got our own troubles."

"Zoo," he said, "where'd you get this?"

She was kneeling on the floor cursing quietly as she shoveled ashes out of the stove. The firelight rippled over her black face and danced a yellow light in her foxgrape eyes which now cut sideways questioningly. "My box?" she said. "Mister Randolph gimme it one Christmas way long ago. He make it hisself, makes lotsa pretty dodads long that line."

Joel studied the compact with awed respect; he would've sworn it was store-bought. Distastefully he recalled his own attempts at hand-made gifts: necktie racks, tool kits, and the like; they were mighty sorry by comparison. He comforted himself with the thought that Cousin Randolph must be older than he'd supposed.

"I usta been usin it for cheek-red," said Zoo, advancing to claim her treasure. She dipped more snuff before re-depositing it down her dress-front. "But seein as I don't go over to Noon City no more (ain't been in two years), I reckoned it'd do to keep my Happy Dip good 'n dry. Sides, no sense paintin up less there's mens round a lady is innerested in . . . which there ain't." A mean expression pinched her face as she gazed at the sunspots freckling the linoleum. "That Keg Brown, the one what landed on the chain gang cause he did me a bad turn, I hope they got him out swingin a ninety-pound pick under this hot sun." And, as if it were sore, she touched her long neck lightly. "Well," she sighed, "spec I best get to tendin Papadaddy: I'm gonna take him some hoecake and molasses: he must be powerful hungry."

Joel watched apathetically while she broke off a cold slab of cornbread, and poured a preserve jar half-full of thick molasses. "How come you don't fix yourself a sling-shot, and go out and kill a mess of birds?" she suggested.

"Dad will probably want me in a minute," he told her. "Miss Amy said she'd see, so I guess I'd better stick around here."

"Mister Randolph likes the dead birds, the kinds with pretty feathers. Won't do you no good squattin in this dark ol kitchen." Her naked feet were soundless as she moved away. "You be at the Service, you hear?"

The fire had waned to ashes, and, while the old broken clock ticked like an invalid heart, the sunspots on the floor spread and darkened; the shadows of the fig leaves trellising the walls swelled to an enormous quivering shape, like the crystal flesh of a jellyfish. Flies skittered along the table, rubbing their restless hair-feet, and zoomed and sang round Joel's ears. When, two hours later, two that seemed five, he raised the clock off its battered face it promptly stopped beating and all sense of life faded from the kitchen; three-twenty its bent hands recorded: three, the empty, middle hour of an endless afternoon. She was not coming. Joel plowed his fingers through his hair. She was not coming, and it was all some crazy trick.

His leg had gone numb from resting so long in one position, and it tingled bloodlessly as he got up and limped out of the kitchen, and down the hall, calling plaintively: "Miss Amy. Miss Amy."

He swished the lavender curtains apart, and moved into the bleak light filling the barren, polished chamber towards his image floating on the watery-surfaced lookingglass; his formless reflected face was wide-lipped and one-eyed, as if it were a heat-softened wax effigy; the lips were a gauzy line, the eyes a glaring bubble. "Miss Amy . . . anybody!"

Somewhere in a school textbook of Joel's was a statement contending that the earth at one time was probably a white hot sphere, like the sun; now, standing in the scorched garden, he remembered it. He had reached the garden by following a path which led round from the front of the house through the rampart of interlacing trees. And here, in the overgrown confusion, were some plants taller than his head, and others razor-sharp with thorns; brittle sun-curled leaves crackled under his cautious step. The dry, tangled weeds grew waist high. The sultry smells of summer and sweet shrub and dark earth were heavy, and the itchy whirr of bumblebees stung the silence. He could hardly raise his eyes upward, for the sky was pure blue fire. The wall of the house rising above the garden was like a great yellow cliff, and patches of Virginia creeper greenly framed all its eight overlooking windows.

Joel trampled down the tough undergrowth till he came up flat against the house. He was bored, and figured he might as well play Blackmail, a kind of peeping-tom game members of the Secret Nine had fooled around with when there was absolutely nothing else to do. Blackmail was practiced in New Orleans only after sunset, inasmuch as daylight could be fatal for a player, the idea being to approach a strange house and peer invisibly through its windows. On these dangerous evening patrols, Joel had witnessed many peculiar specta-cles, like the night he'd watched a young girl waltzing stark naked to victrola music; and again, an old lady drop dead while puffing at a fairyland of candles burning on a birthday cake; and most puzzling of all, two grown men standing in an ugly little room kissing each other.

The parlor of Skully's Landing ran the ground-floor's length; gold draperies tied with satin tassels obscured the greater part of its dusky, deserted interior, but Joel, his nose mashed against a pane, could make out a group of heavy chairs clustered like fat dowagers round a teatable. And a gilded loveseat of lilac velvet, an Empire sofa next to a marble fireplace, and a cabinet, one of three, the others of which were indistinct, gleaming with china figurines and ivory fans and curios. On top of a table directly before him were a Japanese pagoda, and an ornate shepherd lamp, chandelier prisms dangling from its geranium globe like jeweled icicles.

He slipped away from the window and crossed the garden to the slanting shade of a willow. The diamond glitter of the afternoon hurt his eyes, and he was as slippery with sweat as a greased wrestler; it stood to reason such weather would have to break. A rooster crowed beyond the garden, and it had for him the same sad, woebegone sound as a train whistle wailing late at night. A train. He sure wished he were aboard one headed far from here. If he could get to see his father! Miss Amy, she was a mean old bitch. Stepmothers always were. Well, just let her try and lay a hand on him. He'd tell her off soon as look at her, by God. He was pretty brave. Who was it licked Sammy Silverstein to a frazzle a year ago come next October? But gee, Sammy was a good kid, kind of. And he wondered what devilment old Sammy was up to right this minute. Probably sitting in the Nemo Theatre stuffing his belly with popcorn; yeah, that's where you'd find him, because this was the matinee they were going to show that spook picture about a batty scientist changing Lucky Rogers into a murderous gorilla. Of all the pictures he would have to miss that one. Hell! Now supposing he did suddenly decide to make dust tracks on the road? Maybe it would be fun to own a barrel organ and a monkey. And there was always the soda-jerking business: anybody that liked ice-cream sodas as much as he did ought to be able to make one. Hell!

"Ra ta ta ta," went his machine gun as he charged toward the five broken porch columns. And then, midway between the pillars and a clump of golden-rod, he discovered the bell. It was a bell like those used in slave-days to summon fieldhands from work; the metal had turned a mildewed green, and the platform on which it rested was rotten. Fascinated, Joel squatted Indian-style and poked his head inside the bell's flared mouth; the lint of withered spider webs hung everywhere, and a delicate green lizard, racing liquidly round the rusty hollow, swerved, flicked its tongue, and nailed its pinpoint eyes on Joel, who withdrew in disordered haste.

Rising, he glanced up at the yellow wall of the house, and speculated as to which of the top-floor windows belonged to him, his father, Cousin Randolph. It was at this point that he saw the queer lady. She was holding aside the curtains of the left corner window, and smiling and nodding at him, as if in greeting or approval; but she was no one Joel had ever known: the hazy substance of her face, the suffused marshmallow features, brought to mind his own vaporish reflection in the wavy chamber mirror. And her white hair was like the wig of a character from history: a towering pale pompadour with fat dribbling curls. Whoever she was, and Joel could not imagine, her sudden appearance seemed to throw a trance across the garden: a butterfly, poised on a dahlia stem, ceased winking its wings, and the rasping F of the bumblebees droned into nothing.

When the curtain fell abruptly closed, and the window was again empty, Joel, reawakening, took a backward step and stumbled against the bell: one raucous, cracked note rang out, shattering the hot stillness.

Three

"Hey, Lord!" STAMP. "Hey, Lord!" STAMP. "Don't wanna ride on the devil's side . . . jus wanna ride with You!"

Zoo squeezed the music from a toylike accordion, and pounded her flat foot on the rickety cabin-porch floor. "Oh devil done weep, devil done cried, cause he gonna miss me on my last lonesome ride." A prolonged shout: the fillet of gold glistened in the frightening volcano of her mouth, and the little mail-order accordion, shoved in, shoved out, was like a lung of pleated paper and pearl shell. "Gonna miss me . . ."

For some time the rainbird had shrilled its cool promise from an elderberry lair, and the sun was locked in a tomb of clouds, tropical clouds that nosed across the low sky, massing into a mammoth grey mountain.

Jesus Fever sat surrounded by a mound of beautiful scrapquilt pillows in a rocker fashioned out of old barrel-staves; his reverent falsetto quavered like a broken ocarina-note, and occasionally he raised his hands to give a feeble, soundless clap.

". . . on my ride!"

Perched on a toadstool-covered stump growing level with the porch, Joel alternated his interest between Zoo's highjinks and the changing weather; the instant of petrified violence that sometimes foreruns a summer storm saturated the hushed yard, and in the unearthly tinseled light rusty buckets of trailing fern which were strung round the porch like party lanterns appeared illuminated by a faint green inward flame. A damp breeze, tuning in the boles of waterbays, carried the fresh mixed scent of rain, of pine and June flowers blooming in far-off fields. The cabin door swung open, banged closed, and there came the muffled rattle of the Landing's window-shutters being drawn.

Zoo mashed out a final gaudy chord, and put the accordion aside. She had varnished her upended hair with brilliantine, and exchanged the polka-dot neckerchief for a frayed red ribbon. Different colored threads darned her white dress in a dozen spots, and she'd jeweled her ears with a pair of rhinestone earrings.

"If you gotta thirst, and the water done gone, PRAY to the Lord, pray on and on." Outstretching her arms, balanced like a tightrope walker, she stepped into the yard, and strutted round Joel's tree stump. "If you gotta lover, and the lover done gone, PRAY to the Lord, pray on and on."

High in chinaberry towers the wind moved swift as a river, the frenzied leaves, caught in its current, frothed like surf on the sky's shore. And slowly the land came to seem as though it were submerged in dark deep water. The fern undulated like sea-floor plants, the cabin loomed mysterious as a sunken galleon hulk, and Zoo, with her fluid, insinuating grace, could only be, Joel thought, the mermaid bride of an old drowned pirate.

"If you gotta hunger, and the food done gone, PRAY to the Lord, pray on and on."

A yellow tabby loped across the yard, and sprang nimbly into Jesus Fever's lap; it was the cat Joel had seen skulking in the garden lilac. Clambering to the old man's shoulder, it smooched its crafty mug next to the puny cheek, its tawny astonished eyes blazing at Joel. It rumbled as the little Negro stroked the striped belly. Minus his derby hat, Jesus Fever's skull, except for sparse sprouts of motheaten wool, was like a ball of burnished metal; a black suit double his size sagged dilapidatedly on his delicate frame, and he wore tiny high-button shoes of orange leather. The spirit of the service was rousing him mightily, and, from time to time, he honked his nose between his fingers, tossing the discharge into the fern.

The rhythmic chain of Zoo's half-sung, half-shouted phrases rose and fell like her pounding foot, and her earrings, dangling with the sway of her head, shot flecks of sparkle. "Listen oh Lord when us pray, kindly hear what us has to say. . . ."

Silent lightning zigzagged miles away, then another bolt, this a dragon of crackling white, now not too distant, was followed by a crawling thunder-roll. A bantam rooster raced for the safety of a well-shed, and the triangular shadow of a crow flock cut the sky.

"I cold," complained Jesus petulantly. "Leg all swole up with rain. I cold. . . ." The cat curled in his lap, its head flopped over his knee like a wilted dahlia.

The off-on flash of Zoo's gold tooth made Joel's heart suddenly like a rock rattling in his chest, for it suggested to him a certain winking neon sign: *R. R. Oliver's Funeral Estb.* Darkness. *R. R. Oliver's Funeral Estb.* Darkness. "Downright tacky, but they don't charge too outlandish," that's what Ellen had said, standing before the plate window where a fan of gladiolas blushed livid under the electric letters publicizing a cheap but decent berth en route to the kingdom and the glory. Now here again he'd locked the door and thrown away the key: there was conspiracy abroad, even his father had a grudge against him, even God. Somewhere along the line he'd been played a mean trick. Only he didn't know who or what to blame. He felt separated, without identity, a stone-boy mounted on the rotted stump: there was no connection linking himself and the waterfall of elderberry leaves cascading on the ground, or, rising beyond, the Landing's steep, intricate roof.

"I cold. I wants to wrap up in the bed. It gonna storm."

"Hold your tater, Papadaddy."

Then an unusual thing occurred: as if following the directions of a treasure map, Zoo took three measured paces toward a dingy little rose bush, and, frowning up at the sky, discarded the red ribbon binding her throat. A narrow scar circled her neck like a necklace of purple wire; she traced a finger over it lightly.

"When the time come for that Keg Brown to go, Lord, just you send him back in a hounddog's nasty shape, ol hound ain't nobody wants to trifle with: a haunted dog."

It was as though a brutal hawk had soared down and clawed away Joel's eyelids, forcing him to gape at her throat. Zoo. Maybe she was like him, and the world had a grudge against her, too. But christamighty he didn't want to end up with a scar like that. Except what chance have you got when there is always trickery in one hand, and danger in the other. No chance whatsoever. None. A coldness went along his spine. Thunder boomed overhead. The earth shook. He leaped off the stump, and made for the house, his loosened shirt-tail flying behind; run, run, run, his heart told him, and wham! he'd pitched headlong into a briar patch. This was a kind of freak accident. He'd seen the patch, known it for an obstacle, and yet, as though deliberately, he'd thrown himself upon it. But the stinging briar scratches seemed to cleanse him of bewilderment and misery, just as the devil, in fanatic cults, is supposedly, through self-imposed pain, driven from the soul. Realizing the tender concern in Zoo's face as she helped him to his feet, he felt a fool: she was, after all, his friend, and there was no need to be afraid. "Here, little old bad boy," she said kindly, plucking briar needles off his breeches, "how come you act so ugly? Huh, hurt me and Papadaddy's feelins." She took his hand, and led him to the porch.

"Hee hee hee," cackled Jesus, "I tumble thataway, I bust every bone."

Zoo picked up her accordion and, reclining against a porch-pole, presently, with careless effort, produced a hesitant, discordant melody. And her grandfather, in a disappointed child's wheedling singsong, reiterated his grievances: he was about to perish of chill, but what matter; who gave a goldarn whether he lived or died? and why didn't Zoo, inasmuch as he'd performed his Sabbath duty, tuck him in his good warm bed and leave him in peace? oh there were cruel folk in this world, and heartless ways.

"Hush up and bow that head, Papadaddy," said Zoo. "We gonna end this meetin proper-like. We gonna tell Him our prayers. Joel, honey, bow that head."

The trio on the porch were figures in a woodcut engraving; the Ancient on his throne of splendid pillows, a yellow pet relaxed in his lap gazing gravely in the drowning light at the small servant bowed at its master's feet, and the arms of the black arrow-like daughter lifted above them all, as if in benediction.

But there was no prayer in Joel's mind; rather, nothing a net of words could capture, for, with one exception, all his prayers of the past had been simple concrete requests: God, give me a bicycle, a knife with seven blades, a box of oil paints. Only how, how, could you say something so indefinite, so meaningless as this: God, let me be loved.

"Amen," whispered Zoo.

And in this moment, like a swift intake of breath, the rain came.

Four

"Can't we be more specific?" said Randolph, languidly pouring a glass of sherry. "Was she fat, tall, lean?"

"It was hard to tell," said Joel.

Outside in the night, rain washed the roof with close slanted sounds, but here kerosene lamps spun webs of mellow light in the darkest corner, and the kitchen-window mirrored the scene like a golden lookingglass. So far Joel's first supper at the Landing had gone along well enough. He felt very much at ease with Randolph, who, at each conversational lag, introduced topics which might interest and flatter a boy of thirteen: Joel found himself holding forth exceedingly well (he thought) on Do Human Beings Inhabit Mars? How Do You Suppose Egyptians Really Mummified Folks? Are Headhunters Still Active? and other controversial subjects. It was due more or less to an overdose of sherry (disliking the taste, but goaded by the hope of getting sure enough drunk . . . now wouldn't he have something to write Sammy Silverstein! . . . three thimble glasses had been drained) that Joel mentioned the Lady.

"Heat," said Randolph. "Exposing one's bare head to the sun occasionally results in minor hallucinations. Dear me, yes. Once, some years ago, while airing in the garden, I seemed quite distinctly to see a sunflower transformed into a man's face, the face of a scrappy little boxer I admired at one point, a Mexican named Pepe Alvarez." He fondled his chin reflectively, and wrinkled his nose, as if to convey that this name had for him particular implications. "Stunning experience, so impressive I cut the flower, and pressed it in a book;

even now, if I come across it, I fancy . . . but that is neither here nor there. It was the sun, I'm sure. Amy, dearest, what do you think?"

Amy, who was brooding over her food, glanced up, rather startled. "No more for me, thank you," she said.

Randolph frowned in mock annoyance. "As usual, out picking the little blue flower of forgetfulness."

Her narrow face softened with pleasure. "Silver-tongued devil," she said, unreserved adoration brightening her sharp little eyes, and making them, for an instant, almost beautiful.

"To begin at the beginning, then," he said, and burped (*"Excusez-moi, s'il vous plaît.* Blackeyed peas, you understand; most indigestible"). He patted his lips daintily. "Now where was I, oh yes . . . Joel refuses to be persuaded we at the Landing aren't harboring spirits."

"That isn't what I said," Joel protested.

"Some of Missouri's chatter," was Amy's calm opinion. "Just a hotbed of crazy nigger-notions, that girl. Remember when she wrung the neck off every chicken on the place? Oh, it isn't funny, don't laugh. I've sometimes wondered what would happen if it got into her head *his* soul inhabited one of us."

"Keg?" said Joel. "You mean Keg's soul?"

"Don't tell me!" cried Randolph, and giggled in the prim, suffocated manner of an old maid. "Already?"

"I didn't think it was so funny," said Joel resentfully. "He did a bad thing to her."

Amy said: "Randolph's only cutting up."

"You malign me, angel."

"It wasn't funny," said Joel.

Squinting one eye, Randolph studied the spokes of amber light whirling out from the sherry as he raised and revolved his glass. "Not funny, dear me, no. But the story has a certain bizarre interest: would you care to hear it?"

"How unnecessary," said Amy. "The child's morbid enough."

"All children are morbid: it's their one saving grace," said Randolph, and went right ahead. "This happened more than a decade ago, and in a cold, very cold November. There was working for me at the time a strapping young buck, splendidly proportioned, and with skin the color of swamp honey." A curious quality about Randolph's voice had worried Joel from the first, but not till now could he put a finger on it: Randolph spoke without an accent of any kind: his weary voice was free of regional defects, yet there was an emotional undercurrent, a caustic lilt of sarcasm which gave it a rather emphatic personality.

"He was, however, a little feeble-minded. The feeble-minded, the neurotic, the criminal, perhaps, also, the artist, have unpredictability and perverted innocence in common." His expression became smugly remote, as though, having made an observation he thought superior, he must pause and listen admiringly while it reverberated in his head. "Let's compare them to a Chinese chest: the sort, you remember, that opens into a second box, another, still another, until at length you come upon the last . . . the latch is touched, the lid springs open to reveal . . . what unsuspected cache?" He smiled wanly, and tasted the sherry. Then, from the breastpocket of the taffy-silk pyjama top that he wore, he extracted a cigarette, and struck a match. The cigarette had a strange, medicinal odor, as though the tobacco had been long soaked in the juice of acid herbs: it was the smell that identifies a house where asthma reigns. As he puckered his lips to blow a smoke ring, the pattern of his talcumed face was suddenly complete: it seemed composed now of nothing but circles: though not fat, it was round as a coin, smooth and hairless; two discs of rough pink colored his cheeks, and his nose had a broken look, as if once punched by a strong angry fist; curly, very blond, his fine hair fell in childish yellow ringlets across his forehead, and his wide-set, womanly eyes were like sky-blue marbles.

"So they were in love, Keg and Missouri, and we had the wedding here, the bride all clothed in family lace . . ."

"Nice as any white girl, I'll tell you," said Amy. "Pretty as a picture."

Joel said: "But if he was crazy . . ."

"She was never one for reasoning," sighed Randolph. "Only fourteen, of course, a child, but decidedly stubborn: she wanted to marry, and so she did. We lent them a room here in the house the week of their honeymoon, and let them use the yard to have a fishfry for their friends."

"And my dad . . . was he at the wedding?"

Randolph, looking blank, tapped ash onto the floor. "But then one night, very late . . ." Lowering his eyelids sleepily, he drew a finger round the rim of his glass. "Does Amy, by chance, recall the very *original* thing I did when we heard Missouri scream?"

Amy couldn't make up her mind whether she did or not. Ten years, after all, was a long time.

"We were sitting like this in the parlor, doesn't that come back? And I said: it's the wind. Of course I knew it wasn't." He paused, and sucked in his cheeks, as though the memory proved too exquisitely humorous for him to maintain a straight face. He aimed a gun-like finger at Joel, and cocked his thumb: "So I put a roller in the pianola, and it played the Indian Love Call."

"Such a sweet song," said Amy. "So sad. I don't know why you never let me play the pianola any more."

"Keg cut her throat," said Joel, a mood of panic bubbling up, for he couldn't follow the peculiar turn Randolph's talk had taken; it was like trying to decipher some tale being told in a senseless foreign language, and he despised this left-out feeling, just when he'd begun to feel close to Randolph. "I saw her scar," he said, and all but shouted for attention, "that's what Keg did."

"Uh yes, absolutely."

"It went like this," and Amy hummed: "When I'm calling yoo hoo de da dum de da . . ."

"... from ear to ear: ruined a roseleaf quilt my great-great aunt in Tennessee lost her eyesight stitching."

"Zoo says he's on the chain gang, and she hopes he never gets off: she told the Lord to make him into an old dog."

"Will you answer da de de da ... that isn't quite the tune, is it, Randolph?"

"A little off-key."

"But how should it go?"

"Haven't the faintest notion, angel."

Joel said: "Poor Zoo."

"Poor everybody," said Randolph, languidly pouring another sherry.

Greedy moths flattened their wings against the lamp funnels. Near the stove rain seeped through a leak in the roof, dripping with dismal regularity into an empty coal scuttle. "It's the kind of thing that happens when you tamper with the smallest box," observed Randolph, the sour smoke from his cigarette spiraling toward Joel, who, with discreet handwaves, directed it elsewhere.

"I do wish you'd let me play the pianola," said Amy wistfully. "But I don't suppose you realize how much I enjoy it, what a comfort it is."

Randolph cleared his throat, and grinned, dimples denting his cheeks. His face was like a round ripe peach. He was considerably younger than his cousin: somewhere, say, in his middle thirties. "Still, we haven't exorcized Master Knox's ghost."

"It wasn't any ghost," muttered Joel. "There isn't any such of a thing: this was a real live lady, and I saw her."

"And what did she look like, dear?" said Amy, her tone indicating her thoughts were fastened on less far-fetched matters. It reminded Joel of Ellen and his mother: they also had used this special distant voice when suspicious of his stories, only allowing him to proceed for the sake of peace. The old trigger-quick feeling of guilt came over him: a liar, that's what the two of them, Amy and Randolph, were thinking, just a natural-born liar, and believing this he began to elaborate his description embarrassingly: she had the eyes of a fiend, the lady did, wild witch-eyes, cold and green as the bottom of the North Pole sea; twin to the Snow Queen, her face was pale, wintry, carved from ice, and her white hair towered on her head like a wedding cake. She had beckoned to him with a crooked finger, beckoned ...

"Gracious," said Amy, nibbling a cube of watermelon pickle. "You really saw such a person!"

While talking, Joel had noticed with discomfort her cousin's amused, entertained expression: earlier, when he'd given his first flat account, Randolph had heard him out in the colorless way one listens to a stale joke, for he seemed, in some curious manner, to have advance knowledge of the facts.

"You know," said Amy slowly, and suspended the watermelon pickle midway between plate and mouth, "Randolph, have you been ..." she paused, her eyes sliding sideways to confront the smooth, amused peachface. "Well, that *does* sound like . . ."

Randolph kicked her under the table; he accomplished this maneuver so skillfully it would have escaped Joel altogether had Amy's response been less extreme: she jerked back as though lightning had rocked the chair, and, shielding her eyes with the gloved hand, let out a pitiful wail: "Snake a snake I thought it was a snake bit me crawled under the table bit me foot you fool never forgive bit me my heart a snake," repeated over and over the words began to rhyme, to hum from wall to wall where giant moth shadows jittered.

Joel went all hollow inside; he thought he was going to wee wee right there in his breeches, and he wanted to hop up and run, just as he had at Jesus Fever's. Only he couldn't, not this time. So he looked hard at the window where fig leaves tapped a wet windy message, and tried with all his might to find the far-away room.

"Stop it this instant," commanded Randolph, making no pretense of his disgust. But when she could not seem to regain control he reached over and slapped her across the mouth. Then gradually she tapered off to a kind of hiccuping sob.

Randolph touched her arm solicitously. "All better, angel?" he said. "Dear me, you gave us a fright." Glancing at Joel, he added: "Amy is so very highstrung."

"So very," she agreed. "It was just that I thought . . . I hope I haven't upset the child."

But the walls of Joel's room were too thick for Amy's voice to penetrate. Now for a long time he'd been unable to find the far-away room; always it had been difficult, but never so hard as in the last year. So it was good to see his friends again. They were all here, including Mr Mystery, who wore a crimson cape, a plumed Spanish hat, a glittery monocle, and had all his teeth made of solid gold: an elegant gentleman, though given to talking tough from the side of his mouth, and an artist, a great magician: he played the vaudeville downtown in New Orleans twice a year, and did all kinds of eerie tricks. This is how they got to be such buddies. One time he picked Joel from the audience, brought him up on the stage, and pulled a whole basketful of cotton-candy clean out of his ears; thereafter, next to little Annie Rose Kuppermann, Mr Mystery was the most welcome visitor to the other room. Annie Rose was the cutest thing you ever saw. She had jet black hair and a real permanent wave. Her mother kept her dressed in snow white on Sundays and all clear down to her socks. In real life, Annie Rose was too stuck up and sassy to even tell him the time of day, but here in the far-away room her cute little voice jingled on and on: "I love you, Joel. I love you a bushel and a peck and a hug around the neck." And there was someone else who rarely failed to show up, though seldom appearing as the same person twice; that is, he came in various costumes and disguises, sometimes as a circus strong-man, sometimes as a big swell millionaire, but always his name was Edward Q. Sansom.

Randolph said: "She seeks revenge: out of the goodness of my heart I'm going to endure a few infernal minutes of the pianola. Would you mind, Joel, dear, helping with the lamps?"

Like the kitchen, Mr Mystery and little Annie Rose Kuppermann slipped into darkness when the lifted lamps passed through the hall to the parlor.

Ragtime fingers danced spectrally over the upright's yellowed ivories, the carnival strains of "Over the Waves" gently vibrating a girandole's crystal prism-fringe. Amy sat on the piano stool, cooling her little white face with a blue lace fan which she'd taken from the curio cabinet, and rigidly watched the mechanical thumping of the pianola keys.

"That's a parade song," said Joel. "I rode a float in the Mardi Gras once, all fixed up like a Chink with a long black pigtail, only a drunk man yanked it off, and set to whipping his ladyfriend with it right smack in the street."

Randolph inched nearer to Joel on the loveseat. Over his pyjamas he wore a seersucker kimono with butterfly sleeves, and his plumpish feet were encased in a pair of tooled-leather sandals: his exposed toenails had a manicured gloss. Up close, he had a delicate lemon scent, and his hairless face looked not much older than Joel's. Staring straight ahead, he groped for Joel's hand, and hooked their fingers together.

Amy closed her fan with a reproachful snap. "You never thanked me," she said.

"For what, dearheart?"

Holding hands with Randolph was obscurely disagreeable, and Joel's fingers tensed with an impulse to dig his nails into the hot dry palm; also, Randolph wore a ring which pressed painfully between Joel's knuckles. This was a lady's ring, a smoky rainbow opal clasped by sharp silver prongs.

"Why, the feathers," reminded Amy. "The nice bluejay feathers."

"Lovely," said Randolph, and blew her a kiss.

Satisfied, she spread the fan and worked it furiously. Behind her, the girandole quivered, and shedding lilac, loosened by the ragged pounding of the pianola, scattered on a table. A lamp had been placed by the empty hearth, so that it glowed out like a wavery ashen fire. "This is the first year a cricket hasn't visited," she said. "Every summer one has always hidden in the fireplace, and sang till autumn: remember, Randolph, how Angela Lee would never let us kill it?"

Joel quoted: "Hark to the crickets crying in grass, Hear them serenading in the sassafras."

Randolph bent forward. "A charming boy, little Joel, dear Joel," he whispered. "Try to be happy here, try a little to like me, will you?"

Joel was used to compliments, imaginary ones originating in his head, but to have some such plainly spoken left him with an uneasy feeling: was he being poked fun at, teased? So he questioned the round innocent eyes, and saw his own boy-face focused as in double camera lenses. Amy's cousin was in earnest. He looked down at the opal ring, touched and sorry he could've ever had a mean thought like wanting to dig his nails into Randolph's palm. "I like you already," he said.

Randolph smiled and squeezed his hand.

"What are you two whispering about?" said Amy jealously. "I declare you're rude." Suddenly the pianola was silent, the trembling girandole still. "May I play something else, Randolph, oh please?"

"I think we've had quite enough . . . unless Joel would care to hear another."

Joel bided time, tasting his power; then, recalling the miserable lonesome afternoon, spitefully gave a negative nod.

Amy pursed her lips. ". . . the last chance you'll ever have to humiliate me," she told Randolph, flouncing over to the curio cabinet, and replacing her blue fan. Joel had inspected the contents of this cabinet before supper, and had yearned to have as his own such treasures as a jolly Buddha with a fat jade belly, a two-headed china crocodile, the program of a Richmond ball dated 1862 and autographed by Robert E. Lee, a tiny wax Indian in full war regalia, and several plush-framed daintily painted miniatures of virile dandies with villainous mustaches. "It's your house, I'm perfectly aware . . ."

But a queer sound interrupted: a noise like the solitary thump of an over-sized raindrop, it drum-drummed down the stairsteps. Randolph stirred uneasily. "Amy," he said, and coughed significantly. She did not move. "Is it the lady?" asked Joel, but neither answered, and he was sorry he'd drunk the sherry: the parlor, when he did not concentrate hard, had a bent tilted look, like the topsy-turvy room in the crazyhouse at Pontchartrain. The thumping stopped, an instant of quiet, then an ordinary red tennis ball rolled silently through the archway.

With a curtsy, Amy picked it up, and, balancing it in her gloved hand, brought it under close scrutiny, as if it were a fruit she was examining for worms. She exchanged a troubled glance with Randolph.

"Shall I come with you?" he said, as she hurried out.

"Later, when you've sent the boy to bed." Her footsteps resounded on the black stairs; somewhere overhead a doorlatch clicked.

Randolph turned to Joel with a desperately cheerful expression. "Do you play parcheesi?"

Joel was still puzzling over the tennis ball. He concluded, finally, that it would be best just to pretend as though it were the most commonplace thing in the world to have a tennis ball come rolling into your room out of nowhere. He wanted to laugh. Only it wasn't funny. He couldn't believe in the way things were turning out: the difference between this happening, and what he'd expected was too great. It was like paying your fare to see a wild-west show, and walking in on a silly romance picture instead. If that happened, he would feel cheated. And he felt cheated now.

"Or shall I read your fortune?"

Joel held up a clenched hand; the grimy fingers unfurled like the leaves of an opening flower, and the pink of his palm was dotted with sweat-beads. Once, thinking how ideal a career it would make, he'd ordered from a concern in New York City a volume called *Techniques of Fortune-Telling*, authored by an alleged gypsy whose greasy earringed photo adorned the jacket; lack of funds, however, cut short this project, for, in order to become a bonafide fortune-teller, he had to buy, it developed, a generous amount of costly equipment.

"Sooo," mused Randolph, drawing the hand out of shadow nearer lamplight. "Is it important that I see potential voyages, adventure, an alliance with the pretty daughter of some Rockefeller? The future is to me strangely unexciting: long ago I came to realize my life was meant for other times."

"But it's the future I want to know," said Joel.

Randolph shook his head, and his sleepy sky-blue eyes, contemplating Joel, were sober, serious. "Have you never heard what the wise men say: all of the future exists in the past."

"At least may I ask a question?" and Joel did not wait for any judgment: "There are just two things I'd like to know, one is: when am I going to see my dad?" And the quietness of the dim parlor seemed to echo when? when?

Gently releasing the hand, Randolph, a set smile stiffening his face, rose and strolled to a window, his loose kimono swaying about him; he folded his arms like a Chinaman into the butterfly sleeves, and stood very still. "When you are quite settled," he said. "And the other?"

Eyes closed: a dizzy well of stars. Open: a bent tilted room where twin kimonoed figures with curly yellow hair glided back and forth across the lopsided floor. "I saw that Lady, and she was real, wasn't she?" but this was not the question he'd intended.

Randolph opened the window. The rain had stopped, and cicadas were screaming in the wet summer dark. "A matter of viewpoint, I suppose," he said, and yawned. "I know her fairly well, and to me she is a ghost." The night wind blew in from the garden, flourishing the drapes like faded gold flags.

Five

Wednesday, after breakfast, Joel shut himself in his room, and went about the hard task of thinking up letters. It was a hot dull morning, and the Landing, though now and again Randolph's sick cough rattled behind closed doors, seemed, as usual, too quiet, too still. A fat horsefly dived toward the Red Chief tablet where Joel's scrawl wobbled loosely over the paper: at school this haphazard style had earned him an F in penmanship. He twitched, twirled his pencil, paused twice to make water in the china slopjar so artistically festooned with pink-bottomed cupids clutching watercolor bouquets of ivy and violet; eventually, then, the first letter, addressed to his good friend Sammy Silverstein, read, when finished, as follows:

"You would like the house I am living in Sammy as it is a swell house and you would like my dad as he knows all about airplanes like you do. He doesn't look much like your dad though. He doesn't wear specs or smoke cigars, but is tall like Mr Mystery (if Mr Mystery comes to the Nemo this summer write and tell all about it) and smokes a pipe and is very young. He gave me a .22 and when winter comes we will hunt possum and eat possum stew. I wish you could come and visit me as we would have a real good time. One thing we could do is get drunk with my cousin Randolf. We drink alcohol bevrages (sp?) and he is a lot of fun. Its sure not like New Orleans, Sammy. Out here a person old as us is a grown up person. You owe me 20¢. I will forget this det if you will write all news every week. Hello to the gang, remember to write your friend . . ."

and with masterly care he signed his name in a new manner: J.H.K. Sansom. Several times he read it aloud; it had a distinguished, adult sound, a name he could readily imagine prefixed by such proud titles as General, Judge, Governor, Doctor. Doctor J.H.K. Sansom, the celebrated operating specialist; Governor J.H.K. Sansom, the people's choice ("Hello, warden, this is the Governor, just called to say I've given Zoo Fever a reprieve). And then of course the world and all its folks would love him, and Sammy, well, Sammy could sell this old letter for thousands of dollars.

But searching for i's not dotted, t's uncrossed, it came to him that almost all he'd written were lies, big lies poured over the paper like a thick syrup. There was no accounting for them. These things he'd said, they should be true, and they weren't. At home, Ellen was forever airing unwelcome advice, but now he wished he could close his eyes, open them, and see her standing there. She would know what to do.

His pencil traveled so fast occasional words linked: how sorry he was not to have written sooner; he hoped Ellen was o.k., and ditto the kids . . . he missed them all, did they miss him? "It is nicehere," he wrote, but a pain twinged him, so he got up to walk the floor and knock his hands together nervously. How was he going to tell her? He stopped by the window and looked down at the garden where, except for Jesus Fever's tomcat, parading before the ruined columns, all seemed stagnant, painted: the lazy willows, shadowless in the morning sunshine; the hammered slave-bell muffled in the high weeds. Joel shook his head, as if to rock his thoughts into sensible order, then returned to the table, and, angrily pencilling out "It is nicehere," wrote: "Ellen, I hate this place. I don't know where he is and nobody will tell me. Willyou believe it Ellen when I say I have notseen him? Honest; Amy says he's sick but I don't believe oneword as I don't likeher. She lookslike that mean Miss Addie down the street that use to be making suchalot of unecesary stink. Another thing is, there are no radios, picture shows, funny papers and if you want to take a bath you got to fill a washtub with water from the well. I can't see how Randolf keeps clean as he does. I like him o.k. but I don't like it here onebit. Ellen did mama leave enough $ so as I could go away to a school where you can live? Like a military school. Ellen I miss you. Ellen please tell me what to do. Love from Joel XXXXXXXX."

He felt better now, easier in his mind; say what you will, Ellen had never let him down. He felt so good that, stuffing the letters in their envelopes, he began to whistle, and it was the tune the twins had taught him: *when the north wind doth blow, and we shall have snow* . . . What was her name? And that other one, the tomboy? Florabel and Idabel. There was no reason why he had to mope around here all day: hadn't they invited him to visit? Florabel and Idabel and Joel, he thought, whistling happy, whistling loud.

"Quiet in there," came Randolph's muffled complaint. "I'm desperately, desperately ill . . ." and broke off into coughing.

Ha ha! Randolph could go jump in the lake. Ha ha! Joel laughed inwardly as he went to the old bureau where the lacquered chest, containing now his bullet, the bluejay feather, and coins amounting to seventy-eight cents, was hidden in the bottom drawer. Inasmuch as he had no stamps, he figured it would be legal simply to put six cents cash money in the r.f.d. box. So he wadded a nickel and a penny in toilet tissue, gathered his letters and started downstairs, still whistling.

Down by the mailbox he ran into Zoo, and she was not alone, but stood talking with a short bullet-headed Negro. It was Little Sunshine, the hermit. Joel knew this, for Monday night at suppertime Little Sunshine had appeared tapping at the kitchen window; he'd come to call on Randolph, for they were, so Randolph said, "dear friends." He was extra-polite, Little Sunshine, and had brought gifts to all the family: a bucket of swamp honey, two gallons of home-brew, and a wreath of pine needles and tiger lilies which Randolph stuck on his head and galavanted around in the whole evening. Even though he lived far in the dark woods, even though he was a kind of hermit, and everybody knows hermits are evil crazy folks, Joel was not afraid of him. "Little Sunshine, he got more purentee sense 'n most anybody," said Zoo. "Tell the truth, honey, if my brain was like it oughta be, why, I'd marry him like a shot." Only Joel couldn't picture such a marriage; in the first place, Little Sunshine was too old, not so ancient as Jesus Fever, to be sure, but old all the same. And ugly. He had a blue cataract in one eye, hardly a tooth in his head, and smelled bad: while he was in the kitchen, Amy kept the gloved hand over her nose like a sachet-handkerchief, and when Randolph had carted him away to his room (from which sounds of drunken conversation came till dawn), she'd breathed a sigh of relief.

Little Sunshine raised his arm: "Hurry, child, make a cross," he said in a trombone voice, "cause you done come up on me in the lighta day." Awed, Joel crossed himself. A smile stretched the hermit's thick wrinkled lips: "Spin round, boy, and you is saved."

Meanwhile Zoo tried unsuccessfully to conceal a necklace-like ornament the hermit had knotted about her giraffish neck. She looked very put out when Joel asked: "What's that you've got on, Zoo?"

"Hit's a charm," volunteered the hermit proudly.

"Hush up," snapped Zoo. "Done just told me it don't work iffen I goes round tellin everbody." She turned to Joel. "Honey, I spec you best run along; got business with the man."

O.K., if that's how she felt. And she was supposed to be his friend! He stalked over to the mailbox, threw up the red flag, and put his letters inside, using the tissue-wrapped coins as a paperweight. Then, determining from memory the general direction of the twins' house, he trudged off down the road.

. . .

Sand dust eddied about his feet where he walked in the misty forest shade skimming the road's edge. The sun was white in a milkglass sky. Passing a shallow creek rushing swift and cool from the woods, he paused, tempted to take off his tight shoes and go wading where soggy leaves rotated wildly in pebbled whirlpools, but then he heard his name called, and it scared him. Turning, he saw Little Sunshine.

The hermit hobbled forward, throwing his weight against a hickory cane; he carried this cane always, though Joel could not see its necessity since, aside from the fact they were very bowed, nothing seemed wrong with his legs; but his arms were so long his fingertips touched his knees. He wore ripped overalls, no shirt, no hat, no shoes. "Gawd Amighty, you walks fast, boy," he said, panting up alongside. "Else hit's me what ain't use to this daytime; ain't nothin coulda got me out cept Zoo needed that charm mighty bad."

Joel realized that his curiosity was being purposely aroused. So he pretended to be uninterested. And presently, as he expected, Little Sunshine, of his own accord, added: "Hit's a charm guarantee no turrible happenins gonna happen; makes it myself outa frog powder 'n turtle bones."

Joel slackened his gait, for the hermit moved slow as a cripple; in certain ways he was like Jesus Fever: indeed, might have been his brother. But there was about his broad ugly face a slyness the old man's lacked. "Little Sunshine," he said, "would you make *me* a charm?"

The hermit sucked his toothless gums, and the sun shone dull in his gluey blue eye. "They's many kinda charms: love charms, money charms, what kind you speakin of?"

"One like Zoo's," he said, "one that'll keep anything terrible from happening."

"Dog take it!" crowed the hermit, and stopped still in his tracks. He jabbed the road with the cane, and wagged his big bald head. "What kinda troubles a little boy like you got?"

Joel's gaze wandered past the ugly man, who was rocking on his cane, and into the bordering pines. "I don't know," he said, then fixed his eyes on the hermit, trying to make him understand how much this charm meant. "Please, Little Sunshine . . ."

And Little Sunshine, after a long moment, indicated, with a tilt of his head, that yes, the charm would be made, but: "You gotta come fetch it yoself, cause ain't no tellin when Little Sunshine gonna be up thisaway soon. Sides, thing is, trouble charms won't work noways less you wears them when theys most needed."

But how would Joel ever find the hermit's place? "I'd get lost," he argued, as they continued along the road, the dust rising about them, the sun spinning toward noon.

"Naw you ain't: humans go huntin Little Sunshine, the devilman guide they feet." He lifted his cane skyward, and pointed to a sailing shark-like cloud: "Lookayonder," he said, "hit travelin west, gonna past right over Drownin Pond; once you gets to Drownin Pond, can't miss the hotel."

All the hermits Joel had ever heard about were unfriendly say-nothings. Not Little Sunshine: he must've been born talking. Joel thought how, on lonesome evenings in the woods, he must chatter to toads and trees and the cold blue stars, and this made him feel tenderly toward the old man, who began now an account of why Drownin Pond had so queer a name.

Years past, sometime before the turn of the century, there had been, he boasted, a splendid hotel located in these very woods, The Cloud Hotel, owned by Mrs Jimmy Bob Cloud, a widow lady bloodkin to the Skullys. Then known as Cloud Lake, the pond was a diamond eye spouting crystal cold from subterranean limestone springs, and Mrs Jimmy Bob's hotel housed gala crowds come immense distances to parade the wide white halls. Mulberry parasols held aloft by silk-skirted ladies drifted all summer long over the lawns rolling round the water. While feather fans rustled the air, while velvet dancing slippers polished the ballroom floor, scarlet-coated househands glided in and out among the guests, wine spilling redly on silver trays. In May they came, October went, the guests, taking with them memories, leaving tall stacks of gold. Little Sunshine, the stable boy who brushed the gleaming coats of their fine teams, had lain awake many a starry night listening to the furry blend of voices. Oh but then! but then! one August afternoon, this was 1893, a child, a creole boy of Joel's years, having taken a dare to dive into the lake from a hundred-foot oak, crushed his head like a shell between two sunken logs. Soon afterwards there was a second tragedy when a crooked gambler, in much trouble with the law, swam out and never came back. So winter came, passed, another spring. And then a honeymoon couple, out rowing on the lake, claimed that a hand blazing with rubies (the gambler had sported a ruby ring) reached from the depths to capsize their boat. Others followed suit: a swimmer said his legs had been lassoed by powerful arms, another maintained he'd seen the two of them, the gambler and the child, seen them clear as day shining below the surface, naked now, and their hair long, green, tangled as seaweed. Indignant ladies snapped their fans, assembled their silks with fearful haste. The nights were still, the lawns deserted, the guests forever gone; and it broke Mrs Jimmy Bob's heart: she ordered a net sent from Biloxi, and had the lake dragged: "Tol her it ain't no use, tol her she ain't never gonna catch them two cause the devilman, he watch over his own." So Mrs Jimmy Bob went to St. Louis, rented herself a room, poured kerosene all over the bed, lay down and struck a match. Drownin Pond. That was the name colored folks gave it. Slowly old creek-slime, filtering through the limestone springs, had dyed the water an evil color; the lawns, the road, the paths all turned wild; the wide veranda caved in; the chimneys sank low in the swampy earth; storm-uprooted trees leaned against the porch; and water-snakes slithering across the strings made night-songs on the ballroom's decaying piano. It was a terrible, strange-looking hotel. But Little Sunshine stayed on: it was his rightful home, he said, for if he went away, as he had once upon a time, other voices, other rooms, voices lost and clouded, strummed his dreams.

The story made for Joel a jumbled picture of cracked windows reflecting a garden of ghosts, a sunset world where twisting ivy trickled down broken columns, where arbors of spidersilk shrouded all.

Miss Florabel Thompkins pulled a comb through her red waist-length hair, the blunt noon-sun paling each strand, and said: "Now don't you know I'm just tickled to see you. Why, only this morning I was telling sister: 'Sister, I got a feeling we're going to have company.' Said, 'So let's wash our hair,' which naturally made no hit whatsoever: never washes nothing, that girl. Idabel? Oh, she's off to the creek, gone to get the melon we've got cooling down there: first of the summer; Papa planted early this year." Florabel wasn't nearly so pretty as moonlight had made her seem. Her face was flat and freckled, like her sister's. She was kind of snaggletoothed, and her lips pouted in prissy discontent. She was half-reclining in a hammock ("Mama made it herself, and she makes all my lovely clothes, except for my dotted swiss, but she doesn't make any for sister: like Mama says, it's better to let Idabel troop around in what-have-you cause she can't keep a decent rag decent: I tell you this frankly, Mister Knox, Idabel's a torment to our souls, Mama's and mine. We could've been so cute dressed alike, but . . .") swung between shady pecan trees in a corner of the yard. She picked up a pair of Kress tweezers and, with a pained expression, began plucking her pink eyebrows. "Sister's avowed . . . ouch! . . . ambition is she wants to be a farmer."

Joel, who was squatting on the grass nibbling a leaf, stretched his legs, and said: "What's wrong with that?"

"Now, Mister Knox, surely you're just teasing," said Florabel. "Whoever heard of a decent white girl wanting to be a farmer? Mama and me are too disgraced. Course I know what goes on in the back of her mind." Florabel gave him a conniving look, and lowered her voice. "She thinks when Papa dies he'll leave her the place to do with like she pleases. Oh, she doesn't fool me one minute."

Joel glanced about at what Idabel hoped to inherit: the house stood far away in a grove of shade trees; it was a nice house, simple, solid-looking, painted a white now turned slightly grey; an open shotgun hall ran front to back, and on the porch were geranium boxes, and a swing. A small shed housing a green 1934 Chevrolet was at one side. Chickens pecked around in the clean yard of flowerbeds and arranged rocks. At the rear was a smoke house, a water-pump windmill, and the first swelling slope of a cottonfield.

"Ouch!" cried Florabel, and tossed the tweezers aside. She gave the hammock a push and swung to and fro, her lips pouting absurdly. "Now me, I want to be an actor . . . or a schoolteacher," she said. "Only if I become an actor I don't know what we'll do about sister. When somebody's famous like that they dig up all the facts on their past life. I really don't want to sound mean about her, Mister Knox, but the reason I bring this matter up is she's got a crush on you . . ." Florabel dropped her gaze demurely, "and, well, the poor child does have a reputation."

Though he would never have admitted it, not even secretly, Joel felt sweetly flattered. "A reputation for what?" he said, careful not to smile.

Florabel straightened up. "Please, sir," she intoned, her old-lady mannerisms frighteningly accurate. "I thought you were a gentleman of the world." Suddenly, looking rather alarmed, she collapsed back in the hammock. Then: "Why, hey there, sister . . . look who's come to call."

"Howdy," said Idabel, surprise or pleasure very absent from her woolly voice. She carried a huge watermelon, and an old black-and-white bird dog trotted close at her heels. She rolled the melon on the grass, rubbed back her cowlicked bangs, and, slumping against a tree, cocked her thumbs in the belt rungs of the dungarees which she wore. She had on also a pair of plowman's boots, and a sweatshirt with the legend DRINK COCA-COLA fading on its front. She looked first at Joel, then at her sister, and, as though making some rude comment, spit expertly between her fingers. The old dog flopped down beside her. "This here's Henry," she told Joel, gently stroking the dog's ribs with her foot. "He's fixing to take a nap, so let's us not talk loud, hear?"

"Pshaw!" said the other twin. "Mister Knox oughta see what happens when I'm trying to get a wink in edgewise: wham bang whomp!"

"Henry feels kinda poorly," explained Idabel. "I'm fraid he's right sick."

"Well, I'm right sick myself. I'm sick of lotsa things."

Joel imagined that Idabel smiled at him. She did not smile in the fashion of ordinary people, but gave one corner of her mouth a cynical crook: it was like Randolph's trick of arching an eyebrow. She hitched up her pants leg and commenced picking the scab off a knee-sore. "How you making out over at the Landing, son?"

"Yes," said Florabel, bending forward with a rather sly smirk, "haven't you *seen* things?"

"Nothing except that it's a nice place," he said discreetly.

"But . . ." Florabel slid out of the hammock, and sat down beside him with her elbow propped against the melon. "But what I mean is . . ."

"Watch out," warned Idabel, "she's only trying to pick you."

And this gave Joel an opportunity to ease the moment with a laugh. Among his sins were lying and stealing and bad thoughts; disloyalty, however, was not part of his nature. He saw how cheap it would be to confide in Florabel, though there was nothing he needed more now than a sympathetic ear. "Does it hurt?" he asked her sister, anxious to show his gratitude by assuming an interest in the sore.

"Why, this old thing?" she said, and clawed the scab. "Shoot, boy, one time I had me a rising on my butt big as a baseball, and didn't pay it any mind whatsoever."

"Hmm, squalled loud enough when Mama smacked you and it busted," reminded Florabel, bunching her lips prissily. She thumped the melon and it made a ripe hollow report. "Hmn, sounds green as grass to me." With her fingernails she scratched her initials on the rind, drew a ragged heart, arrowed it, and carved M.S., which, eyeing Joel coyly, she announced stood for Mysterious Stranger.

Idabel displayed a jackknife. "Look," she demanded, releasing a thin vicious blade. "I could kill somebody, couldn't I?" And with one murderous stab the melon cracked, spraying icy juice as she chopped off generous portions. "Leave Papa a hunk," she said, retiring under the tree to gorge in peace.

"Cold," said Joel, a trickle of red dyeing his shirt. "That creek must be freezing like an icebox; where's it come from: does it flow down from Drownin Pond?"

Florabel looked at Idabel and Idabel looked at Florabel. Neither seemed able to make up her mind which should answer. Idabel spit pulp, and said: "Who told you?"

"Told me?"

"About Drownin Pond?"

A touch of hostility in her tone made him wary. But in this case he could not see where the truth would cost more than a lie. "Oh, the man who lives there. He's a friend of mine."

Idabel responded with a hoarse, sarcastic laugh. "I'm the only person in these parts that'll go anywhere near that creepy hotel; and, son, I've never even got so much as a peek at him."

"Sister's right," added Florabel. "She's always had a hankering to see the hermit; Mama used to say he'd grab us good if we didn't act proper. But lately I've come to think he's just somebody grown people made up."

It was Joel's turn for sarcasm. "If you'd been out on the road an hour ago I would've been glad to introduce you. His name is Little Sunshine, and he's going to make me . . ." but he recalled that to mention the charm was forbidden.

Against such testimony Idabel had no comeback. She was stumped. And jealous. "Huh," she snorted, and shoved a chunk of melon in her mouth.

Rings of sunlight, sifting through the tree, dappled the dark grass like fallen gold fruit; bluebottle flies swarmed over melon rinds, and a cowbell, somewhere beyond the windmill, tolled lazily and long. Henry was having a nightmare. His fretful snores seemed to annoy Florabel; she spit seed into her hand, and, chanting, "Nasty old nasty," hurled them at him.

Idabel did nothing for a moment. Then, rising, she closed the blade of her knife, and stuck it in her pocket. Slowly, without expression, she moved toward her sister, who went quite pink in the face and began to giggle nervously.

Hands on hips, Idabel stared at her with eyes like granite. She did not say a word, but her breathing hissed between clenched teeth, and a vein throbbed in the hollow of her neck. The old dog padded forward, and looked at Florabel reproachfully. Joel inched several feet backwards: he didn't want to become involved in any family fracas.

"You're going to bug-out those eyes too far someday," sassed Florabel. But as the rock-like stare continued her impertinent pose gradually dissolved. "I don't see why you want to take on about that nasty hound thisaway," she said, looping a curl in her strawberry hair, blinking her eyes innocently. "Mama's going to make Papa shoot him anyway cause he's liable to give us all some mortal disease."

Idabel sucked in her breath, and lunged, and over and over they rolled tussling on the grass. Florabel's skirt got hiked up so high Joel's cheeks reddened: then, scratching, kicking, screaming, she managed to break loose. "Sister, please . . . please, sister . . . I beg of you!" She ran behind a pecan tree: like figures on a two-ponied carousel they whirled around the trunk, first one way, then the other. "Mama, get Mama . . . oh, Mister Knox, she's loony . . . DO something!" Henry set up a barking commotion, and commenced to chase his tail. "Mister KNOX . . ."

But Joel was afraid of Idabel himself. She was about the maddest human he ever saw, and the quickest: nobody at home would believe a girl could move this fast. Also, he knew from experience that, if he interfered, the finger of blame would ultimately point in his direction: *he* started the whole thing, that's how the tale would read. Besides, Florabel had no call to throw those seeds: deep in his heart he didn't care if she got the daylight whammed out of her.

She cut across the yard, and made a desperate sprint for the house, but it was useless, for Idabel hedged her off. Close together they went whooping past Joel, who suddenly became, like the pecan tree, and through no fault of his own, a shield. Idabel tried to push him aside: when he did not budge, she tossed her sweaty hair, and fixed him angrily with her bold green eyes: "Outa the way, sissy-britches."

Joel thought of the knife in her pocket, and despite Florabel's pleas, concluded it might be wise to move elsewhere.

So they went off again, running in circles, zigzagging between trees, Florabel's hair jouncing on her back. When they reached the pecan tree, tallest of two, she began to climb. Idabel pulled off her clumsy boots. "Ha, won't get far that way," she hollered, and agile as a monkey shinnied up the trunk.

The branches swayed, broken twigs, torn leaves showered at Joel's feet: as he darted around hunting a clearer view the sky seemed to crash bluely through the tree, and the twins, climbing nearer the sun, grew smaller and dizzy bright.

Florabel had gone as far as she could, the top; but it was a safe and fortified position: here, balanced in the crotch of forked limbs, she was immune to any assault, for to force the enemy's retreat she had only to kick.

"I can wait," said Idabel, and straddled a branch. She glanced down at Joel irritably. "Go on home, you."

"Please disregard her altogether, Mister Knox."

"Go on home and cut out paper dolls, sissy-britches."

Joel stood there hating her, wishing she'd fall from the tree and bust her neck. Like every other tomboy, Idabel was mean, just gut-mean: the haircut man in Noon City sure had her number. So did the husky woman with the wart. So did Florabel. Then he shrugged, and hung his head.

"Come back when *she's* not around," called Florabel as he started for home. "And Mister Knox, remember what I said about you-know-what. Well, a word to the wise . . ."

A pair of chicken hawks wheeled with stiffened wings above smoke, dimly yellow in the distance, rising spirelike out the Landing's kitchen chimney: that would be Zoo fixing dinner, he guessed, pausing by the roadside to stampede a colony of ants feeding on a dead frog. He was tired of Zoo's cooking: always the same stuff, collards, yams, black-eyed peas, cornbread. Right now he would like to meet up with the Snowball Man. Every afternoon at home in New Orleans the Snowball Man came pushing his delicious cart, tinkling his delicious bell; and for pennies you could have a dunce-hat of flaked ice flavored with a dozen syrups, cherry and chocolate, grape and blackberry all mingling like a rainbow.

The ants scurried like shooting sparks: thinking of Idabel, he hopped about mashing them underfoot, but this sinful dance did nothing toward lessening the hurt of her insults. Wait! Wait till he was Governor: he'd sic the law on her, have her locked in a dungeon cell with a little trapdoor cut in the ceiling where he could look down and laugh.

But when the Landing came in full view, its rambling outline darkened by foliage, he forgot Idabel.

Like kites being reeled in, the chicken hawks circled lower till their shadows revolved over the slanting shingled roof. The shaft of smoke lifting from the chimney mounted unbroken in the hot windless air; a sign, at least, that people lived here. Joel had known and explored other houses quiet with emptiness, but none so deserted-looking, silent: it was as though the place were captured under a cone of glass; inside, waiting to claim him, was an afternoon of endless boredom: each step, and his shoes were heavy as though soled with stone, carried him closer. A whole afternoon. And how many more for how many months?

Then, approaching the mailbox, seeing its cheerful red flag still upraised, the good feeling came back: Ellen would make things different, she would fix it so he could go away to a school where everybody was like everybody else. Singing the song about snow and the north wind, he stopped and jerked open the mailbox; deep inside lay a thick stack of letters, sealed, as he found, in watergreen envelopes. It was like the stationery his father had used when writing Ellen. And the spidery handwriting was identical: Mr Pepe Alvarez, c/o the postmaster, Monterrey, Mexico. Then Mr Pepe Alvarez, c/o the postmaster, Fukuoka, Japan. Again, again. Seven letters, all addressed to Mr Pepe Alvarez, in care of postmasters in: Camden, New Jersey; Lahore, India; Copenhagen, Denmark; Barcelona, Spain; Keokuk, Iowa.

But his letters were not among these. He certainly remembered putting them in the box. Little Sunshine had seen him. And Zoo. So where were they? Of course: the mailman must've come along already. But why hadn't he heard or seen the mailman's car? It was a half-wrecked Ford and made considerable racket. Then, in the dust at his feet, torn from the toilet-paper wrapping, he saw his coins, a nickel and a penny sparkling up at him like uneven eyes.

At this same instant the sound of bullet fire cracked whiplike on the quiet: Joel, stooping for his money, turned a paralyzed face toward the house: there was no one on the porch, the path, not a sign of life anywhere. Another shot. The wings of the hawks raged as they fled over tree tops, their shadows sweeping across the road's broiling sand like islands of dark.

Two

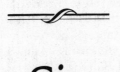

Six

"Hold still," said Zoo, her eyes like satin in the kitchen lamplight. "Never saw such a fidget; best hold still and let me cut this hair: can't have you runnin round here lookin like some ol gal: first thing you know, boy, folks is gonna say you got to wee wee squattin down." Garden shears snipped round the rim of the bowl, a blue bowl fitted on Joel's head like a helmet. "You got such pretty fine molasses hair seems like we oughta could sell it to them wigmakers."

Joel squirmed. "So what did you say after she said that?" he asked, anxious she return to a previous topic.

"Said what?"

"Said you've got a big nerve shooting off rifles when Randolph's so sick."

"Huh," Zoo grunted, "why, I just come right out and tol her, tol her: 'Miss Amy, them hawks fixin to steal the place off our hands less we shoo em away.' Said, 'Done fly off with a dozen fat fryers this spring a'ready, and Mister Randolph, he gonna take mighty little pleasure in his sickness if his stomach stay growl-empty.' "

Removing the bowl, making a telescope of her hands, she roamed around Joel's chair viewing his haircut from all angles. "Now that's what I calls a good trim," she said. "Go look in the window."

Evening silvered the glass, and his face reflected transparently, changed and mingled with moth-moving lamp yellow; he saw himself, and through himself, and beyond: a night bird whistled in the fig leaves, a whippoorwill, and fireflies sprinkled the blue-flooded air, rode the dark like ship lights. The haircut was disfiguring, for it made him in silhouette resemble those idiots with huge world-globe heads, and now, because of Randolph's flattery, he was self-conscious about his looks. "It's awful," he said.

"Huh," said Zoo, dishing supper scraps into a lard can reserved for pig slop, "you is as ignorant as that Keg Brown. Course he was the most ignorant human in my acquaintance. But you is both ignorant."

Joel, imitating Randolph, arched an eyebrow, and said: "I daresay I know some things I daresay you don't."

Zoo's elegant grace disappeared as she strode about clearing the kitchen: the floor creaked under her animal footfall, and, as she bent to lower the lamp, the hurt sadness of her long face gleamed like a mask. "I daresays," she said, plucking at her neckerchief, and not looking at Joel. "I daresays you is smarter'n Zoo, but I reckon as she knows better about folks feelins; leastwise, she don't go round makin folks feel no-count for no cause whatsoever."

"Aw," said Joel, "aw, I was just joking, honest," and, hugging her, smothered his face against her middle; she smelled sweet, a curious dark sour sweet, and her fingers, gliding through his hair, were cool, strong. "I love you because you've got to love me because you've got to."

"Lord, Lord," said Zoo, disengaging herself, "you is nothin but a kitty now, but comes the time you is full growed . . . what a Tom you gonna be."

Standing in the doorway he watched her lamp divide the dark, saw Jesus Fever's windows color: here he was, and there she was, and there was all of night between them. It had been a curious evening, for Randolph kept to his room, and Amy, fixing supper trays, one for Randolph and the other, presumably, Mr Sansom's (she'd said: "Mr Sansom won't eat cold peas"), had stopped at the table only long enough to swallow a tumbler of buttermilk. But Joel had talked, and in talking eased away his worries, and Zoo told tales, tall funny sad, and now and again their voices had met and made a song, a summer kitchen ballad.

From the first he'd noticed in the house complex sounds, sounds on the edge of silence, settling sighs of stone and board, as though the old rooms inhaled-exhaled constant wind, and he'd heard Randolph say: "We're sinking, you know, sank four inches last year." It was drowning in the earth, this house, and they, all of them, were submerging with it: Joel, moving through the chamber, imagined moles tracing silver tunnels down eclipsed halls, lank pink sliding through earth-packed rooms, lilac bleeding out the sockets of a skull: Go away, he said, climbing toward a lamp which threw nervous light over the stairsteps, Go Away, he said, for his imagination was too tricky and terrible. But was it possible for a whole house to disappear? Yes, he'd heard of such things. All Mr Mystery had to do was snap his fingers, and whatever was *there* went whisk. And human beings, too. They could go right off the face of the earth. That was what had happened to his father; he was gone, not in a sad respectable way like his mother, but just gone, and Joel had no reason to suppose he would ever find him. So why did they pretend? Why didn't they say right out, "There is no Mr Sansom, you have no father," and send him away. Ellen was always talking of the decent Christian thing to do; he'd wondered what she meant, and now he knew: to speak truth was a decent Christian thing. He took the steps slowly, awake but dreaming, and in the dream he saw the Cloud Hotel, saw its leaning molding rooms, its wind-cracked windows hung with draperies of blackwidow web, and realized suddenly this was not a hotel; indeed, had never been: this was the place folks came when they went off the face of the earth, when they died but were not dead. And he thought of the ballroom Little Sunshine had described: there nightfall covered the walls like a tapestry, and the dry delicate skeletons of bouquet leaves littering the wavy floor powdered under his dreamed footstep: he walked in the dark in the dust of thorns listening for a name, his own, but even here no father claimed him. The shadow of a grand piano spotted the vaulted ceiling like a luna moth wing, and at the keyboard, her eyes soaked white with moonlight, her wig of cold white curls askew, sat the Lady: was this the ghost of Mrs Jimmy Bob Cloud? Mrs Cloud, who'd cremated herself in a St. Louis boarding house? Was that the answer?

It struck his knee, and all that happened happened quickly: a brief blur of light flashed as a door banged in the hall above, and then he felt something hit him, go past, go bumping down the steps, and it was suddenly as though all his bones had unjoined, as though all the vital parts of him had unraveled like the springs of a sprung watch. A little red ball, it was rolling and knocking on the chamber floor, and he thought of Idabel: he wished he were as brave as Idabel; he wished he had a brother, sister, somebody; he wished he were dead.

Randolph bent over the top banister; his hands were folded into the sleeves of a kimono; his eyes were flat and glazed, drunk-looking, and if he saw Joel he made no sign. Presently, his kimono rustling, he crossed the hall and opened a door where the eccentric light of candles floated on his face. He did not go inside, but stood there moving his hands in a queer way; then, turning, he started down the stairs and when finally he came against Joel he only said: "Bring a glass of water, please." Without a second word he went back up and into the room, and Joel, unable to move, waited on the stairs a long while: there were voices in the walls, settling sighs of stone and board, sounds on the edge of silence.

"Come in." Amy's voice echoed through the house, and Joel, waiting on the threshold, felt his heart separate.

"Careful there, my dear," said Randolph, lolling at the foot of a canopied bed, "don't spill the water."

But he could not keep his hand from shaking, or focus his eyes properly: Amy and Randolph, though some distance apart, were fused like Siamese twins: they seemed a kind of freak animal, half-man half-woman. There were candles, a dozen or so, and the heat of the night made them lean limp and crooked. A limestone fireplace gleamed in their shine, and a menagerie of crystal chimes, set in motion by Joel's entrance, tinkled on the mantel like brookwater. The air was strong with the smell of asthma cigarettes, used linen, and whiskey breath. Amy's starched face was in coinlike profile against a closed window where insects thumped with a watchbeat's regularity: intent upon embroidering a sampler, she rocked back and forth in a little sewing chair, her needle, held in the gloved hand, stabbing lilac cloth rhythmically. She looked like a kind of wax machine, a life-sized doll, and the concentration of her work was unnatural: she was like a person pretending to read, though the book is upside down. And Randolph, cleaning his nails with a goosequill, was as stylized in his attitude as she: Joel felt as though they interpreted his presence here as somehow indecent, but it was impossible to withdraw, impossible to advance. On a table by the bed there were two rather arresting objects, an illuminated globe of rose frost glass depicting scenes of Venice: golden gondolas, wicked gondoliers and lovers drifting past glorious palaces on a canal of saccharine blue; and a milkglass nude suspending a tiny silver mirror. Reflected in this mirror were a pair of eyes: the instant Joel became aware of them his gaze dismissed all else.

The eyes were a teary grey; they watched Joel with a kind of dumb glitter, and soon, as if to acknowledge him, they closed in a solemn double wink, and turned . . . so that he saw them only as part of a head, a shaved head lying with invalid looseness on unsanitary pillows.

"He wants the water," said Randolph, scraping the quill under his thumb nail. "You'll have to feed him: poor Eddie, absolutely helpless."

And Joel said: "Is that him?"

"Mr Sansom," said Amy, her lips tight as the rosebud she stitched. "It is Mr Sansom."

"But you never told me."

Randolph, clutching the bedpost, heaved to his feet: the kimono swung out, exposing pink substantial thighs, hairless legs. Like many heavy men he could move with unexpected nimbleness, but he'd had more than enough to drink, and as he came toward Joel, a numb smile bunching his features, he looked as if he were about to fall. He stooped down to Joel's size, and whispered: "Tell you what, baby?"

The eyes covered the glass again, their image twitching in the tossing light, and a hand trimmed with wedding gold poked out from under quilts to let go a red ball: it was like a cue, a challenge, and Joel, ignoring Randolph, went briskly forward to meet it.

Seven

She came up the road, kicking stones, whistling. A bamboo pole, balanced on her shoulder, pointed toward the late noon sun. She carried a molasses bucket, and wore a pair of toylike dark glasses. Henry, the hound, paced beside her, his red tongue dangling hotly. And Joel, who'd been waiting for the mailman, hid behind a pine tree; just wait, this was going to be good: he'd scare the . . . there, she was almost near enough.

Then she stopped, and took off the sun-glasses, and polished them on her khaki shorts. Shielding her eyes, she looked straight at Joel's tree, and beyond it: there was no one on the Landing's porch, not a sign of life. She shrugged her shoulders. "Henry," she said, and his eyes rolled sadly up, "Henry, I leave it to you: do we want him with us or don't we?" Henry yawned: a fly buzzed inside his mouth and he swallowed it whole. "Henry," she continued, scrutinizing a certain pine, "did you ever notice what funny shadows some trees have?" A pause. "O.K., my fine dandy, come on out."

Sheepishly Joel stepped into the daylight. "Hello, Idabel," he said, and Idabel laughed, and this laugh of hers was rougher than barbed wire. "Look here, son," she said, "the last boy that tried pulling tricks on Idabel is still picking up the pieces." She put back on her dark glasses, and gave her shorts a snappy hitch. "Henry and me, we're going down to catch us a mess of catfish: if you can make yourself helpful you're welcome to come."

"How do you mean helpful?"

"Oh, put worms on the hook . . . ." tilting up the bucket, she showed him its white, writhing interior.

Joel, disgusted, averted his eyes; but thought: yes, he'd like to go with Idabel, yes, anything not to be alone: hook worms, or kiss her feet, it did not matter.

"You'd better change clothes," said Idabel; "you're fixed up like it was Sunday."

Indeed, he was wearing his finest suit, white flannels bought for Dancing Class; he'd put them on because Randolph had promised to paint his picture. But at dinner Amy had said Randolph was sick. "Poor child, and in all this heat; it does seem to me if he'd lose a little weight he wouldn't suffer so. Angela Lee was that way, too: the heat just laid her out." As for Angela Lee, Zoo had told him this queer story: "Honey, a mighty peculiar thing happen to that old lady, happen just before she die: she grew a beard; it just commence pouring out her face, real sure enough hair; a yeller color, it was, and strong as wire. Me, I used to shave her, and her paralyzed from head to toe, her skin like a dead man's. But it growed so quick, this beard, I couldn't hardly keep up, and when she died, Miss Amy hired the barber to come out from town. Well, sir, that man took one look, and walked right back down them stairs, and right out the front door. I tell you I mean I had to laugh!"

"It's just my old suit," he said, afraid to go back and change, for Amy might say no he could not go, might, instead, make him read to his father. And his father, like Angela Lee, was paralyzed, helpless; he could say a few words (boy, why, kind, bad, ball, ship), move his head a little (yes, no), and one arm (to drop a tennis ball, the signal for attention). All pleasure, all pain, he communicated with his eyes, and his eyes, like windows in summer, were seldom shut, always open and staring, even in sleep.

Idabel gave him the worm bucket to carry. Crossing a cane field, climbing a thread of path, passing a Negro house where in the yard there was a naked child fondling a little black goat, they passed into the woods through an avenue of bitter wild cherry trees. "We get drunk as a coot on those," she said, meaning cherries. "Greedy old wildcats get so drunk they scream all night: you ought to hear them . . . hollering crazy with the moon and cherry juice." Invisible birds prowling in leaves rustled, sang; beneath the still facade of forest restless feet trampled plushlike moss where limelike light sifted to stain the natural dark. Idabel's bamboo pole scraped low limbs, and the hound, eager and suspicious, careened through nets of blackberry bush. Henry, the sentry; Idabel, the guide; Joel, the captive: three explorers on a solemn trek over earth sloping steadily downward. Black, orange-trimmed butterflies wheeled over wheel-sized ponds of stagnant rain water, the glide of their wings traced on green reflecting surfaces; a rattlesnake's cellophane-like sheddings littered the trail, and broken silver spiderweb covered like cauls dead fallen branches. They passed a little human grave: on its splintered headcross was printed a legend: Toby, Killed by the Cat. Sunken, a stretch of sycamore root growing from its depth, it was, you could tell, an old grave. "What's that mean," said Joel, "killed by the cat?"

"It happened before I was born," said Idabel, as if this explained everything. She turned off the path into an area deep with last winter's leaves: a skunk skittered in the distance, and Henry boomed forward. "This Toby, you see, she was a nigger baby, and her mama worked for old Mrs Skully like Zoo does now. She was Jesus Fever's wife, and Toby was their baby. Old Mrs Skully had a big fine Persian cat, and one day when Toby was asleep the cat sneaked in and put its mouth against Toby's mouth and sucked away all her breath."

Joel said he didn't believe it; but if it was true, it was certainly the most horrible tale he'd ever heard. "I didn't know Jesus Fever had ever been married."

"There's lots you don't know. All kinds of strange things . . . mostly they happened before we were born: that makes them seem to me so much more real."

Before birth; yes, what time was it then? A time like now, and when they were dead, it would be still like now: these trees, that sky, this earth, those acorn seeds, sun and wind, all the same, while they, with dust-turned hearts, change only. Now at thirteen Joel was nearer a knowledge of death than in any year to come: a flower was blooming inside him, and soon, when all tight leaves unfurled, when the noon of youth burned whitest, he would turn and look, as others had, for the opening of another door. In the woods they walked the tireless singings of larks had sounded a century, and more, and floods of frogs had galloped in moonlight bands; stars had fallen here, and Indian arrows, too; prancing blacks had played guitars, sung ballads of bandit-buried gold, sung songs grieving and ghostly, ballads of long ago: before birth.

"Not for me: that makes it not so real," said Joel, and stopped, struck still by the truth of this: Amy, Randolph, his father, they were all outside time, all circling the present like spirits: was this why they seemed to him so like a dream? Idabel reached back and jerked his hand. "Wake up," she said. He looked at her, his eyes wide with alarm. "But I can't. I can't." "Can't what?" she said sourly. "Oh, nothing." Early voyagers, they descended together.

"Take my colored glasses," Idabel offered. "Everything looks a lot prettier."

The grass-colored lenses tinted the creek where nervous minnow schools stitched the water like needles; occasionally, in deeper pools, a chance shaft of sunlight illuminated bigger game: fat clumsy perch moving slowly, blackly below the surface. Idabel's fishline quivered in the midstream current, but now, after an hour, she'd had not even a nibble, so, rooting the pole firmly between two stumps, she leaned back, pillowing her head on a clump of moss. "O.K., give 'em back," she demanded.

"Where did you get them?" he said, wishing he had a pair.

"At the travelin-show," she said. "Travelin-show comes every year in August; it's not such a big one, but they've got a flying jinny, and a ferris wheel. And they've got a two-headed baby inside a bottle, too. The way I got these glasses was I won them; I used to wear them all the time, even nighttime, but Papa, he said I was going to put out my eyes. Want a cigarette?"

There was only one, a crumpled *Wing;* dividing it, she struck a match.

"Look," she said, "I can blow one smoke ring through another." The rings mounted in the air, blue and perfect; it was so still, yet all around there was the feeling of movement, subtle, secret, shifting: dragonflies skidded on the water, some sudden unseen motion loosened snowdrop bells brown now all withered and scentless.

Joel said, "I don't think we're going to catch anything."

"I never expect to," said Idabel. "I just like to come here and think about my worries; nobody ever comes hunting for me here. It's a nice place . . . just to lie and take your ease."

"What kind of worries do you worry about?" he asked.

"That's my business. And you know something . . . you're an awful poke-nose. You don't ever catch me prying, hell, no. Anybody else in the country, why, they'd eat you alive, you being a stranger, and living at the Landing and all. Look at Florabel. What a snoop she is."

"I think she's very pretty," said Joel, just to be aggravating.

Idabel made no comment. She flipped away her cigarette, and, forking her fingers between her lips, whistled boylike: Henry, padding along the creek's shallow edge, scrambled up the bank, his coat shining soggy wet. "Pretty on the outside, sure, but it's what's on the inside that counts," she said, hugging the hound. "She keeps telling Papa he ought to do away with Henry, says he's got a mortal disease: that's what she's like on the inside."

The white face of afternoon took shape in the sky; his enemy, Joel thought, was there, just behind those glasslike, smokelike clouds; whoever, whatever this enemy was, his was the face imaged there brightly blank. And in this respect Idabel could be envied; she at least knew her enemies: you and you, she could say, such and such and so and so. "Were you ever afraid of losing your mind?"

"Never thought about it," she said, and laughed. "To hear *them* tell it, I haven't got a mind no ways."

Joel said: "You're not being serious. Here's what I mean: do you ever see things, like people, like whole houses, see them and feel them and know for certain they're real . . . only . . ."

"Only they're not," said Idabel. "The time that snake bit me, I lived a week in a terrible place where everything was crawling, the floors and walls, every-thing. Now all that was plain foolishness. But then it was a peculiar thing, because last summer I went with Uncle August (he's the one that's so afraid of girls he won't look at one; he says I'm not a girl; I do love my Uncle August: we're like brothers) . . . we went down to Pearl River . . . and one day we were rowing in this dark place and came on an island of snakes; it was real little, just one tree, but alive with old copperheads: they were even hanging off the branches. I tell you it was right spooky. And when folks talk about dreams-come-true, I guess I know what they mean."

"That's not like what I was saying," said Joel, his voice small, bewildered. "Dreams are different, dreams you can lose. But if you see something . . . a lady, say, and you see her where nobody should be, then she follows you around inside your head. I mean like this: the other night Zoo was scared; she'd heard a dog howl, and she said it was her husband come back, and she went to the window: 'I see him,' she said, 'he's squatting under the fig tree,' she said, 'and his eyes are all yellow in the dark.' But then when I looked there was nothing but nothing."

All this Idabel seemed to find rather unexceptional. "Oh, shoot!" she said, tossing her head, the chopped red hair swishing wonderful fire, "everybody knows Zoo's crazy for true. One time, and it was hot as now, I was passing on the road, and she was there by the mailbox with this dumb look, and she says: 'What a fine snow we had last night.' Always talking about snow, always seeing things, that Zoo, that crazy Zoo."

Joel regarded Idabel with malice: what a mean liar she was. Zoo was not crazy. She was not. Yet he remembered the snow of their first conversation: it fell swiftly all about him: the woods dazzled whitely, and Idabel's voice, speaking now, sounded soft, and snow-hushed: "It's Ivory," she said. "It floats."

"What for?" he said, accepting a cake of soap she'd taken from her pocket.

"To wash with, stupid," she told him. "And don't look so prissy. Everytime I come down here, I always take a scrub. Here, you put your clothes on that stump where the fishpole is."

Joel looked shyly at the designated place. "But you're a girl."

With an exceedingly contemptuous expression, Idabel drew up to her full height. "Son," she said, and spit between her fingers, "what you've got in your britches is no news to me, and no concern of mine: hell, I've fooled around with nobody but boys since first grade. I never think like I'm a girl; you've got to remember that, or we can't never be friends." For all its bravado, she made this declaration with a special and compelling innocence; and when she knocked one fist against the other, as, frowning, she did now, and said: "I want so much to be a boy: I would be a sailor, I would . . ." the quality of her futility was touching.

Joel stood up and began to unbutton his shirt.

He lay there on a bed of cold pebbles, the cool water washing, rippling over him; he wished he were a leaf, like the current-carried leaves riding past: leaf-boy, he would float lightly away, float and fade into a river, an ocean, the world's great flood. Holding his nose, he put his head underwater: he was six years old, and his penny-colored eyes were round with terror: Holy Ghost, the preacher said, pressing him down into baptism water; he screamed, and his mother, watching from a front pew, rushed forward, took him in her arms, held him, whispered softly: my darling, my darling. He lifted his face from the great stillness, and, as Idabel splashed a playful wave, seven years vanished in an instant.

"You look like a plucked chicken," said Idabel. "So skinny and white."

Joel's shoulders contracted self-consciously. Despite Idabel's quite genuine lack of interest in his nakedness, he could not make so casual an adjustment to the situation as she seemed to expect.

Idabel said: "Hold still, now, and I'll shampoo your hair." Her own was a maze of lather-curls like cake icing. Without clothes, her figure was, if anything, more boyish: she seemed mostly legs, like a crane, or a walker on modified stilts, and freckles, dappling her rather delicate shoulders, gave her a curiously wistful look. But already her breast had commenced to swell, and there was about her hips a mild suggestion of approaching width. Joel, having conceived of Idabel as gloomy, and cantankerous, was surprised at how funny and gay she could be: working her fingers rhythmically over his scalp, she kept laughing and telling jokes, some of them quite bawdy: ". . . so the farmer said: 'Sure she's a pretty baby; oughta be, after having been strained through a silk handkerchief.' "

When he did not laugh, she said: "What's the matter? Don't you get it?" Joel shook his head. "And you from the city, too," she sighed.

"What did he mean . . . strained through a silk handkerchief?"

"Skip it, son," said Idabel, rinsing his hair, "you're too young." Joel thought then that the points of Idabel's jokes were even for her none too clear: the manner in which she told them was not altogether her own; she was imitating someone, and, wondering who, he asked: "Where'd you hear that joke?"

"Billy Bob told me," she said.

"Who's that?"

"He's just Billy Bob."

"Do you like him?" said Joel, not understanding why he felt so jealous.

"Sure I like him," she said, rising up and wading toward land; her eyes fixed on the water, she was, moving slowly and with such grace, like a bird in search of food. "Sure: he's practically my best friend. He's awful tough, Billy Bob is. I remember back in fourth grade we had that mean Miss Aikens, and she used to beat Billy Bob's hands raw with a ruler, and he never cried once."

They sat down in a sunny place to dry, and she put on her dark glasses.

"I never cry," Joel lied.

She turned on her stomach, and, fingering moss, said with gentle matter-of-factness: "Well, I do. I cry sometimes." She looked at him earnestly. "But you don't ever tell anybody, hear."

He wanted to say: no, Idabel, dear Idabel, I am your good true friend. And he wanted to touch her, to put his arms around her, for this seemed suddenly the only means of expressing all he felt. Pressing closer, he reached and, with breathtaking delicacy, kissed her cheek. There was a hush; tenuous moods of light and shade seem to pass between them like the leaf-shadow trembling on their bodies. Then Idabel tightened all over. She grabbed hold of his hair and started to pull, and when she did this a terrible, and puzzled rage went through Joel. This was the real betrayal. And so he fought back; tangled and wrestling, the sky turning, descending, revolving, they rolled over, over. The dark glasses fell off, and Joel, falling back, felt them crush beneath and cut his buttocks. "Stop," he panted, "please stop, I'm bleeding." Idabel was astride him, and her strong hands locked his wrists to the ground. She brought her red, angry face close to his: "Give up?"

"I'm bleeding," was all Joel would say.

Presently, after releasing him, she brought water, and washed his cut. "You'll be all right," she said, as if nothing had happened. And, indefinably, it was as if nothing had: neither, of course, would ever be able to explain why they had fought.

Joel said: "I'm sorry about your glasses."

The broken pieces sprinkled the ground like green raindrops. Stooping, she started picking them up; then, seeming to think better of this, she spilled them back. "It's not your fault," she said sadly. "Maybe . . . maybe some day I'll win another pair."

Eight

Randolph dipped his brush into a little water-filled vinegar jar, and tendrils of purple spread like some fast-growing vine. "Don't smile, my dear," he said. "I'm not a photographer. On the other hand, I could scarcely be called an artist; not, that is, if you define *artist* as one who sees, takes and purely transmits: always for me there is the problem of distortion, and I never paint so much what I see as what I think: for example, some years ago, this was in Berlin, I drew a boy not much older than yourself, and yet in my picture he looked more aged than Jesus Fever, and whereas in reality his eyes were childhood blue, the eyes I saw were bleary and lost. And what I saw was indeed the truth, for little Kurt, that was his name, turned out to be a perfect horror, and tried twice to murder me . . . exhibiting both times, I must say, admirable ingenuity. Poor child, I wonder whatever became of him . . . or, for that matter, me. Now that is a most interesting question: whatever became of me?" As if to punctuate his sentences he kept, all the while he talked, thrusting the brush inside the jar, and the water, continually darkening, had at its center, like a hidden flower, a rope of red. "Very well, sit back, we'll relax a minute now."

Sighing, Joel glanced about him. It was the first time he'd been in Randolph's room; after two hours, he still could not quite take it in, for it was so unlike anything he'd ever known before: faded gold and tarnished silk reflecting in ornate mirrors, it all made him feel as though he'd eaten too much candy. Large as the room was, the barren space in it amounted to no more than one foot; carved tables, velvet chairs, candelabras, a German music box, books and paintings seemed to spill each into the other, as if the objects in a flood had floated through the windows and sunk here. Behind his liver-shaped desk unframed foreign postcards crusted the walls; six of these, a series from Japan, were for Joel an education, even though to some extent he knew already the significance of what they depicted. Like a museum exhibit, there was spread out on a long, black, tremendously heavy table a display consisting in part of antique dolls, some with missing arms, legs, some without heads, others whose bead-eyes stared glass-blank though their innards, straw and sawdust, showed through open wounds; all, however, were costumed, and exquisitely, in a variety of velvet, lace, linen. Now set in the center of this table was a little photograph in a silver frame so elaborate as to be absurd; it was a cheap photograph, obviously taken at a carnival or amusement park, for the persons concerned, three men and a girl, were posed against a humorous backdrop of cross-eyed baboons and leering kangaroos; though he was thinner in this scene and more handsome, Joel, without much effort, recognized Randolph, and another of the men looked familiar, too. . . . was it his father? Certainly the face was only mildly reminiscent of the man across the hall. The third man, taller than his companions, cut an amazing figure; he was powerfully made and, even in so faded a print, very dark, almost Negroid; his eyes, narrow and sly and black, glittered beneath brows thick as mustaches, and his lips, fuller than any woman's, were caught in a cocky smile which intensified the dashing, rather vaudeville effect of a straw hat he wore, a cane he carried. He had his arm around the girl, and she, an anemic faunlike creature, was gazing up at him with the completest adoration.

"Oh, yes," said Randolph, stretching his legs, lighting a mentholated cigarette, "do not take it seriously, what you see here: it's only a joke played on myself by myself . . . it amuses and horrifies . . . a rather gaudy grave, you might say. There is no daytime in this room, nor night; the seasons are changeless here, and the years, and when I die, if indeed I haven't already, then let me be dead drunk and curled, as in my mother's womb, in the warm blood of darkness. Wouldn't that be an ironic finale for one who, deep in his goddamned soul, sought the sweetly clean-limbed life? bread and water, a simple roof to share with some beloved, nothing more." Smiling, smoothing the back of his hair, he put out the cigarette, and picked up his brush. "Inasmuch as I was born dead, how ironic that I should die at all; yes, born dead, literally: the midwife was perverse enough to slap me into life. Or did she?" He looked at Joel in an amused way. "Answer me: did she?"

"Did she what?" said Joel, for, as usual, he did not understand: Randolph seemed always to be carrying on in an unfathomable vocabulary secret dialogues with someone unseen. "Randolph," he said, "please don't be mad with me: it's only that you say things in such a funny way."

"Never mind," said Randolph, "all difficult music must be heard more than once. And if what I tell you now sounds senseless, it will in retrospect seem far too clear; and when this happens, when those flowers in your eyes wither, irrecoverable as they are, why, though no tears helped dissolve my own co-coon, I shall weep a little for you." Rising, going to a huge baroque bureau, he dabbed on lemon cologne, combed his polished curls, and, posturing some-what, studied himself in a mirror; while duplicating him in all essentials, the mirror, full-length and of French vintage, seemed to absorb his color, to pare and change his features: the man in the mirror was not Randolph, but what-ever personality imagination desired him to resemble, and he, as if corroborat-ing such a theory, said: "They can romanticize us so, mirrors, and that is their secret: what a subtle torture it would be to destroy all the mirrors in the world: where then could we look for reassurance of our identities? I tell you, my dear, Narcissus was no egotist . . . he was merely another of us who, in our unshatter-able isolation, recognized, on seeing his reflection, the one beautiful comrade, the only inseparable love . . . poor Narcissus, possibly the only human who was ever honest on this point."

A shy rap at the door interrupted. "Randolph," said Amy, "is that boy in there with you?"

"We're busy. Go away, go away . . ."

"But Randolph," she whined, "don't you think he ought to come read to his father?"

"I said: go away."

Joel let his face reveal neither relief nor gratitude: to obscure emotion was becoming for him a natural reflex; it helped him sometimes not to feel at all. Still there was one thing he could not do, for there is no known way of making the mind clear-blank, and whatever he obliterated in daytime rose up at night in dreams to sleep beside him with an iron embrace. As for reading to his father, he'd made an odd discovery: Mr Sansom never really listened: a list of prices recited from a Sears Roebuck interested him, Joel had found by experi-ment, as much as any wild-west story.

"Before it happened," said Randolph, resuming his seat, "before then, Ed was very different . . . very sporting, and, if your standards are not too distinguished, handsome (there, in that photograph you can see for yourself), but, to be truthful, I never much liked him, quite the contrary; for one thing, his owning Pepe, or being, that is, his manager, complicated our relations. Pepe Alvarez, he is the one with the straw hat, and the girl, well, that is Dolores. It is not of course a very accurate picture: so innocent: who could imagine that only two days after it was taken one of us fell down a flight of stairs with a bullet in his back?" Pausing to adjust the drawing board, he stared at Joel, one eye squinting like a watchmaker's. "Careful now, don't speak, I'm doing your lips." Rustling the ribbon-dressed dolls, a breeze came through the windows bringing here in the velvet shade sunshine smells of outside, and Joel wanted to be out there where right now Idabel might be splashing through a field of grass, running with Henry at her heels. The circular composition of Ran-dolph's face lengthened in concentration; he worked silently a great while until at last, and it was as if all that had gone before had indescribably led up to this, he said:

"Let me begin by telling you that I was in love. An ordinary statement, to be sure, but not an ordinary fact, for so few of us learn that love is tenderness, and tenderness is not, as a fair proportion suspect, pity; and still fewer know that happiness in love is not the absolute focusing of all emotion in another: one has always to love a good many things which the beloved must come only to symbolize; the true beloveds of this world are in their lover's eyes lilac opening, ship lights, school bells, a landscape, remembered conversations, friends, a child's Sunday, lost voices, one's favorite suit, autumn and all seasons, memory, yes, it being the earth and water of existence, memory. A nostalgic list, but then, of course, where could one find a more nostalgic subject? When one is your age most subtleties go unobserved; even so, I imagine you think it incredible, looking at me as I am now, that I should've had ever the innocence to feel such love; nevertheless, when I was twenty-three . . .

It is the girl in the picture, Dolores. And we met in Madrid. But she was not Spanish; at least I do not believe so, though actually I never knew precisely where she came from: her English was quite perfect. As for me, I had been in Europe then two years, living, as it were, and for the most part, in museums: I wonder really whether anyone ever copied so many Masters? There was almost no painting of which I could not do a most engaging facsimile . . . still, when it came to something of my own, I went quite dead, and it was as though I had no personal perception, no interior life whatever: I was like the wind-flower whose pollen will not mate at all.

Dolores, on the other hand, was one of those from whom such as I manage occasionally to borrow energy: always with her I knew very much that I was alive, and came finally to believe in my own validity: for the first time I saw things without distortion and complete. That fall we went to Paris, and then to Cuba, where we lived high above the bay of Matanzas in a house . . . how should I describe it? . . . it was cloud-pink stone with rooms strewn like gold and white flowers on a vine of high corridors and crumbling blue steps; with the windows wide and the wind moving through it was like an island, cool and most silent. She was like a child there, and sweet as an orange is sweet, and lazy, deliciously lazy; she liked to sit naked in the sun, and draw tiny little animals, toads and bees and chipmunks, and read astrology magazines, and chart the stars, and wash her hair (this she did no less than three times a day); she was a gambler, too, and every afternoon we went down to the village and bought lottery tickets, or a new guitar: she had over thirty guitars, and played all of them, I must admit, quite horridly.

And there was this other thing: we very seldom talked; I can never remember having with Dolores a sustained conversation; there was always between us something muted, hushed; still our silence was not of a secret kind, for in itself it communicated that wonderful peace those who understand each other very well sometimes achieve . . . yet neither knew the other truly, for at that time we did not really know ourselves.

However . . . toward the end of winter I discovered the dream book. Every morning Dolores wrote out her night's dreams in a big scrapbook she kept concealed under a mattress; she wrote them sometimes in French, more often in German or English, but whatever the language, the content was always shockingly malevolent, and I could make no sense of them, for it seemed impossible to identify Dolores with her ruthless dreams. And I was always in them, always fleeing before her, or hiding in the shadow, and each day while she lay naked in the sun I would find the newest page and read how much closer her pursuit had come, for in early dreams she'd murdered in Madrid a lover she called L., and I knew . . . that when she found R. . . . she would kill him, too.

We slept in a bed with a canopy veil that kept out mosquitoes and sifted the moonlight, and I would lie there awake in the dark watching her sleep, afraid of being trapped in that dream-choked head; and when morning came she would laugh and tease and pull my hair, and presently, after I'd gone, write . . . well, there is this I remember: 'R. is hiding behind a giant clock. Its tick is like thunderstrokes, like the pulsebeat of God, and the hands, shaped like pointing fingers, stand at seventeen past three; come six I will find him, for he does not know it is from me he hides, but imagines it is himself. I do not wish him harm, and I would run away if I could, but the clock demands a sacrifice, or it will never stop, and life must cease somewhere, for who among us can long endure its boom?'

Aside from all else, there is some truth in that; clocks indeed must have their sacrifice: what is death but an offering to time and eternity?

Now, oddly enough, our lives were more than ever interlocked: there were any number of times I could have left, gone away, never seen her again; however, to desert would've been to deny love, and if I did not love Dolores, then no emotion of mine has been anything but spurious. I think now she was not altogether human (a trance-child, if such there be, or a dream herself), nor was I . . . though for reasons of youth, and youth is hardly human: it can't be, for the young never believe they will die . . . especially would they never believe that death comes, and often, in forms other than the natural one.

In the spring we sailed for Florida; Dolores had never been before to the States, and we went to New York, which she did not like, and Philadelphia, which she thought equally tiresome. At last, in New Orleans, where we took a charming patio apartment, she was happy, as indeed was I. And during our peregrinations the dream book disappeared: where she could have hidden it I do not know, for I searched every possible place: it was in a way a relief really not to find it. Then one afternoon, walking home from the market and carrying, if you please, a fine live hen, I saw her talking with a man there in the shade by the cathedral; there was an intimacy in their attitude which made me still inside: this I knew was no simple tourist asking direction, and later, when I told her what I'd seen, she said, oh, very casually, yes, it was a friend, someone she'd met in a café, a prizefighter: would I care to meet him?

Now after an injury, physical, spiritual, whatever, one always believes had one obeyed a premonition (there is usually in such instances an imagined premonition) nothing would have happened; still, had I had absolute fore-knowledge, I should have gone right ahead, for in every lifetime there occur situations when one is no more than a thread in a design willfully woven by . . . who should I say? God?

It was one Sunday that they came, the prizefighter, Pepe Alvarez, and Ed Sansom, his manager. A mercilessly hot day, as I recall, and we sat in the patio with fans and cold drinks: you could scarcely select a group with less in common than we four; had it not been for Sansom, who was something of a buffoon and therefore distracting, it would all have been rather too tense, for one couldn't ignore the not very discreet interplay between Dolores and the young Mexican: they were lovers, even slow-witted Amy could've perceived this, and I was not surprised: Pepe was so extraordinary: his face was alive, yet dreamlike, brutal, yet boyish, foreign but familiar (as something from childhood is familiar), both shy and aggressive, both sleeping and awake. But when I say he and Dolores were lovers, perhaps I exaggerate: lovers implies, to some extent, reciprocity, and Dolores, as became apparent, could never love anyone, so caught was she within a trance; then, too, other than that they performed a pleasurable function, she had no personal feeling or respect for men or the masculine personality . . . that personality which, despite legend, can only be most sensitively appreciated by its own kind. As it was getting dark in the patio, I looked at Pepe: his Indian skin seemed to hold all the light left in the air, his flat animal-shrewd eyes, bright as though with tears, regarded Dolores exclusively; and suddenly, with a mild shock, I realized it was not she of whom I was jealous, but him.

Afterwards, and though at first I was careful not to show the quality of my feelings, Dolores understood intuitively what had happened: 'Strange how long it takes us to discover ourselves; I've known since first I saw you,' she said, adding, 'I do not think, though, that he is the one for you; I've known too many Pepes: love him if you will, it will come to nothing.' The brain may take advice, but not the heart, and love, having no geography, knows no boundaries: weight and sink it deep, no matter, it will rise and find the surface: and why not? any love is natural and beautiful that lies within a person's nature; only hypocrites would hold a man responsible for what he loves, emotional illiterates and those of righteous envy, who, in their agitated concern, mistake so frequently the arrow pointing to heaven for the one that leads to hell.

It was different, this love of mine for Pepe, more intense than anything I felt for Dolores, and lonelier. But we are alone, darling child, terribly, isolated each from the other; so fierce is the world's ridicule we cannot speak or show our tenderness; for us, death is stronger than life, it pulls like a wind through the dark, all our cries burlesqued in joyless laughter; and with the garbage of loneliness stuffed down us until our guts burst bleeding green, we go screaming round the world, dying in our rented rooms, nightmare hotels, eternal homes of the transient heart. There were moments, wonderful moments, when I thought I was free, that I could forget him and that sleepy violent face, but then he would not let me, no, he was always there, sitting in the patio, or listening to her play the guitar, laughing, talking, near but remote, always there, as I was in Dolores' dreams. I could not endure to see him suffer; it was an agony to watch him fight, prancing quick and cruel, see him hit, the glare, the blood and the blueness. I gave him money, bought him cream-colored hats, gold bracelets (which he adored, and wore like a woman), shoes in bright Negro colors, candy silk shirts, and I gave all these things to Ed Sansom, too: how they despised me, both of them, but not enough to refuse a gift, oh never. And Dolores continued with Pepe in her queer compulsive way, not really interested one way or another, not caring whether he stayed or went; like some brainless plant, she lived (existed) beyond her own control in that reckless book of dreams. She could not help me. What we most want is only to be held ... and told ... that everything (everything is a funny thing, is baby milk and Papa's eyes, is roaring logs on a cold morning, is hoot-owls and the boy who makes you cry after school, is Mama's long hair, is being afraid and twisted faces on the bedroom wall) ... everything is going to be all right.

One night Pepe came to the house very drunk, and proceeded with the boldest abandon to a) beat Dolores with his belt, b) piss on the rug and on my paintings, c) call me horrible hurting names, d) break my nose, e and f and otherwise. And I walked in the streets that night, and along the docks, and talked aloud pleading with myself to go away, be alone again, I said, as if I were not alone, rent another room in another life. I sat in Jackson Square; except for the tolling of train bells, it was quiet and all the Cabildo was like a haunted palace; there was a blond misty boy sitting beside me, and he looked at me, and I at him, and we were not strangers: our hands moved towards each other to embrace. I never heard his voice, for we did not speak; it is a shame, I should so like the memory of it. Loneliness, like fever, thrives on night, but there with him light broke, breaking in the trees like birdsong, and when sunrise came, he loosened his fingers from mine, and walked away, that misty boy, my friend.

Always now we were together, Dolores, Pepe, Ed and I, Ed and his jokes, we other three and our silences. Grotesque quadruplets (born of what fantastic parent?) we fed upon one another, as cancer feeds upon itself, and yet, will you believe this? there are a medley of moments I remember with the kind of nostalgia reserved usually for sweeter things: Pepe (I see) is lighting a match with his thumbnail, is trying with a bare hand to snatch a goldfish from the fountain, we are at a picture-show eating popcorn from the same bag, he has fallen asleep and leans against my shoulder, he is laughing because I wince at a boxing-cut on his lip, I hear him whistling on the stairs, I hear him mounting toward me and his footsteps are not so loud as my heart. Days, fast fading as snowflakes, flurry into autumn, fall all around like November leaves, the sky, cold red with winter, frightens with the light it sheds: I sleep all day, the shutters closed, the covers drawn above my eyes. Now it is Mardi Gras, and we are going to a ball; everyone has chosen his costume but me: Ed is a Franciscan monk (gnawing a cigar), Pepe is a bandit and Dolores a ballerina; but I cannot think what to wear and this becomes a dilemma of disproportionate importance. Dolores appears the night of the ball with a tremendous pink box: transformed, I am a Countess and my king is Louis XVI; I have silver hair and satin slippers, a green mask, am wrapped in silk pistachio and pink: at first, before the mirror, this horrifies me, then pleases to rapture, for I am very beautiful, and later, when the waltz begins, Pepe, who does not know, begs a dance, and I, oh sly Cinderella, smile beneath my mask, thinking: Ah, if I were really me! Toad into prince, tin into gold; fly, feathered serpent, the hour grows old: so ends a part of my saga.

Another spring, and they were gone; it was April, the sixth of that rainy lilac April, just two days after our happy trip to Pontchartrain . . . where the picture was taken, and where, in symbolic dark, we'd drifted through the tunnel of love. All right, listen: late that afternoon when I woke up rain was at the window and on the roof: a kind of silence, if I may say, was walking through the house, and, like most silence, it was not silent at all: it rapped on the doors, echoed in the clocks, creaked on the stairs, leaned forward to peer into my face and explode. Below a radio talked and sang, yet I knew no one heard it: she was gone, and Pepe with her.

Her room was overturned; as I searched through the wreckage, a guitar string broke, its twang vibrating every nerve. I hurried to the top of the stairs, my mouth open but no sound coming out: all the control centers of my mind were numb; the air undulated, and the floor expanded like an accordion. Someone was coming towards me. I felt them like a pressure climbing the steps; unrecognized, they seemed to walk straight into my eyes. First I thought it was Dolores, then Ed, then Pepe. Whoever it was, they shook me, pleading and swearing: that bastard, they said, gone, sonofabitchinbastard, gone, with the car, all the clothes and money, gone, forever and ever and ever. But who was it? I couldn't see: a blinding Jesus-like glow burned around him: Pepe, is it you? Ed? Dolores? I pushed myself free, ran back into the bedroom and shut the door: it was no use: the doorknob began to turn, and suddenly everything was crazy plain: Dolores had at last caught me in her dreams.

So I found a gun I kept wrapped in an old sock. The rain had stopped. The windows were open, and the room was cool and sweet with lilac. Downstairs the radio was singing, and in my ears there was the roar a seashell makes. The door opened; I fired once, and again, and Jesus dissolved, became nothing but Ed in a dirty linen suit; doubled over, he stumbled toward the stairs, and rolled down the steps loose like a ragdoll.

For two days he lay crumpled on the couch, bleeding all over himself, moaning and shouting and running a rosary through his fingers. He called for you, and his mother, and the Lord. There was nothing I could do. And then Amy came from the Landing. She was very good. She found a doctor, a little Negro dwarf not too particular. Abruptly the weather was like July, but those weeks were the winter of our lives; the veins froze and cracked with coldness, and in the sky the sun was like a lump of ice. That little doctor, waddling around on his six-inch legs, laughed and laughed and kept the radio playing comedy programs. Every day I woke up saying, 'If I die . . .,' not realizing how dead I was already, and only a memory tagging along with Dolores and Pepe . . . wherever they were: I grieved for Pepe, not because I'd lost him (yes, that a little), but because in the end I knew Dolores would find him, too: it is easy to escape daylight, but night is inevitable, and dreams are the giant cage.

To be brief: Ed and Amy were married in New Orleans. It was, you see, her fantasy come true; she was at last what she'd always wanted to be, a nurse . . . with a more or less permanent position. Then we all came back to the Landing; Amy's idea, and the only solution, for he would never be well again. I suppose we shall go on together until the house sinks, until the garden grows up and weeds hide us in their depth."

Randolph, pushing aside his drawing board, slumped over on the desk; dusk had come while he talked, and swept the room bluely; outside, sparrows were calling to roost, their nightfall chatter punctuated by a solemn frog. Pretty soon Zoo would be ringing the supper bell. None of this was apparent to Joel; he was not even aware of any stiffness from having sat so long in one position: it was as though Randolph's voice continued saying in his head things that were real enough, but not necessary to believe. He was confused because the story had been like a movie with neither plot nor motive: had Randolph really shot his father? And, most important of all, where was the ending? What had happened to Dolores and old awful Pepe Alvarez? That is what he wanted to know, and that is what he asked.

"If I knew . . ." said Randolph, pausing, holding a match to a candle; the sudden light flattered his face, made the pink hairless skin more impeccably young. "But, my dear, so few things are fulfilled: what are most lives but a series of incompleted episodes? *We work in the dark, we do what we can, we give what we have. Our doubt is our passion, and our passion is our task . . .*' It is wanting to know the end that makes us believe in God, or witchcraft, believe, at least, in something."

Joel still wanted to know: "Didn't you ever even try to find out where they got off to?"

"Over there," said Randolph with a tired smile, "is a five-pound volume listing every town and hamlet on the globe; it is what I believe in, this almanac: day by day I've gone through it writing Pepe always in care of the postmaster;

just notes, nothing but my name and what we will for convenience call address. Oh, I know that I shall never have an answer. But it gives me something to believe in. And that is peace."

Downstairs the supper bell sounded. Randolph did not move. His face seemed to contract with a look of sad guilt. "I've been very weak this afternoon, very wicked," he said, rising for Joel to accept an invitation of open arms. "Do forgive me, darling Joel." Then, in a voice as urgent as the bell, he added: "And please, tell me what I want to hear."

Joel remembered. "Everything," he said gently, "everything is going to be all right."

Nine

Jesus Fever was a sick man. For over a week he'd been unable to hold anything on his stomach. His skin was parched like an old leaf, and his eyes, milky with film, saw strange things: Randolph's father, he swore, was lurking in a corner of the cabin; all the funny papers and Coca-Cola pictures plastering the walls were, he complained, crooked and aggravating; a noise like the crack of a whip snapped in his head; a bouquet of sunflowers Joel had brought became suddenly a flock of canaries crazily singing and circling the room; he was worried to frenzy by a stranger staring at him from a gloomy little mirror hung above the mantel. Little Sunshine, arriving to give what aid he could, covered the mirror with a flour sack in order that, as he explained, Jesus Fever's soul could not be trapped there; he hung a charm around the old man's neck, sprinkled magic ginger powder in the air, and disappeared before moonrise. "Zoo, child," said Jesus, "how come you let me freeze thisaway? Fix the fire, child, it's colder'n a well-bottom."

Zoo took a reasoning tone. "Papadaddy, now honey, we all us gonna melt . . . so hot Mister Randolph done change clothes three times today." But Jesus would not listen, and asked for a quilt to wrap around his legs, a wool sock to stretch over his head: the whole house, he argued, was rattling with wind: why, look, there was old Mr Skully, his fine red beard turned white with frost. So Zoo went out in the dark of the yard to find an armful of kindling.

Joel, left in charge, started when Jesus beckoned to him secretively. The old man was sitting in a rattan rocker, a worn scrapquilt of velvet flowers covering his knees. He could not stay in bed: a horizontal position interfered with his breathing. "Rock my rocker, son," he said in a reedy voice, "it's kinda restful like . . . makes me feel I'm ridin in a wagon an got a long way to go." A kerosene lamp burned in the room. The chair, shadowed on the wall, swished a gentle drowsy sound. "Can't you feel the cold, son?"

"Mama was always cold, too," said Joel, prickly chill tingling his spine. Don't die, he thought, and as he pushed the chair back and forth the runners whispered, don't die, don't die. For if Jesus Fever died, then Zoo would go away, and there would be no one but Amy, Randolph, his father. It was not so much these three, however, but the Landing, and the fragile hush of living under a glass bell. Maybe Randolph would take him away: there had been some mention of a trip. And he'd written Ellen again, surely something would come of that.

"Papadaddy," said Zoo, lugging in a bundle of wood, "you is mighty thoughtless makin me hunt round out there in the dark where theys all kinda wild creatures crawling just hungry for a nip outa tasty me. They is a wildcat smell on the air, they is, I declare. And who knows but what Keg's done runaway from the chain gang? Joel, honey, latch the door."

When the fire commenced to burn Jesus asked that his chair be brought nearer the hearth. "I used to could play the fiddle," he said, wistfully watching the flames slide upward ". . . rheumatism stole all the music outa my fingers." He shook his head, and sucked his gums, and spit into the fire. "Don't fuss with me, child," he complained as Zoo tried to adjust the quilt. "Tell you now, bring me my sword." She returned from the other room bearing a beautiful sword with a silver handle: across the blade there was inscribed, Unsheath Me Not Without Reason—Sheath Me Not Without Honor. "Mister Randolph's granddaddy gimme this, that be more 'n sixty year ago." In the past days he'd one by one called forth all his treasures: a dusty cracked violin, his derby with the feather, a Mickey Mouse watch, his high-button orange shoes, three little monkeys who neither saw, heard nor spoke evil, these and other precious things lay strewn around the cabin, for he would not allow them to be put again out of sight.

Zoo presented Joel with a handful of pecans and gave him a pair of pliers to crack them with. "I'm not hungry," he said and rested his head in her lap. It was not a comfortable lap like Ellen's. You could feel too precisely tensed muscle and sharp bone. But she played her fingers through his hair, and that was sweet. "Zoo," he said softly, not wanting the old man to hear, "Zoo, he's going to die, isn't he?"

"I spec so," she said, and there was little feeling in her voice.

"And then will you go away?"

"I reckon."

At this Joel straightened and looked at her angrily. "But why, Zoo?" he demanded. "Tell me why!"

"Hush, child, speak quiet." A slow moment followed in which she twisted her neckerchief, felt for and found the charm Little Sunshine had given her. "Ain't gonna hold good forever," she said, tapping the charm. "Someday he gonna come back here lookin for to slice me up. I knows it good as anythin. I seen it in my dreams, and the floor don't creak but what my heart stops. Every time a dog howls I think, that's him, that's him on his way, on accounta dogs just naturally hate that Keg and start to holler time they smell him."

"I'd protect you, Zoo," he pleaded. "Honest, I'd never let nobody hurt you."

Zoo laughed, and her laugh seemed to fly around the room like a frightening black bird. "Why, Keg could drop you with just the look of his eyes!" She began to shiver in the suffocating room. "One day he gonna come crawlin through that window, and won't nobody hear nothin; else I'll find him waitin in the dark tween here and the house, gotta long shiny razor: Lawd, I seen it a million times. So I gotta run, gotta go where there's snow and he ain't gonna catch me."

Joel squeezed her wrist. "If you'd let me go with you, Zoo . . . oh, we could have such a lot of fun."

"Don't talk foolishness, baby."

The yellow tabby scooted from under the bed, darted before the fire, arched its back and hissed. "What he see?" cried Jesus, pointing his sword: firelight ran up the gaunt blade like a gold spider. "Answer me, cat, you see somethin?" The cat relaxed on its haunches, and fixed the old man coldly. Jesus giggled. "Try to joke ol Jesus," he said, wagging his finger. "Try to scare him." His blindlike blue-looking eyes closed; he tilted back his head so that the stocking-foot dangled like a Chinese pigtail, sighed and said: "Ain't got no time left for to joke, cat." And then, holding the sword to his chest: "Mister Skully gimme this my weddin day; me and my woman, us just jumped over a broom, and Mister Skully, he say, 'All right now, Jesus, you is married.' Travelin Preacher come tell me and my woman that ain't proper, say the Lawd ain't gonna put up with it: sure enough, the cat done killed Toby, and my woman grieves herself so she hangs on a tree, big cozy lady got the branch bent double: back when I was just so high my daddy cut his switches offen that tree . . ." remembering, it was as if his mind were an island in time, the past surrounding sea.

Joel cracked a pecan, and tossed the hull into the fire. "Zoo," he said, "did you ever hear of anybody called Alcibiades?"

"Who that you say?"

"Alcibiades. I don't know. It's somebody Randolph says I look like."

Zoo considered. "You musta heard wrong, honey. The name he most likely said is Alicaster. Alicaster Jones is a Paradise Chapel boy what used to sing in the choir. Looks like a white angel, so pretty he got the preacher and all kinda mens and ladies lovin him up. Leastwise, that's what folks say."

"I'll bet I can sing better than him," said Joel. "You know, I bet I could sing in vaudeville shows and make a whole lot of money, enough money to buy you a fur coat, Zoo, and dresses like they show in the Sunday papers."

"I want red dresses," said Zoo, entering the spirit. "Look real nice in red, I do. We gonna have us a car?"

Joel was delirious. It seemed so real. There he was bathed by spotlights, and wearing a tuxedo with a gardenia in his lapel. But there was only one song he knew how to sing all the way through. So he said, "Listen, Zoo," and sang, "Silent Night, Holy Night, all is calm, all is bright, round yon Vir . . ." his voice, up to this point high and sweet like a girl's, broke in an ugly, mystifying way.

"Uh huh," Zoo nodded knowingly. "Little tadpole growin to be a fish."

In the fireplace a log, cracking dramatically, sent out a sizzle of sparks; then, with no warning, a nest of newborn chimney sweeps fell into the flames and quite swiftly split with fire: the little birds burned without sound or movement. Joel, somewhat stunned, remained silent, and Zoo's face was blankly surprised. Only Jesus spoke: "In fire," he said, and had it not been so quiet you could not have heard him, "first comes water, and last comes the fire. Don't say no place in the Good Book why we's in tween. Do it? Can't member . . . not nothin. You," his voice rose shrilly, "you-all! It's gettin powerful warm, it's gettin fire!"

Ten

One grey curiously cool afternoon a week later Jesus Fever died. It was as if someone had been tickling his ribs, for he died in a spasm of desperate giggles. "Maybe," as Zoo said, "God done told somethin funny." She dressed him in his little suspender suit, his orange-leather shoes and derby hat; she squeezed a bunch of dogtooth violets in his hand, and put him in a cedar chest: there he remained for two days while Amy, with Randolph's aid, decided the location of his grave: under the moon tree, they said finally. The moon tree, so named for its round ivory blooms, grew in a lonely place far back from the Landing, and here Zoo shoveled away with no one to help but Joel: the mild excavation they managed at last to make reminded him of all the backyard swimming pools dug in summers that seemed now so long ago. Transporting the cedar chest was an arduous business; in the end they hitched a rope to John Brown, the old mule, and he hauled it to the foot of the grave. "Papadaddy would be mighty tickled could he know who it is is pullin him home," said Zoo. "Papadaddy surely did love you, John Brown: trustiest mule he ever saw, he said so many a time: now you member that." At the last minute Randolph sent word he could not be present for the funeral, and Amy, who brought this message, said a prayer in his name, mumbled, that is, a sentence or so, and made a cross: she wore for the occasion a black glove. But for Jesus there were no mourners: the three in the moon-tree shade were like some distracted group assembled at a depot to wish a friend goodbye, and, as such gatherings long for the whistle of the train that will release them, they wanted to hear the first thud of earth upon the cedar lid. It seemed odd to Joel nature did not reflect so solemn an event: flowers of cottonboll clouds within a sky as scandalously blue as kitten-eyes were offensive in their sweet disrespect: a resident of over a hundred years in so narrow a world deserved higher homage. The cedar chest capsized as they lowered it into the grave, but Zoo said, "Pay no mind, honey, we ain't got the strenth of heathen giants." She shook her head. "Pore Papa-daddy, goin to heaven face down." Unfolding her accordion, she spread her legs wide apart, threw back her head, hollered: "Lawd, take him to thy bosom, tote him all around, Lawd don't you never, don't you never put him down, Lawd, he seen the glory, Lawd, he seen the light . . ." Up until now Joel had not altogether accepted Jesus Fever's death; anybody who'd lived that long just couldn't die; way back in his mind he kind of felt the old man was playing possum; but when the last note of Zoo's requiem became stillness, then it was true, then Jesus was really dead.

That night sleep was like an enemy; dreams, a winged avenging fish, swam rising and diving until light, drawing toward daybreak, opened his eyes. Hurriedly buttoning his breeches, he crept down through the quiet house and out the kitchen door. Above, the moon paled like a stone receding below water, tangled morning color rushed up the sky, trembled there in pastel uncertainty.

"Ain't I gotta donkey's load?" cried Zoo, as he crossed the yard to where she stood on the cabin porch. A quilt stuffed fat with belongings bulged on her back; the accordion was tied to her belt and hung there like a caterpillar; aside from this she had a quite large jellyjar box. "Time I gets to Washington D.C. gonna be a humpback," she said, sounding as though she'd swallowed a gallon of wine, and her joy, in the dimness of sunup, was to him disgusting: what right had she to be so happy?

"You can't carry all that. You look like a fool, for one thing."

But Zoo just flexed her arms, and stamped her foot. "Honey, I feels like ninety-nine locomotives; gonna light outa here goin licketysplit: why, I figures to be in Washington D.C. fore dark." She drew back into a kind of pose, and, as if she were about to curtsey, held out her starched calico skirt: "Pretty, huh?"

Joel squinted critically. Her face was powdered with flour, a sort of reddish oil inflamed her cheeks, she'd scented herself with vanilla flavoring, and greased her hair shiny. About her neck she sported a lemon silk scarf. "Turn around," he said; then, after she'd done so, he moved away, pointedly suppressing comment.

She placidly accepted this affront, but said: "How come you gotta go pull such a long face, and take on in any such way? Do seem to me like you'd be glad on my account, us being friends and all."

He yanked loose a trailing arm of ivy, and this set swinging all the porch-eave pots: bumping against each other they raised a noise like a series of closing doors. "Oh, you're awful funny. Ha ha ha." He gave her one of Randolph's cool arched looks. "You were never my friend. But after all why should anyone such as me have anything in common with such as you?"

"Baby, baby . . ." said Zoo, her voice rocking in a tender way ". . . baby, I make you a promise: whenever I gets all fixed . . . I'm gonna send for you and take care you all the resta your years. Before the Almighty may He strike me dead if this promise ain't made."

Joel jerked away, flung himself against a porch-pole, embraced it, clung there as though it alone understood and loved him.

"Hold on there now," she told him firmly. "You is almost a growed man; idea, takin on like some little ol gal! Why, you mortify me, I declare. Here was bout to give you Papadaddy's fine handsome sword . . . seen now you is not man enough for to own it."

Parting the curtain of ivy, Joel stepped through and into the yard; to walk straight off, and not look back, that would punish her. But when he reached the tree stump, and still she had not relented, not called him back, he stopped, retraced his steps onto the porch, and, looking seriously into her African eyes, said: "You will send for me?"

Zoo smiled and half picked him up. "Time I gets a place to put our heads." She reached down into her quilt-covered bundle, and brought out the sword. "This here was Papadaddy's proudest thing," she said. "Now don't you bring it no disgrace."

He strapped it to his waist. It was a weapon against the world, and he tensed with the cold grandeur of its sheath along his leg: suddenly he was most powerful, and unafraid. "I thank you kindly, Zoo," he said.

Gathering the quilt, and jellyjar box, she staggered down the steps. Her breath came in grunts, and with every loping movement the accordion, bouncing up and down, sprinkled a rainfall of discordant notes. They walked through the garden wilderness, and to the road. The sun was traveling the green-rimmed distance: as far as you could see daybreak blueness lifted over trees, layers of light unrolled across the land. "I spec to be down past Paradise Chapel fore dew's off the ground: good I got my quilt handy, may be lotsa snow round Washington D.C." And that was the last she said. Joel stopped by the mailbox. "Goodbye," he called, and stood there watching until she grew pinpoint small, lost, and the accordion soundless, gone.

". . . no gratitude," Amy sniffed. "Good and kind, that's how we were, always, and what does she do? Runs off, God knows where, leaving me with a houseful of sick people, not one of whom has sense enough to empty a slopjar. Furthermore, whatever else I may be, I'm a lady: I was brought up to be a lady, and I had my full four years at the Normal School. And if Randolph thinks I'm going to play nursemaid to orphans and idiots . . . damn Missouri!" Her mouth worked in a furious ugly way. "Niggers! Angela Lee warned me time and again, said never trust a nigger: their minds and hair are full of kinks in equal measure. Still, does seem like she could've stayed to fix breakfast." She took a pan of biscuits from the oven, and, along with a bowl of grits, a pot of coffee, arranged them on a tray. "Here now, trot this up to Cousin Randolph and trot right back: poor Mr Sansom has to be fed too, heaven help us; yes, may the Lord in his wisdom . . ."

Randolph was propped up in bed, naked, and with the covers stripped back; his skin seemed translucently pink in the morning light, his round smooth face bizarrely youthful. There was a small Japanese table set across his legs, and on it were a mound of bluejay feathers, a paste pot, a sheet of cardboard. "Isn't this delightful?" he said, smiling up at Joel. "Now put down the tray and have a visit."

"There isn't time," said Joel a little mysteriously.

"Time?" Randolph repeated. "Dear me, I thought that was where we were overstocked."

Pausing between words, Joel said: "Zoo's gone." He was anxious that the announcement should have a dramatic effect. Randolph, however, gave him no satisfaction, for, contrary to Amy, he seemed not at all upset, even surprised. "How tiresome of her," he sighed, "and how absurd, too. Because she can't come back, one never can."

"She wouldn't want to anyway," answered Joel impertinently. "She wasn't happy here; I don't think nothing would make her come back."

"Darling child," said Randolph, dipping a bluejay feather in the paste, "happiness is relative, and," he continued, fitting the feather on the cardboard, "Missouri Fever will discover that all she has deserted is her proper place in a rather general puzzle. Like this." He held up the cardboard in order that Joel could see: there feathers were so arranged the effect was of a living bird transfixed. "Each feather has, according to size and color, a particular position, and if one were the slightest awry, why, it would not look at all real."

A memory floated like a feather in the air; Joel's mental eye saw the bluejay beating its wings up the wall, and Amy's ladylike lifting of a poker. "What good is a bird that can't fly?" he said.

"I beg your pardon?"

Joel was himself uncertain what he meant. "The other one, the real one, it could fly. But this one can't do anything . . . except maybe look like it was alive."

Tossing the cardboard aside, Randolph lay drumming his fingers on his chest. He lowered his eyelids, and with his eyes closed he looked peculiarly defenseless. "It is pleasanter in the dark," he said, as if talking in his sleep. "Would it inconvenience you, my dear, to bring from the cabinet a bottle of sherry? And then, on tiptoe, mind you, draw all the shades, and then, oh very quietly please, shut the door." As Joel fulfilled the last of these requests, he rose up to say: "You are quite right: my bird can't fly."

Some while later, Joel, his stomach still jittery from having fed Mr Sansom's breakfast to him mouthful by mouthful, sat reading aloud in rapid flat tones. The story, such as it was, involved a blonde lady and a brunette man who lived in a house sixteen floors high; most of the stuff the lady said was embarrassing to repeat: "Darling," he read, "I love you as no woman ever loved, but Lance, my dearest, leave me now while our love is still a shining thing." And Mr Sansom smiled continuously through even the saddest parts; glancing at him, his son remembered a threat Ellen had delivered whenever he'd made an ugly face: "Mark my word," she'd say, "it's going to freeze that way." Such a fate had apparently descended upon Mr Sansom, for his ordinarily expressionless face had been grinning now no less than eight days. Finishing off the beautiful lady and lovely man, who were left honeymooning in Bermuda, Joel went on to a recipe for banana custard pie: it was all the same to Mr Sansom, romance or recipe, he gave each of them staring unequaled attention.

What was it like almost never to shut your eyes, always to be forever reflecting the same ceiling, light, faces, furniture, dark? But if the eyes could not escape you, neither could you avoid them; they seemed indeed sometime to permeate the room, their damp greyness covering all like mist; and if those eyes were to make tears they would not be normal tears, but something grey, perhaps green, a color at any rate, and solid, like ice.

Downstairs in the parlor was a collection of old books, and exploring there Joel had come upon a volume of Scottish legends. One of these concerned a man who compounded a magic potion unwisely enabling him to read the thoughts of other men and see deep into their souls; the evil he saw, and the shock of it, turned his eyes into open sores: thus he remained the rest of his life. It impressed Joel to the extent that he was half-convinced Mr Sansom's eyes knew exactly what went on inside his head, and he attempted, for this reason, to keep his thoughts channeled in impersonal directions. ". . . mix sugar, flour, salt and add egg yolks. Stir constantly while pouring on scalded milk . . ." Every once in a while he was tantalized by a sense of guilt: he ought to feel more for Mr Sansom than he did, he ought to try and love him. If only he'd never seen Mr Sansom! Then he could have gone on picturing him as looking this and that wonderful way, as talking in a kind strong voice, as being really his father. Certainly this Mr Sansom was not his father. This Mr Sansom was nobody but a pair of crazy eyes. ". . . turn into baked pieshell. Cover with . . . it says meringay or something like that . . . and bake. Makes nine-inch pie." He put down the magazine, a journal for females to which Amy subscribed, and began straightening Mr Sansom's pillows. Mr Sansom's head lolled back and forth, as if saying no no no; actually, and his voice sounded prickly as though a handful of pins were lodged in his throat, he said, "Boy kind kind boy kind," over and over, "ball kind ball," he said, dropping one of his red tennis balls, and, as Joel retrieved it, his set smile became more glassy: it ached on his grey skeleton face. Then all at once a whistle broke through the shut windows. Joel turned to listen. Three short blasts and a hoot-owl wail. He went to the window. It was Idabel; she was in the garden below, and Henry was with her. The window was stuck, so he signaled to her, but she could not see him, and he hurried to the door. "Bad," said Mr Sansom, and let go every tennis ball in the bed, "boy bad bad!"

Detouring into his room long enough to strap on his sword, he ran downstairs, outside and into the garden. For the first time since he'd known her Joel felt Idabel was glad to see him: a look of serious relief cleared her face, and for a moment he thought she might embrace him: her arms lifted as if to do so, then instead she stooped and hugged Henry, squeezed his neck until the old hound whined. "Is something wrong?" he said, for she had not spoken, nor, in a sense, taken notice of him, not enough, that is, even to mention his sword, and when she said, "We were scared you weren't home," all the rough spirit seemed to have drained from her voice. Joel felt stronger than she, and sure of himself as he'd never been with that other Idabel, the tomboy. He squatted down beside her there in the shade of the house where tulip stalks leaned around, and elephant leaves, streaked with silver snail tracks, hung above their heads like parasols. She was pale beneath her freckles, and a ridge of fingernail-scratch stood out across her cheek. "How'd you get that?" he said.

Her lips whitened, she spit the answer: "Florabel. That damned bastard."

"A girl can't be a bastard," he said.

"Oh, she's a bastard all right. But I didn't mean her." Idabel pulled the hound onto her lap; sleepily submissive, he lay there allowing her to pick fleas off his belly. "I meant that old bastard daddy of mine. We had us a knock-down drag-out fight, him and me and Florabel. On account of he tried to shoot Henry here; Florabel put him up to it. . . . says Henry's got a mortal disease, which is a low-down lie from start to finish. I figure I broke her nose and some teeth, too; leastwise, she was bleeding like a pig when me and Henry took off. We been walking around in the dark all night." Suddenly she laughed in her woolly familiar way. "And up around sunrise, know who we saw? Zoo Fever. She couldn't hardly breathe, she was carrying so much junk: golly, we were right sorry to hear about Jesus. It's funny for that old man to die and nobody hear a word. But like I told you, who knows what goes on at the Landing?"

Joel thought: who knows what goes on anywhere? Except Mr Sansom. He knew everything; in some trick way his eyes traveled the whole world over: they this very instant were watching him, of that he had no doubt. And it was probable, too, that, if he had a mind, he could reveal to Randolph Pepe Alvarez's whereabouts.

"Don't you fret none, Henry," said Idabel, popping a flea. "They'll never lay a hand on you."

"But what are you going to do?" Joel asked. "You've got to go home sometime."

She rubbed her nose, and considered him with eyes exaggeratedly wide and appealing: if it had been anyone but Idabel, Joel would've thought she was making up to him. "Maybe," she said, "and maybe not; that's what I came to see you for." Abruptly businesslike, she shoved the dog off her lap, and took a hearty comrade-grip on Joel's shoulders: "How would you like to run away?" But before he could say what he'd like she hurried on: "We could go to town tonight when it's dark. The travelin-show's in town, and there'll be a big crowd. I do want to see the travelin-show one more time; they've got a ferris wheel this year somebody said, and . . ."

"But where would we go?" he said.

Idabel's mouth opened, closed. Apparently she hadn't given this much thought, and with the wide world to choose from, all she could find to say was: "Outside; we'll just walk around outside till we come on a nice place."

"We could go to California and pick grapes," he suggested. "Out West you don't have to be but twelve years old to get married."

"I don't want to get married," said Idabel, coloring. "Who the hell said I wanted to get married? Now you listen, boy: you behave decent, you behave like we're brothers, or don't you behave at all. Anyway, we don't want to do no sissy thing like pick grapes. I thought maybe we could join the navy; else we could teach Henry tricks and get in the circus: say, couldn't you learn magic tricks?"

Which reminded him: he'd never gone after the charm Little Sunshine had promised; certainly, if he were running off with Idabel, they would need this magic, and so he asked if she knew the way to the Cloud Hotel. "Kind of," she said, "down through the woods and the sweetgum hollow and then across the creek where the mill is . . . oh, it's a long way. Why'd we want to go anyhow?" But of course he could not say, for Little Sunshine had warned him never to mention the charm. "I've got important business with the man there," he said, and then, wanting a little to frighten her: "Otherwise something terrible will happen to us."

They both jumped. "Don't hide, I know you're out there, I heard you." It was Amy, and she was calling from a window directly above: she could not see them, though, for the elephant leaves were a camouflage. "The idea, leaving Mr Sansom in this fix, are you completely out of your mind?" They crawled from under the leaves, crept along the side of the house, then raced for the road, the woods. "I know you're there, Joel Knox, come up this instant, sir!"

Deep in the hollow, dark syrup crusted the bark of vine-roped sweetgums; like pale apple leaves green witch butterflies sank and rose there and there; a breezy lane of trumpet lilies (Saints and Heroes, these alone, or so old folks said, could hear their mythical flourish) beckoned like hands lace-gloved and ghostly. Idabel kept waving her arms, for the mosquitoes were fierce: everywhere, like scraps of a huge shattered mirror, mosquito pools of marsh water gleamed and broke in Henry's jogging path.

"I've got some money," said Idabel. "Fact is, I've got near about four bits." Joel thought of the change he'd stored away in the box, and bragged that he had more than that. "We'll spend it all at the travelin-show," she said, and took a froggish jump over a crocodile-looking log. "Who needs money any-how? Leastwise, not right always we don't . . . except for dopes. We ought to save enough so as we can have a dope every day cause my brains get fried if I can't have myself an ice-cold dope. And cigarettes. I surely do appreciate a smoke. Dopes and smokes and Henry are the onliest things I love."

"You like me some, don't you?" he said, without meaning really to speak aloud. In any case, Idabel, chanting ". . . the big baboon by the light of the moon was combing his auburn hair . . ." did not answer.

They stopped to scrape off chews of sweetgum, and while they stood there she said: "My daddy'll be out rooting up the country for me; I bet he'll go down and ask Mr Bluey for the loan of his old bloodhound." She laughed and sweetgum juice trickled out the corners of her mouth; a green butterfly lighted on her head, held like a ribbon to a lock of her hair. "One time they were hunting for an escaped convict (right here in this very hollow), Mr Bluey and his hound and Sam Radclif and Roberta Lacey and the Sheriff and all those dogs from the farm; when it got dark we could see their lamps shining way off here in the woods, and hear the dogs howling; it was like a holiday: daddy and all the men and Roberta Lacey got hollering drunk, you could hear old Roberta's hee-haw clear to Noon City and back . . . and you know, I was real sorry for that convict, and afraid for him: I kept thinking I was him and he was me and it was both of us they were out to catch." She spit the gum like tobacco, and hooked her thumbs in the belt rungs of her khaki shorts. "But he got away. They never did find him. Some folks hold that he's still about . . . hiding in the Cloud Hotel, maybe, or living at the Landing."

"There *is* someone living at the Landing," Joel said excitedly, and then, with some disappointment, added: "Except it's not a convict, it's a lady."

"A lady? You mean Miss Amy?"

"Another lady," he told her, and regretted mentioning the matter. "She has a tall white wig, and wears a lovely old-time dress, but I don't know who she is or even if she is real." But Idabel just looked at him as if he were a fool, so he smiled uneasily and said: "I'm only joking, I only wanted to scare you." And, not wanting to answer questions, he ran a little ahead, the sword spanking his thigh. It seemed to him they had come a far way, and he played with the notion that they were lost: probably there was no such place as this hotel whose name evoked a kind of mist-white palace floating foglike through the woods. Then, facing a fence of brambles, he unsheathed his sword and cut an opening. "After you, my dear Idabel," he said, bowing low, and Idabel, whis-tling for Henry, stepped through. Off a short distance on the other side lay a roughly pebbled beach along which the creek, here rather more of a river, ran sluggishly. A yellowed cane-break obscured at first the sight of a broken dam, and, below this, a queer house straddling the water on high stilts: it was made of unpainted plank gone grey now, and had a strange unfinished look, as though its builder had been frightened and fled his job midway. Three sunning buzzards sat hunched on what remained of the roof, butterflies went in and out of blue skybright windows. Joel was sorely let-down, for he thought this alas was the Cloud Hotel, but then Idabel said no, it was an old forsaken mill, a place where, years since, farmers had brought corn to be ground. "There used to be a road, one that went to the Cloud Hotel; nothing but woods now, not even a path to show the way." She seized a rock, and threw it up at the buzzards; they glided off the roof, glided over the beach, their shadows making there lazy interlocking circles.

The water, deeper here than where he and Idabel had taken their bath, was also darker, a muddy bottomless olive, and when he knew they did not have to swim over, his relief gave him courage enough to travel down under the mill where there was a heavy but rotting beam on which they might cross.

"I'd better go first," said Idabel. "It's pretty old and liable to bust."

But Joel pushed in front of her and started over; after all, no matter what Idabel said, he was a boy and she was a girl and he was damned if she were going to get the upper hand again. "You and Henry come after me," he called, his voice hollow in the sudden cellar-like dark. Luminous water-shadows snaked up the cracked and eaten columns supporting the mill-house; copper waterbugs swung on intricate trapezes of insect's thread, and fungus flowered fist-size on the wet decrepit wood. Joel, stepping gingerly, using his sword to balance, made his eyes avoid the dizzy deep creek moving so closely below, kept them, instead, aimed on the opposite bank where, in sunshine, laden gourdvine burst from red clay green and promising. Still all at once he felt he would never reach the other side: always he would be balanced here suspended between land, and in the dark, and alone. Then, feeling the board shake as Idabel started across, he remembered he had someone to be together with. Only. And his heart turned over, skipped: every part of him went like iron.

Idabel shouted: "What's wrong? What're you stopping for?"

But he could not tell her. Nor bring himself to make any sound, motion. For piled no more than a foot beyond was a cotton-mouth thick as his leg, long as a whip; its arrow-shaped head slid out, the seed-like eyes alertly pointed, and all over Joel began to sting, as though already bitten. Idabel, coming up behind him, looked over his shoulder. "Jesus," she breathed, "oh Jesus," and at the touch of her hand he broke up inside: the creek froze, was like a horizontal cage, and his feet seemed to sink, as though the beam on which they stood was made of quicksand. How did Mr Sansom's eyes come to be in a moccasin's head?

"Hit him," Idabel demanded. "Hit him with your sword."

It was this way: they were bound for the Cloud Hotel, yes, the Cloud Hotel, where a man with a ruby ring was swimming underwater, yes, and Randolph was looking through his almanac and writing letters to Hongkong, to Port-o'-Spain, yes, and poor Jesus was dead, killed by Toby the cat (no, Toby was a baby), by a nest of chimney sweeps falling in a fire. And Zoo: was she in Washington yet? And was it snowing? And why was Mr Sansom staring at him so hard? It was really very, very rude (as Ellen would say), really very rude indeed of Mr Sansom never to close his eyes.

The snake, unwinding with involved grace, stretched toward them in a rolling way, and Idabel screamed, "Hit him, hit him!" but Joel of course was concerned only with Mr Sansom's stare.

Spinning him around, and pushing him safely behind her, she pulled the sword out of his hand. "Big granddaddy bastard," she jeered, thrusting at the snake. For an instant it seemed paralyzed; then, invisibly swift, and its whole length like a wire singingly tense, it hooked back, snapped forward. "Bastard," she hollered, closing her eyes, swinging the blade like a sickle, and the cotton-mouth, slapped into the air, turned, plunged, flattened on the water: belly up, white and twisted, it was carried by the current like a torn lily root. "No," said Joel when, some while later, Idabel, calm in her triumph, tried to coax him on across. "No," he said, for what use could there be now in finding Little Sunshine? His danger had already been, and he did not need a charm.

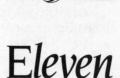

Eleven

During supper Amy announced: "It is my birthday. Yes," she said, "it is indeed, and not a soul to remember. Now if Angela Lee were here, I should've had an immense cake with a prize in every slice: tiny gold rings, and a pearl for my add-a-pearl, and little silver shoebuckles: oh when I think!"

"Happy birthday," said Joel, though what he wished her was hardly happiness, for when he'd come home she'd rushed down the hall with every intention, or so she'd said, of breaking an umbrella over his head; whereupon Randolph, throwing open his door, had warned her, and very sincerely, that if ever she touched him he'd wring her damned neck.

Randolph went right on chewing a pig's knuckle, and Amy, ignoring Joel, glared at him, her eyebrows going up and up, her lips pursed and trembling. "Eat, go on and eat, get fat as a hog," she said, and slammed down her gloved hand: hitting the table it knocked like wood, and the old alarm clock, touched off by this commotion, began to ring: all three sat motionless until it whined itself silent. Then, the lines of her face becoming prominent as veins, Amy, with a preposterously maudlin sob, broke into tears and hiccups. "You silly toad," she panted, "who else has ever helped you? Angela Lee would sooner have seen you hanged! But no, I've given up my life." Spouting intermittent pardon-me's, she hiccuped in succession a dozen times. "I tell you this, Randolph, I would sooner go off and clean house for a bunch of tacky niggers than stay here another instant; don't think I couldn't earn my way, the mothers of any town in America would send their children to me and we would play organized games, blind man's bluff and musical chairs and pin the tail, and I would charge each child ten cents: I could make a good living. No, I need not depend on you; in fact, if I had a particle of sense I'd sit down and write a letter to the Law."

Randolph crossed his knife and fork, and patted his lips with his kimono sleeve. "I'm sorry, my dear," he said, "but I'm afraid I haven't been following: exactly where is it you fancy me at fault?"

His cousin shook her head, took a deep, nervous breath; the tears stopped coming, the hiccups ceased, and all at once she turned on a shy smile. "It's my birthday," she said, her voice reduced to a waver.

"How very odd. Joel, does it seem to you peculiarly warm for January?"

Joel was listening for sounds above their voices: three short whistles and a hoot-owl wail, Idabel's signal. In his impatience it was as if the clock, having unwound, had stopped time altogether.

"January, yes; and you, my dear, were born (if one believes a family Bible, though I'll admit one never should, so many weddings being listed an erroneous nine months early) one January New Year's."

Amy's neck dipped turtlewise into shoulders timidly contracting, and her hiccups racked up again, but less indignant now, more mournful. "But Randolph . . . Randolph I *feel* as though it was my birthday."

"A little wine, then," he said, "and a song on the pianola; look in the cupboard, too, I'm certain you'll find a box of stale animal crackers with little silver worms in every crumb." Carrying lamps, they moved into the parlor, and Joel, sent upstairs to fetch the wine, crossed Randolph's room quickly, and raised the window. Below, bonfires of newly bloomed roses burned like flower-eyes in the August twilight, their sweetness filling the air like a color. He whistled, whispered, "Idabel, Idabel," and with Henry she appeared between the leaning columns. "Joel," she said, unsure, and behind her it was as though the falling night slipped a glove over the five stone fingers which, curling in shadow, seemed bendingly to reach her; when he answered, she hurried beyond their grasp, came safely under the window. "Are you ready?" She'd plaited a collar of white roses for Henry, and there was a rose hung awkwardly in her hair. Idabel, he thought, you look real beautiful. "Go to the mailbox," he said, "I'll meet you there." It was too dark now to maneuver without light. He lit a candle on Randolph's desk, and went to the cabinet, searching there until he located an unopened bottle of sherry. Stooping to extinguish the candle, he noticed a sheet of green tissue-thin stationery, and on it, in a handwriting daintily familiar, was written only a salutation: "My dearest Pepe." Randolph, then, had composed the letters to Ellen, but how could he have supposed that Mr Sansom could ever have written a word? In the black hall, lamplight rimmed Mr Sansom's door, which, as he waited, a cross-draft commenced to swing open, and it was as though he were seeing his father's room through reversed binoculars, for, in its yellow clarity, it was like a miniature: the hand with the wedding ring slouched over the bed's side; scenes of Venice, projected by the frost-glass globe, tinted the walls, the crocheted spread, and there in the mirror whirled his eyes, his smile. Joel entered on tiptoe and went on his knees beside the bed. Downstairs the pianola had begun pounding its raggedy carnival tune, yet somehow it did not interfere with the stillness and secrecy of this moment. Tenderly he took Mr Sansom's hand and put it against his cheek and held it there until there was warmth between them; he kissed the dry fingers, and the wedding ring whose gold had been meant to encircle them both. "I'm leaving, Father," he said, and it was, in a sense, the first time he'd acknowledged their blood; slowly he rose up and pressed his palms on either side of Mr Sansom's face and brought their lips together: "My only father," he whispered, turning, and, descending the stairs, he said it again, but this time all to himself.

He set the bottle of sherry on the hall-tree in the chamber, and, hidden by a curtain, peered into the parlor; neither Amy nor Randolph had heard him come down the stairs: she was sitting on the pianola stool, studiously working an ivory fan, tiresomely tapping her foot, and Randolph, bored to limpness, was staring at the archway where Joel was scheduled presently to present himself. He was gone now, and running toward the mailbox, Idabel, outside. The road was like a river to float upon, and it was as if a roman-candle, ignited by the sudden breath of freedom, had zoomed him away in a wake of star-sparks. "Run!" he cried, reaching Idabel, for to stop before the Landing stood forever out of sight was an idea unendurable, and she was racing before him, her hair pulling back in windy stiffness: as the road humped into a hill it was as though she mounted the sky on a moon-leaning ladder; beyond the hill they came to a standstill, panting, tossing their heads. "Was they chasing us?" asked Idabel, petals from her hair-rose shedding in the air, and he said: "Nobody will catch us now never." Staying to the road, even when they passed close by her house, they walked with Henry between them: roses, strewn from the wreath about the dog's neck, soaked the colors of a stony moon, and Idabel said she was hungry enough to eat a rose, "or grass and toadstools." Well, he said, well, when they reached town he'd splurge and treat her to a barbecue at R. V. Lacey's Princely Place. And they talked of the night he'd first come along this road and heard her in the distance singing with her sister. His eyes nailed down with stars, an old wagon had carried him over a ledge of sleep, a wintry slumber dispelled in the exhilaration of recent waking: meantime, there had taken place a dream, from whose design, unraveling now swifter than memory could reweave it, only Idabel remained, all else and others having dimmed-out as shadows do in dark. "I remember," she said, "and I thought you was a mess just like Florabel; to be honest to God, I never did much change-mind till today." Seeming then ashamed, she scampered down the road-bank, and scooped up drinks of water from a thread of creek which trickled there; abruptly she straightened, and, with a finger to her lips, motioned for Joel to join her. "Hear it?" she whispered. Behind the foliage, a bull-toned voice, and another, this like a guitar, blended as raindrops caress to sound a same rhythm;

an intricate wind of rustling murmurs, small laughter followed sighs not sad and silences deeper than space. Moss cushioned their footsteps as they moved through the leafy thickness, and came to pause at the edge of an opening: two Negroes, caught in a filmy skein of moon and fern, lay unclothed and enfolded, the man's caramel-colored body braceleted with his darker lover's arms, legs, his lips nuzzling her nipples: oo-we, oo-we, sweet Simon, she sighed, love shivering her voice, love rolling through her like thunder; easy, Simon, sweet Simon, easy honey, she crooned, and tensed then, her arms lifting as if to embrace the moon; her lover sank across her, and there together, limbs akimbo, they made on the bloom of moss a black fallen star. Idabel retreated with splashful, rowdy haste, and Joel, trying to keep up, went shh! shh!, thinking how wrong to frighten the lovers, and wishing, too, that she'd waited longer, for watching them it had been as if his heart were beating all over his body, and all undefined whisperings had gathered into one yearning roar: he knew now, and it was not a giggle or a sudden white-hot word; only two people with each other in withness, and it was as though a tide had receded leaving him dry on a beach white as bone, and it was good at last to have come from so grey so cold a sea. He wanted to walk with Idabel's hand in his, but she had them doubled like knots, and when he spoke to her she looked at him mean and angry and scared; it was as if their positions of the afternoon had somehow reversed: she'd been the hero under the mill, but now he had no weapon with which to defend her, and even if this were not true he wouldn't have known what it was she wanted killed.

A whirl of ferris-wheel lights revolved in the distance; rockets rose, burst, fell over Noon City like showering rainbows; gawky kids and their elders, all beautiful in their Sunday summer finest, traipsed back and forth with reflections of the carnival starring their eyes; a young Negro watched sadly from the isolation of the jail, and a rhinestoned colored girl, red-silk stockings flashing on her legs, swished by shouting lewdly up at him. On the porch of the cracked ancient house old people recalled traveling-shows in other years, and little boys, going behind hedges to pee, lingered to laugh and pinch each other. Ice-cream cones slipped from grimy fingers, crackerjack split and so did tears, but nobody was unhappy, nobody thought of chores beyond the moment.

Hiya, Idabel—Watcha say, Idabel? but not a soul spoke to him, he was no part of them, they did not know him; only R. V. Lacey remembered. "Look, babylove!" she said, when they appeared in the door of her Princely Place, and those assembled there, beribboned sassy-faced town-tarts and rednecked farmboys with cow-dumb eyes, paused in their jukebox shuffling; one girl advanced to tickle him under the chin. "Where'd you find this, Idabel? He's cute."

"Mind your own business, punk," Idabel said, seating herself at the counter.

Miss Roberta Lacey wagged her finger. "Idabel Thompkins, I warned you time and again, none of that gangster talk in my establishment. Furthermore, I have many times put into words the fact you are not to set foot inside my place, acting as you do like Baby Face Floyd, and dressing as you do in no proper way befitting a young lady: now skidaddle, and take that filthy hound with you."

"Please, Miss Roberta," said Joel, "Idabel's awful hungry."

"Then she oughta be home learning to fix a man his vittels (laughter); besides which this here's a grown-folks café (applause). Romeo, remind me to put up a sign to that effect. Whatismore, Idabel, your daddy has been round here inquirin as to your whereabouts, and it is my serious opinion he means to burn up that saucy little butt of yours (laughter)."

Idabel leveled a slant-eyed look at the proprietress, then, as though this seemed to her the most expressive retort, she spit on the floor, shoved her hands in her pockets and swaggered out. Joel started to follow, but R. V. Lacey clamped a hand on his shoulder. "Babylove," she said, toying with the long black hair extending from her chin-wart, "Angelboy, you're keeping kinda peculiar company. Idabel's daddy said she's done broke her pretty sweet little sister's nose, and knocked out most her teeth." Grinning, scratching under her armpits like a baboon, she added, "Now don't go saying Roberta's a hard woman; she's soft on you," and handed him a bag of salted peanuts. "No charge."

Idabel told him what he could do with those old Roberta goobers, but she relented, to be sure, and devoured the sack solo. She let him take her arm, and they descended on the gala beehive acre where the traveling-show buzzed. The merry-go-round, a sorry battered toy, turned to a jingling sound of bells, and colored folks, who were not allowed to ride, stood clustered at a distance getting more fun from its magical whirl than those astride saddles. Idabel shelled out 35¢ at the dart-throw game, all in order to win a pair of dark glasses like the ones Joel had broken, and what a ruckus she raised when the straw-hat man tried to palm off a walking cane! You bet she got those specs, but, being too large for her, they kept sliding down her nose. At the 10¢ Tent they saw a four-legged chicken (stuffed), and the two-headed baby floating in a glass tank like a green octopus: Idabel studied it a long while, and when she turned away her eyes were moist: "Poor little baby," she said, "poor little thing." The Duck Boy cheered her up; he sure was a comedy all right, quack-quack-quacking, making dopey faces and flapping his hands, the fingers of which were webbed together; at one point he opened his shirt to reveal a white feathery chest. Joel preferred Miss Wisteria, a darling little girl, he thought, and so did Idabel; they did not quite believe she was a midget, though Miss Wisteria herself claimed to be twenty-five years old, and just back from a grand tour of Europe where she'd appeared before all the crowned heads: her own sweet little gold head sported a twinkling crown; she wore elegant silver slippers (it was a marvel the way she could walk on her toes); her dress was a drape of purple silk tied about the middle with a yellow silk sash. She hopped and skipped and giggled and sang a song and said a poem, and when she came off the platform, Idabel, more excited than Joel had ever seen her, rushed up and asked, please, wouldn't she have some sodapop with them. "Charmed," said Miss Wisteria, twisting her gold sausage curls, "charmed." Idabel humbled herself; she bought cokes, found them a place to sit, and made Henry keep his distance, for Miss Wisteria confessed to a fear of animals. "Frankly," she lisped, "I do not think God intended them." Except for rouged kewpie-doll lips, her baby-plump face was pale, enameled; her hands flitted about so that they seemed to have a separate life of their own, and she glanced at them now and again as if they deeply puzzled her; they were smaller than a child's these hands, but thin, mature, and the fingernails were painted. "Well, this is surely a treat," she said. "Now lots of showpeople are just plain put-ons, but I don't hold with any put-on, I like to bring my art to the people . . . lots of whom don't see how come I jog around with an outfit like this . . . look, they say to me, there you were out in Hollywood pulling down a thousand dollars a week as Shirley Temple's stand-in . . . but I say to them: the road to happiness isn't always a highway." Draining her coke, she took out a lipstick and reshaped her kewpie-bow; then a queer thing happened: Idabel, borrowing the lipstick, painted an awkward clownish line across her mouth, and Miss Wisteria, clapping her little hands, shrieked with a kind of sassy pleasure. Idabel met this merriment with a dumb adoring smile. Joel could not understand what had taken her. Unless it was that the midget had cast a spell. But as she continued to fawn over tiny yellow-haired Miss Wisteria it came to him that Idabel was in love. No, she would not consider leaving, there was a world of time. "Charmed," said Miss Wisteria to a suggestion they ride the ferris-wheel, "charmed."

A rash of lightning rattled the stars; Miss Wisteria's royal headgear caught fire in this brief tinseled burst, the glass jewels glittering roselike in the pink lights of the ferris-wheel, and Joel, left below, could see her white winglike hands alight on Idabel's hair, flutter away, squeeze the dark as if eating its very substance. They swung low, their laughter rippling like Miss Wisteria's long sash, and, rising toward a new flush of lightning, dissolved; still he could hear the midget's pennyflute voice purring persistent as a mosquito above every fairground noise: Idabel, come back, he thought, thinking he would never see her again, that she would travel on into the sky with Miss Wisteria at her side, Idabel, come back, I love you. So then she was there, telling him, "You can see way off, you can almost touch the sky," so then he was aboard the ferris-wheel, alone with Miss Wisteria, and together they watched Idabel diminish as the rocking rickety car started to climb.

Wind swung them like a lantern; it is wind, Joel thought, for he could see the pennants trembling above the tents, trash-paper scurrying animal-like along the ground, and over there, on the walls of the old house where a Yankee bandit had murdered three women, raggedy posters danced a skeleton jig. The car in front contained a sunbonneted mother and her little girl, who nursed a corncob doll; they waved to a farmer waiting below. "Y'all better get offen that thing," he called back, "hitsa fixin to rain." Around they went, wind rustling Miss Wisteria's purple silk. "Run away, is it?" she said, a smile displaying rabbity teeth. "Well, I said to her, and I say to you: the world is a frightening place." She gestured her arms in an arc, and in that moment she seemed to him Outside, to be, that is, geography, earth and sea and all the cities in Randolph's almanac: her queer little hands, twittering midair, encompassed the globe. "And oh a lonesome place. Once I ran away. I had four sisters (Maudy went to Atlantic City as Miss Maryland, she's that beautiful), tall lovely girls, and my mother, bless her soul, stood nearly six feet in her stockings. We lived in a big house in Baltimore, the nicest on our street, and I never went to school; I was so little I could sit in my mother's sewing basket, and she used to joke that I could crawl through the eye of her needle; there was a beau of Maudy's who could balance me in the palm of his hand, and when I was seventeen I still had to sit in a highchair to eat my supper. They said I need not play alone, there are other little people, they said, go out and find them, they live in flowers. Many's the petal I've peeled but lilac is lilac and no one lives in any rose I ever saw; a spot of grease is all a wishbone leaves, and there is only candy in a Christmas stocking. Then I was twenty, and Mama said it wasn't right I shouldn't have a beau, and she sat right down and wrote a letter to the Sweethearts Matrimonial Agency in Newark, New Jersey. And do you know a man came to marry me: he was much too big, though, and much too ugly, and he was seventy-seven years old; well, even so, I might have married him except when he saw how little I was he said bye-bye and took the train back to from whence he'd come. I never have found a sweet little person. There are children; but I cry sometimes to think little boys must grow tall." Her voice, while making this memoir, had stiffened solemnly, and her hands folded themselves quietly in her lap. Idabel waved, shouted, but wind carried her words another way, and sadly Miss Wisteria said: "Poor child, is it that she believes she is a freak, too?" She placed her hand on his thigh, and then, as though she had no control over them whatsoever, her fingers crept up inside his legs: she stared at the hand with shocked intensity but seemed unable to remove it, and Joel, disturbed but knowing now he wanted never to hurt anyone, not Miss Wisteria, nor Idabel, nor the little girl with the corncob doll, wished so much he could say: it doesn't matter, I love you, I love your hand. The world was a frightening place, yes, he knew: unlasting, what could be forever? or only what it seemed? rock corrodes, rivers freeze, fruit rots; stabbed, blood of black and white bleeds alike; trained parrots tell more truth than most, and who is lonelier: the hawk or the worm? every flowering heart shrivels dry and pitted as the herb from which it bloomed, and while the old man grows spinsterish, his wife assumes a mustache; moment to moment, changing, changing, like the cars on the ferris-wheel. Grass and love are always greener; but remember Little Three Eyes? show her love and apples ripen gold, love vanquishes the Snow Queen, its presence finds the name, be it Rumpelstiltskin or merely Joel Knox: that is constant.

A wall of rain pushed toward them from the distance; you could hear it long before it came, humming like a horde of locusts. The operator of the ferris-wheel began letting off his passengers. "Oh, we'll be last," wailed Miss Wisteria, for they were suspended near the top. The rain-wall leaned over them, and she threw up her hands as if to hold it back. Idabel, everyone, fled as down it toppled like a tidal wave.

Presently only a hatless man stood there in the emptiness below. Joel, his eyes searching so frenziedly for Idabel, did not at first altogether see him. But the carnival lights short-circuited with a crackling flare, and when this happened it was suddenly as though the man turned phosphorescent: he seemed to Joel no more than a hand's space away. "Randolph," he whispered, and the name gripped him at the root of his throat. It was a momentary vision, for the lights all fizzled out, and as the ferris-wheel descended to a last stop, he could not see Randolph anywhere.

"Wait," demanded Miss Wisteria, assembling her drenched costume, "wait for me." But Joel leaped past her, and hurried from one shelter to the next; Idabel was not in the 10¢ Tent: no one was there but the Duck Boy, who was playing solitaire by candlelight. Nor was she in the group huddled on the merry-go-round. He went to the livery stable. He went to the Baptist church. And soon, there being scarcely another possibility, he found himself on the porch of the old house. Leaves, gathering in a coil, spiralled hissingly across its deserted expanse; empty rocking chairs tilted gently back and forth; a Prince Albert poster swept like a bird through the air and struck him in the face: he fought to free himself, but it was as though it were alive, and, struggling with it, it suddenly frightened him more than had the sight of Randolph: he would never rid himself of either. But then, what was there in Randolph to fear? The fact that he'd found him proved he was only a messenger for a pair of telescopic eyes. Randolph would never bring him harm (still, but, and yet). He let down his arms: it was curious, for so soon as he did this, Prince Albert, of his own accord, flew off howling in the hoarse rain. And could he, with equal ease, appease that other fury, the nameless one whose envoy appeared in Randolph's guise? Vine from the Landing's garden had stretched these miles to entwine his wrists, and he saw their plans, his and Idabel's, break apart like the thunder-split sky: not yet, not if he could find her, and he ran into the house: "Idabel, you are here, you are!"

A boom of silence answered him; here, there, a marginal sound: rain like wings in the chimney, mice feet on fallen glass, maidenly steps of her who always walks the stair, and wind, opening doors, closing them, wind conversing sadly on the ceiling, blowing its damp sour breath in his face, breathing out its lungs through the rooms: he let himself be carried in its course: his head was light as a balloon, and as hollow-feeling; ice as eyes, thorns as teeth, flannel as tongue; he'd seen sunrise that morning, but, each step directing him nearing a precipice permanent in shadowed intent (or so it seemed), it was not likely he would see another: sleep was like smoke, he inhaled it deeply, but it went back on the air in rings of color, spots, sparks, whose fire restrained him from falling in a bundle on the floor: warnings, they were, these starry flies, stay awake, Joel, in eskimoland sleep is death, is all, remember? She was cold, his mother, she passed to sleep with dew of snowflakes scenting her hair; if he could have but thawed open her eyes here now she would be to hold him and say, as he'd said to Randolph, "Everything is going to be all right"; no, she'd splintered like frozen crystal, and Ellen, gathering the pieces, had put them in a box surrounded by gladiolas fifty cents the dozen.

Somewhere he owned a room, he had a bed: their promise quivered before him like heat waves. Oh Idabel, why have you done this terrible thing!

There were footsteps on the porch; he could hear the squish-sqush of soggy shoes; abruptly a flashlight beam poked through a parlor window, and for an instant settled on a flecked decaying mantel-mirror: shining there, the mirror was like a slab of jelly, and the figure from outside fumed indistinctly on its surface: no one could've said who it was, but Joel, seeing the light slide away, hearing the steps enter the hall, knew for certain it was Randolph. And there came over him the humiliating probability that not once since he'd left the Landing had he made a movement unobserved: how amusing his goodbye must've seemed to Mr Sansom!

He crouched behind a door; through the hinged slit he could see into the hall where the light crawled like a burning centipede. It did not matter now if Randolph found him, he would welcome it. Still something kept him from calling out. The squshing steps moved toward the parlor threshold, and he heard, "Little boy, little boy," a whimper of despair.

Miss Wisteria stood so near he could smell the rancid wetness of her shriveled silk; her curls had uncoiled, the little crown had slipped awry, her yellow sash was fading its color on the floor. "Little boy," she said, swerving her flashlight over the bent, broken walls where her midget image mingled with the shadows of things in flight. "Little boy," she said, the resignation of her voice intensifying its pathos. But he dared not show himself, for what she wanted he could not give: his love was in the earth, shattered and still, dried flowers where eyes should be, and moss upon the lips, his love was faraway feeding on the rain, lilies frothing from its ruin. Withdrawing, she went up the stairs, and Joel, who listened to her footfalls overhead as she in her need of him searched the jungle of rooms, felt for himself ferocious contempt: what was his terror compared with Miss Wisteria's? He owned a room, he had a bed, any minute now he would run from here, go to them. But for Miss Wisteria, weeping because little boys must grow tall, there would always be this journey through dying rooms until some lonely day she found her hidden one, the smiler with the knife.

Three

Twelve

He sentenced himself: he was guilty: his own hands set about to expedite the verdict: magnetized, they found a bullet, the one thefted from Sam Radclif (Mr Radclif, forgive me, please, I never meant to steal) and, inserting it in Major Knox's old Indian pistol (Child, how many times have I told you not to touch that nasty thing?—Mama, don't scold me now, mama, my bones hurt, I'm on fire— The good die cold, the wicked in flames: the winds of hell are blue with the sweet ether of fever-flowers, horned snake-tongued children dance on lawns that are the surface of the sun, all loot from thievery tied to their tails like cat-cans, tokens of a life in crime) and put the bullet through his head: oh dear, there was nothing but a tickling, oh dear, now what? When lo! he was where he'd never imagined to find himself again: the secret hideaway room in which, on hot New Orleans afternoons, he'd sat watching snow sift through scorched August trees: the run of reindeer hooves came crisply tinkling down the street, and Mr Mystery, elegantly villainous in his black cape, appeared in their wake riding a most beautiful boatlike sleigh: it was made of scented wood, a carved red swan graced the front, and silver bells were strung like beads to make a sail: swinging, billowing-out, what shivering melodies it sang as the sleigh, with Joel aboard and warm in the folds of Mr Mystery's cape, cut over snowdeep fields and down unlikely hills.

But all at once his powers to direct adventures in the secret room failed: an ice-wall rose before them, the sleigh raced on to certain doom, that night radios would sadden the nation: Mr Mystery, esteemed magician, and Joel Harrison

Knox, beloved by one and all, were killed today in an accident which also claimed the lives of six reindeer who . . . r-r-rip, the ice tore like cellophane, the sleigh slid through into the Landing's parlor.

A strange sort of party seemed in progress there. These were among those present: Mr Sansom, Ellen Kendall, Miss Wisteria, Randolph, Idabel, Florabel, Zoo, Little Sunshine, Amy, R. V. Lacey, Sam Radclif, Jesus Fever, a man naked except for boxing-gloves (Pepe Alvarez), Sydney Katz (proprietor of the Morning Star Café in Paradise Chapel), a thick-lipped convict who wore a long razor on a chain around his neck like some sinister crucifix (Keg Brown), Romeo, Sammy Silverstein and three other members of the St. Deval Street Secret Nine. Most were dressed in black, rather formal attire; the pianola was playing Nearer My God to Thee. Not noticing the sleigh, they moved in a leaning black procession around a gladiola-garlanded cedar chest into which each dropped an offering: Idabel her dark glasses, Randolph his almanac, R. V. Lacey the snipped hair from her wart, Jesus Fever his fiddle, Florabel her Kress tweezers, Mr Sansom his tennis balls, Little Sunshine a magic charm, and so on: inside the chest lay Joel himself, all dressed in white, his face powdered and rouged, his goldbrown hair arranged in damp ringlets: Like an angel, they said, more beautiful than Alcibiades, more beautiful, said Randolph, and Idabel wailed: Believe me, I tried to save him, but he wouldn't move, and snakes are so very quick. Miss Wisteria, fitting her little crown upon his head, leaned so far over she nearly fell into the chest: Listen, she whispered, I'm no fool, I know you're alive: unless you give me the answer, I shan't save you, I shan't say a word: are the dead as lonesome as the living? Whereupon the room commenced to vibrate slightly, then more so, chairs overturned, the curio cabinet spilled its contents, a mirror cracked, the pianola, composing its own doomed jazz, held a haywire jamboree: down went the house, down into the earth, down, down, past Indian tombs, past the deepest root, the coldest stream, down, down, into the furry arms of horned children whose bumblebee eyes withstand forests of flame.

He knew too well the rhythm of a rocking-chair; aramp-arump, hour on hour he'd heard one for how long? traveling through space, and the cedar chest became at last confused with its sway: if you fall you fall forever, back and forth together, the ceaseless chair, the cedar chest: he squeezed pillows, gripped the posters of the bed, for on seas of lamplight it rode the rolling rocker's waves whose rocking was the tolling of a bellbuoy; and who was the pirate inching toward him in the seat? His eyes stung as he tasked them to identify: lace masks confounded, frost glass intervened, now the chair's passenger was Amy, now Randolph, then Zoo. But Zoo could not be here; she was walking for Washington, her accordion announcing every step of the way. An unrecognized voice quarreled with him, teased, taunted, revealed secrets he'd scarcely made known to himself: shut up, he cried, and wept, trying to silence it, but, of course, the voice belonged to him: "I saw you under the ferris-wheel," it accused the pirate in the chair; "No," said the pirate, "I never left here, sweet child, sweet Joel, all night I waited for you sitting on the stairs."

Always he was gnawing bitter spoons, or struggling to breathe through scarves soaked in lemon water. Hands coaxed down curtains of slumbering dusk; fingers leanly firm like Zoo's rambled through his hair, and other fingers, too, these with a touch cooler, more spun than sea spray: Randolph's voice, in tones still gentler, augmented their soothing traceries.

One afternoon the rocking chair became precisely that; scissors seemed to cut round the edges of his mind, and as he peeled away the dead discardings, Randolph, taking shape, shone blessedly near.

"Randolph," he said, reaching out to him, "do you hate me?" Smiling, Randolph whispered: "Hate you, baby?" "Because I went away," said Joel, "went way away and left your sherry on the hall-tree." Randolph took him in his arms, kissed his forehead, and Joel, pained, grateful, said, "I'm sick and so sick," and Randolph replied, "Lie back, my darling, lie still."

He drifted deep into September; the blissful depths of the bed seemed future enough, every pore absorbed its cool protection. And when he thought of himself he affixed the thought to a second person, another Joel Knox about whom he was interested in the moderate way one would be in a childhood snapshot: what a dumbbell! he would gladly be rid of him, this old Joel, but not quite yet, he somehow needed him still. For long periods each day he studied his face in a hand mirror: a disappointing exercise, on the whole, for nothing he saw concretely affirmed his suspicions of emerging manhood, though about his face there were certain changes: baby-fat had given way to a true shape, the softness of his eyes had hardened: it was a face with a look of innocence but none of its charm, an alarming face, really, too shrewd for a child, too beautiful for a boy. It would be difficult to say how old he was. All that displeased him was the brown straightness of his hair. He wished it were curly gold like Randolph's.

He did not know when Randolph slept; he seemed to vacate the rocking-chair only when it was time for Joel to eat or commit some function; and sometimes, waking with the moon watching at the window like a bandit's eye, he would see Randolph's asthmatic cigarette still pulsing in the dark: though the house had sunk, he was not alone, another had survived, not a stranger, but one more kind, more good than any had ever been, the friend whose nearness is love. "Randolph," he said, "were you ever as young as me?" And Randolph said: "I was never so old." "Randolph," he said, "do you know something? I'm very happy." To which his friend made no reply. The reason for this happiness seemed to be simply that he did not feel unhappy; rather, he knew all through him a kind of balance. There was so little to cope with. The mist which for him overhung so much of Randolph's conversation, even that had lifted, at least it was no longer troubling, for it seemed as though he understood him absolutely. Now in the process of, as it were, discovering someone, most people experience simultaneously an illusion they are discovering themselves: the other's eyes reflect their real and glorious value. Such a feeling was with Joel, and inestimably so because this was the first time he'd ever known the triumph, false or true, of seeing through to a friend. And he did not want any more to be responsible, he wanted to put himself in the hands of his friend, be, as here in the sickbed, dependent upon him for his very life. Looking in the handglass became, consequently, an ordeal: it was as if now only one eye examined for signs of maturity, while the other, gradually of the two the more attentive, gazed inward wishing him always to remain as he was.

"There is an October chill in the air today," said Randolph, settling overblown roses in a vase by the bed. "These are the last, I'm afraid, they are quite falling apart, even the bees have lost interest. And here, I've brought an autumn specimen, a sycamore leaf." Another day, and though the air was mild, he built a fire by which they toasted marshmallows and sipped tea from cups two hundred years old. Randolph did imitations. He was Charlie Chaplin to a T, Mae West too, and his cruel take-off on Amy made Joel double up on the bed, finally absorbed in laughter for its own sake, and Randolph said ha! ha! he would show him something really funny: "I'll have to fix up, though," he said, his eyes quickly alive, and made as if to leave the room; then, releasing the doorknob, he looked back. "But if I do . . . you mustn't laugh." And Joel's answer was a laugh, he couldn't stop, it was like hiccups. Randolph's smile ran off his face like melted butter, and when Joel cried, "Go on, you promised," he sat down, nursing his round pink head between his hands: "Not now," he said wearily, "some other time."

One morning Joel received the first mail he'd ever had at the Landing; it was a picture postcard, and Randolph, appearing with a copy of *Macbeth*, which they'd planned to read aloud, brought it to him. "It's from the little girl down the road," he said, and Joel's breath caught: long-legged and swaggering, Idabel walked from the wall, rocked in the chair. He'd not directly thought of her since the night of the traveling-show, an omission for which he couldn't account, but which did not strike him as freakish: she was, after all, one with the others covered over when the house sank, those whose names concerned the old Joel, whose names now in gnarled October freckling leaves spelled on the wind. Still Idabel was back, a ghost, perhaps, but here, and in the room: Idabel the hoodlum out to stone a one-armed barber, and Idabel with roses, Idabel with sword, Idabel who said she sometimes cried: all of autumn was the sycamore leaf and its red the red of her hair and its stem the rusty color of her rough voice and its jagged shape the pattern, the souvenir of her face.

The card, which showed joyful cottonpickers, was postmarked from Alabama, and it said: "Mrs Collie 1/2 sister an hes the baptis prechur Last Sunday

I past the plate at church! papa and F shot henry They put me to life here. why did you Hide? write to IDABEL THOMPKINS."

Well, frankly, he didn't believe her; she'd put herself to life, and it was with Miss Wisteria, not a baptis prechur. He handed the card to Randolph who, in turn, passed it to the fire; for an instant, as Idabel and her cottonpickers crinkled, he would have lost his hands to retrieve them, but Randolph, adjusting gold reading glasses, began: "First witch. When shall we three meet again In thunder, lightning, or in rain?" and he settled down to listen, he fell asleep and woke up with a holler, for he'd climbed up the chimney after Idabel, and there was only smoke where she'd been, sky. "Hush, now, hush," said Randolph slowly, softly, a voice like dying light, and he was glad for Randolph, calm in the center of his mercy.

So sometimes he came near to speaking out his love for him; but it was unsafe ever to let anyone guess the extent of your feelings or knowledge: suppose, as he often had, that he were kidnaped; in which case the wisest defense would be not to let the kidnaper know you recognized him as such. If concealment is the single weapon, then a villain is never a villain: one smiles to the very end.

And even if he spoke to Randolph, to whom would he be confessing love? Faceted as a fly's eye, being neither man nor woman, and one whose every identity cancelled the other, a grab-bag of disguises, who, what was Randolph? X, an outline in which with crayon you color in the character, the ideal hero: whatever his role, it is pitched by you into existence. Indeed, try to conceive of him alone, unseen, unheard, and he becomes invisible, he is not to be imagined. But such as Randolph justify fantasy, and if a genii should appear, certainly Joel would have asked that these sealed days continue through a century of calendars.

They ended, though, and at the time it seemed Randolph's fault. "Very soon we're going to visit the Cloud Hotel," he said. "Little Sunshine wants to see us; you are quite well enough, I think: it's absurd to pretend you're not." Urgency underscored his voice, an enthusiasm in which Joel could not altogether believe, for he sensed the plan was motivated by private, no doubt unpleasant reasons, and these, whatever they were, opposed Randolph's actual desires. And he said: "Let's stay right here, Randolph, let's don't ever go anywhere." And when the plea was rejected old galling grindful thoughts about Randolph came back. He felt grumpy enough to quarrel; that, of course, was a drawback in being dependent: he could never quarrel with Randolph, for anger seemed, if anything, more unsafe than love: only those who know their own security can afford either. Even so, he was on the point of risking cross words when an outside sound interrupted, and rolled him backward through time: "Why are you staring that way?" said Randolph.

"It's Zoo . . . I hear her," he said: through the evening windows came an accordion refrain. "Really I do."

Randolph was annoyed. "If she must be musical, heaven knows I'd prefer she took up the harmonica."

"But she's gone." And Joel sat up on his knees. "Zoo walked away to Washington . . ."

"I thought you knew," said Randolph, fingering the ribbon which marked the pages of *Macbeth*. "During the worst of it, when you were the most sick, she sat beside you with a fan: can't you remember at all?"

So Zoo was back; it was not long before he saw her for himself: at noon the next day she brought his broth; no greetings passed between them, nor smiles, it was as if each felt too much the fatigued embarrassment of anticlimax. Only with her it was still something more: she seemed not to know him, but stood there as if waiting to be introduced. "Randolph told me you couldn't come back," he said. "I'm glad he was wrong."

In answer there came a sigh so stricken it seemed to have heaved up from the pits of her being. She leaned her forehead on the bed-post, and it was then that with a twinge he realized her neckerchief was missing: exposed, her slanted scar leered like crooked lips, and her neck, divided this way, had lost its giraffe-like grandeur. How small she seemed, cramped, as if some reduction of the spirit had taken double toll and made demands upon the flesh: with that illusion of height was gone the animal grace, arrow-like dignity, defiant emblem of her separate heart.

"Zoo," he said, "did you see snow?"

She looked at him, but her eyes appeared not to make a connection with what they saw; in fact, there was about them a cross-eyed effect, as though they fixed on a solacing inner vision. "Did I see snow?" she repeated, trying hard, it seemed, to understand. "Did I see snow!" and she broke into a kind of scary giggle, and threw back her head, lips apart, like an open-mouthed child hoping to catch rain. "There ain't none," she said, violently shaking her head, her black greased hair waving with a windy rasp like scorched grass. "Hit's all a lotta foolery, snow and such: that sun! it's everywhere."

"Like Mr Sansom's eyes," said Joel, off thinking by himself.

"Is a nigger sun," she said, "an my soul, it's black." She took the broth bowl, and looked down into it, as if she were a gypsy reading tea-leaves. "I rested by the road; the sun poked down my eyes till I'm near-bout blind . . ."

And Joel said: "But Zoo, if there wasn't any snow, what was it you saw in Washington, D.C.? I mean now, didn't you meet up with any of those men from the newsreels?"

". . . an was holes in my shoes where the rocks done cut through the jackodiamonds and the aceohearts; walked all day, an here it seemed like I ain't come no ways, and here I'm sittin by the road with my feets afire an ain't a soul in sight." Two tears, following the bony edges of her face, faded, leaving silver stains. "I'm so tired ain't no feelin what tells me iffen I pinch myself, and I go on sittin there in that lonesome place till I looks up an see the Big Dipper: right about now along come a red truck with big bug lights coverin me head to toe." There were four men in the truck, she said, three white boys, and a Negro who rode in back squatting on top of a mountain of watermelons. The driver of the truck got out: "A real low man puffin a cigar like a bull; he ain't wearin no shirt an all this red hair growin even on his shoulders an hands; so quiet he walks through the grass, an looks at me so sweet I reckon maybe he sorry my feets is cut an maybe's gonna ax me why don't I ride in his fine car?" Go on, he told her, tapping his cigar so the ash was flung in her face, go on, gal, get down in the ditch; never mind why, says the man, and shoved her so she rolled over the embankment, landing on her back helpless as a junebug. "Lord, I sure commenced to hoop n' holler an this little bull-man says I hush up else he's gonna bust out my brains." She got up and started to run, but those other two boys, answering the driver's whistle, jumped down into the ditch and cut her off at either end; both these boys wore panama hats, and one had on a pair of sailor pants and a soldier's shirt: it was he who caught her and called for the Negro to bring a rifle. "That mean nigger look a whole lot like Keg, an he put that rifle up side my ear, an the man, he done tore my pretty dress straight down the front, an tells them panama boys theys to set to: I hear the Lord's voice talkin down that gun barrel, an the Lord said Zoo, you done took the wrong road and come the wrong way, you et of the apple, he said, an hits pure rotten, an outa the sky my Lord look down an brung comfort, an whilst them devils went jerkin like billygoats right then and there in all my shameful sufferin I said holy words: Yea, though I walk through the valley of the shadow of death, I'll fear no evil, for you is with me Lord, yea verily, I say, an them fools laughed, but my Lord took that sailor boy's shape, an us, me and the Lord, us loved." The boys had removed their panama hats; now they put them on again, and one said to the driver, well, what was wrong with him? and the driver sucked his cigar and scratched behind his ear and said, well, to tell the truth, he wasn't much one for being watched; O. K., said the boys, and climbed back up the bank, the Negro following after them, all three laughing, which made the driver's cheek twitch and his eyes "go yellow like an ol tomcat; an it was peculiar, cause he was one scared man." He did not move to touch her, but squatted impotent at her side like a bereaved lover, like an idol, then the truck-horn blew, the boys called, and he bent close: "He pushed that cigar in my bellybutton, Lord, in me was born fire like a child . . ."

Joel plugged his ears; what Zoo said was ugly, he was sick-sorry she'd ever come back, she ought to be punished. "Stop that, Zoo," he said, "I won't listen, I wont . . ." but Zoo's lips quivered, her eyes blindly twisted toward the inner vision; and in the roar of silence she was a pantomime: the joy of Jesus demented her face and glittered like a sweat, like a preacher her finger shook the air, agonies of joy jerked her breasts, her lips bared for a lowdown shout: in sucked her guts, wide swung her arms embracing the eternal: she was a cross, she was crucified. He saw without hearing, and it was more terrible for that, and after she'd gone, docilely taking the broth bowl with her, he kept his fingers in his ears till the ringing grew so loud it deafened even the memory of sound.

They were sure John Brown would never make it up the hill: "If he simply lay down and rolled over on us, I wouldn't blame him," said Randolph, and Joel tightened his muscles, hoping this might make the mule's load lighter. They had a croquer sack for saddle and rope for reins, nevertheless they managed to stay astride, though Randolph wobbled perilously, grunting all the while, and eating endless hardboiled eggs which Joel handed him from a picnic basket he held. "Another egg, my dear, I'm feeling most frightfully seasick again: if you feel something coming up always put something down."

It was a smoky day, the sky like a rained-on tinroof, the sun, when you saw it, fishbelly pale, and Joel, who had been routed out of bed and rushed away with such inconsiderate haste, he'd not had time in which to dress decently, was goosepimpled with cold, for he wore a thin T-shirt (turned inside out), and a pair of summer knickers with most of the buttons busted off the fly. At least he had on regular shoes, whereas Randolph wore only carpet slippers. "My feet have expanded so ominously it's all I can do to squeeze them into these; really, in the light of day what a ghoul I must look: I have the damnedest sensation that every time this sad beast moves my hair falls in floods, and my eyes: are they spinning like dice? Of course I reek of mothballs . . ." The suit he wore gave off their odor like a gas; a shrunken linen suit stiff with starch and ironed shiny, it bulged and creaked like medieval armor, and he handled himself with exaggerated gingerness, for the seams kept announcing bawdy intentions.

Toward twelve they dismounted, and spread their picnic under a tree. Randolph had brought along a fruit-jar of scuppernong wine; he gargled it like mouthwash, and when there was no more, Joel made use of the empty jar to trap ants: The Pious Insect, Randolph called them, and said: "They fill me with oh so much admiration and ah so much gloom: such puritan spirit in their mindless march of Godly industry, but can so anti-individual a government admit the poetry of what is past understanding? Certainly the man who refused to carry his crumb would find assassins on his trail, and doom in every smile. As for me, I prefer the solitary mole: he is no rose dependent upon thorn and root, nor ant whose time of being is organized by the unalterable herd: sightless, he goes his separate way, knowing truth and freedom are attitudes of the spirit." He smoothed his hair, and laughed: at himself, it seemed. "If I were as wise as the mole, if I were free and equal, then what an admirable whorehouse I should be the Madame of; more likely, though, I would end up just Mrs Nobody in Particular, a dumpy corsetless creature with a brickhead husband and stepladder brats and a pot of stew on the stove." Hurriedly, as if bringing an important message, an ant climbed up his neck, and disappeared into his ear. "There's an ant inside your head," said Joel, but Randolph, with the briefest nod, went on talking. So Joel cuddled up to him and, politely as he could, peered into his ear. The idea of an ant swimming inside a human head so enthralled him that it was some while before he became aware of silence, and the tense prolonged asking of Randolph's eyes: it was a look which made Joel prickle mysteriously. "I was looking for the ant," he said. "It went inside your ear; that could be dangerous, I mean, like swallowing a pin."

"Or defeat," said Randolph, his face sinking into sugary folds of resignation.

The gentle jog of John Brown's trot set ajar the brittle woods; sycamores released their spice-brown leaves in a rain of October: like veins dappled trails veered through storms of showering yellow; perched on dying towers of jack-in-the-pulpit cranberry beetles sang of their approach, and tree-toads, no bigger than dewdrops, skipped and shrilled, relaying the news through the light that was dusk all day. They followed the remnants of a road down which once had spun the wheels of lacquered carriages carrying verbena-scented ladies who twittered like linnets in the shade of parasols, and leathery cotton-rich gentlemen gruffing at each other through a violet haze of Havana smoke, and their children, prim little girls with mint crushed in their handkerchiefs, and boys with mean blackberry eyes, little boys who sent their sisters screaming with tales of roaring tigers. Gusts of autumn, exhaling through the inheriting weeds, grieved for the cruel velvet children and their virile bearded fathers: Was, said the weeds, Gone, said the sky, Dead, said the woods, but the full laments of history were left to the Whippoorwill.

As seagulls inform the sailor of land's nearness, so a twist of smoke unfurling beyond a range of pines announced the Cloud Hotel. John Brown's hoofs made a sucking sound in the swamp mud as they circled the green shores of Drownin Pond: Joel looked over the water, hoping to glimpse the creole or the gambler; alas, those sly and slimy fellows did not show themselves. But anchored off shore was a bent, man-shaped tree with moss streaming from its crown like scarecrow hair; sunset birds, hullabalooing around this island roost, detonated the desolate scene with cheerless cries, and only catfish bubbles ruffled the level eel-like slickness of the pond: in a burst, like the screaming of the birds, Joel heard the lovely laughing splashful girls splashing diamond fountains, the lovely harp-voiced girls, silent now, gone to the arms of their lovers, the creole and the gambler.

The hotel rose before them like a mound of bones; a widow's-walk steepled the roof, and leaning over its fence was Little Sunshine, who had a telescope trained upon the path; as they came closer he began a furious gesturing which at first seemed a too frantic welcome, but as his frenzy dissipated not at all, they soon realized he was warning them off. Curbing John Brown, they waited in the seeping twilight while the hermit descended through the trapdoor of the widow's-walk, presently reappearing on a slide of steps which tinkled over wastes of feudal lawn down to the water's rim. Brandishing his hickory cane, he advanced along the shore with a creeping bowlegged hobble, and Joel's eyes played a trick: he saw Little Sunshine as the old pond-tree come alive.

Still yards away, the hermit stopped and, stooping on his cane, fixed them
with a gluey stare. Then Randolph said his name, and the old man, blinking
with disbelief, broke into frisky giggles: "Well, now, ain't you the mischief!
Can't see worth nothin, an there I was with my ol spyglass axin: who that
a-comin where they ain't got no place? Well, now, this be a sweet todo!
Step-long, step-long, follow me right careful, plenty quicksand."

They walked single-file, Joel, who led the mule, going last, and wondering,
as he followed the sog of Randolph's footprints, why he'd been lied to, for it
was plain that Little Sunshine had not been expecting them.

Swan stairs soft with mildewed carpet curved upward from the hotel's lobby;
the diabolic tongue of a cuckoo bird, protruding out of a wall-clock, mutely
proclaimed an hour forty years before, and on the room clerk's splintery desk
stood dehydrated specimens of potted palm. After tying a spittoon onto John
Brown's leg, this in order that they could hear him should he wander off, they
left him in the lobby, and filed through the ballroom, where a fallen chandelier
jeweled the dust, and weather-ripped draperies lay bunched on the waltz-
waved floor like curtsying ladies. Passing a piano, over which web was woven
like the gauzy covering of a museum exhibit, Joel struck the keys expecting
Chopsticks in return; instead, there came a glassy rattle of scuttling feet.

Beyond the ballroom, and in what had once been Mrs Cloud's private
apartment, were two simply furnished, spacious rooms, both beautifully clean,
and this was where Little Sunshine lived: the evident pride he took in these
quarters increased the charm of their surprise, and when he closed the door
he made nonexistent the ruin surrounding them. Firelight polished sherry-red
wood, gilded the wings of a carved angel, and the hermit, bringing forth a
bottle of homemade whiskey, put it where the light could lace its comforting
promise. "It is been a mighty long while since you come here, Mister Randolph," he said, drawing chairs about the fire. "You was justa child, like this
sweet boy." He pinched Joel's cheek, and his fingernails were so long they
nearly broke the skin. "Usta come here totin them drawin books; I wisht you'd
come again like that." Randolph inclined his face toward the shadows of his
chair: "How silly, my dear; don't you know that if I came here as a child, then
most of me never left? I've always been, so to speak, a non-paying guest. At
least I hope so, I should so dislike thinking I'd left myself somewhere else."
Joel slumped like a dog on the floor before the hearth, and the hermit handed
him a pillow for his head; all day, after the weeks in bed, it had been as if he
were bucking a whirlpool, and now, lullabyed to the bone with drowsy
warmth, he let go, let the rivering fire sweep him over its fall; in the eyelid-blue
betweenness the wordy sounds of the whiskey-drinkers spilled distantly: more
distinct and real were whisperings behind the walls, above the ceiling: rotate
of party slippers answering a violin's demand, and the children passing to and
fro, their footsteps linking in a dance, and up and down the stairs going-coming
humming heel-clatter of chattering girls, and rolling broken beads, busted
pearls, the bored snores of fat fathers, and the lilt of fans tapped in tune and

the murmur of gloved hands as the musicians, like bridegrooms in their angel-cake costumes, rise to take a bow. (He looked into the fire, longing to see their faces as well, and the flames erupted an embryo; a veined, vacillating shape, its features formed slowly, and even when complete stayed veiled in dazzle; his eyes burned tar-hot as he brought them nearer: tell me, tell me, who are you? are you someone I know? are you dead? are you my friend? do you love me? But the painted, disembodied head remained unborn beyond its mask, and gave no clue. Are you someone I am looking for? he asked, not knowing whom he meant, but certain that for him there must be such a person, just as there was for everybody else: Randolph with his almanac, Miss Wisteria and her search by flashlight, Little Sunshine remembering other voices, other rooms, all of them remembering, or never having known. And Joel drew back. If he recognized the figure in the fire, then what ever would he find to take its place? It was easier not to know, better holding heaven in your hand like a butterfly that is not there at all.) *Goodnight ladies, sweet dreams ladies, farewell ladies, we're going to leave you now!* Farewell sighs of folding fans, the brute fall of male boots, and the furtive steps of tittering Negro girls tiptoeing through the vast honeycomb snuffing candles and drawing shades against the night: echoes of the orchestra strum a house of sleep.

Then over the floors an unearthly clangclang dragging commenced, and Joel, wide-eyed at this uproar, turned to the others; they'd heard it, too. Randolph, flushed with whiskey and talk, frowned and put down his glass. "It be the mule," said Little Sunshine with an inebriated giggle, "he out there walkin round." And Joel recalled the spittoon they'd tied to John Brown's leg: it banged on the stairs, seemed to pass overhead, become remote, grow near.

"How'd he get up yonder?" said the hermit, worried now. "Ain't no place for him to be: damn fool gonna kill hisself." He held a hunk of kindling in the fire. Using it as a torch, he stumbled out into the ballroom. Joel tagged bravely after him. But Randolph was too drunk to move.

Around the torch swooped white choirs of singing wings which made to leap and sway all within range of the furious light: humped greyhounds hurtled through the halls, their silent shadow-feet trampling flowerbeds of spiders, and in the lobby lizards loomed like dinosaurs; the coral-tongued cuckoo bird, forever stilled at three o'clock, spread wings hawk-wide, falcon-fierce.

They halted at the foot of the stairs. The mule was nowhere to be seen: the banging of the telltale spittoon had stopped. "John Brown . . . John Brown," Joel's voice enlarged the quiet: he shivered to think that in every room some sleepless something listened. Little Sunshine held his torch higher, and brought into view a balcony which overlooked the lobby: there, iron-stiff and still, stood the mule. "You hear me, suh, come down offen there!" commanded the hermit, and John Brown reared back, snorted, pawed the floor; then, as if insane with terror, he came at a gallop, and lunged, splintering the balcony's rail. Joel primed himself for a crash which never came; when he looked again, the mule, hung to a beam by the rope-reins twisted about his neck, was swinging in mid-air, and his big lamplike eyes, lit by the torch's blaze, were golden with death's impossible face, the figure in the fire.

Morning collected in the room, exposing a quilt-wrapped bundle huddled in a corner: Little Sunshine, sound asleep. "Don't wake him," whispered Randolph who, in rising, knocked over three empty whiskey bottles. But the hermit did not stir. As they crept out through the hotel Joel closed his eyes, and let Randolph lead him, for he did not want to see the mule: a sharp intake of breath was Randolph's only comment, and never once did he refer to the accident, nor ask a question: it was as if from the outset they'd planned to return to the Landing on foot. The morning was like a slate clean for any future, and it was as though an end had come, as if all that had been before had turned into a bird, and flown there to the island tree: a crazy elation caught hold of Joel, he ran, he zigzagged, he sang, he was in love, he caught a little tree-toad because he loved it and because he loved it he set it free, watched it bounce, bound like the immense leaping of his heart; he hugged himself, alive and glad, and socked the air, butted like a goat, hid behind a bush, jumped out: Boo! "Look, Randolph," he said, folding a turban of moss about his head, "look, who am I?"

But Randolph would have no part of him. His mouth was set in a queer, grim way. As if he walked the deck of a tossing ship, he lurched forward, leaning from side to side, and his eyes, raw with bloodshot, acted as a poor compass, for he seemed not to know in which direction he was going.

"I am me," Joel whooped. "I am Joel, we are the same people." And he looked about for a tree to climb: he would go right to the very top, and there, midway to heaven, he would spread his arms and claim the world. Running far ahead of Randolph, he shinnied up a birch, but when he reached the middle branches, he clasped the trunk of the tree, suddenly dizzy; from this altitude he looked back and saw Randolph, who was walking in a circle, his hands stretched before him as if he were playing blind man's bluff: his carpet slippers fell off, but he did not notice; now and then he shook himself, like a wet animal. And Joel thought of the ant. Hadn't he warned him? Hadn't he told him it was dangerous? Or was it only corn whiskey swimming in his head? Except Randolph was being so quiet. And drunk folks were never quiet. It was peculiar. It was as though Randolph were in a trance of some kind.

And Joel realized then the truth; he saw how helpless Randolph was: more paralyzed than Mr Sansom, more childlike than Miss Wisteria, what else could he do, once outside and alone, but describe a circle, the zero of his nothingness? Joel slipped down from the tree; he had not made the top, but it did not matter, for he knew who he was, he knew that he was strong.

He puzzled out the rest of the way back to the Landing the best way he could. Randolph did not say a word. Twice he fell down, and sat there on the ground, solemn and baby-eyed, until Joel helped him up. Another time he walked straight into an old stump: after that, Joel took hold of his coat-tail and steered him.

Long, like a cathedral aisle, and weighted with murky leaf-light, a path appeared, then a landmark: Toby, Killed by the Cat. Passing the moon tree, beneath which Jesus Fever was buried, no sign marking his grave, they came upon the Landing from the rear, and entered the garden.

A ridiculous scene presented itself: Zoo, crouched near the broken columns, was tugging at the slave-bell, trying, it seemed, to uproot it, and Amy, her hair disarranged and dirt streaking her face like war paint, paced back and forth, directing Zoo's efforts. "Lift it, stupid, lift it . . . why, any child! . . . now try again." Then she saw Randolph; her face contorted, a tick started in her cheek, and she shouted at him: "Don't think you're going to stop me because you're not; you don't own everything; it's just as much mine as it is yours and more so if the truth were known, and I'm going to do just what I please; you leave me alone, Randolph, or I'm going to do something to you. I'll go to the sheriff, I'll travel around the country, I'll make speeches. You don't think I will, but I will, I will . . ."

Randolph did not look at her, but went on across the garden quite as if he had no idea she was there, and she ran after him, pulling at his sleeve, pleading now: "Let me have it, Randolph, please. Oh, I was so good, I did just what you told me: I said they'd gone away, I said they'd gone off on a long squirrel hunt; I wore my nice grey dress, Randolph, and made little tea-cakes, and the house was so clean, and really she liked me, Randolph, she said she did, and she told me about this store in New Orleans where I could sell my girandoles and the bell and the mirror in the hall: you aren't listening, Randolph!" She followed him into the house.

As soon as she was gone, Zoo spit vindictively on the bell, and gave it such a kick it overturned with a mighty bong. "Ain't nobody gonna pay cash-money for that piece-a mess. She plumb outa sense, the one done told Miss Amy any such of a thing."

Joel tapped the bell like a tomtom. "Who was it that told her?"

"Was . . . I don't know who." And it was as if Zoo walked away while standing still; her voice, when she spoke again, seemed slowed down, distant: "Was some lady from New Orleans . . . had a ugly little child what wore a machine in her ear: was a little deaf child. I don't know. They went away."

"My cousin Louise, she's deaf," said Joel, thinking how he used to hide her hearing aid, of how mean he'd been to her: the times he'd made that kid cry! He wished he had a penny. But when he saw her again, why, he'd be so kind; he'd talk real loud so that she could hear every word, and he'd play those card games with her. Still, it would be fun to make her mad. Just once. But Ellen had never answered his letters. The hell with her. He didn't care any more. His own bloodkin. And she'd made so many promises. And she'd said she loved him. But she forgot. All right, so had he, sure, you forget, o.k., who cares? And she'd said she loved him. "Zoo . . ." he said, and looked up in time to see her retreating through the arbor-vitae hedge, which shivered, and was still.

A sound, as if the bell had suddenly tolled, and the shape of loneliness, greenly iridescent, whitely indefinite, seemed to rise from the garden, and Joel, as though following a kite, bent back his head: clouds were coming over the sun: he waited for them to pass, thinking that when they had, when he looked back, some magic would have taken place: perhaps he would find himself sitting on the curb of St. Deval Street, or studying next week's attractions outside the Nemo: why not? it was possible, for everywhere the sky is the same and it is down that things are different. The clouds traveled slower than a clock's hands, and, as he waited, became thunder-dark, became John Brown and horrid boys in panama hats and the Cloud Hotel and Idabel's old hound, and when they were gone, Mr Sansom was the sun. He looked down. No magic had happened; yet something had happened; or was about to. And he sat numb with apprehension. Before him stood a rose stalk throwing shadow like a sundial: an hour traced itself, another, the line of dark dissolved, all the garden began to mingle, move.

It was as if he had been counting in his head and, arriving at a number, decided through certain intuitions, thought: now. For, quite abruptly, he stood up and raised his eyes level with the Landing's windows.

His mind was absolutely clear. He was like a camera waiting for its subject to enter focus. The wall yellowed in the meticulous setting of the October sun, and the windows were rippling mirrors of cold, seasonal color. Beyond one, someone was watching him. All of him was dumb except his eyes. They knew. And it was Randolph's window. Gradually the blinding sunset drained from the glass, darkened, and it was as if snow were falling there, flakes shaping snow-eyes, hair: a face trembled like a white beautiful moth, smiled. She beckoned to him, shining and silver, and he knew he must go: unafraid, not hesitating, he paused only at the garden's edge where, as though he'd forgotten something, he stopped and looked back at the bloomless, descending blue, at the boy he had left behind.

Breakfast
at
Tiffany's

For Jack Dunphy

I am always drawn back to places where I have lived, the houses and their neighborhoods. For instance, there is a brownstone in the East Seventies where, during the early years of the war, I had my first New York apartment. It was one room crowded with attic furniture, a sofa and fat chairs upholstered in that itchy, particular red velvet that one associates with hot days on a train. The walls were stucco, and a color rather like tobacco-spit. Everywhere, in the bathroom too, there were prints of Roman ruins freckled brown with age. The single window looked out on a fire escape. Even so, my spirits heightened whenever I felt in my pocket the key to this apartment; with all its gloom, it still was a place of my own, the first, and my books were there, and jars of pencils to sharpen, everything I needed, so I felt, to become the writer I wanted to be.

It never occurred to me in those days to write about Holly Golightly, and probably it would not now except for a conversation I had with Joe Bell that set the whole memory of her in motion again.

Holly Golightly had been a tenant in the old brownstone; she'd occupied the apartment below mine. As for Joe Bell, he ran a bar around the corner on Lexington Avenue; he still does. Both Holly and I used to go there six, seven times a day, not for a drink, not always, but to make telephone calls: during the war a private telephone was hard to come by. Moreover, Joe Bell was good about taking messages, which in Holly's case was no small favor, for she had a tremendous many.

Of course this was a long time ago, and until last week I hadn't seen Joe Bell in several years. Off and on we'd kept in touch, and occasionally I'd stopped by his bar when passing through the neighborhood; but actually we'd never been strong friends except in as much as we were both friends of Holly Golightly. Joe Bell hasn't an easy nature, he admits it himself, he says it's because he's a bachelor and has a sour stomach. Anyone who knows him will tell you he's a hard man to talk to. Impossible if you don't share his fixations, of which Holly is one. Some others are: ice hockey, Weimaraner dogs, *Our Gal Sunday* (a soap serial he has listened to for fifteen years), and Gilbert and Sullivan—he claims to be related to one or the other, I can't remember which.

And so when, late last Tuesday afternoon, the telephone rang and I heard "Joe Bell here," I knew it must be about Holly. He didn't say so, just: "Can you rattle right over here? It's important," and there was a croak of excitement in his froggy voice.

I took a taxi in a downpour of October rain, and on my way I even thought she might be there, and I would see Holly again.

But there was no one on the premises except the proprietor. Joe Bell's is a quiet place compared to most Lexington Avenue bars. It boasts neither neon nor television. Two old mirrors reflect the weather from the streets; and behind the bar, in a niche surrounded by photographs of ice-hockey stars, there is always a large bowl of fresh flowers that Joe Bell himself arranges with matronly care. That is what he was doing when I came in.

"Naturally," he said, rooting a gladiola deep into the bowl, "naturally I wouldn't have got you over here if it wasn't I wanted your opinion. It's peculiar. A very peculiar thing has happened."

"You heard from Holly?"

He fingered a leaf, as though uncertain of how to answer. A small man with a fine head of coarse white hair, he has a bony, sloping face better suited to someone far taller; his complexion seems permanently sunburned: now it grew even redder. "I can't say exactly heard from her. I mean, I don't know. That's why I want your opinion. Let me build you a drink. Something new. They call it a White Angel," he said, mixing one-half vodka, one-half gin, no vermouth. While I drank the result, Joe Bell stood sucking on a Tums and turning over in his mind what he had to tell me. Then: "You recall a certain Mr. I. Y. Yunioshi? A gentleman from Japan."

"From California," I said, recalling Mr. Yunioshi perfectly. He's a photographer on one of the picture magazines, and when I knew him he lived in the studio apartment on the top floor of the brownstone.

"Don't go mixing me up. All I'm asking, you know who I mean? Okay. So last night who comes waltzing in here but this selfsame Mr. I. Y. Yunioshi. I haven't seen him, I guess it's over two years. And where do you think he's been those two years?"

"Africa."

Joe Bell stopped crunching on his Tums, his eyes narrowed. "So how did you know?"

"Read it in Winchell." Which I had, as a matter of fact.

He rang open his cash register, and produced a manila envelope. "Well, see did you read this in Winchell."

In the envelope were three photographs, more or less the same, though taken from different angles: a tall delicate Negro man wearing a calico skirt and with a shy, yet vain smile, displaying in his hands an odd wood sculpture, an elongated carving of a head, a girl's, her hair sleek and short as a young man's, her smooth wood eyes too large and tilted in the tapering face, her mouth wide, overdrawn, not unlike clown-lips. On a glance it resembled most primitive carving; and then it didn't, for here was the spit-image of Holly Golightly, at least as much of a likeness as a dark still thing could be.

"Now what do you make of that?" said Joe Bell, satisfied with my puzzlement.

"It looks like her."

"Listen, boy," and he slapped his hand on the bar, "it *is* her. Sure as I'm a man fit to wear britches. The little Jap knew it was her the minute he saw her."

"He saw her? In Africa?"

"Well. Just the statue there. But it comes to the same thing. Read the facts for yourself," he said, turning over one of the photographs. On the reverse was written: Wood Carving, S Tribe, Tococul, East Anglia, Christmas Day, 1956.

He said, "Here's what the Jap says," and the story was this: On Christmas day Mr. Yunioshi had passed with his camera through Tococul, a village in the tangles of nowhere and of no interest, merely a congregation of mud huts with monkeys in the yards and buzzards on the roofs. He'd decided to move on when he saw suddenly a Negro squatting in a doorway carving monkeys on a walking stick. Mr. Yunioshi was impressed and asked to see more of his work. Whereupon he was shown the carving of the girl's head: and felt, so he told Joe Bell, as if he were falling in a dream. But when he offered to buy it the Negro cupped his private parts in his hand (apparently a tender gesture, comparable to tapping one's heart) and said no. A pound of salt and ten dollars, a wristwatch and two pounds of salt and twenty dollars, nothing swayed him. Mr. Yunioshi was in all events determined to learn how the carving came to be made. It cost him his salt and his watch, and the incident was conveyed in African and pig-English and finger-talk. But it would seem that in the spring of that year a party of three white persons had appeared out of the brush riding horseback. A young woman and two men. The men, both red-eyed with fever, were forced for several weeks to stay shut and shivering in an isolated hut, while the young woman, having presently taken a fancy to the woodcarver, shared the woodcarver's mat.

"I don't credit that part," Joe Bell said squeamishly. "I know she had her ways, but I don't think she'd be up to anything as much as that."

"And then?"

"Then nothing," he shrugged. "By and by she went like she come, rode away on a horse."

"Alone, or with the two men?"

Joe Bell blinked. "With the two men, I guess. Now the Jap, he asked about her up and down the country. But nobody else had ever seen her." Then it was as if he could feel my own sense of letdown transmitting itself to him, and he wanted no part of it. "One thing you got to admit, it's the only *definite* news in I don't know how many"—he counted on his fingers: there weren't enough —"years. All I hope, I hope she's rich. She must be rich. You got to be rich to go mucking around in Africa."

"She's probably never set foot in Africa," I said, believing it; yet I could see her there, it was somewhere she would have gone. And the carved head: I looked at the photographs again.

"You know so much, where is she?"

"Dead. Or in a crazy house. Or married. I think she's married and quieted down and maybe right in this very city."

He considered a moment. "No," he said, and shook his head. "I'll tell you why. If she was in this city I'd have seen her. You take a man that likes to walk, a man like me, a man's been walking in the streets going on ten or twelve years, and all those years he's got his eye out for one person, and nobody's ever her, don't it stand to reason she's not there? I see pieces of her all the time, a flat little bottom, any skinny girl that walks fast and straight—" He paused, as though too aware of how intently I was looking at him. "You think I'm round the bend?"

"It's just that I didn't know you'd been in love with her. Not like that."

I was sorry I'd said it; it disconcerted him. He scooped up the photographs and put them back in their envelope. I looked at my watch. I hadn't any place to go, but I thought it was better to leave.

"Hold on," he said, gripping my wrist. "Sure I loved her. But it wasn't that I wanted to touch her." And he added, without smiling: "Not that I don't think about that side of things. Even at my age, and I'll be sixty-seven January ten. It's a peculiar fact—but, the older I grow, that side of things seems to be on my mind more and more. I don't remember thinking about it so much even when I was a youngster and it's every other minute. Maybe the older you grow and the less easy it is to put thought into action, maybe that's why it gets all locked up in your head and becomes a burden. Whenever I read in the paper about an old man disgracing himself, I know it's because of this burden. But" —he poured himself a jigger of whiskey and swallowed it neat—"I'll never disgrace myself. And I swear, it never crossed my mind about Holly. You can love somebody without it being like that. You keep them a stranger, a stranger who's a friend."

Two men came into the bar, and it seemed the moment to leave. Joe Bell followed me to the door. He caught my wrist again. "Do you believe it?"

"That you didn't want to touch her?"

"I mean about Africa."

At that moment I couldn't seem to remember the story, only the image of her riding away on a horse. "Anyway, she's gone."

"Yeah," he said, opening the door. "Just gone."

Outside, the rain had stopped, there was only a mist of it in the air, so I turned the corner and walked along the street where the brownstone stands. It is a street with trees that in the summer make cool patterns on the pavement; but now the leaves were yellowed and mostly down, and the rain had made them slippery, they skidded underfoot. The brownstone is midway in the block, next to a church where a blue tower-clock tolls the hours. It has been sleeked up since my day; a smart black door has replaced the old frosted glass, and gray elegant shutters frame the windows. No one I remember still lives there except Madame Sapphia Spanella, a husky coloratura who every afternoon went roller-skating in Central Park. I know she's still there because I went up the steps and looked at the mailboxes. It was one of these mailboxes that had first made me aware of Holly Golightly.

I'd been living in the house about a week when I noticed that the mailbox belonging to Apt. 2 had a name-slot fitted with a curious card. Printed, rather Cartier-formal, it read: *Miss Holiday Golightly;* and, underneath, in the corner, *Traveling.* It nagged me like a tune: *Miss Holiday Golightly, Traveling.*

One night, it was long past twelve, I woke up at the sound of Mr. Yunioshi calling down the stairs. Since he lived on the top floor, his voice fell through the whole house, exasperated and stern. "Miss Golightly! I must protest!"

The voice that came back, welling up from the bottom of the stairs, was silly-young and self-amused. "Oh, darling, I *am* sorry. I lost the goddamn key."

"You cannot go on ringing my bell. You must please, please have yourself a key made."

"But I lose them all."

"I work, I have to sleep," Mr. Yunioshi shouted. "But always you are ringing my bell . . ."

"Oh, *don't* be angry, you *dear* little man: I *won't* do it again. And if you promise not to be angry"—her voice was coming nearer, she was climbing the stairs—"I might let you take those pictures we mentioned."

By now I'd left my bed and opened the door an inch. I could hear Mr. Yunioshi's silence: hear, because it was accompanied by an audible change of breath.

"When?" he said.

The girl laughed. "Sometime," she answered, slurring the word.

"Any time," he said, and closed his door.

I went out into the hall and leaned over the banister, just enough to see without being seen. She was still on the stairs, now she reached the landing, and the ragbag colors of her boy's hair, tawny streaks, strands of albino-blond and yellow, caught the hall light. It was a warm evening, nearly summer, and she wore a slim cool black dress, black sandals, a pearl choker. For all her chic thinness, she had an almost breakfast-cereal air of health, a soap and lemon cleanness, a rough pink darkening in the cheeks. Her mouth was large, her nose upturned. A pair of dark glasses blotted out her eyes. It was a face beyond childhood, yet this side of belonging to a woman. I thought her anywhere between sixteen and thirty; as it turned out, she was shy two months of her nineteenth birthday.

She was not alone. There was a man following behind her. The way his plump hand clutched at her hip seemed somehow improper; not morally, aesthetically. He was short and vast, sun-lamped and pomaded, a man in a buttressed pin-stripe suit with a red carnation withering in the lapel. When they reached her door she rummaged her purse in search of a key, and took no notice of the fact that his thick lips were nuzzling the nape of her neck. At last, though, finding the key and opening her door, she turned to him cordially: "Bless you, darling—you were sweet to see me home."

"Hey, baby!" he said, for the door was closing in his face.

"Yes, Harry?"

"Harry was the other guy. I'm Sid. Sid Arbuck. You like me."

"I worship you, Mr. Arbuck. But good night, Mr. Arbuck."

Mr. Arbuck stared with disbelief as the door shut firmly. "Hey, baby, let me in, baby. You like me, baby. I'm a liked guy. Didn't I pick up the check, five people, *your* friends, I never seen them before? Don't that give me the right you should like me? You like me, baby."

He tapped on the door gently, then louder; finally he took several steps back, his body hunched and lowering, as though he meant to charge it, crash it down. Instead, he plunged down the stairs, slamming a fist against the wall. Just as he reached the bottom, the door of the girl's apartment opened and she poked out her head.

"Oh, Mr. *Ar*buck . . ."

He turned back, a smile of relief oiling his face: she'd only been teasing.

"The next time a girl wants a little powder-room change," she called, not teasing at all, "take my advice, darling: *don't* give her twenty-cents!"

She kept her promise to Mr. Yunioshi; or I assume she did not ring his bell again, for in the next days she started ringing mine, sometimes at two in the morning, three and four: she had no qualms at what hour she got me out of bed to push the buzzer that released the downstairs door. As I had few friends, and none who would come around so late, I always knew that it was her. But on the first occasions of its happening, I went to my door, half-expecting bad news, a telegram; and Miss Golightly would call up: "Sorry, darling—I forgot my key."

Of course we'd never met. Though actually, on the stairs, in the street, we often came face-to-face; but she seemed not quite to see me. She was never without dark glasses, she was always well groomed, there was a consequential good taste in the plainness of her clothes, the blues and grays and lack of luster that made her, herself, shine so. One might have thought her a photographer's model, perhaps a young actress, except that it was obvious, judging from her hours, she hadn't time to be either.

Now and then I ran across her outside our neighborhood. Once a visiting relative took me to "21," and there, at a superior table, surrounded by four men, none of them Mr. Arbuck, yet all of them interchangeable with him, was Miss Golightly, idly, publicly combing her hair; and her expression, an unrealized yawn, put, by example, a dampener on the excitement I felt over dining at so swanky a place. Another night, deep in the summer, the heat of my room sent me out into the streets. I walked down Third Avenue to Fifty-first Street, where there was an antique store with an object in its window I admired: a palace of a bird cage, a mosque of minarets and bamboo rooms yearning to be filled with talkative parrots. But the price was three hundred and fifty dollars. On the way home I noticed a cab-driver crowd gathered in front of P. J. Clark's saloon, apparently attracted there by a happy group of whiskey-eyed Australian army officers baritoning, "Waltzing Matilda." As they sang they took turns spin-dancing a girl over the cobbles under the El; and the girl, Miss Golightly, to be sure, floated round in their arms light as a scarf.

But if Miss Golightly remained unconscious of my existence, except as a doorbell convenience, I became, through the summer, rather an authority on hers. I discovered, from observing the trash-basket outside her door, that her regular reading consisted of tabloids and travel folders and astrological charts; that she smoked an esoteric cigarette called Picayunes; survived on cottage cheese and melba toast; that her vari-colored hair was somewhat self-induced. The same source made it evident that she received V-letters by the bale. They were always torn into strips like bookmarks. I used occasionally to pluck myself a bookmark in passing. *Remember* and *miss you* and *rain* and *please write* and *damn* and *goddamn* were the words that recurred most often on these slips; those, and *lonesome* and *love*.

Also, she had a cat and she played the guitar. On days when the sun was strong, she would wash her hair, and together with the cat, a red tiger-striped tom, sit out on the fire escape thumbing a guitar while her hair dried. Whenever I heard the music, I would go stand quietly by my window. She played very well, and sometimes sang too. Sang in the hoarse, breaking tones of a boy's adolescent voice. She knew all the show hits, Cole Porter and Kurt Weill; especially she liked the songs from *Oklahoma!,* which were new that summer and everywhere. But there were moments when she played songs that made you wonder where she learned them, where indeed she came from. Harsh-tender wandering tunes with words that smacked of pineywoods or prairie. One went: *Don't wanna sleep, Don't wanna die, Just wanna go a-travelin' through the pastures of the sky;* and this one seemed to gratify her the most, for often she continued it long after her hair had dried, after the sun had gone and there were lighted windows in the dusk.

But our acquaintance did not make headway until September, an evening with the first ripple-chills of autumn running through it. I'd been to a movie, come home and gone to bed with a bourbon nightcap and the newest Simenon: so much my idea of comfort that I couldn't understand a sense of unease that multiplied until I could hear my heart beating. It was a feeling I'd read about, written about, but never before experienced. The feeling of being watched. Of someone in the room. Then: an abrupt rapping at the window, a glimpse of ghostly gray: I spilled the bourbon. It was some little while before I could bring myself to open the window, and ask Miss Golightly what she wanted.

"I've got the most terrifying man downstairs," she said, stepping off the fire escape into the room. "I mean he's sweet when he isn't drunk, but let him start lapping up the vino, and oh God quel beast! If there's one thing I loathe, it's men who bite." She loosened a gray flannel robe off her shoulder to show me evidence of what happens if a man bites. The robe was all she was wearing. "I'm sorry if I frightened you. But when the beast got so tiresome I just went out the window. I think he thinks I'm in the bathroom, not that I give a damn what he thinks, the hell with him, he'll get tired, he'll go to sleep, my God he should, eight martinis before dinner and enough wine to wash an elephant. Listen, you can throw me out if you want to. I've got a gall barging in on you like this. But that fire escape was damned icy. And you looked so cozy. Like my brother Fred. We used to sleep four in a bed, and he was the only one that ever let me hug him on a cold night. By the way, do you mind if I call you Fred?" She'd come completely into the room now, and she paused there, staring at me. I'd never seen her before not wearing dark glasses, and it was obvious now that they were prescription lenses, for without them her eyes had an assessing squint, like a jeweler's. They were large eyes, a little blue, a little green, dotted with bits of brown: vari-colored, like her hair; and, like her hair, they gave out a lively warm light. "I suppose you think I'm very brazen. Or très fou. Or something."

"Not at all."

She seemed disappointed. "Yes, you do. Everybody does. I don't mind. It's useful."

She sat down on one of the rickety red-velvet chairs, curved her legs underneath her, and glanced round the room, her eyes puckering more pronouncedly. "How can you bear it? It's a chamber of horrors."

"Oh, you get used to anything," I said, annoyed with myself, for actually I was proud of the place.

"I don't. I'll never get used to anything. Anybody that does, they might as well be dead." Her dispraising eyes surveyed the room again. "What do you do here all day?"

I motioned toward a table tall with books and paper. "Write things."

"I thought writers were quite old. Of course Saroyan isn't old. I met him at a party, and really he isn't old at all. In fact," she mused, "if he'd give himself a closer shave . . . by the way, is Hemingway old?"

"In his forties, I should think."

"That's not bad. I can't get excited by a man until he's forty-two. I know this idiot girl who keeps telling me I ought to go to a head-shrinker; she says I have a father complex. Which is so much *merde.* I simply *trained* myself to like older men, and it was the smartest thing I ever did. How old is W. Somerset Maugham?"

"I'm not sure. Sixty-something."

"That's not bad. I've never been to bed with a writer. No, wait: do you know Benny Shacklett?" She frowned when I shook my head. "That's funny. He's written an awful lot of radio stuff. But quel rat. Tell me, are you a real writer?"

"It depends on what you mean by real."

"Well, darling, does anyone *buy* what you write?"

"Not yet."

"I'm going to help you," she said. "I can, too. Think of all the people I know who know people. I'm going to help you because you look like my brother Fred. Only smaller. I haven't seen him since I was fourteen, that's when I left home, and he was already six-feet-two. My other brothers were more your size, runts. It was the peanut butter that made Fred so tall. Everybody thought it was dotty, the way he gorged himself on peanut butter; he didn't care about anything in this world except horses and peanut butter. But he wasn't dotty, just sweet and vague and terribly slow; he'd been in the eighth grade three years when I ran away. Poor Fred. I wonder if the Army's generous with their peanut butter. Which reminds me, I'm starving."

I pointed to a bowl of apples, at the same time asked her how and why she'd left home so young. She looked at me blankly, and rubbed her nose, as though it tickled: a gesture, seeing often repeated, I came to recognize as a signal that one was trespassing. Like many people with a bold fondness for volunteering intimate information, anything that suggested a direct question, a pinning-down, put her on guard. She took a bite of apple, and said: "Tell me something you've written. The story part."

"That's one of the troubles. They're not the kind of stories you *can* tell."

"Too dirty?"

"Maybe I'll let you read one sometime."

"Whiskey and apples go together. Fix me a drink, darling. Then you can read me a story yourself."

Very few authors, especially the unpublished, can resist an invitation to read aloud. I made us both a drink and, settling in a chair opposite, began to read to her, my voice a little shaky with a combination of stage fright and enthusiasm: it was a new story, I'd finished it the day before, and that inevitable sense of shortcoming had not had time to develop. It was about two women who share a house, schoolteachers, one of whom, when the other becomes engaged, spreads with anonymous notes a scandal that prevents the marriage. As I read, each glimpse I stole of Holly made my heart contract. She fidgeted. She picked apart the butts in an ashtray, she mooned over her fingernails, as though longing for a file; worse, when I did seem to have her interest, there was actually a telltale frost over her eyes, as if she were wondering whether to buy a pair of shoes she'd seen in some window.

"Is that the *end?*" she asked, waking up. She floundered for something more to say. "Of course I like dykes themselves. They don't scare me a bit. But stories about dykes bore the bejesus out of me. I just can't put myself in their shoes. Well really, darling," she said, because I was clearly puzzled, "if it's not about a couple of old bull-dykes, what the hell *is* it about?"

But I was in no mood to compound the mistake of having read the story with the further embarrassment of explaining it. The same vanity that had led to such exposure, now forced me to mark her down as an insensitive, mindless show-off.

"Incidentally," she said, "do you happen to *know* any nice lesbians? I'm looking for a roommate. Well, don't laugh. I'm so disorganized, I simply can't afford a maid; and really, dykes are wonderful homemakers, they love to do all the work, you never have to bother about brooms and defrosting and sending out the laundry. I had a roommate in Hollywood, she played in Westerns, they called her the Lone Ranger; but I'll say this for her, she was better than a man around the house. Of course people couldn't help but think I must be a bit of a dyke myself. And of course I am. Everyone is: a bit. So what? That never discouraged a man yet, in fact it seems to goad them on. Look at the Lone Ranger, married twice. Usually dykes only get married once, just for the name. It seems to carry such cachet later on to be called Mrs. Something Another. That's not true!" She was staring at an alarm clock on the table. "It can't be four-thirty!"

The window was turning blue. A sunrise breeze bandied the curtains.

"What is today?"

"Thursday."

"*Thursday.*" She stood up. "My God," she said, and sat down again with a moan. "It's too gruesome."

I was tired enough not to be curious. I lay down on the bed and closed my eyes. Still it was irresistible: "What's gruesome about Thursday?"

"Nothing. Except that I can never remember when it's coming. You see, on Thursdays I have to catch the eight forty-five. They're so particular about visiting hours, so if you're there by ten that gives you an hour before the poor men eat lunch. Think of it, lunch at eleven. You *can* go at two, and I'd so much rather, but he likes me to come in the morning, he says it sets him up for the rest of the day. I've *got* to stay awake," she said, pinching her cheeks until the roses came, "there isn't time to sleep, I'd look consumptive, I'd sag like a tenement, and that wouldn't be fair: a girl can't go to Sing Sing with a green face."

"I suppose not." The anger I felt at her over my story was ebbing; she absorbed me again.

"All the visitors *do* make an effort to look their best, and it's very tender, it's sweet as hell, the way the women wear their prettiest everything, I mean the old ones and the really poor ones too, they make the dearest effort to look nice and smell nice too, and I love them for it. I love the kids too, especially the colored ones. I mean the kids the wives bring. It should be sad, seeing the kids there, but it isn't, they have ribbons in their hair and lots of shine on their shoes, you'd think there was going to be ice cream; and sometimes that's what it's like in the visitors' room, a party. Anyway it's not like the movies: you know, grim whisperings through a grille. There isn't any grille, just a counter between you and them, and the kids can stand on it to be hugged; all you have to do to kiss somebody is lean across. What I like most, they're so happy to see each other, they've saved up so much to talk about, it isn't possible to be dull, they keep laughing and holding hands. It's different afterwards," she said. "I see them on the train. They sit so quiet watching the river go by." She stretched a strand of hair to the corner of her mouth and nibbled it thoughtfully. "I'm keeping you awake. Go to sleep."

"Please. I'm interested."

"I know you are. That's why I want you to go to sleep. Because if I keep on, I'll tell you about Sally. I'm not sure that would be quite cricket." She chewed her hair silently. "They never *told* me not to tell anyone. In so many words. And it *is* funny. Maybe you could put it in a story with different names and whatnot. Listen, Fred," she said, reaching for another apple, "you've got to cross your heart and kiss your elbow—"

Perhaps contortionists can kiss their elbow; she had to accept an approximation.

"Well," she said, with a mouthful of apple, "you may have read about him in the papers. His name is Sally Tomato, and I speak Yiddish better than he speaks English; but he's a darling old man, terribly pious. He'd look like a monk if it weren't for the gold teeth; he says he prays for me every night. Of course he was never my lover; as far as that goes, I never knew him until he was already in jail. But I adore him now, after all I've been going to see him every Thursday for seven months, and I think I'd go even if he didn't pay me. This one's mushy," she said, and aimed the rest of the apple out the window. "By the way, I *did* know Sally by sight. He used to come to Joe Bell's bar, the one around the corner: never talked to anybody, just stand there, like the kind of man who lives in hotel rooms. But it's funny to remember back and realize how closely he must have been watching me, because right after they sent him up (Joe Bell showed me his picture in the paper. Blackhand. Mafia. All that mumbo jumbo: but they gave him five years) along came this telegram from a lawyer. It said to contact him immediately for information to my advantage."

"You thought somebody had left you a million?"

"Not at all. I figured Bergdorf was trying to collect. But I took the gamble and went to see this lawyer (if he *is* a lawyer, which I doubt, since he doesn't seem to have an office, just an answering service, and he always wants to meet you in Hamburg Heaven: that's because he's fat, he can eat ten hamburgers and two bowls of relish and a whole lemon meringue pie). He asked me how I'd like to cheer up a lonely old man, at the same time pick up a hundred a week. I told him look, darling, you've got the wrong Miss Golightly, I'm not a nurse that does tricks on the side. I wasn't impressed by the honorarium either; you can do as well as that on trips to the powder room: any gent with the slightest chic will give you fifty for the girl's john, and I always ask for cab fare too, that's another fifty. But then he told me his client was Sally Tomato. He said dear old Sally had long admired me *à la distance,* so wouldn't it be a good deed if I went to visit him once a week. Well, I couldn't say no: it was too romantic."

"I don't know. It doesn't sound right."

She smiled. "You think I'm lying?"

"For one thing, they can't simply let *any*one visit a prisoner."

"Oh, they don't. In fact they make quite a boring fuss. I'm supposed to be his niece."

"And it's as simple as that? For an hour's conversation he gives you a hundred dollars?"

"He doesn't, the lawyer does. Mr. O'Shaughnessy mails it to me in cash as soon as I leave the weather report."

"I think you could get into a lot of trouble," I said, and switched off a lamp; there was no need of it now, morning was in the room and pigeons were gargling on the fire escape.

"How?" she said seriously.

"There must be something in the law books about false identity. After all, you're *not* his niece. And what about this weather report?"

She patted a yawn. "But it's nothing. Just messages I leave with the answering service so Mr. O'Shaughnessy will know for sure that I've been up there. Sally tells me what to say, things like, oh, 'there's a hurricane in Cuba' and 'it's snowing in Palermo.' Don't worry, darling," she said, moving to the bed, "I've taken care of myself a long time." The morning light seemed refracted through her: as she pulled the bed covers up to my chin she gleamed like a transparent child; then she lay down beside me. "Do you mind? I only want to rest a moment. So let's don't say another word. Go to sleep."

I pretended to, I made my breathing heavy and regular. Bells in the tower of the next-door church rang the half-hour, the hour. It was six when she put her hand on my arm, a fragile touch careful not to waken. "Poor Fred," she whispered, and it seemed she was speaking to me, but she was not. "Where are you, Fred? Because it's cold. There's snow in the wind." Her cheek came to rest against my shoulder, a warm damp weight.

"Why are you crying?"

She sprang back, sat up. "Oh, for God's sake," she said, starting for the window and the fire escape, "I *hate* snoops."

. . .

The next day, Friday, I came home to find outside my door a grand-luxe Charles & Co. basket with her card: *Miss Holiday Golightly, Traveling:* and scribbled on the back in a freakishly awkward, kindergarten hand: *Bless you darling Fred. Please forgive the other night. You were an angel about the whole thing. Mille tendresse—Holly. P.S. I won't bother you again.* I replied, *Please do,* and left this note at her door with what I could afford, a bunch of street-vendor violets. But apparently she'd meant what she said; I neither saw nor heard from her, and I gathered she'd gone so far as to obtain a downstairs key. At any rate she no longer rang my bell. I missed that; and as the days merged I began to feel toward her certain far-fetched resentments, as if I were being neglected by my closest friend. A disquieting loneliness came into my life, but it induced no hunger for friends of longer acquaintance: they seemed now like a salt-free, sugarless diet. By Wednesday thoughts of Holly, of Sing Sing and Sally Tomato, of worlds where men forked over fifty dollars for the powder room, were so constant that I couldn't work. That night I left a message in her mailbox: *Tomorrow is Thursday.* The next morning rewarded me with a second note in the play-pen script: *Bless you for reminding me. Can you stop for a drink tonight 6-ish?*

I waited until ten past six, then made myself delay five minutes more.

A creature answered the door. He smelled of cigars and Knize cologne. His shoes sported elevated heels; without these added inches, one might have taken him for a Little Person. His bald freckled head was dwarf-big: attached to it were a pair of pointed, truly elfin ears. He had Pekingese eyes, unpitying and slightly bulged. Tufts of hair sprouted from his ears, from his nose; his jowls were gray with afternoon beard, and his handshake almost furry.

"Kid's in the shower," he said, motioning a cigar toward a sound of water hissing in another room. The room in which we stood (we were standing because there was nothing to sit on) seemed as though it were being just moved into; you expected to smell wet paint. Suitcases and unpacked crates were the only furniture. The crates served as tables. One supported the mixings of a martini; another a lamp, a Libertyphone, Holly's red cat and a bowl of yellow roses. Bookcases, covering one wall, boasted a half-shelf of literature. I warmed to the room at once, I liked its fly-by-night look.

The man cleared his throat. "You expected?"

He found my nod uncertain. His cold eyes operated on me, made neat, exploratory incisions. "A lot of characters come here, they're not expected. You know the kid long?"

"Not very."

"So you don't know the kid long?"

"I live upstairs."

The answer seemed to explain enough to relax him. "You got the same layout?"

"Much smaller."

He tapped ash on the floor. "This is a dump. This is unbelievable. But the kid don't know how to live even when she's got the dough." His speech had a jerky metallic rhythm, like a teletype. "So," he said, "what do you think: is she or ain't she?"

"Ain't she what?"

"A phony."

"I wouldn't have thought so."

"You're wrong. She is a phony. But on the other hand you're right. She isn't a phony because she's a *real* phony. She believes all this crap she believes. You can't talk her out of it. I've tried with tears running down my cheeks. Benny Polan, respected everywhere, Benny Polan tried. Benny had it on his mind to marry her, she don't go for it, Benny spent maybe thousands sending her to head-shrinkers. Even the famous one, the one can only speak German, boy, did he throw in the towel. You can't talk her out of these"—he made a fist, as though to crush an intangible—"ideas. Try it sometime. Get her to tell you some of the stuff she believes. Mind you," he said, "I like the kid. Everybody does, but there's lots that don't. I do. I sincerely like the kid. I'm sensitive, that's why. You've got to be sensitive to appreciate her: a streak of the poet. But I'll tell you the truth. You can beat your brains out for her, and she'll hand you horseshit on a platter. To give an example—who is she like you see her today? She's strictly a girl you'll read where she ends up at the bottom of a bottle of Seconals. I've seen it happen more times than you've got toes: and those kids, they weren't even nuts. She's nuts."

"But young. And with a great deal of youth ahead of her."

"If you mean future, you're wrong again. Now a couple of years back, out on the Coast, there was a time it could've been different. She had something working for her, she had them interested, she could've really rolled. But when you walk out on a thing like that, you don't walk back. Ask Luise Rainer. And Rainer was a star. Sure, Holly was no star; she never got out of the still department. But that was before *The Story of Dr. Wassell*. Then she could've really rolled. I know, see, cause I'm the guy was giving her the push." He pointed his cigar at himself. "O.J. Berman."

He expected recognition, and I didn't mind obliging him, it was all right by me, except I'd never heard of O.J. Berman. It developed that he was a Hollywood actor's agent.

"I'm the first one saw her. Out at Santa Anita. She's hanging around the track every day. I'm interested: professionally. I find out she's some jock's regular, she's living with the shrimp. I get the jock told Drop It if he don't want conversation with the vice boys: see, the kid's fifteen. But stylish: she's okay, she comes across. Even when she's wearing glasses *this* thick; even when she opens her mouth and you don't know if she's a hillbilly or an Okie or what. I still don't. My guess, nobody'll ever know where she came from. She's such a goddamn liar, maybe she don't know herself any more. But it took us a year to smooth out that accent. How we did it finally, we gave her

French lessons: after she could imitate French, it wasn't so long she could imitate English. We modeled her along the Margaret Sullavan type, but she could pitch some curves of her own, people were interested, big ones, and to top it all, Benny Polan, a respected guy, Benny wants to marry her. An agent could ask for more? Then wham! *The Story of Dr. Wassell.* You see that picture? Cecil B. DeMille. Gary Cooper. Jesus. I kill myself, it's all set: they're going to test her for the part of Dr. Wassell's nurse. One of his nurses, anyway. Then wham! The phone rings." He picked a telephone out of the air and held it to his ear. "She says, this is Holly, I say honey, you sound far away, she says I'm in New York, I say what the hell are you doing in New York when it's Sunday and you got the test tomorrow? She says I'm in New York cause I've never been to New York. I say get your ass on a plane and get back here, she says I don't want it. I say what's your angle, doll? She says you got to want it to be good and I don't want it, I say well, what the hell do you want, and she says when I find out you'll be the first to know. See what I mean: horseshit on a platter."

The red cat jumped off its crate and rubbed against his leg. He lifted the cat on the toe of his shoe and gave him a toss, which was hateful of him except he seemed not aware of the cat but merely his own irritableness.

"*This* is what she wants?" he said, flinging out his arms. "A lot of characters they aren't expected? Living off tips. Running around with bums. So maybe she could marry Rusty Trawler? You should pin a medal on her for that?"

He waited, glaring.

"Sorry, I don't know him."

"You don't know Rusty Trawler, you can't know much about the kid. Bad deal," he said, his tongue clucking in his huge head. "I was hoping you maybe had influence. Could level with the kid before it's too late."

"But according to you, it already is."

He blew a smoke ring, let it fade before he smiled; the smile altered his face, made something gentle happen. "I could get it rolling again. Like I told you," he said, and now it sounded true, "I sincerely like the kid."

"What scandals are you spreading, O.J.?" Holly splashed into the room, a towel more or less wrapped round her and her wet feet dripping footmarks on the floor.

"Just the usual. That you're nuts."

"Fred knows that already."

"But you don't."

"Light me a cigarette, darling," she said, snatching off a bathing cap and shaking her hair. "I don't mean you, O.J. You're such a slob. You always nigger-lip."

She scooped up the cat and swung him onto her shoulder. He perched there with the balance of a bird, his paws tangled in her hair as if it were knitting yarn; and yet, despite these amiable antics, it was a grim cat with a pirate's cutthroat face; one eye was gluey-blind, the other sparkled with dark deeds.

"O.J. is a slob," she told me, taking the cigarette I'd lighted. "But he does know a terrific lot of phone numbers. What's David O. Selznick's number, O.J.?"

"Lay off."

"It's not a joke, darling. I want you to call him up and tell him what a genius Fred is. He's written barrels of the most marvelous stories. Well, don't blush, Fred: you didn't say you were a genius, I did. Come on, O.J. What are you going to do to make Fred rich?"

"Suppose you let me settle that with Fred."

"Remember," she said, leaving us, "I'm his agent. Another thing: if I holler, come zipper me up. And if anybody knocks, let them in."

A multitude did. Within the next quarter-hour a stag party had taken over the apartment, several of them in uniform. I counted two Naval officers and an Air Force colonel; but they were outnumbered by graying arrivals beyond draft status. Except for a lack of youth, the guests had no common theme, they seemed strangers among strangers; indeed, each face, on entering, had struggled to conceal dismay at seeing others there. It was as if the hostess had distributed her invitations while zigzagging through various bars; which was probably the case. After the initial frowns, however, they mixed without grumbling, especially O.J. Berman, who avidly exploited the new company to avoid discussing my Hollywood future. I was left abandoned by the bookshelves; of the books there, more than half were about horses, the rest baseball. Pretending an interest in *Horseflesh and How to Tell It* gave me sufficiently private opportunity for sizing Holly's friends.

Presently one of these became prominent. He was a middle-aged child that had never shed its baby fat, though some gifted tailor had almost succeeded in camouflaging his plump and spankable bottom. There wasn't a suspicion of bone in his body; his face, a zero filled in with pretty miniature features, had an unused, a virginal quality: it was as if he'd been born, then expanded, his skin remaining unlined as a blown-up balloon, and his mouth, though ready for squalls and tantrums, a spoiled sweet puckering. But it was not appearance that singled him out; preserved infants aren't all that rare. It was, rather, his conduct; for he was behaving as though the party were his: like an energetic octopus, he was shaking martinis, making introductions, manipulating the phonograph. In fairness, most of his activities were dictated by the hostess herself: *Rusty, would you mind; Rusty, would you please.* If he was in love with her, then clearly he had his jealousy in check. A jealous man might have lost control, watching her as she skimmed around the room, carrying her cat in one hand but leaving the other free to straighten a tie or remove lapel lint; the Air Force colonel wore a medal that came in for quite a polish.

The man's name was Rutherfurd ("Rusty") Trawler. In 1908 he'd lost both his parents, his father the victim of an anarchist and his mother of shock, which double misfortune had made Rusty an orphan, a millionaire, and a celebrity, all at the age of five. He'd been a stand-by of the Sunday supplements ever since, a consequence that had gathered hurricane momentum when, still a schoolboy, he had caused his godfather-custodian to be arrested on charges of sodomy. After that, marriage and divorce sustained his place in the tabloid-sun. His first wife had taken herself, and her alimony, to a rival of Father Divine's. The second wife seems unaccounted for, but the third had sued him in New York State with a full satchel of the kind of testimony that entails. He himself divorced the last Mrs. Trawler, his principal complaint stating that she'd started a mutiny aboard his yacht, said mutiny resulting in his being deposited on the Dry Tortugas. Though he'd been a bachelor since, apparently before the war he'd proposed to Unity Mitford, at least he was supposed to have sent her a cable offering to marry her if Hitler didn't. This was said to be the reason Winchell always referred to him as a Nazi; that, and the fact that he attended rallies in Yorkville.

I was not told these things. I read them in *The Baseball Guide,* another selection off Holly's shelf which she seemed to use for a scrapbook. Tucked between the pages were Sunday features, together with scissored snippings from gossip columns. *Rusty Trawler and Holly Golightly two-on-the-aisle at "One Touch of Venus" preem.* Holly came up from behind, and caught me reading: *Miss Holiday Golightly, of the Boston Golightlys, making every day a holiday for the 24-karat Rusty Trawler.*

"Admiring my publicity, or are you just a baseball fan?" she said, adjusting her dark glasses as she glanced over my shoulder.

I said, "What was this week's weather report?"

She winked at me, but it was humorless: a wink of warning, "I'm all for horses, but I loathe baseball," she said, and the sub-message in her voice was saying she wished me to forget she'd ever mentioned Sally Tomato. "I hate the sound of it on a radio, but I have to listen, it's part of my research. There're so few things men can talk about. If a man doesn't like baseball, then he must like horses, and if he doesn't like either of them, well, I'm in trouble anyway: he don't like girls. And how are you making out with O.J.?"

"We've separated by mutual agreement."

"He's an opportunity, believe me."

"I do believe you. But what have I to offer that would strike him as an opportunity?"

She persisted. "Go over there and make him think he isn't funny-looking. He really can help you, Fred."

"I understand you weren't too appreciative." She seemed puzzled until I said: "*The Story of Doctor Wassell.*"

"He's still harping?" she said, and cast across the room an affectionate look at Berman. "But he's got a point, I *should* feel guilty. Not because they would have given me the part or because I would have been good: they wouldn't and I wouldn't. If I do feel guilty, I guess it's because I let him go on dreaming when I wasn't dreaming a bit. I was just vamping for time to make a few self-improvements: I knew damn well I'd never be a movie star. It's too hard; and if you're intelligent, it's too embarrassing. My complexes aren't inferior enough: being a movie star and having a big fat ego are supposed to go hand-in-hand; actually, it's essential not to have any ego at all. I don't mean I'd mind being rich and famous. That's very much on my schedule, and someday I'll try to get around to it; but if it happens, I'd like to have my ego tagging along. I want to still be me when I wake up one fine morning and have breakfast at Tiffany's. You need a glass," she said, noticing my empty hands. "Rusty! Will you bring my friend a drink?"

She was still hugging the cat. "Poor slob," she said, tickling his head, "poor slob without a name. It's a little inconvenient, his not having a name. But I haven't any right to give him one: he'll have to wait until he *belongs* to somebody. We just sort of took up by the river one day, we don't belong to each other: he's an independent, and so am I. I don't want to own anything until I know I've found the place where me and things belong together. I'm not quite sure where that is just yet. But I know what it's like." She smiled, and let the cat drop to the floor. "It's like Tiffany's," she said. "Not that I give a hoot about jewelry. Diamonds, yes. But it's tacky to wear diamonds before you're forty; and even that's risky. They only look right on the really old girls. Maria Ouspenskaya. Wrinkles and bones, white hair and diamonds: I can't wait. But that's not why I'm mad about Tiffany's. Listen. You know those days when you've got the mean reds?"

"Same as the blues?"

"No," she said slowly. "No, the blues are because you're getting fat or maybe it's been raining too long. You're sad, that's all. But the mean reds are horrible. You're afraid and you sweat like hell, but you don't know what you're afraid of. Except something bad is going to happen, only you don't know what it is. You've had that feeling?"

"Quite often. Some people call it *angst.*"

"All right. *Angst.* But what do you do about it?"

"Well, a drink helps."

"I've tried that. I've tried aspirin, too. Rusty thinks I should smoke marijuana, and I did for a while, but it only makes me giggle. What I've found does the most good is just to get into a taxi and go to Tiffany's. It calms me down right away, the quietness and the proud look of it; nothing very bad could happen to you there, not with those kind men in their nice suits, and that lovely smell of silver and alligator wallets. If I could find a real-life place that made me feel like Tiffany's, then I'd buy some furniture and give the cat a name. I've thought maybe after the war, Fred and I—" She pushed up her dark glasses, and her eyes, the differing colors of them, the grays and wisps of blue and green, had taken on a far-seeing sharpness. "I went to Mexico once. It's wonderful country for raising horses. I saw one place near the sea. Fred's good with horses."

Rusty Trawler came carrying a martini; he handed it over without looking at me. "I'm hungry," he announced, and his voice, retarded as the rest of him, produced an unnerving brat-whine that seemed to blame Holly. "It's seven-thirty, and I'm hungry. You know what the doctor said."

"Yes, Rusty. I know what the doctor said."

"Well, then break it up. Let's go."

"I want you to behave, Rusty." She spoke softly, but there was a governess threat of punishment in her tone that caused an odd flush of pleasure, of gratitude, to pink his face.

"You don't love me," he complained, as though they were alone.

"Nobody loves naughtiness."

Obviously she'd said what he wanted to hear; it appeared to both excite and relax him. Still he continued, as though it were a ritual: "Do you love me?"

She patted him. "Tend to your chores, Rusty. And when I'm ready, we'll go eat wherever you want."

"Chinatown?"

"But that doesn't mean sweet and sour spareribs. You know what the doctor said."

As he returned to his duties with a satisfied waddle, I couldn't resist reminding her that she hadn't answered his question. "*Do* you love him?"

"I told you: you can make yourself love anybody. Besides, he had a stinking childhood."

"If it was so stinking, why does he cling to it?"

"Use your head. Can't you see it's just that Rusty feels safer in diapers than he would in a skirt? Which is really the choice, only he's awfully touchy about it. He tried to stab me with a butter knife because I told him to grow up and face the issue, settle down and play house with a nice fatherly truck driver. Meantime, I've got him on my hands; which is okay, he's harmless, he thinks girls are dolls literally."

"Thank God."

"Well, if it were true of most men, I'd hardly be thanking God."

"I meant thank God you're not going to marry Mr. Trawler."

She lifted an eyebrow. "By the way, I'm not pretending I don't know he's rich. Even land in Mexico costs something. Now," she said, motioning me forward, "let's get hold of O.J."

I held back while my mind worked to win a postponement. Then I remembered: "Why *Traveling?*"

"On my card?" she said, disconcerted. "You think it's funny?"

"Not funny. Just provocative."

She shrugged. "After all, how do I know where I'll be living tomorrow? So I told them to put *Traveling.* Anyway, it was a waste of money, ordering those cards. Except I felt I owed it to them to buy some little *some*thing. They're from Tiffany's." She reached for my martini, I hadn't touched it; she drained it in two swallows, and took my hand. "Quit stalling. You're going to make friends with O.J."

An occurrence at the door intervened. It was a young woman, and she entered like a wind-rush, a squall of scarves and jangling gold. "H-H-Holly," she said, wagging a finger as she advanced, "you miserable h-h-hoarder. Hogging all these simply r-r-riveting m-m-men!"

She was well over six feet, taller than most men there. They straightened their spines, sucked in their stomachs; there was a general contest to match her swaying height.

Holly said, "What are you doing here?" and her lips were taut as drawn string.

"Why, n-n-nothing, sugar. I've been upstairs working with Yunioshi. Christmas stuff for the *Ba-ba-zaar.* But you sound vexed, sugar?" She scattered a roundabout smile. "You b-b-boys not vexed at me for butting in on your p-p-party?"

Rusty Trawler tittered. He squeezed her arm, as though to admire her muscle, and asked her if she could use a drink.

"I surely could," she said. "Make mine bourbon."

Holly told her, "There *isn't* any." Whereupon the Air Force colonel suggested he run out for a bottle.

"Oh, I declare, don't let's have a f-f-fuss. I'm happy with ammonia. Holly, honey," she said, slightly shoving her, "don't you bother about me. I can introduce myself." She stopped toward O. J. Berman, who, like many short men in the presence of tall women, had an aspiring mist in his eye. "I'm Mag W-w-wildwood, from Wild-w-w-wood, Arkansas. That's hill country."

It seemed a dance, Berman performing some fancy footwork to prevent his rivals cutting in. He lost her to a quadrille of partners who gobbled up her stammered jokes like popcorn tossed to pigeons. It was a comprehensible success. She was a triumph over ugliness, so often more beguiling than real beauty, if only because it contains paradox. In this case, as opposed to the scrupulous method of plain good taste and scientific grooming, the trick had been worked by exaggerating defects; she'd made them ornamental by admitting them boldly. Heels that emphasized her height, so steep her ankles trembled; a flat tight bodice that indicated she could go to a beach in bathing trunks; hair that was pulled straight back, accentuating the spareness, the starvation of her fashion-model face. Even the stutter, certainly genuine but still a bit laid on, had been turned to advantage. It was the master stroke, that stutter; for it contrived to make her banalities sound somehow original, and secondly, despite her tallness, her assurance, it served to inspire in male listeners a protective feeling. To illustrate: Berman had to be pounded on the back because she said, "Who can tell me w-w-where is the j-j-john?"; then, completing the cycle, he offered an arm to guide her himself.

"That," said Holly, "won't be necessary. She's been here before. She knows where it is." She was emptying ashtrays, and after Mag Wildwood had left the room, she emptied another, then said, sighed rather: "It's really very sad." She paused long enough to calculate the number of inquiring expressions; it was sufficient. "And so mysterious. You'd think it would show more. But heaven knows, she *looks* healthy. So, well, *clean.* That's the extraordinary part. Wouldn't you," she asked with concern, but of no one in particular, "wouldn't you say she *looked* clean?"

Someone coughed, several swallowed. A Naval officer, who had been holding Mag Wildwood's drink, put it down.

"But then," said Holly, "I hear so many of these Southern girls have the same trouble." She shuddered delicately, and went to the kitchen for more ice.

Mag Wildwood couldn't understand it, the abrupt absence of warmth on her return; the conversations she began behaved like green logs, they fumed but would not fire. More unforgivably, people were leaving without taking her telephone number. The Air Force colonel decamped while her back was turned, and this was the straw too much: he'd asked her to dinner. Suddenly she was blind. And since gin to artifice bears the same relation as tears to mascara, her attractions at once dissembled. She took it out on everyone. She called her hostess a Hollywood degenerate. She invited a man in his fifties to fight. She told Berman, Hitler was right. She exhilarated Rusty Trawler by stiff-arming him into a corner. "You know what's going to happen to you?" she said, with no hint of a stutter. "I'm going to march you over to the zoo and feed you to the yak." He looked altogether willing, but she disappointed him by sliding to the floor, where she sat humming.

"You're a bore. Get up from there," Holly said, stretching on a pair of gloves. The remnants of the party were waiting at the door, and when the bore didn't budge Holly cast me an apologetic glance. "Be an angel, would you, Fred? Put her in a taxi. She lives at the Winslow."

"Don't. Live Barbizon. Regent 4-5700. Ask for Mag Wildwood."

"You *are* an angel, Fred."

They were gone. The prospect of steering an Amazon into a taxi obliterated whatever resentment I felt. But she solved the problem herself. Rising on her own steam, she stared down at me with a lurching loftiness. She said, "Let's go Stork. Catch lucky balloon," and fell full-length like an axed oak. My first thought was to run for a doctor. But examination proved her pulse fine and her breathing regular. She was simply asleep. After finding a pillow for her head, I left her to enjoy it.

The following afternoon I collided with Holly on the stairs. "*You*" she said, hurrying past with a package from the druggist. "There she is, on the verge of pneumonia. A hang-over out to here. And the mean reds on top of it." I gathered from this that Mag Wildwood was still in the apartment, but she gave me no chance to explore her surprising sympathy. Over the weekend, mystery deepened. First, there was the Latin who came to my door: mistakenly, for he was inquiring after Miss Wildwood. It took a while to correct his error, our accents seemed mutually incoherent, but by the time we had I was charmed. He'd been put together with care, his brown head and bullfighter's figure had an exactness, a perfection, like an apple, an orange, something nature has made just right. Added to this, as decoration, were an English suit and a brisk cologne and, what is still more unlatin, a bashful manner. The second event of the day involved him again. It was toward evening, and I saw him on my way out to dinner. He was arriving in a taxi; the driver helped him totter into the house with a load of suitcases. That gave me something to chew on: by Sunday my jaws were quite tired.

Then the picture became both darker and clearer.

Sunday was an Indian summer day, the sun was strong, my window was open, and I heard voices on the fire escape. Holly and Mag were sprawled there on a blanket, the cat between them. Their hair, newly washed, hung lankly. They were busy, Holly varnishing her toenails, Mag knitting on a sweater. Mag was speaking.

"If you ask me, I think you're l-l-lucky. At least there's one thing you can say for Rusty. He's an American."

"Bully for him."

"*Sugar.* There's a war on."

"And when it's over, you've seen the last of me, boy."

"I don't feel that way. I'm p-p-proud of my country. The men in my family were great soldiers. There's a statue of Papadaddy Wildwood smack in the center of Wildwood."

"Fred's a soldier," said Holly. "But I doubt if he'll ever be a statue. Could be. They say the more stupid you are the braver. He's pretty stupid."

"Fred's that boy upstairs? I didn't realize he was a soldier. But he *does* look stupid."

"Yearning. Not stupid. He wants awfully to be on the inside staring out: anybody with their nose pressed against a glass is liable to look stupid. Anyhow, he's a different Fred. Fred's my brother."

"You call your own f-f-flesh and b-b-blood stupid?"

"If he is he is."

"Well, it's poor taste to say so. A boy that's fighting for you and me and all of us."

"What is this: a bond rally?"

"I just want you to know where I stand. I appreciate a joke, but underneath I'm a s-s-serious person. Proud to be an American. That's why I'm sorry about José." She put down her knitting needles. "You *do* think he's terribly good-looking, don't you?" Holly said Hmn, and swiped the cat's whiskers with her lacquer brush. "If only I could get used to the idea of m-m-marrying a Brazilian. And *being* a B-b-brazilian myself. It's such a canyon to cross. Six thousand miles, and not knowing the language—"

"Go to Berlitz."

"Why on earth would they be teaching P-p-portuguese? It isn't as though anyone spoke it. No, my only chance is to try and make José forget politics and become an American. It's such a useless thing for a man to want to be: the p-p-president of *Brazil.*" She sighed and picked up her knitting. "I must be madly in love. You saw us together. Do you think I'm madly in love?"

"Well. Does he bite?"

Mag dropped a stitch. "Bite?"

"You. In bed."

"Why, no. *Should* he?" Then she added, censoriously: "But he does laugh."

"Good. That's the right spirit. I like a man who sees the humor; most of them, they're all pant and puff."

Mag withdrew her complaint; she accepted the comment as flattery reflecting on herself. "Yes. I suppose."

"Okay. He doesn't bite. He laughs. What else?"

Mag counted up her dropped stitch and began again, knit, purl, purl.

"I said—"

"I heard you. And it isn't that I don't want to tell you. But it's so difficult to remember. I don't d-d-dwell on these things. The way you seem to. They go out of my head like a dream. I'm sure that's the n-n-normal attitude."

"It may be normal, darling; but I'd rather be natural." Holly paused in the process of reddening the rest of the cat's whiskers. "Listen. If you can't remember, try leaving the lights on."

"Please understand me, Holly. I'm a very-very-very *conventional* person."

"Oh, balls. What's wrong with a decent look at a guy you like? Men are beautiful, a lot of them are, José is, and if you don't even want to *look* at him, well, I'd say he's getting a pretty cold plate of macaroni."

"L-l-lower your voice."

"You can't possibly be in love with him. Now. Does that answer your question?"

"No. Because I'm not a cold plate of m-m-macaroni. I'm a warm-hearted person. It's the basis of my character."

"Okay. You've got a warm heart. But if I were a man on my way to bed, I'd rather take along a hot-water bottle. It's more tangible."

"You won't hear any squawks out of José," she said complacently, her needles flashing in the sunlight. "What's more, I *am* in love with him. Do you realize I've knitted ten pairs of Argyles in less than three months? And this is the second sweater." She stretched the sweater and tossed it aside. "What's the point, though? Sweaters in Brazil. I ought to be making s-s-sun helmets."

Holly lay back and yawned. "It must be winter sometime."

"It *rains,* that I know. Heat. Rain. J-j-jungles."

"Heat. Jungles. Actually, I'd like that."

"Better you than me."

"Yes," said Holly, with a sleepiness that was not sleepy. "Better me than you."

On Monday, when I went down for the morning mail, the card on Holly's box had been altered, a name added: Miss Golightly and Miss Wildwood were now traveling together. This might have held my interest longer except for a letter in my own mailbox. It was from a small university review to whom I'd sent a story. They liked it; and, though I must understand they could not afford to pay, they intended to publish. Publish: that meant *print*. Dizzy with excitement is no mere phrase. I had to tell someone: and, taking the stairs two at a time, I pounded on Holly's door.

I didn't trust my voice to tell the news; as soon as she came to the door, her eyes squinty with sleep, I thrust the letter at her. It seemed as though she'd had time to read sixty pages before she handed it back. "I wouldn't let them do it, not if they don't pay you," she said, yawning. Perhaps my face explained she'd misconstrued, that I'd not wanted advice but congratulations: her mouth shifted from a yawn into a smile. "Oh, I see. It's wonderful. Well, come in," she said. "We'll make a pot of coffee and celebrate. No. I'll get dressed and take you to lunch."

Her bedroom was consistent with her parlor: it perpetuated the same camping-out atmosphere; crates and suitcases, everything packed and ready to go, like the belongings of a criminal who feels the law not far behind. In the parlor there was no conventional furniture, but the bedroom had the bed itself, a double one at that, and quite flashy: blond wood, tufted satin.

She left the door of the bathroom open, and conversed from there; between the flushing and the brushing, most of what she said was unintelligible, but the gist of it was: she *supposed* I knew Mag Wildwood had moved in, and wasn't that *convenient?* because if you're going to *have* a roommate, and she *isn't* a dyke, then the next best thing is a *perfect* fool, which Mag *was,* because then you can dump the lease on them *and* send them out for the laundry.

One could see that Holly had a laundry problem; the room was strewn, like a girl's gymnasium.

"—and you know, she's quite a successful model: isn't that *fan*tastic? But a good thing," she said, hobbling out of the bathroom as she adjusted a garter. "It ought to keep her out of my hair most of the day. And there shouldn't be too much trouble on the man front. She's engaged. Nice guy, too. Though there's a tiny difference in height: I'd say a foot, her favor. Where the hell—" She was on her knees poking under the bed. After she'd found what she was looking for, a pair of lizard shoes, she had to search for a blouse, a belt, and it was a subject to ponder, how, from such wreckage, she evolved the eventual effect: pampered, calmly immaculate, as though she'd been attended by Cleopatra's maids. She said, "Listen," and cupped her hand under my chin, "I'm glad about the story. Really I am."

That Monday in October, 1943. A beautiful day with the buoyancy of a bird. To start, we had Manhattans at Joe Bell's; and, when he heard of my good luck, champagne cocktails on the house. Later, we wandered toward Fifth Avenue, where there was a parade. The flags in the wind, the thump of military bands and military feet, seemed to have nothing to do with war, but to be, rather, a fanfare arranged in my personal honor.

We ate lunch at the cafeteria in the park. Afterwards, avoiding the zoo

(Holly said she couldn't bear to see anything in a cage), we giggled, ran, sang along the paths toward the old wooden boathouse, now gone. Leaves floated on the lake; on the shore, a park-man was fanning a bonfire of them, and the smoke, rising like Indian signals, was the only smudge on the quivering air. Aprils have never meant much to me, autumns seem that season of beginning, spring; which is how I felt sitting with Holly on the railings of the boathouse porch. I thought of the future, and spoke of the past. Because Holly wanted to know about my childhood. She talked of her own, too; but it was elusive, nameless, placeless, an impressionistic recital, though the impression received was contrary to what one expected, for she gave an almost voluptuous account of swimming and summer, Christmas trees, pretty cousins and parties: in short, happy in a way that she was not, and never, certainly, the background of a child who had run away.

Or, I asked, wasn't it true that she'd been out on her own since she was fourteen? She rubbed her nose. "That's true. The other isn't. But really, darling, you made such a tragedy out of *your* childhood I didn't feel I should compete."

She hopped off the railing. "Anyway, it reminds me: I ought to send Fred some peanut butter." The rest of the afternoon we were east and west worming out of reluctant grocers cans of peanut butter, a wartime scarcity; dark came before we'd rounded up a half-dozen jars, the last at a delicatessen on Third Avenue. It was near the antique shop with the palace of a bird cage in its window, so I took her there to see it, and she enjoyed the point, its fantasy: "But still, it's a cage."

Passing a Woolworth's, she gripped my arm: "Let's steal something," she said, pulling me into the store, where at once there seemed a pressure of eyes, as though we were already under suspicion. "Come on. Don't be chicken." She scouted a counter piled with paper pumpkins and Halloween masks. The saleslady was occupied with a group of nuns who were trying on masks. Holly picked up a mask and slipped it over her face; she chose another and put it on mine; then she took my hand and we walked away. It was as simple as that. Outside, we ran a few blocks, I think to make it more dramatic; but also because, as I'd discovered, successful theft exhilarates. I wondered if she'd often stolen. "I used to," she said. "I mean I had to. If I wanted anything. But I still do it every now and then, sort of to keep my hand in."

We wore the masks all the way home.

I have a memory of spending many hither and yonning days with Holly; and it's true, we did at odd moments see a great deal of each other; but on the whole, the memory is false. Because toward the end of the month I found a job: what is there to add? The less the better, except to say it was necessary and lasted from nine to five. Which made our hours, Holly's and mine, extremely different.

Unless it was Thursday, her Sing Sing day, or unless she'd gone horseback riding in the park, as she did occasionally, Holly was hardly up when I came home. Sometimes, stopping there, I shared her wake-up coffee while she dressed for the evening. She was forever on her way out, not always with Rusty Trawler, but usually, and usually, too, they were joined by Mag Wildwood and the handsome Brazilian, whose name was José Ybarra-Jaegar: his mother was German. As a quartet, they struck an unmusical note, primarily the fault of Ybarra-Jaegar, who seemed as out of place in their company as a violin in a jazz band. He was intelligent, he was presentable, he appeared to have a serious link with his work, which was obscurely governmental, vaguely important, and took him to Washington several days a week. How, then, could he survive night after night in La Rue, El Morocco, listening to the Wildwood ch-ch-chatter and staring into Rusty's raw baby-buttocks face? Perhaps, like most of us in a foreign country, he was incapable of placing people, selecting a frame for their picture, as he would at home; therefore all Americans had to be judged in a pretty equal light, and on this basis his companions appeared to be tolerable examples of local color and national character. That would explain much; Holly's determination explains the rest.

Late one afternoon, while waiting for a Fifth Avenue bus, I noticed a taxi stop across the street to let out a girl who ran up the steps of the Forty-second Street public library. She was through the doors before I recognized her, which was pardonable, for Holly and libraries were not an easy association to make. I let curiosity guide me between the lions, debating on the way whether I should admit following her or pretend coincidence. In the end I did neither, but concealed myself some tables away from her in the general reading room, where she sat behind her dark glasses and a fortress of literature she'd gathered at the desk. She sped from one book to the next, intermittently lingering on a page, always with a frown, as if it were printed upside down. She had a pencil poised above paper—nothing seemed to catch her fancy, still now and then, as though for the hell of it, she made laborious scribblings. Watching her, I remembered a girl I'd known in school, a grind, Mildred Grossman. Mildred: with her moist hair and greasy spectacles, her stained fingers that dissected frogs and carried coffee to picket lines, her flat eyes that only turned toward the stars to estimate their chemical tonnage. Earth and air could not be more opposite than Mildred and Holly, yet in my head they acquired a Siamese twinship, and the thread of thought that had sewn them together ran like this: the average personality reshapes frequently, every few years even our bodies undergo a complete overhaul—desirable or not, it is a natural thing that we should change. All right, here were two people who never would. That is what Mildred Grossman had in common with Holly Golightly. They would never change because they'd been given their character too soon; which, like sudden riches, leads to a lack of proportion: the one had splurged herself into a top-heavy realist, the other a lopsided romantic. I imagined them in a restaurant of the future, Mildred still studying the menu for its nutritional values, Holly still gluttonous for everything on it. It would never be different. They would walk through life and out of it with the same determined step that took small notice of those cliffs at the left. Such profound observations made me forget where I was; I came to, startled to find myself in the gloom of the library, and surprised all over again to see Holly there. It was after seven, she was freshening her lipstick and perking up her appearance from what she deemed correct for a library to what, by adding a bit of scarf, some earrings, she considered suitable for the Colony. When she'd left, I wandered over to the table where her books remained; they were what I had wanted to see. *South by Thunderbird. Byways of Brazil. The Political Mind of Latin America.* And so forth.

On Christmas Eve she and Mag gave a party. Holly asked me to come early and help trim the tree. I'm still not sure how they maneuvered that tree into the apartment. The top branches were crushed against the ceiling, the lower ones spread wall-to-wall; altogether it was not unlike the yuletide giant we see in Rockefeller Plaza. Moreover, it would have taken a Rockefeller to decorate it, for it soaked up baubles and tinsel like melting snow. Holly suggested she run out to Woolworth's and steal some balloons; she did: and they turned the tree into a fairly good show. We made a toast to our work, and Holly said: "Look in the bedroom. There's a present for you."

I had one for her, too: a small package in my pocket that felt even smaller when I saw, square on the bed and wrapped with a red ribbon, the beautiful bird cage.

"But, Holly! It's dreadful!"

"I couldn't agree more; but I thought you wanted it."

"The money! Three hundred and fifty dollars!"

She shrugged. "A few extra trips to the powder room. Promise me, though. Promise you'll never put a living thing in it."

I started to kiss her, but she held out her hand. "Gimme," she said, tapping the bulge in my pocket.

"I'm afraid it isn't much," and it wasn't: a St. Christopher's medal. But at least it came from Tiffany's. Holly was not a girl who could keep anything, and surely by now she has lost that medal, left it in a suitcase or some hotel drawer. But the bird cage is still mine. I've lugged it to New Orleans, Nantucket, all over Europe, Morocco, the West Indies. Yet I seldom remember that it was Holly who gave it to me, because at one point I chose to forget: we had a big falling-out, and among the objects rotating in the eye of our hurricane were the bird cage and O.J. Berman and my story, a copy of which I'd given Holly when it appeared in the university review.

Sometime in February, Holly had gone on a winter trip with Rusty, Mag and José Ybarra-Jaegar. Our altercation happened soon after she returned. She was brown as iodine, her hair was sun-bleached to a ghost-color, she'd had a wonderful time: "Well, first of all we were in Key West, and Rusty got mad at some sailors, or vice versa, *any*way he'll have to wear a spine brace the rest of his life. Dearest Mag ended up in the hospital, too. First-degree sunburn.

Disgusting: all blisters and citronella. We couldn't stand the smell of her. So José and I left them in the hospital and went to Havana. He says wait till I see Rio; but as far as I'm concerned Havana can take my money right now. We had an irresistible guide, most of him Negro and the rest of him Chinese, and while I don't go much for one or the other, the combination was fairly riveting: so I let him play kneesie under the table, because frankly I didn't find him at all banal; but then one night he took us to a blue movie, and what do you suppose? There *he* was *on* the screen. Of course when we got back to Key West, Mag was positive I'd spent the whole time sleeping with José. So was Rusty: but he doesn't care about that, he simply wants to hear the details. Actually, things were pretty tense until I had a heart-to-heart with Mag."

We were in the front room, where, though it was now nearly March, the enormous Christmas tree, turned brown and scentless, its balloons shriveled as an old cow's dugs, still occupied most of the space. A recognizable piece of furniture had been added to the room: an army cot; and Holly, trying to preserve her tropic look, was sprawled on it under a sun lamp.

"And you convinced her?"

"That I hadn't slept with José? God, yes. I simply told—but you know: made it sound like an *ago*nized confession—simply told her I was a dyke."

"She couldn't have believed that."

"The hell she didn't. Why do you think she went out and bought this army cot? Leave it to me: I'm always top banana in the shock department. Be a darling, darling, rub some oil on my back." While I was performing this service, she said: "O.J. Berman's in town, and listen, I gave him your story in the magazine. He was quite impressed. He thinks maybe you're worth helping. But he says you're on the wrong track. Negroes and children: who cares?"

"Not Mr. Berman, I gather."

"Well, I agree with him. I read that story twice. Brats and niggers. Trembling leaves. *Description*. It doesn't *mean* anything."

My hand, smoothing oil on her skin, seemed to have a temper of its own: it yearned to raise itself and come down on her buttocks. "Give me an example," I said quietly. "Of something that means something. In your opinion."

"*Wuthering Heights*," she said, without hesitation.

The urge in my hand was growing beyond control. "But that's unreasonable. You're talking about a work of genius."

"It was, wasn't it? *My wild sweet Cathy*. God, I cried buckets. I saw it ten times."

I said, "Oh" with recognizable relief, "oh" with a shameful, rising inflection, "the *movie*."

Her muscles hardened, the touch of her was like stone warmed by the sun. "Everybody has to feel superior to somebody," she said. "But it's customary to present a little proof before you take the privilege."

"I don't compare myself to you. Or Berman. Therefore I can't feel superior. We want different things."

"Don't you want to make money?"

"I haven't planned that far."

"That's how your stories sound. As though you'd written them without knowing the end. Well, I'll tell you: you'd better make money. You have an expensive imagination. Not many people are going to buy you bird cages."

"Sorry."

"You will be if you hit me. You wanted to a minute ago: I could feel it in your hand; and you want to now."

I did, terribly; my hand, my heart was shaking as I recapped the bottle of oil. "Oh no, I wouldn't regret that. I'm only sorry you wasted your money on me: Rusty Trawler is too hard a way of earning it."

She sat up on the army cot, her face, her naked breasts coldly blue in the sun-lamp light. "It should take you about four seconds to walk from here to the door. I'll give you two."

I went straight upstairs, got the bird cage, took it down and left it in front of her door. That settled that. Or so I imagined until the next morning when, as I was leaving for work, I saw the cage perched on a sidewalk ashcan waiting for the garbage collector. Rather sheepishly, I rescued it and carried it back to my room, a capitulation that did not lessen my resolve to put Holly Golightly absolutely out of my life. She was, I decided, "a crude exhibitionist," "a time waster," "an utter fake": someone never to be spoken to again.

And I didn't. Not for a long while. We passed each other on the stairs with lowered eyes. If she walked into Joe Bell's, I walked out. At one point, Madame Sapphia Spanella, the coloratura and roller-skating enthusiast who lived on the first floor, circulated a petition among the brownstone's other tenants asking them to join her in having Miss Golightly evicted: she was, said Madame Spanella, "morally objectionable" and the "perpetrator of all-night gatherings that endanger the safety and sanity of her neighbors." Though I refused to sign, secretly I felt Madame Spanella had cause to complain. But her petition failed, and as April approached May, the open-windowed, warm spring nights were lurid with the party sounds, the loud-playing phonograph and martini laughter that emanated from Apt. 2.

It was no novelty to encounter suspicious specimens among Holly's callers, quite the contrary; but one day late that spring, while passing through the brownstone's vestibule, I noticed a *very* provocative man examining her mailbox. A person in his early fifties with a hard, weathered face, gray forlorn eyes. He wore an old sweat-stained gray hat, and his cheap summer suit, a pale blue, hung too loosely on his lanky frame; his shoes were brown and brand-new. He seemed to have no intention of ringing Holly's bell. Slowly, as though he were reading Braille, he kept rubbing a finger across the embossed lettering of her name.

That evening, on my way to supper, I saw the man again. He was standing across the street, leaning against a tree and staring up at Holly's windows.

Sinister speculations rushed through my head. Was he a detective? Or some underworld agent connected with her Sing Sing friend, Sally Tomato? The situation revived my tenderer feelings for Holly; it was only fair to interrupt our feud long enough to warn her that she was being watched. As I walked to the corner, heading east toward the Hamburg Heaven at Seventy-ninth and Madison, I could feel the man's attention focused on me. Presently, without turning my head, I knew that he was following me. Because I could hear him whistling. Not any ordinary tune, but the plaintive, prairie melody Holly sometimes played on her guitar: *Don't wanna sleep, don't wanna die, just wanna go a-travelin' through the pastures of the sky.* The whistling continued across Park Avenue and up Madison. Once, while waiting for a traffic light to change, I watched him out of the corner of my eye as he stooped to pet a sleazy Pomeranian. "That's a fine animal you got there," he told the owner in a hoarse, countrified drawl.

Hamburg Heaven was empty. Nevertheless, he took a seat right beside me at the long counter. He smelled of tobacco and sweat. He ordered a cup of coffee, but when it came he didn't touch it. Instead, he chewed on a toothpick and studied me in the wall mirror facing us.

"Excuse me," I said, speaking to him via the mirror, "but what do you want?"

The question didn't embarrass him; he seemed relieved to have had it asked. "Son," he said, "I need a friend."

He brought out a wallet. It was as worn as his leathery hands, almost falling to pieces; and so was the brittle, cracked, blurred snapshot he handed me. There were seven people in the picture, all grouped together on the sagging porch of a stark wooden house, and all children, except for the man himself, who had his arm around the waist of a plump blond little girl with a hand shading her eyes against the sun.

"That's me," he said, pointing at himself. "That's her . . ." he tapped the plump girl. "And this one over here," he added, indicating a tow-headed beanpole, "that's her brother, Fred."

I looked at "her" again: and yes, now I could see it, an embryonic resemblance to Holly in the squinting, fat-cheeked child. At the same moment, I realized who the man must be.

"You're Holly's *father.*"

He blinked, he frowned. "Her name's not Holly. She was a Lulamae Barnes. Was," he said, shifting the toothpick in his mouth, "till she married me. I'm her husband. Doc Golightly. I'm a horse doctor, animal man. Do some farming, too. Near Tulip, Texas. Son, why are you laughin'?"

It wasn't real laughter: it was nerves. I took a swallow of water and choked; he pounded me on the back. "This here's no humorous matter, son. I'm a tired man. I've been five years lookin' for my woman. Soon as I got that letter from Fred, saying where she was, I bought myself a ticket on the Greyhound. Lulamae belongs home with her husband and her churren."

"Children?"

"*Them's* her churren," he said, almost shouted. He meant the four other young faces in the picture, two barefooted girls and a pair of overalled boys. Well, of course: the man was deranged. "But Holly can't be the mother of those children. They're older than she is. Bigger."

"Now, son," he said in a reasoning voice, "I didn't claim they was her natural-born churren. Their own precious mother, precious woman, Jesus rest her soul, she passed away July 4th, Independence Day, 1936. The year of the drought. When I married Lulamae, that was in December, 1938, she was going on fourteen. Maybe an ordinary person, being only fourteen, wouldn't know their right mind. But you take Lulamae, she was an exceptional woman. She knew good-and-well what she was doing when she promised to be my wife and the mother of my churren. She plain broke our hearts when she ran off like she done." He sipped his cold coffee, and glanced at me with a searching earnestness. "Now, son, do you doubt me? Do you believe what I'm saying is so?"

I did. It was too implausible not to be fact; moreover, it dovetailed with O.J. Berman's description of the Holly he'd first encountered in California: "You don't know whether she's a hillbilly or an Okie or what." Berman couldn't be blamed for not guessing that she was a child-wife from Tulip, Texas.

"Plain broke our hearts when she ran off like she done," the horse doctor repeated. "She had no cause. All the housework was done by her daughters. Lulamae could just take it easy: fuss in front of mirrors and wash her hair. Our own cows, our own garden, chickens, pigs: son, that woman got positively fat. While her brother growed into a giant. Which is a sight different from how they come to us. 'Twas Nellie, my oldest girl, 'twas Nellie brought 'em into the house. She come to me one morning, and said: 'Papa, I got two wild yunguns locked in the kitchen. I caught 'em outside stealing milk and turkey eggs.' That was Lulamae and Fred. Well, you never saw a more pitiful something. Ribs sticking out everywhere, legs so puny they can't hardly stand, teeth wobbling so bad they can't chew mush. Story was: their mother died of the TB, and their papa done the same—and all the churren, a whole raft of 'em, they been sent off to live with different mean people. Now Lulamae and her brother, them two been living with some mean, no-count people a hundred miles east of Tulip. She had good cause to run off from that house. She didn't have none to leave mine. 'Twas her home." He leaned his elbows on the counter and, pressing his closed eyes with his fingertips, sighed. "She plumped out to be a real pretty woman. Lively, too. Talky as a jaybird. With something smart to say on every subject: better than the radio. First thing you know, I'm out picking flowers. I tamed her a crow and taught it to say her name. I showed her how to play the guitar. Just to look at her made the tears spring to my eyes. The night I proposed, I cried like a baby. She said: 'What you want to cry for, Doc? 'Course we'll be married. I've never been married before.' Well, I had to laugh, hug and squeeze her: *never been married before!*" He chuckled, chewed on his toothpick a moment. "Don't tell me that woman wasn't happy!" he said, challengingly. "We all doted on her. She didn't have to lift a finger, 'cept to eat a piece of pie. 'Cept to comb her hair and send away for all the magazines. We must've had a hunnerd dollars' worth of magazines come into that house. Ask me, that's what done it. Looking at show-off pictures. Reading dreams. That's what started her walking down the road. Every day she'd walk a little further: a mile, and come home. Two miles, and come home. One day she just kept on." He put his hands over his eyes again; his breathing made a ragged noise. "The crow I give her went wild and flew away. All summer you could hear him. In the yard. In the garden. In the woods. All summer that damned bird was calling: Lulamae, Lulamae."

He stayed hunched over and silent, as though listening to the long-ago summer sound. I carried our checks to the cashier. While I was paying, he joined me. We left together and walked over to Park Avenue. It was a cool, blowy evening; swanky awnings flapped in the breeze. The quietness between us continued until I said: "But what about her brother? He didn't leave?"

"No, sir," he said, clearing his throat. "Fred was with us right till they took him in the Army. A fine boy. Fine with horses. He didn't know what got into Lulamae, how come she left her brother and husband and churren. After he was in the Army, though, Fred started hearing from her. The other day he wrote me her address. So I come to get her. I know she's sorry for what she done. I know she wants to go home." He seemed to be asking me to agree with him. I told him that I thought he'd find Holly, or Lulamae, somewhat changed. "Listen, son," he said, as we reached the steps of the brownstone, "I advised you I need a friend. Because I don't want to surprise her. Scare her none. That's why I've held off. Be my friend: let her know I'm here."

The notion of introducing Mrs. Golightly to her husband had its satisfying aspects; and, glancing up at her lighted windows, I hoped her friends were there, for the prospect of watching the Texan shake hands with Mag and Rusty and José was more satisfying still. But Doc Golightly's proud earnest eyes and sweat-stained hat made me ashamed of such anticipations. He followed me into the house and prepared to wait at the bottom of the stairs. "Do I look nice?" he whispered, brushing his sleeves, tightening the knot of his tie.

Holly was alone. She answered the door at once; in fact, she was on her way out—white satin dancing pumps and quantities of perfume announced gala intentions. "Well, idiot," she said, and playfully slapped me with her purse. "I'm in too much of a hurry to make up now. We'll smoke the pipe tomorrow, okay?"

"Sure, Lulamae. If you're still around tomorrow."

She took off her dark glasses and squinted at me. It was as though her eyes were shattered prisms, the dots of blue and gray and green like broken bits of sparkle. "*He* told you that," she said in a small, shivering voice. "Oh, please. *Where* is he?" She ran past me into the hall. "Fred!" she called down the stairs. "Fred! Where are you, darling?"

I could hear Doc Golightly's footsteps climbing the stairs. His head appeared above the banisters, and Holly backed away from him, not as though she were frightened, but as though she were retreating into a shell of disappointment. Then he was standing in front of her, hangdog and shy. "Gosh, Lulamae," he began, and hesitated, for Holly was gazing at him vacantly, as though she couldn't place him. "Gee, honey," he said, "don't they feed you up here? You're so skinny. Like when I first saw you. All wild around the eye."

Holly touched his face; her fingers tested the reality of his chin, his beard stubble. "Hello, Doc," she said gently, and kissed him on the cheek. "Hello, Doc," she repeated happily, as he lifted her off her feet in a rib-crushing grip. Whoops of relieved laughter shook him. "Gosh, Lulamae. Kingdom come."

Neither of them noticed me when I squeezed past them and went up to my room. Nor did they seem aware of Madame Sapphia Spanella, who opened her door and yelled: "Shut up! It's a disgrace. Do your whoring elsewhere."

"*Divorce* him? Of course I never divorced him. I was only fourteen, for God's sake. It couldn't have been *legal.*" Holly tapped an empty martini glass. "Two more, my darling Mr. Bell."

Joe Bell, in whose bar we were sitting, accepted the order reluctantly. "You're rockin' the boat kinda early," he complained, crunching on a Tums. It was not yet noon, according to the black mahogany clock behind the bar, and he'd already served us three rounds.

"But it's Sunday, Mr. Bell. Clocks are slow on Sundays. Besides, I haven't been to bed yet," she told him, and confided to me: "Not to sleep." She blushed, and glanced away guiltily. For the first time since I'd known her, she seemed to feel a need to justify herself: "Well, I had to. Doc really loves me, you know. And I love him. He may have looked old and tacky to *you*. But you don't know the sweetness of him, the confidence he can give to birds and brats and fragile things like that. Anyone who ever gave you confidence, you owe them a lot. I've always remembered Doc in my prayers. Please stop smirking!" she demanded, stabbing out a cigarette. "I *do* say my prayers."

"I'm not smirking. I'm smiling. You're the most amazing person."

"I suppose I am," she said, and her face, wan, rather bruised-looking in the morning light, brightened; she smoothed her tousled hair, and the colors of it glimmered like a shampoo advertisement. "I must look fierce. But who wouldn't? We spent the rest of the night roaming around in a bus station. Right up till the last minute Doc thought I was going to go with him. Even though I kept telling him: But, Doc, I'm not fourteen any more, and I'm not Lulamae. But the terrible part is (and I realized it while we were standing there) I am. I'm still stealing turkey eggs and running through a brier patch. Only now I call it having the mean reds."

Joe Bell disdainfully settled the fresh martinis in front of us.

"Never love a wild thing, Mr. Bell," Holly advised him. "That was Doc's mistake. He was always lugging home wild things. A hawk with a hurt wing. One time it was a full-grown bobcat with a broken leg. But you can't give your heart to a wild thing: the more you do, the stronger they get. Until they're strong enough to run into the woods. Or fly into a tree. Then a taller tree. Then the sky. That's how you'll end up, Mr. Bell. If you let yourself love a wild thing. You'll end up looking at the sky."

"She's drunk," Joe Bell informed me.

"Moderately," Holly confessed. "But Doc knew what I meant. I explained it to him very carefully, and it was something he could understand. We shook hands and held on to each other and he wished me luck." She glanced at the clock. "He must be in the Blue Mountains by now."

"What's she talkin' about?" Joe Bell asked me.

Holly lifted her martini. "Let's wish the Doc luck, too," she said, touching her glass against mine. "Good luck: and believe me, dearest Doc—it's better to look at the sky than live there. Such an empty place; so vague. Just a country where the thunder goes and things disappear."

TRAWLER MARRIES FOURTH. I was on a subway somewhere in Brooklyn when I saw that headline. The paper that bannered it belonged to another passenger. The only part of the text that I could see read: *Rutherfurd "Rusty" Trawler, the millionaire playboy often accused of pro-Nazi sympathies, eloped to Greenwich yesterday with a beautiful*—Not that I wanted to read any more. Holly had married him: well, well. I wished I were under the wheels of the train. But I'd been wishing that before I spotted the headline. For a headful of reasons. I hadn't seen Holly, not really, since our drunken Sunday at Joe Bell's bar. The intervening weeks had given me my own case of the mean reds. First off, I'd been fired from my job: deservedly, and for an amusing misdemeanor too complicated to recount here. Also, my draft board was displaying an uncomfortable interest; and, having so recently escaped the regimentation of a small town, the idea of entering another form of disciplined life made me desperate. Between the uncertainty of my draft status and a lack of specific experience, I couldn't seem to find another job. That was what I was doing on a subway in Brooklyn: returning from a discouraging interview with an editor of the now defunct newspaper, *PM*. All this, combined with the city heat of the summer, had reduced me to a state of nervous inertia. So I more than half meant it when I wished I were under the wheels of the train. The headline made the desire quite positive. If Holly could marry that "absurd foetus," then the army of wrongness rampant in the world might as well march over me. Or, and the question is apparent, was my outrage a little the result of being in love with Holly myself? A little. For I *was* in love with her. Just as I'd once been in love with my mother's elderly colored cook and a postman who let me follow him on his rounds and a whole family named McKendrick. That category of love generates jealousy, too.

When I reached my station I bought a paper; and, reading the tail-end of that sentence, discovered that Rusty's bride was: *a beautiful cover girl from the Arkansas hills, Miss Margaret Thatcher Fitzhue Wildwood.* Mag! My legs went so limp with relief I took a taxi the rest of the way home.

Madame Sapphia Spanella met me in the hall, wild-eyed and wringing her hands. "Run," she said. "Bring the police. She is killing somebody! Somebody is killing her!"

It sounded like it. As though tigers were loose in Holly's apartment. A riot of crashing glass, of rippings and fallings and overturned furniture. But there were no quarreling voices inside the uproar, which made it seem unnatural. "Run," shrieked Madame Spanella, pushing me. "Tell the police murder!"

I ran; but only upstairs to Holly's door. Pounding on it had one result: the racket subsided. Stopped altogether. But pleadings to let me in went unanswered, and my efforts to break down the door merely culminated in a bruised shoulder. Then below I heard Madame Spanella commanding some newcomer to go for the police. "Shut up," she was told, "and get out of my way."

It was José Ybarra-Jaegar. Looking not at all the smart Brazilian diplomat; but sweaty and frightened. He ordered me out of his way, too. And, using his own key, opened the door. "In here, Dr. Goldman," he said, beckoning to a man accompanying him.

Since no one prevented me, I followed them into the apartment, which was tremendously wrecked. At last the Christmas tree had been dismantled, very literally: its brown dry branches sprawled in a welter of torn-up books, broken lamps and phonograph records. Even the icebox had been emptied, its contents tossed around the room: raw eggs were sliding down the walls, and in the midst of the debris Holly's no-name cat was calmly licking a puddle of milk.

In the bedroom, the smell of smashed perfume bottles made me gag. I stepped on Holly's dark glasses; they were lying on the floor, the lenses already shattered, the frames cracked in half.

Perhaps that is why Holly, a rigid figure on the bed, stared at José so blindly, seemed not to see the doctor, who, testing her pulse, crooned: "You're a tired young lady. Very tired. You want to go to sleep, don't you? Sleep."

Holly rubbed her forehead, leaving a smear of blood from a cut finger. "Sleep," she said, and whimpered like an exhausted, fretful child. "He's the only one would ever let me. Let me hug him on cold nights. I saw a place in Mexico. With horses. By the sea."

"With horses by the sea," lullabied the doctor, selecting from his black case a hypodermic.

José averted his face, queasy at the sight of a needle. "Her sickness is only grief?" he asked, his difficult English lending the question an unintended irony. "She is grieving only?"

"Didn't hurt a bit, now did it?" inquired the doctor, smugly dabbing Holly's arm with a scrap of cotton.

She came to sufficiently to focus the doctor. "*Everything* hurts. Where are my glasses?" But she didn't need them. Her eyes were closing of their own accord.

"She is only grieving?" insisted José.

"Please, sir," the doctor was quite short with him, "if you will leave me alone with the patient."

José withdrew to the front room, where he released his temper on the snooping, tiptoeing presence of Madame Spanella. "Don't touch me! I'll call the police," she threatened as he whipped her to the door with Portuguese oaths.

He considered throwing me out, too; or so I surmised from his expression. Instead, he invited me to have a drink. The only unbroken bottle we could find contained dry vermouth. "I have a worry," he confided. "I have a worry that this should cause scandal. Her crashing everything. Conducting like a crazy. I must have no public scandal. It is too delicate: my name, my work."

He seemed cheered to learn that I saw no reason for a "scandal"; demolishing one's own possessions was, presumably, a private affair.

"It is only a question of grieving," he firmly declared. "When the sadness came, first she throws the drink she is drinking. The bottle. Those books. A lamp. Then I am scared. I hurry to bring a doctor."

"But why?" I wanted to know. "Why should she have a fit over Rusty? If I were her, I'd celebrate."

"Rusty?"

I was still carrying my newspaper, and showed him the headline.

"Oh, that." He grinned rather scornfully. "They do us a grand favor, Rusty and Mag. We laugh over it: how they think they break our hearts when all the time we *want* them to run away. I assure you, we were laughing when the sadness came." His eyes searched the litter on the floor; he picked up a ball of yellow paper. "This," he said.

It was a telegram from Tulip, Texas: *Received notice young Fred killed in action overseas stop your husband and children join in the sorrow of our mutual loss stop letter follows love Doc.*

Holly never mentioned her brother again: except once. Moreover, she stopped calling me Fred. June, July, all through the warm months she hibernated like a winter animal who did not know spring had come and gone. Her hair darkened, she put on weight. She became rather careless about her clothes: used to rush round to the delicatessen wearing a rain-slicker and nothing underneath. José moved into the apartment, his name replacing Mag Wildwood's on the mailbox. Still, Holly was a good deal alone, for José stayed in Washington three days a week. During his absences she entertained no one and seldom left the apartment—except on Thursdays, when she made her weekly trip to Ossining.

Which is not to imply that she had lost interest in life; far from it, she seemed more content, altogether happier than I'd ever seen her. A keen sudden un-Holly-like enthusiasm for homemaking resulted in several un-Holly-like purchases: at a Parke-Bernet auction she acquired a stag-at-bay hunting tapestry and, from the William Randolph Hearst estate, a gloomy pair of Gothic "easy" chairs; she bought the complete Modern Library, shelves of classical records, innumerable Metropolitan Museum reproductions (including a statue of a Chinese cat that her own cat hated and hissed at and ultimately broke), a Waring mixer and a pressure cooker and a library of cook books. She spent whole hausfrau afternoons slopping about in the sweatbox of her midget kitchen: "José says I'm better than the Colony. Really, who would have dreamed I had such a great natural talent? A month ago I couldn't scramble eggs." And still couldn't, for that matter. Simple dishes, steak, a proper salad, were beyond her. Instead, she fed José, and occasionally myself, *outré* soups (brandied black terrapin poured into avocado shells) Nero-ish novelties (roasted pheasant stuffed with pomegranates and persimmons) and other dubious innovations (chicken and saffron rice served with a chocolate sauce: "An East Indian classic, *my* dear.") Wartime sugar and cream rationing restricted her imagination when it came to sweets—nevertheless, she once managed something called Tobacco Tapioca: best not describe it.

Nor describe her attempts to master Portuguese, an ordeal as tedious to me as it was to her, for whenever I visited her an album of Linguaphone records never ceased rotating on the phonograph. Now, too, she rarely spoke a sentence that did not begin, "After we're married—" or "When we move to Rio—" Yet José had never suggested marriage. She admitted it. "But, after all, he *knows* I'm preggers. Well, I am, darling. Six weeks gone. I don't see why *that* should surprise you. It didn't me. Not *un peu* bit. I'm delighted. I want to have at least nine. I'm sure some of them will be rather dark—José has a touch of *le nègre,* I suppose you guessed that? Which is fine by me: what could be prettier than a quite coony baby with bright green beautiful eyes? I wish, please don't laugh—but I wish I'd been a virgin for him, for José. Not that I've warmed the multitudes some people say: I don't blame the bastards for *saying* it, I've always thrown out such a jazzy line. Really, though, I toted up the other night, and I've only had eleven lovers—not counting anything that happened before I was thirteen because, after all, that just *doesn't* count. Eleven. Does that make me a whore? Look at Mag Wildwood. Or Honey Tucker. Or Rose Ellen Ward. They've had the old clap-yo'-hands so many times it amounts to applause. Of course I haven't anything *against* whores. Except this: some of them may have an honest tongue but they all have dishonest hearts. I mean, you can't bang the guy and cash his checks and at least not *try* to believe you love him. I never have. Even Benny Shacklett and all those rodents. I sort of hypnotized myself into thinking their sheer rattiness had a certain allure. Actually, except for Doc, if you want to count Doc, José is my first non-rat romance. Oh, he's not my idea of the absolute finito. He tells little lies and he worries what people *think* and he takes about fifty baths a day: men ought to smell *some* what. He's too prim, too cautious to be my guy ideal; he always turns his back to get undressed and he makes too much noise when he eats and I don't like to see him run because there's something funny-looking about him when he runs. If I were free to choose from everybody alive, just snap my fingers and say come here you, I wouldn't pick José. Nehru, he's nearer the mark. Wendell Willkie. I'd settle for Garbo any day. Why not? A person ought to be able to marry men or women or—listen, if you came to me and said you wanted to hitch up with Man o' War, I'd respect your feeling. No, I'm serious. Love should be allowed. I'm all for it. Now that I've got a pretty good idea what it is. Because I *do* love José—I'd stop smoking if he asked me to. He's *friendly,* he can laugh me out of the mean reds, only I don't have them much any more, except sometimes, and even then they're not so hideola that I gulp Seconal or have to haul myself to Tiffany's: I take his suit to the cleaner, or stuff some mushrooms, and I feel fine, just great. Another thing, I've thrown away my horoscopes. I must have spent a dollar on every goddamn star in the goddamn planetarium. It's a bore, but the answer is good things only happen to you if you're good. Good? Honest is more what I mean. Not law-type honest—I'd rob a grave, I'd steal two bits off a dead man's eyes if I thought it would contribute to the day's enjoyment—but unto-thyself-type honest. Be anything but a coward, a pretender, an emotional crook, a whore: I'd rather have cancer than a dishonest heart. Which isn't being pious. Just practical. Cancer *may* cool you, but the other's sure to. Oh, screw it, cookie —hand me my guitar and I'll sing you a *fada* in *the* most perfect Portuguese."

Those final weeks, spanning end of summer and the beginning of another autumn, are blurred in memory, perhaps because our understanding of each other had reached that sweet depth where two people communicate more often in silence than in words: an affectionate quietness replaces the tensions, the unrelaxed chatter and chasing about that produce a friendship's more showy, more, in the surface sense, dramatic moments. Frequently, when *he* was out of town (I'd developed hostile attitudes toward *him,* and seldom used his name) we spent entire evenings together during which we exchanged less than a hundred words; once, we walked all the way to Chinatown, ate a chow-mein supper, bought some paper lanterns and stole a box of joss sticks, then moseyed across the Brooklyn Bridge, and on the bridge, as we watched seaward-moving ships pass between the cliffs of burning skyline, she said: "Years from now, years and years, one of those ships will bring me back, me and my nine Brazilian brats. Because yes, they *must* see this, these lights, the river—I love New York, even though it isn't mine, the way something has to be, a tree or a street or a house, something, anyway, that belongs to me because I belong to it." And I said: "Do shut up," for I felt infuriatingly left out—a tugboat in drydock while she, glittery voyager of secure destination, steamed down the harbor with whistles whistling and confetti in the air.

So the days, the last days, blow about in memory, hazy, autumnal, all alike as leaves: until a day unlike any other I've lived.

. . .

It happened to fall on the 30th of September, my birthday, a fact which had no effect on events, except that, expecting some form of monetary remembrance from my family, I was eager for the postman's morning visit. Indeed, I went downstairs and waited for him. If I had not been loitering in the vestibule, then Holly would not have asked me to go horseback riding; and would not, consequently, have had the opportunity to save my life.

"Come on," she said, when she found me awaiting the postman. "Let's walk a couple of horses around the park." She was wearing a windbreaker and a pair of blue jeans and tennis shoes; she slapped her stomach, drawing attention to its flatness: "Don't think I'm out to lose the heir. But there's a horse, my darling old Mabel Minerva—I can't go without saying good-bye to Mabel Minerva."

"Good-bye?"

"A week from Saturday. José bought the tickets." In rather a trance, I let her lead me down to the street. "We change planes in Miami. Then over the sea. Over the Andes. Taxi!"

Over the Andes. As we rode in a cab across Central Park it seemed to me as though I, too, were flying, desolately floating over snow-peaked and perilous territory.

"But you can't. After all, what about. Well, what about. Well, you can't *really* run off and leave everybody."

"I don't think anyone will miss me. I have no friends."

"I will. Miss you. So will Joe Bell. And oh—millions. Like Sally. Poor Mr. Tomato."

"I loved old Sally," she said, and sighed. "You know I haven't been to see him in a month? When I told him I was going away, he was an angel. *Actually*"—she frowned—"he seemed *delighted* that I was leaving the country. He said it was all for the best. Because sooner or later there might be trouble. If they found out I wasn't his real niece. That fat lawyer, O'Shaughnessy, O'Shaughnessy sent me five hundred dollars. In cash. A wedding present from Sally."

I wanted to be unkind. "You can expect a present from me, too. When, and if, the wedding happens."

She laughed. "He'll marry me, all right. In church. And with his family there. That's why we're waiting till we get to Rio."

"Does he know you're married already?"

"What's the matter with you? Are you trying to ruin the day? It's a beautiful day: leave it alone!"

"But it's perfectly possible—"

"It *isn't* possible. I've told you, that wasn't legal. It *couldn't* be." She rubbed her nose, and glanced at me sideways. "Mention that to a living soul, darling. I'll hang you by your toes and dress you for a hog."

The stables—I believe they have been replaced by television studios—were on West Sixty-sixth Street. Holly selected for me an old sway-back black and white mare: "Don't worry, she's safer than a cradle." Which, in my case, was a necessary guarantee, for ten-cent pony rides at childhood carnivals were the limit of my equestrian experience. Holly helped hoist me into the saddle, then mounted her own horse, a silvery animal that took the lead as we jogged across the traffic of Central Park West and entered a riding path dappled with leaves denuding breezes danced about.

"See?" she shouted. "It's great!"

And suddenly it was. Suddenly, watching the tangled colors of Holly's hair flash in the red-yellow leaf light, I loved her enough to forget myself, my self-pitying despairs, and be content that something she thought happy was going to happen. Very gently the horses began to trot, waves of wind splashed us, spanked our faces, we plunged in and out of sun and shadow pools, and joy, a glad-to-be-alive exhilaration, jolted through me like a jigger of nitrogen. That was one minute; the next introduced farce in grim disguise.

For all at once, like savage members of a jungle ambush, a band of Negro boys leapt out of the shrubbery along the path. Hooting, cursing, they launched rocks and thrashed at the horse's rumps with switches.

Mine, the black and white mare, rose on her hind legs, whinnied, teetered like a tightrope artist, then blue-streaked down the path, bouncing my feet out of the stirrups and leaving me scarcely attached. Her hooves made the gravel stones spit sparks. The sky careened. Trees, a lake with little-boy sailboats, statues went by licketysplit. Nursemaids rushed to rescue their charges from our awesome approach; men, bums and others, yelled: "Pull in the reins!" and "Whoa, boy, whoa!" and "Jump!" It was only later that I remembered these voices; at the time I was simply conscious of Holly, the cowboy-sound of her racing behind me, never quite catching up, and over and over calling encouragements. Onward: across the park and out into Fifth Avenue: stampeding against the noonday traffic, taxis, buses that screechingly swerved. Past the Duke mansion, the Frick Museum, past the Pierre and the Plaza. But Holly gained ground; moreover, a mounted policeman had joined the chase: flanking my runaway mare, one on either side, their horses performed a pincer movement that brought her to a steamy halt. It was then, at last, that I fell off her back. Fell off and picked myself up and stood there, not altogether certain where I was. A crowd gathered. The policeman huffed and wrote in a book: presently he was most sympathetic, grinned and said he would arrange for our horses to be returned to their stable.

Holly put us in a taxi. "Darling. How do you feel?"

"Fine."

"But you haven't *any* pulse," she said, feeling my wrist.

"Then I must be dead."

"No, idiot. This is serious. Look at me."

The trouble was, I couldn't see her; rather, I saw several Holly's, a trio of sweaty faces so white with concern that I was both touched and embarrassed. "Honestly. I don't feel anything. Except ashamed."

"Please. Are you sure? Tell me the truth. You might have been killed."

"But I wasn't. And thank you. For saving my life. You're wonderful. Unique. I love you."

"Damn fool." She kissed me on the cheek. Then there were four of her, and I fainted dead away.

That evening, photographs of Holly were frontpaged by the late edition of the *Journal-American* and by the early editions of both the *Daily News* and the *Daily Mirror*. The publicity had nothing to do with runaway horses. It concerned quite another matter, as the headlines revealed: PLAYGIRL ARRESTED IN NARCOTICS SCANDAL (*Journal-American*), ARREST DOPE-SMUGGLING ACTRESS (*Daily News*), DRUG RING EXPOSED, GLAMOUR GIRL HELD (*Daily Mirror*).

Of the lot, the *News* printed the most striking picture: Holly, entering police headquarters, wedged between two muscular detectives, one male, one female. In this squalid context even her clothes (she was still wearing her riding costume, windbreaker and blue jeans) suggested a gang-moll hooligan: an impression dark glasses, disarrayed coiffure and a Picayune cigarette dangling from sullen lips did not diminish. The caption read: *Twenty-year-old Holly Golightly, beautiful movie starlet and café society celebrity D.A. alleges to be key figure in international drug-smuggling racket linked to racketeer Salvatore "Sally" Tomato. Dets. Patrick Connor and Sheilah Fezzonetti (L. and R.) are shown escorting her into 67th St. Precinct. See story on Pg. 3.* The story, featuring a photograph of a man identified as Oliver "Father" O'Shaughnessy (shielding his face with a fedora), ran three full columns. Here, somewhat condensed, are the pertinent paragraphs: *Members of café society were stunned today by the arrest of gorgeous Holly Golightly, twenty-year-old Hollywood starlet and highly publicized girl-about-New York. At the same time, 2 P.M., police nabbed Oliver O'Shaughnessy, 52, of the Hotel Seabord, W. 49th St., as he exited from a Hamburg Heaven on Madison Ave. Both are alleged by District Attorney Frank L. Donovan to be important figures in an international drug ring dominated by the notorious Mafia-führer Salvatore "Sally" Tomato, currently in Sing Sing serving a five-year rap for political bribery. . . . O'Shaughnessy, a defrocked priest variously known in crimeland circles as "Father" and "The Padre," has a history of arrests dating back to 1934, when he served two years for operating a phony Rhode Island mental institution, The Monastery. Miss Golightly, who has no previous criminal record, was arrested in her luxurious apartment at a swank East Side address. . . . Although the D.A.'s office has issued no formal statement, responsible sources insist the blond and beautiful actress, not long ago the constant companion of multimillionaire Rutherfurd Trawler, has been acting as "liaison" between the imprisoned Tomato and his chief-lieutenant, O'Shaughnessy. . . . Posing as a relative of Tomato's, Miss Golightly is said to have paid weekly visits to Sing Sing, and on these occasions Tomato supplied her with verbally coded messages which she then transmitted to O'Shaughnessy. Via this link, Tomato, believed to have been born in Cefalu, Sicily, in 1874, was able to keep first-hand control of a world-wide narcotics syndicate with outposts in Mexico, Cuba, Sicily, Tangier, Tehran and Dakar. But the D.A.'s office refused to offer any detail on these allegations or even verify them. . . . Tipped off, a large number of reporters were on hand at the E. 67th St. Precinct station when the accused pair arrived for booking. O'Shaughnessy, a burly red-haired man, refused comment and kicked one cameraman in the groin. But Miss Golightly, a fragile eyeful, even though attired like a tomboy in slacks and leather jacket, appeared relatively unconcerned. "Don't ask me what the hell this is about," she told reporters. "Parce-que Je ne sais pas, mes chères. (Because I do not know, my dears).* Yes—I have visited Sally Tomato. I used to go to see him every week. What's wrong with that? He believes in God, and so do I." . . . Then, under the subheading ADMITS OWN DRUG ADDICTION: *Miss Golightly smiled when a reporter asked whether or not she herself is a narcotics user. "I've had a little go at marijuana. It's not half so destructive as brandy. Cheaper, too. Unfortunately, I prefer brandy. No, Mr. Tomato never mentioned drugs to me. It makes me furious, the way these wretched people keep persecuting him. He's a sensitive, a religious person. A darling old man."*

There is one especially gross error in this report: she was not arrested in her "luxurious apartment." It took place in my own bathroom. I was soaking away my horse-ride pains in a tub of scalding water laced with Epsom salts; Holly, an attentive nurse, was sitting on the edge of the tub waiting to rub me with Sloan's liniment and tuck me into bed. There was a knock at the front door. As the door was unlocked, Holly called Come in. In came Madame Sapphia Spanella, trailed by a pair of civilian-clothed detectives, one of them a lady with thick yellow braids roped round her head.

"*Here* she is: the wanted woman!" boomed Madame Spanella, invading the bathroom and leveling a finger, first at Holly's, then my nakedness. "Look. What a whore she is." The male detective seemed embarrassed: by Madame Spanella and by the situation; but a harsh enjoyment tensed the face of his companion—she plumped a hand on Holly's shoulder and, in a surprising baby-child voice, said: "Come along, sister. You're going places." Whereupon Holly coolly told her: "Get them cotton-pickin' hands off of me, you dreary, driveling old bull-dyke." Which rather enraged the lady: she slapped Holly damned hard. So hard, her head twisted on her neck, and the bottle of liniment, flung from her hand, smithereened on the tile floor—where I, scampering out of the tub to enrich the fray, stepped on it and all but severed both big toes. Nude and bleeding a path of bloody footprints, I followed the action as far as the hall. "Don't forget," Holly managed to instruct me as the detectives propelled her down the stairs, "please feed the cat."

Of course I believed Madame Spanella to blame: she'd several times called the authorities to complain about Holly. It didn't occur to me the affair could have dire dimensions until that evening when Joe Bell showed up flourishing the newspapers. He was too agitated to speak sensibly; he caroused the room hitting his fists together while I read the accounts.

Then he said: "You think it's so? She was mixed up in this lousy business?"

"Well, yes."

He popped a Tums in his mouth and, glaring at me, chewed it as though he were crunching my bones. "Boy, that's rotten. And you meant to be her friend. What a bastard!"

"Just a minute. I didn't say she was involved *knowingly*. She wasn't. But there, she did do it. Carry messages and whatnot—"

He said: "Take it pretty calm, don't you? Jesus, she could get ten years. More." He yanked the papers away from me. "You know her friends. These rich fellows. Come down to the bar, we'll start phoning. Our girl's going to need fancier shysters than I can afford."

I was too sore and shaky to dress myself; Joe Bell had to help. Back at his bar he propped me in the telephone booth with a triple martini and a brandy tumbler full of coins. But I couldn't think who to contact. José was in Washington, and I had no notion where to reach him there. Rusty Trawler? Not that bastard! Only: what other friends of hers did I know? Perhaps she'd been right when she'd said she had none, not really.

I put through a call to Crestview 5-6958 in Beverly Hills, the number long-distance information gave me for O.J. Berman. The person who answered said Mr. Berman was having a massage and couldn't be disturbed: sorry, try later. Joe Bell was incensed—told me I should have said it was a life and death matter; and he insisted on my trying Rusty. First, I spoke to Mr. Trawler's butler—Mr. and Mrs. Trawler, he announced, were at dinner and might he take a message? Joe Bell shouted into the receiver: "This is urgent, mister. Life and death." The outcome was that I found myself talking—listening, rather —to the former Mag Wildwood: "Are you starkers?" she demanded. "My husband and I will positively *sue* anyone who attempts to connect our names with that ro-ro-ro*vol*ting and de-de-de*gen*erate girl. I always *knew* she was a hop-hop-head with no more morals than a hound-bitch in heat. Prison is where she belongs. And my husband agrees one thousand percent. We will positively *sue* anyone who—" Hanging up, I remembered old Doc down in Tulip, Texas; but no, Holly wouldn't like it if I called him, she'd kill me good.

I rang California again; the circuits were busy, stayed busy, and by the time O.J. Berman was on the line I'd emptied so many martinis he had to tell me why I was phoning him: "About the kid, is it? I know already. I spoke already to Iggy Fitelstein. Iggy's the best shingle in New York. I said Iggy you take care of it, send me the bill, only keep my name anonymous, see. Well, I owe the kid something. Not that I owe her *any*thing, you want to come down to it. She's crazy. A phony. But a *real* phony, you know? Anyway, they only got her in ten thousand bail. Don't worry, Iggy'll spring her tonight—it wouldn't surprise me she's home already."

. . .

But she wasn't; nor had she returned the next morning when I went down to feed her cat. Having no key to the apartment, I used the fire escape and gained entrance through a window. The cat was in the bedroom, and he was not alone: a man was there, crouching over a suitcase. The two of us, each thinking the other a burglar, exchanged uncomfortable stares as I stepped through the window. He had a pretty face, lacquered hair, he resembled José; moreover, the suitcase he'd been packing contained the wardrobe José kept at Holly's, the shoes and suits she fussed over, was always carting to menders and cleaners. And I said, certain it was so: "Did Mr. Ybarra-Jaegar send you?"

"I am the cousin," he said with a wary grin and just-penetrable accent.

"Where is José?"

He repeated the question, as though translating it into another language. "Ah, *where* she is! She is waiting," he said and, seeming to dismiss me, resumed his valet activities.

So: the diplomat was planning a powder. Well, I wasn't amazed; or in the slightest sorry. Still, what a heartbreaking stunt: "He ought to be horse-whipped."

The cousin giggled, I'm sure he understood me. He shut the suitcase and produced a letter. "My cousin, she ask me leave that for his chum. You will oblige?"

On the envelope was scribbled: *For Miss H. Golightly—Courtesy Bearer.*

I sat down on Holly's bed, and hugged Holly's cat to me, and felt as badly for Holly, every iota, as she could feel for herself.

"Yes, I will oblige."

And I did: without the least wanting to. But I hadn't the courage to destroy the letter; or the will power to keep it in my pocket when Holly very tentatively inquired if, if by any chance, I'd had news of José. It was two mornings later; I was sitting by her bedside in a room that reeked of iodine and bedpans, a hospital room. She had been there since the night of her arrest. "Well, darling," she'd greeted me, as I tiptoed toward her carrying a carton of Picayune cigarettes and a wheel of new-autumn violets, "I lost the heir." She looked not quite twelve years: her pale vanilla hair brushed back, her eyes, for once minus their dark glasses, clear as rain water—one couldn't believe how ill she'd been.

Yet it was true: "Christ, I nearly cooled. No fooling, the fat woman almost had me. She was yakking up a storm. I guess I couldn't have told you about the fat woman. Since I didn't know about her myself until my brother died. Right away I was wondering where he'd gone, what it meant, Fred's dying; and then I saw her, she was there in the room with me, and she had Fred cradled in her arms, a fat mean red bitch rocking in a rocking chair with Fred on her lap and laughing like a brass band. The mockery of it! But it's all that's ahead for us, my friend: this comedienne waiting to give you the old razz. Now do you see why I went crazy and broke everything?"

Except for the lawyer O.J. Berman had hired, I was the only visitor she had been allowed. Her room was shared by other patients, a trio of triplet-like ladies who, examining me with an interest not unkind but total, speculated in whispered Italian. Holly explained that: "They think you're my downfall, darling. The fellow what done me wrong"; and, to a suggestion that she set them straight, replied: "I can't. They don't speak English. Anyway, I wouldn't dream of spoiling their fun." It was then that she asked about José.

The instant she saw the letter she squinted her eyes and bent her lips in a tough tiny smile that advanced her age immeasurably. "Darling," she instructed me, "would you reach in the drawer there and give me my purse. A girl doesn't read this sort of thing without her lipstick."

Guided by a compact mirror, she powdered, painted every vestige of twelve-year-old out of her face. She shaped her lips with one tube, colored her cheeks from another. She penciled the rims of her eyes, blued the lids, sprinkled her neck with 4711; attached pearls to her ears and donned her dark glasses; thus armored, and after a displeased appraisal of her manicure's shabby condition, she ripped open the letter and let her eyes race through it while her stony small smile grew smaller and harder. Eventually she asked for a Picayune. Took a puff: "Tastes bum. But divine," she said and, tossing me the letter: "Maybe this will come in handy—if you ever write a rat-romance. Don't be hoggy: read it aloud. I'd like to hear it myself."

It began: "My dearest little girl—"

Holly at once interrupted. She wanted to know what I thought of the handwriting. I thought nothing: a tight, highly legible, uneccentric script. "It's him to a T. Buttoned up and constipated," she declared. "Go on."

"My dearest little girl, I have loved you knowing you were not as others. But conceive of my despair upon discovering in such a brutal and public style how very different you are from the manner of woman a man of my faith and career could hope to make his wife. Verily I grief for the disgrace of your present circumstance, and do not find it in my heart to add my condemn to the condemn that surrounds you. So I hope you will find it in your heart not to condemn me. I have my family to protect, and my name, and I am a coward where those institutions enter. Forget me, beautiful child. I am no longer here. I am gone home. But may God always be with you and your child. May God be not the same as—José."

"Well?"

"In a way it seems quite honest. And even touching."

"*Touching?* That square-ball jazz!"

"But after all, he *says* he's a coward; and from his point of view, you must see—"

Holly, however, did not want to admit that she saw; yet her face, despite its cosmetic disguise, confessed it. "All right, he's not a rat without reason. A super-sized, King Kong-type rat like Rusty. Benny Shacklett. But oh gee, golly goddamn," she said, jamming a fist into her mouth like a bawling baby, "I *did* love him. The rat."

The Italian trio imagined a lover's *crise* and, placing the blame for Holly's groanings where they felt it belonged, tut-tutted their tongues at me. I was flattered: proud that anyone should think Holly cared for me. She quieted when I offered her another cigarette. She swallowed and said: "Bless you, Buster. And bless you for being such a bad jockey. If I hadn't had to play Calamity Jane I'd still be looking forward to the grub in an unwed mama's home. Strenuous exercise, that's what did the trick. But I've scared *la merde* out of the whole badge-department by saying it was because Miss Dykeroo slapped me. Yessir, I can sue them on several counts, including false arrest."

Until then, we'd skirted mention of her more sinister tribulations, and this jesting reference to them seemed appalling, pathetic, so definitely did it reveal how incapable she was of recognizing the bleak realities before her. "Now, Holly," I said, thinking: be strong, mature, an uncle. "Now, Holly. We can't treat it as a joke. We have to make plans."

"You're too young to be stuffy. Too small. By the way, what business is it of yours?"

"None. Except you're my friend, and I'm worried. I mean to know what you intend doing."

She rubbed her nose, and concentrated on the ceiling. "Today's Wednesday, isn't it? So I suppose I'll sleep until Saturday, really get a good *schluffen*. Saturday morning I'll skip out to the bank. Then I'll stop by the apartment and pick up a nightgown or two and my Mainbocher. Following which, I'll report to Idlewild. Where, as you damn well know, I have a perfectly fine reservation on a perfectly fine plane. And since you're such a friend I'll let you wave me off. *Please* stop shaking your head."

"Holly. Holly. You can't do that."

"*Et pourquoi pas?* I'm not hot-footing after José, if that's what you suppose. According to my census, he's strictly a citizen of Limboville. It's only: why should I waste a perfectly fine ticket? Already paid for? Besides, I've never been to Brazil."

"Just what kind of pills have they been feeding you here? Can't you realize, you're under a criminal indictment. If they catch you jumping bail, they'll throw away the key. Even if you get away with it, you'll never be able to come home."

"Well, so, tough titty. Anyway, home is where you feel at home. I'm still looking."

"No, Holly, it's stupid. You're innocent. You've got to stick it out."

She said, "Rah, team, rah," and blew smoke in my face. She was impressed, however; her eyes were dilated by unhappy visions, as were mine: iron rooms, steel corridors of gradually closing doors. "Oh, screw it," she said, and stabbed out her cigarette. "I have a fair chance they *won't* catch me. Provided *you* keep your *bouche fermez.* Look. Don't despise me, darling." She put her hand over mine and pressed it with sudden immense sincerity. "I haven't much choice. I talked it over with the lawyer: oh, I didn't tell *him* anything *re* Rio—he'd tip the badgers himself, rather than lose his fee, to say nothing of the nickels O.J. put up for bail. Bless O.J.'s heart; but once on the coast I helped him win more than ten thou in a single poker hand: we're square. No, here's the real shake: all the badgers want from me is a couple of free grabs and my services as a state's witness against Sally—nobody has any intention of prosecuting me, they haven't a ghost of a case. Well, I may be rotten to the core, Maude, *but:* testify against a friend I will not. Not if they can prove he doped Sister Kenny. My yardstick is how somebody treats me, and old Sally, all right he wasn't absolutely white with me, say he took a slight advantage, just the same Sally's an okay shooter, and I'd let the fat woman snatch me sooner than help the law-boys pin him down." Tilting her compact mirror above her face, smoothing her lipstick with a crooked pinkie, she said: "And to be honest, that isn't all. Certain shades of limelight wreck a girl's complexion. Even if a jury gave me the Purple Heart, this neighborhood holds no future: they'd still have up every rope from LaRue to Perona's Bar and Grill—take my word, I'd be about as welcome as Mr. Frank E. Campbell. And if you lived off my particular talents, Cookie, you'd understand the kind of bankruptcy I'm describing. Uh, uh, I don't just fancy a fade-out that finds me belly-bumping around Roseland with a pack of West Side hillbillies. While the excellent Madame Trawler sashayes her twat in and out of Tiffany's. I couldn't take it. Give me the fat woman any day."

A nurse, soft-shoeing into the room, advised that visiting hours were over. Holly started to complain, and was curtailed by having a thermometer popped in her mouth. But as I took leave, she unstoppered herself to say: "Do me a favor, darling. Call up the *Times,* or whatever you call, and get a list of the fifty richest men in Brazil. I'm *not* kidding. The fifty richest: regardless of race or color. Another favor—poke around my apartment till you find that medal you gave me. The St. Christopher. I'll need it for the trip."

The sky was red Friday night, it thundered, and Saturday, departing day, the city swayed in a squall-like downpour. Sharks might have swum through the air, though it seemed improbable a plane could penetrate it.

But Holly, ignoring my cheerful conviction that her flight would not go, continued her preparations—placing, I must say, the chief burden of them on me. For she had decided it would be unwise of her to come near the brownstone. Quite rightly, too: it was under surveillance, whether by police or reporters or other interested parties one couldn't tell—simply a man, sometimes men, who hung around the stoop. So she'd gone from the hospital to a bank and straight then to Joe Bell's bar. "She don't figure she was followed," Joe Bell told me when he came with a message that Holly wanted me to meet her there as soon as possible, a half-hour at most, bringing: "Her jewelry. Her guitar. Toothbrushes and stuff. And a bottle of hundred-year-old brandy: she says you'll find it hid down in the bottom of the dirty-clothes basket. Yeah, oh, and the cat. She wants the cat. But hell," he said, "I don't know we should help her at all. She ought to be protected against herself. Me, I feel like telling the cops. Maybe if I go back and build her some drinks, maybe I can get her drunk enough to call it off."

Stumbling, skidding up and down the fire escape between Holly's apartment and mine, wind-blown and winded and wet to the bone (clawed to the bone as well, for the cat had not looked favorably upon evacuation, especially in such inclement weather) I managed a fast, first-rate job of assembling her going-away belongings. I even found the St. Christopher's medal. Everything was piled on the floor of my room, a poignant pyramid of brassières and dancing slippers and pretty things I packed in Holly's only suitcase. There was a mass left over that I had to put in paper grocery bags. I couldn't think how to carry the cat; until I thought of stuffing him in a pillowcase.

Never mind why, but once I walked from New Orleans to Nancy's Landing, Mississippi, just under five hundred miles. It was a light-hearted lark compared to the journey to Joe Bell's bar. The guitar filled with rain, rain softened the paper sacks, the sacks split and perfume spilled on the pavement, pearls rolled in the gutter: while the wind pushed and the cat scratched, the cat screamed —but worse, I was frightened, a coward to equal José: those storming streets seemed aswarm with unseen presences waiting to trap, imprison me for aiding an outlaw.

The outlaw said: "You're late, Buster. Did you bring the brandy?"

And the cat, released, leaped and perched on her shoulder: his tail swung like a baton conducting rhapsodic music. Holly, too, seemed inhabited by melody, some bouncy *bon voyage* oompahpah. Uncorking the brandy, she said: "This was meant to be part of my hope chest. The idea was, every anniversary we'd have a swig. Thank Jesus I never bought the chest. Mr. Bell, sir, three glasses."

"You'll only need two," he told her. "I won't drink to your foolishness."

The more she cajoled him ("Ah, Mr. Bell. The lady doesn't vanish every day. Won't you toast her?"), the gruffer he was: "I'll have no part of it. If you're going to hell, you'll go on your own. With no further help from me." An inaccurate statement: because seconds after he'd made it a chauffeured limousine drew up outside the bar, and Holly, the first to notice it, put down her brandy, arched her eyebrows, as though she expected to see the District Attorney himself alight. So did I. And when I saw Joe Bell blush, I had to think: by God, he *did* call the police. But then, with burning ears, he announced: "It's nothing. One of them Carey Cadillacs. I hired it. To take you to the airport."

He turned his back on us to fiddle with one of his flower arrangements. Holly said: "Kind, dear Mr. Bell. Look at me, sir."

He wouldn't. He wrenched the flowers from the vase and thrust them at her; they missed their mark, scattered on the floor. "Good-bye," he said; and, as though he were going to vomit, scurried to the men's room. We heard the door lock.

The Carey chauffeur was a worldly specimen who accepted our slapdash luggage most civilly and remained rock-faced when, as the limousine swished uptown through a lessening rain, Holly stripped off her clothes, the riding costume she'd never had a chance to substitute, and struggled into a slim black dress. We didn't talk: talk could have only led to argument; and also, Holly seemed too preoccupied for conversation. She hummed to herself, swigged brandy, she leaned constantly forward to peer out the windows, as if she were hunting an address—or, I decided, taking a last impression of a scene she wanted to remember. It was neither of these. But this: "Stop here," she ordered the driver, and we pulled to the curb of a street in Spanish Harlem. A savage, a garish, a moody neighborhood garlanded with poster-portraits of movie stars and Madonnas. Sidewalk litterings of fruit-rind and rotted newspaper were hurled about by the wind, for the wind still boomed, though the rain had hushed and there were bursts of blue in the sky.

Holly stepped out of the car; she took the cat with her. Cradling him, she scratched his head and asked. "What do you think? This ought to be the right kind of place for a tough guy like you. Garbage cans. Rats galore. Plenty of cat-bums to gang around with. So scram," she said, dropping him; and when he did not move away, instead raised his thug-face and questioned her with yellowish pirate-eyes, she stamped her foot: "I said beat it!" He rubbed against her leg. "I said fuck off!" she shouted, then jumped back in the car, slammed the door, and: "Go," she told the driver. "Go. Go."

I was stunned. "Well, you *are*. You *are* a bitch."

We'd traveled a block before she replied. "I told you. We just met by the river one day: that's all. Independents, both of us. We never made each other any promises. We never—" she said, and her voice collapsed, a tic, an invalid whiteness seized her face. The car had paused for a traffic light. Then she had the door open, she was running down the street; and I ran after her.

But the cat was not at the corner where he'd been left. There was no one, nothing on the street except a urinating drunk and two Negro nuns herding a file of sweet-singing children. Other children emerged from doorways and ladies leaned over their window sills to watch as Holly darted up and down the block, ran back and forth chanting: "You. Cat. Where are you? Here, cat." She kept it up until a bumpy-skinned boy came forward dangling an old tom by the scruff of its neck: "You wants a nice kitty, miss? Gimme a dollar."

The limousine had followed us. Now Holly let me steer her toward it. At the door, she hesitated; she looked past me, past the boy still offering his cat ("Halfa dollar. Two-bits, maybe? Two-bits, it ain't much"), and she shuddered, she had to grip my arm to stand up: "Oh, Jesus God. We did belong to each other. He was mine."

Then I made her a promise, I said I'd come back and find her cat: "I'll take care of him, too. I promise."

She smiled: that cheerless new pinch of a smile. "But what about me?" she said, whispered, and shivered again. "I'm very scared, Buster. Yes, at last. Because it could go on forever. Not knowing what's yours until you've thrown it away. The mean reds, they're nothing. The fat woman, she nothing. This, though: my mouth's so dry, if my life depended on it I couldn't spit." She stepped in the car, sank in the seat. "Sorry, driver. Let's go."

TOMATO'S TOMATO MISSING. And: DRUG-CASE ACTRESS BE-LIEVED GANGLAND VICTIM. In due time, however, the press reported: FLEEING PLAYGIRL TRACED TO RIO. Apparently no attempt was made by American authorities to recover her, and soon the matter diminished to an occasional gossip-column mention; as a news story, it was revived only once: on Christmas Day, when Sally Tomato died of a heart attack at Sing Sing. Months went by, a winter of them, and not a word from Holly. The owner of the brownstone sold her abandoned possessions, the white-satin bed, the tapestry, her precious Gothic chair; a new tenant acquired the apartment, his name was Quaintance Smith, and he entertained as many gentlemen callers of a noisy nature as Holly ever had—though in this instance Madame Spanella did not object, indeed she doted on the young man and supplied filet mignon whenever he had a black eye. But in the spring a postcard came: it was scribbled in pencil, and signed with a lipstick kiss: *Brazil was beastly but Buenos Aires the best. Not Tiffany's, but almost. Am joined at the hip with duhvine $enor. Love? Think so. Anyhoo am looking for somewhere to live ($enor has wife, 7 brats) and will let you know address when I know it myself. Mille tendresse.* But the address, if it ever existed, never was sent, which made me sad, there was so much I wanted to write her: that I'd *sold* two stories, had read where the Trawlers were countersuing for divorce, was moving out of the brownstone because it was haunted. But mostly, I wanted to tell about her cat. I had kept my promise; I had found him. It took weeks of after-work roaming through those Spanish Harlem streets, and there were many false alarms—flashes of tiger-striped fur that, upon inspection, were not him. But one day, one cold sunshiny Sunday winter afternoon, it was. Flanked by potted plants and framed by clean lace curtains, he was seated in the window of a warm-looking room: I wondered what his name was, for I was certain he had one now, certain he'd arrived somewhere he belonged. African hut or whatever. I hope Holly has, too.

Music
for
Chameleons

For Tennessee Williams

Preface

My life—as an artist, at least—can be charted as precisely as a fever: the highs and lows, the very definite cycles.

I started writing when I was eight—out of the blue, uninspired by any example. I'd never known anyone who wrote; indeed, I knew few people who read. But the fact was, the only four things that interested me were: reading books, going to the movies, tap dancing, and drawing pictures. Then one day I started writing, not knowing that I had chained myself for life to a noble but merciless master. When God hands you a gift, he also hands you a whip; and the whip is intended solely for self-flagellation.

But of course I didn't know that. I wrote adventure stories, murder mysteries, comedy skits, tales that had been told me by former slaves and Civil War veterans. It was a lot of fun—at first. It stopped being fun when I discovered the difference between good writing and bad, and then made an even more alarming discovery: the difference between very good writing and true art; it is subtle, but savage. And after that, the whip came down!

As certain young people practice the piano or the violin four and five hours a day, so I played with my papers and pens. Yet I never discussed my writing with anyone; if someone asked what I was up to all those hours, I told them I was doing my school homework. Actually, I never did any homework. My literary tasks kept me fully occupied: my apprenticeship at the altar of technique, craft; the devilish intricacies of paragraphing, punctuation, dialogue placement. Not to mention the grand overall design, the great demanding arc of middle-beginning-end. One had to learn so much, and from so many sources: not only from books, but from music, from painting, and just plain everyday observation.

In fact, the most interesting writing I did during those days was the plain everyday observations that I recorded in my journal. Descriptions of a neighbor. Long verbatim accounts of overheard conversations. Local gossip. A kind of reporting, a style of "seeing" and "hearing" that would later seriously influence me, though I was unaware of it then, for all my "formal" writing, the stuff that I polished and carefully typed, was more or less fictional.

By the time I was seventeen, I was an accomplished writer. Had I been a pianist, it would have been the moment for my first public concert. As it was, I decided I was ready to publish. I sent off stories to the principal literary quarterlies, as well as to the national magazines, which in those days published the best so-called "quality" fiction—*Story, The New Yorker, Harper's Bazaar, Mademoiselle, Harper's, Atlantic Monthly*—and stories by me duly appeared in those publications.

Then, in 1948, I published a novel: *Other Voices, Other Rooms.* It was well received critically, and was a best seller. It was also, due to an exotic photograph of the author on the dust jacket, the start of a certain notoriety that has kept close step with me these many years. Indeed, many people attributed the commercial success of the novel to the photograph. Others dismissed the book as though it were a freakish accident: "Amazing that anyone so young can write that well." Amazing? I'd only been writing day in and day out for fourteen years! Still, the novel was a satisfying conclusion to the first cycle in my development.

A short novel, *Breakfast at Tiffany's,* ended the second cycle in 1958. During the intervening ten years I experimented with almost every aspect of writing, attempting to conquer a variety of techniques, to achieve a technical virtuosity as strong and flexible as a fisherman's net. Of course, I failed in several of the areas I invaded, but it is true that one learns more from a failure than one does from a success. I know I did, and later I was able to apply what I had learned to great advantage. Anyway, during that decade of exploration I wrote short-story collections *(A Tree of Night, A Christmas Memory),* essays and portraits *(Local Color, Observations,* the work contained in *The Dogs Bark),* plays *(The Grass Harp, House of Flowers),* film scripts *(Beat the Devil, The Innocents),* and a great deal of factual reportage, most of it for *The New Yorker.*

In fact, from the point of view of my creative destiny, the most interesting writing I did during the whole of this second phase first appeared in *The New Yorker* as a series of articles and subsequently as a book entitled *The Muses Are Heard.* It concerned the first cultural exchange between the U.S.S.R. and the U.S.A.: a tour, undertaken in 1955, of Russia by a company of black Americans in *Porgy and Bess.* I conceived of the whole adventure as a short comic "nonfiction novel," the first.

Some years earlier, Lillian Ross had published *Picture,* her account of the making of a movie, *The Red Badge of Courage*; with its fast cuts, its flash forward and back, it was itself like a movie, and as I read it I wondered what would happen if the author let go of her hard linear straight-reporting discipline and handled her material as if it were fictional—would the book gain or lose? I decided, if the right subject came along, I'd like to give it a try: *Porgy and Bess* and Russia in the depths of winter seemed the right subject.

The Muses Are Heard received excellent reviews; even sources usually unfriendly to me were moved to praise it. Still, it did not attract any special notice, and the sales were moderate. Nevertheless, that book was an important event for me: while writing it, I realized I just might have found a solution to what had always been my greatest creative quandary.

For several years I had been increasingly drawn toward journalism as an art form in itself. I had two reasons. First, it didn't seem to me that anything truly innovative had occurred in prose writing, or in writing generally, since the 1920s; second, journalism as art was almost virgin terrain, for the simple reason that very few literary artists ever wrote narrative journalism, and when they did, it took the form of travel essays or autobiography. *The Muses Are Heard* had set me to thinking on different lines altogether: I wanted to produce a journalistic novel, something on a large scale that would have the credibility of fact, the immediacy of film, the depth and freedom of prose, and the precision of poetry.

It was not until 1959 that some mysterious instinct directed me toward the subject—an obscure murder case in an isolated part of Kansas—and it was not until 1966 that I was able to publish the result, *In Cold Blood*.

In a story by Henry James, I think *The Middle Years,* his character, a writer in the shadows of maturity, laments: "We live in the dark, we do what we can, the rest is the madness of art." Or words to that effect. Anyway, Mr. James is laying it on the line there; he's telling us the truth. And the darkest part of the dark, the maddest part of the madness, is the relentless gambling involved. Writers, at least those who take genuine risks, who are willing to bite the bullet and walk the plank, have a lot in common with another breed of lonely men —the guys who make a living shooting pool and dealing cards. Many people thought I was crazy to spend six years wandering around the plains of Kansas; others rejected my whole concept of the "nonfiction novel" and pronounced it unworthy of a "serious" writer; Norman Mailer described it as a "failure of imagination"—meaning, I assume, that a novelist should be writing about something imaginary rather than about something real.

Yes, it was like playing high-stakes poker; for six nerve-shattering years I didn't know whether I had a book or not. Those were long summers and freezing winters, but I just kept on dealing the cards, playing my hand as best I could. Then it turned out I *did* have a book. Several critics complained that "nonfiction novel" was a catch phrase, a hoax, and that there was nothing really original or new about what I had done. But there were those who felt differently, other writers who realized the value of my experiment and moved swiftly to put it to their own use—none more swiftly than Norman Mailer, who has made a lot of money and won a lot of prizes writing nonfiction novels *(The Armies of the Night, Of a Fire on the Moon, The Executioner's Song),* although he has always been careful never to describe them as "nonfiction novels." No matter; he is a good writer and a fine fellow and I'm grateful to have been of some small service to him.

The zigzag line charting my reputation as a writer had reached a healthy height, and I let it rest there before moving into my fourth, and what I expect will be my final, cycle. For four years, roughly from 1968 through 1972, I spent most of my time reading and selecting, rewriting and indexing my own letters, other people's letters, my diaries and journals (which contain detailed accounts of hundreds of scenes and conversations) for the years 1943 through 1965. I intended to use much of this material in a book I had long been planning: a variation on the nonfiction novel. I called the book *Answered Prayers,* which is a quote from Saint Thérèse, who said: "More tears are shed over answered prayers than unanswered ones." In 1972 I began work on this book by writing the last chapter first (it's always good to know where one's going). Then I wrote the first chapter, "Unspoiled Monsters." Then the fifth, "A Severe Insult to the Brain." Then the seventh, "La Côte Basque." I went on in this manner, writing different chapters out of sequence. I was able to do this only because the plot—or rather plots—was true, and all the characters were real: it wasn't difficult to keep it all in mind, for I hadn't invented anything. And yet *Answered Prayers* is not intended as any ordinary roman à clef, a form where facts are disguised as fiction. My intentions are the reverse: to remove disguises, not manufacture them.

In 1975 and 1976 I published four chapters of the book in *Esquire* magazine. This aroused anger in certain circles, where it was felt I was betraying confidences, mistreating friends and/or foes. I don't intend to discuss this; the issue involves social politics, not artistic merit. I will say only that all a writer has to work with is the material he has gathered as the result of his own endeavor and observations, and he cannot be denied the right to use it. Condemn, but not deny.

However, I did stop working on *Answered Prayers* in September 1977, a fact that had nothing to do with any public reaction to those parts of the book already published. The halt happened because I was in a helluva lot of trouble: I was suffering a creative crisis and a personal one at the same time. As the latter was unrelated, or very little related, to the former, it is only necessary to remark on the creative chaos.

Now, torment though it was, I'm glad it happened; after all, it altered my entire comprehension of writing, my attitude toward art and life and the balance between the two, and my understanding of the difference between what is true and what is *really* true.

To begin with, I think most writers, even the best, overwrite. I prefer to underwrite. Simple, clear as a country creek. But I felt my writing was becoming too dense, that I was taking three pages to arrive at effects I ought to be able to achieve in a single paragraph. Again and again I read all that I had written of *Answered Prayers,* and I began to have doubts—not about the material or my approach, but about the texture of the writing itself. I reread *In Cold Blood* and had the same reaction: there were too many areas where I was not writing as well as I could, where I was not delivering the total potential. Slowly, but with accelerating alarm, I read every word I'd ever published, and decided that never, not once in my writing life, had I completely exploded all the energy and esthetic excitements that material contained. Even when it was good, I could see that I was never working with more than half, sometimes only a third, of the powers at my command. Why?

The answer, revealed to me after months of meditation, was simple but not very satisfying. Certainly it did nothing to lessen my depression; indeed, it thickened it. For the answer created an apparently unsolvable problem, and if I couldn't solve it, I might as well quit writing. The problem was: how can a writer successfully combine within a single form—say the short story—all he knows about every other form of writing? For this was why my work was often insufficiently illuminated; the voltage was there, but by restricting myself to the techniques of whatever form I was working in, I was not using everything I knew about writing—all I'd learned from film scripts, plays, reportage, poetry, the short story, novellas, the novel. A writer ought to have all his colors, all his abilities available on the same palette for mingling (and, in suitable instances, simultaneous application). But how?

I returned to *Answered Prayers.* I removed one chapter and rewrote two others. An improvement, definitely an improvement. But the truth was, I had to go back to kindergarten. Here I was—off again on one of those grim gambles! But I was excited; I felt an invisible sun shining on me. Still, my first experiments were awkward. I truly felt like a child with a box of crayons.

From a technical point, the greatest difficulty I'd had in writing *In Cold Blood* was leaving myself completely out of it. Ordinarily, the reporter has to use himself as a character, an eyewitness observer, in order to retain credibility. But I felt that it was essential to the seemingly detached tone of that book that the author should be absent. Actually, in all my reportage, I had tried to keep myself as invisible as possible.

Now, however, I set myself center stage, and reconstructed, in a severe, minimal manner, commonplace conversations with everyday people: the superintendent of my building, a masseur at the gym, an old school friend, my dentist. After writing hundreds of pages of this simple-minded sort of thing, I eventually developed a style. I had found a framework into which I could assimilate everything I knew about writing.

Later, using a modified version of this technique, I wrote a nonfiction short novel *(Handcarved Coffins)* and a number of short stories. The result is the present volume: *Music for Chameleons.*

And how has all this affected my other work-in-progress, *Answered Prayers*? Very considerably. Meanwhile, I'm here alone in my dark madness, all by myself with my deck of cards—and, of course, the whip God gave me.

I
Music for
Chameleons

1
Music for Chameleons

She is tall and slender, perhaps seventy, silver-haired, soigné, neither black nor white, a pale golden rum color. She is a Martinique aristocrat who lives in Fort de France but also has an apartment in Paris. We are sitting on the terrace of her house, an airy, elegant house that looks as if it was made of wooden lace: it reminds me of certain old New Orleans houses. We are drinking iced mint tea slightly flavored with absinthe.

Three green chameleons race one another across the terrace; one pauses at Madame's feet, flicking its forked tongue, and she comments: "Chameleons. Such exceptional creatures. The way they change color. Red. Yellow. Lime. Pink. Lavender. And did you know they are very fond of music?" She regards me with her fine black eyes. "You don't believe me?"

During the course of the afternoon she had told me many curious things. How at night her garden was filled with mammoth night-flying moths. That her chauffeur, a dignified figure who had driven me to her house in a dark green Mercedes, was a wife-poisoner who had escaped from Devil's Island. And she had described a village high in the northern mountains that is entirely inhabited by albinos: "Little pink-eyed people white as chalk. Occasionally one sees a few on the streets of Fort de France."

"Yes, of course I believe you."

She tilts her silver head. "No, you don't. But I shall prove it."

So saying, she drifts into her cool Caribbean salon, a shadowy room with gradually turning ceiling fans, and poses herself at a well-tuned piano. I am still sitting on the terrace, but I can observe her, this chic, elderly woman, the product of varied bloods. She begins to perform a Mozart sonata.

Eventually the chameleons accumulated: a dozen, a dozen more, most of them green, some scarlet, lavender. They skittered across the terrace and scampered into the salon, a sensitive, absorbed audience for the music played. And then not played, for suddenly my hostess stood and stamped her foot, and the chameleons scattered like sparks from an exploding star.

Now she regards me. *"Et maintenant? C'est vrai?"*

"Indeed. But it seems so strange."

She smiles. *"Alors.* The whole island floats in strangeness. This very house is haunted. Many ghosts dwell here. And not in darkness. Some appear in the bright light of noon, saucy as you please. Impertinent."

"That's common in Haiti, too. The ghosts there often stroll about in daylight. I once saw a horde of ghosts working in a field near Petionville. They were picking bugs off coffee plants."

She accepts this as fact, and continues: *"Oui. Oui.* The Haitians work their dead. They are well known for that. Ours we leave to their sorrows. And their frolics. So coarse, the Haitians. So Creole. And one can't bathe there, the sharks are so intimidating. And their mosquitoes: the size, the audacity! Here in Martinique we have no mosquitoes. None."

"I've noticed that; I wondered about it."

"So do we. Martinique is the only island in the Caribbean not cursed with mosquitoes, and no one can explain it."

"Perhaps the night-flying moths devour them all."

She laughs. "Or the ghosts."

"No. I think ghosts would prefer moths."

"Yes, moths are perhaps more ghostly fodder. If I was a hungry ghost, I'd rather eat anything than mosquitoes. Will you have more ice in your glass? Absinthe?"

"Absinthe. That's something we can't get at home. Not even in New Orleans."

"My paternal grandmother was from New Orleans."

"Mine, too."

As she pours absinthe from a dazzling emerald decanter: "Then perhaps we are related. Her maiden name was Dufont. Alouette Dufont."

"Alouette? Really? Very pretty. I'm aware of two Dufont families in New Orleans, but I'm not related to either of them."

"Pity. It would have been amusing to call you cousin. *Alors.* Claudine Paulot tells me this is your first visit to Martinique."

"Claudine Paulot?"

"Claudine and Jacques Paulot. You met them at the Governor's dinner the other night."

I remember: he was a tall, handsome man, the First President of the Court of Appeals for Martinique and French Guiana, which includes Devil's Island.

"The Paulots. Yes. They have eight children. He very much favors capital punishment."

"Since you seem to be a traveler, why have you not visited here sooner?"

"Martinique? Well, I felt a certain reluctance. A good friend was murdered here."

Madame's lovely eyes are a fraction less friendly than before. She makes a slow pronouncement: "Murder is a rare occurrence here. We are not a violent people. Serious, but not violent."

"Serious. Yes. The people in restaurants, on the streets, even on the beaches have such severe expressions. They seem so preoccupied. Like Russians."

"One must keep in mind that slavery did not end here until 1848."

I fail to make the connection, but do not inquire, for already she is saying: "Moreover, Martinique is *très cher*. A bar of soap bought in Paris for five francs costs twice that here. The price of everything is double what it should be because everything has to be imported. If these troublemakers got their way, and Martinique became independent of France, then that would be the close of it. Martinique could not exist without subsidy from France. We would simply perish. *Alors,* some of us have serious expressions. Generally speaking, though, do you find the population attractive?"

"The women. I've seen some amazingly beautiful women. Supple, suave, such beautifully haughty postures; bone structure as fine as cats. Also, they have a certain alluring aggressiveness."

"That's the Senegalese blood. We have much Senegalese here. But the men —you do not find them so appealing?"

"No."

"I agree. The men are not appealing. Compared to our women, they seem irrelevant, without character: *vin ordinaire*. Martinique, you understand, is a matriarchal society. When that is the case, as it is in India, for example, then the men never amount to much. I see you are looking at my black mirror."

I am. My eyes distractedly consult it—are drawn to it against my will, as they sometimes are by the senseless flickerings of an unregulated television set. It has that kind of frivolous power. Therefore, I shall overly describe it—in the manner of those "avant-garde" French novelists who, having chosen to discard narrative, character, and structure, restrict themselves to page-length paragraphs detailing the contours of a single object, the mechanics of an isolated movement: a wall, a white wall with a fly meandering across it. So: the object in Madame's drawing room is a black mirror. It is seven inches tall and six inches wide. It is framed within a worn black leather case that is shaped like a book. Indeed, the case is lying open on a table, just as though it were a deluxe edition meant to be picked up and browsed through; but there is nothing there to be read or seen—except the mystery of one's own image projected by the black mirror's surface before it recedes into its endless depths, its corridors of darkness.

"It belonged," she is explaining, "to Gauguin. You know, of course, that he lived and painted here before he settled among the Polynesians. That was his black mirror. They were a quite common artifact among artists of the last century. Van Gogh used one. As did Renoir."

"I don't quite understand. What did they use them for?"

"To refresh their vision. Renew their reaction to color, the tonal variations. After a spell of work, their eyes fatigued, they rested themselves by gazing into these dark mirrors. Just as gourmets at a banquet, between elaborate courses, reawaken their palates with a *sorbet de citron.*" She lifts the small volume containing the mirror off the table and passes it to me. "I often use it when my eyes have been stricken by too much sun. It's soothing."

Soothing, and also disquieting. The blackness, the longer one gazes into it, ceases to be black, but becomes a queer silver-blue, the threshold to secret visions; like Alice, I feel on the edge of a voyage through a looking-glass, one I'm hesitant to take.

From a distance I hear her voice—smoky, serene, cultivated: "And so you had a friend who was murdered here?"

"Yes."

"An American?"

"Yes. He was a very gifted man. A musician. A composer."

"Oh, I remember—the man who wrote operas! Jewish. He had a mustache."

"His name was Marc Blitzstein."

"But that was long ago. At least fifteen years. Or more. I understand you are staying at the new hotel. La Bataille. How do you find it?"

"Very pleasant. In a bit of a turmoil because they are in the process of opening a casino. The man in charge of the casino is called Shelley Keats. I thought it was a joke at first, but that really happens to be his name."

"Marcel Proust works at Le Foulard, that fine little seafood restaurant in Schoelcher, the fishing village. Marcel is a waiter. Have you been disappointed in our restaurants?"

"Yes and no. They're better than anywhere else in the Caribbean, but too expensive."

"*Alors.* As I remarked, everything is imported. We don't even grow our own vegetables. The natives are too lackadaisical." A hummingbird penetrates the terrace and casually balances on the air. "But our sea-fare is exceptional."

"Yes and no. I've never seen such enormous lobsters. Absolute whales; prehistoric creatures. I ordered one, but it was tasteless as chalk, and so tough to chew that I lost a filling. Like California fruit: splendid to look at, but without flavor."

She smiles, not happily: "Well, I apologize"—and I regret my criticism, and realize I'm not being very gracious.

"I had lunch at your hotel last week. On the terrace overlooking the pool. I was shocked."

"How so?"

"By the bathers. The foreign ladies gathered around the pool wearing nothing above and very little below. Do they permit that in your country? Virtually naked women parading themselves?"

"Not in so public a place as a hotel pool."

"Exactly. And I don't think it should be condoned here. But of course we can't afford to annoy the tourists. Have you bothered with any of our tourist attractions?"

"We went yesterday to see the house where Empress Josephine was born."

"I never advise anyone to visit there. That old man, the curator, what a chatterbox! And I can't say which is worse—his French or his English or his German. Such a bore. As though the journey getting there weren't tiring enough."

Our hummingbird departs. Far off we hear steel-drum bands, tambourines, drunken choirs (*"Ce soir, ce soir nous danserons sans chemise, sans pantalons"*: Tonight, tonight we dance without shirts, without pants), sounds reminding us that it is Carnival week in Martinique.

"Usually," she announces, "I leave the island during Carnival. It's impossible. The racket, the stench."

When planning for this Martinique experience, which included traveling with three companions, I had not known our visit would coincide with Carnival; as a New Orleans native, I've had my fill of such affairs. However, the Martinique variation proved surprisingly vital, spontaneous and vivid as a bomb explosion in a fireworks factory. "We're enjoying it, my friends and I. Last night there was one marvelous marching group: fifty men carrying black umbrellas and wearing silk tophats and with their torsos painted with phosphorescent skeleton bones. I love the old ladies with gold-tinsel wigs and sequins pasted all over their faces. And all those men wearing their wives' white wedding gowns! And the millions of children holding candles, glowing like fireflies. Actually, we did have one near-disaster. We borrowed a car from the hotel, and just as we arrived in Fort de France, and were creeping through the midst of the crowds, one of our tires blew out, and immediately we were surrounded by red devils with pitchforks—"

Madame is amused: *"Oui. Oui.* The little boys who dress as red devils. That goes back centuries."

"Yes, but they were dancing all over the car. Doing terrific damage. The roof was a positive samba floor. But we couldn't abandon it, for fear they'd wreck it altogether. So the calmest of my friends, Bob MacBride, volunteered to change the tire then and there. The problem was that he had on a new white linen suit and didn't want to ruin it."

"Therefore, he disrobed. Very sensible."

"At least it was funny. To watch MacBride, who's quite a solemn sort of fellow, stripped to his briefs and trying to change a tire with Mardi Gras madness swirling around him and red devils jabbing at him with pitchforks. Paper pitchforks, luckily."

"But Mr. MacBride succeeded."

"If he hadn't, I doubt that I'd be here abusing your hospitality."

"Nothing would have happened. We are not a violent people."

"Please. I'm not suggesting we were in any danger. It was just—well, part of the fun."

"Absinthe? *Un peu?*"

"A mite. Thank you."

The hummingbird returns.

"Your friend, the composer?"

"Marc Blitzstein."

"I've been thinking. He came here once to dinner. Madame Derain brought him. And Lord Snowdon was here that evening. With his uncle, the Englishman who built all those houses on Mustique—"

"Oliver Messel."

"*Oui. Oui.* It was while my husband was still alive. My husband had a fine ear for music. He asked your friend to play the piano. He played some German songs." She is standing now, moving to and fro, and I am aware of how exquisite her figure is, how ethereal it seems silhouetted inside a frail green lace Parisian dress. "I remember that, yet I can't recall how he died. Who killed him?"

All the while the black mirror has been lying in my lap, and once more my eyes seek its depths. Strange where our passions carry us, floggingly pursue us, forcing upon us unwanted dreams, unwelcome destinies.

"Two sailors."

"From here? Martinique?"

"No. Two Portuguese sailors off a ship that was in harbor. He met them in a bar. He was here working on an opera, and he'd rented a house. He took them home with him—"

"I *do* remember. They robbed him and beat him to death. It was dreadful. An appalling tragedy."

"A tragic accident." The black mirror mocks me: Why did you say that? It wasn't an accident.

"But our police caught those sailors. They were tried and sentenced and sent to prison in Guiana. I wonder if they are still there. I might ask Paulot. He would know. After all, he is the First President of the Court of Appeals."

"It really doesn't matter."

"Not matter! Those wretches ought to have been guillotined."

"No. But I wouldn't mind seeing them at work in the fields in Haiti, picking bugs off coffee plants."

Raising my eyes from the mirror's demonic shine, I notice my hostess has momentarily retreated from the terrace into her shadowy salon. A piano chord echoes, and another. Madame is toying with the same tune. Soon the music lovers assemble, chameleons scarlet, green, lavender, an audience that, lined out on the floor of the terra-cotta terrace, resembles a written arrangement of musical notes. A Mozartean mosaic.

2

Mr. Jones

During the winter of 1945 I lived for several months in a rooming house in Brooklyn. It was not a shabby place, but a pleasantly furnished, elderly brownstone kept hospital-neat by its owners, two maiden sisters.

Mr. Jones lived in the room next to mine. My room was the smallest in the house, his the largest, a nice big sunshiny room, which was just as well, for Mr. Jones never left it: all his needs, meals, shopping, laundry, were attended to by the middle-aged landladies. Also, he was not without visitors; on the average, a half-dozen various persons, men and women, young, old, in-between, visited his room each day, from early morning until late in the evening. He was not a drug dealer or a fortuneteller; no, they came just to talk to him and apparently they made him small gifts of money for his conversation and advice. If not, he had no obvious means of support.

I never had a conversation with Mr. Jones myself, a circumstance I've often since regretted. He was a handsome man, about forty. Slender, black-haired, and with a distinctive face; a pale, lean face, high cheekbones, and with a birthmark on his left cheek, a small scarlet defect shaped like a star. He wore gold-rimmed glasses with pitch-black lenses: he was blind, and crippled, too —according to the sisters, the use of his legs had been denied him by a childhood accident, and he could not move without crutches. He was always dressed in a crisply pressed dark grey or blue three-piece suit and a subdued tie—as though about to set off for a Wall Street office.

However, as I've said, he never left the premises. Simply sat in his cheerful room in a comfortable chair and received visitors. I had no notion of why they came to see him, these rather ordinary-looking folk, or what they talked about, and I was far too concerned with my own affairs to much wonder over it. When I did, I imagined that his friends had found in him an intelligent, kindly man, a good listener in whom to confide and consult with over their troubles: a cross between a priest and a therapist.

Mr. Jones had a telephone. He was the only tenant with a private line. It rang constantly, often after midnight and as early as six in the morning.

I moved to Manhattan. Several months later I returned to the house to collect a box of books I had stored there. While the landladies offered me tea and cakes in their lace-curtained "parlor," I inquired of Mr. Jones.

The women lowered their eyes. Clearing her throat, one said: "It's in the hands of the police."

The other offered: "We've reported him as a missing person."

The first added: "Last month, twenty-six days ago, my sister carried up Mr. Jones's breakfast, as usual. He wasn't there. All his belongings were there. But he was gone."

"It's odd—"

"—how a man totally blind, a helpless cripple—"

Ten years pass.

Now it is a zero-cold December afternoon, and I am in Moscow. I am riding in a subway car. There are only a few other passengers. One of them is a man sitting opposite me, a man wearing boots, a thick long coat and a Russian-style fur cap. He has bright eyes, blue as a peacock's.

After a doubtful instant, I simply stared, for even without the black glasses, there was no mistaking that lean distinctive face, those high cheekbones with the single scarlet star-shaped birthmark.

I was just about to cross the aisle and speak to him when the train pulled into a station, and Mr. Jones, on a pair of fine sturdy legs, stood up and strode out of the car. Swiftly, the train door closed behind him.

3
A Lamp
in a
Window

Once I was invited to a wedding; the bride suggested I drive up from New York with a pair of other guests, a Mr. and Mrs. Roberts, whom I had never met before. It was a cold April day, and on the ride to Connecticut the Robertses, a couple in their early forties, seemed agreeable enough—no one you would want to spend a long weekend with, but not bad.

However, at the wedding reception a great deal of liquor was consumed, I should say a third of it by my chauffeurs. They were the last to leave the party —at approximately II P.M.—and I was most wary of accompanying them; I knew they were drunk, but I didn't realize *how* drunk. We had driven about twenty miles, the car weaving considerably, and Mr. and Mrs. Roberts insulting each other in the most extraordinary language (really, it was a moment out of *Who's Afraid of Virginia Woolf?*), when Mr. Roberts, very understandably, made a wrong turn and got lost on a dark country road. I kept asking them, finally begging them, to stop the car and let me out, but they were so involved in their invectives that they ignored me. Eventually the car stopped of its own accord (temporarily) when it swiped against the side of a tree. I used the opportunity to jump out the car's back door and run into the woods. Presently the cursed vehicle drove off, leaving me alone in the icy dark. I'm sure my hosts never missed me; Lord knows I didn't miss them.

But it wasn't a joy to be stranded out there on a windy cold night. I started walking, hoping I'd reach a highway. I walked for half an hour without sighting a habitation. Then, just off the road, I saw a small frame cottage with a porch and a window lighted by a lamp. I tiptoed onto the porch and looked in the window; an elderly woman with soft white hair and a round pleasant face was sitting by a fireside reading a book. There was a cat curled in her lap, and several others slumbering at her feet.

I knocked at the door, and when she opened it I said, with chattering teeth: "I'm sorry to disturb you, but I've had a sort of accident; I wonder if I could use your phone to call a taxi."

"Oh, dear," she said, smiling. "I'm afraid I don't have a phone. Too poor. But please, come in." And as I stepped through the door into the cozy room, she said: "My goodness, boy. You're freezing. Can I make coffee? A cup of tea? I have a little whiskey my husband left—he died six years ago."

I said a little whiskey would be very welcome.

While she fetched it I warmed my hands at the fire and glanced around the room. It was a cheerful place occupied by six or seven cats of varying alley-cat colors. I looked at the title of the book Mrs. Kelly—for that was her name, as I later learned—had been reading: it was *Emma* by Jane Austen, a favorite writer of mine.

When Mrs. Kelly returned with a glass of ice and a dusty quarter-bottle of bourbon, she said: "Sit down, sit down. It's not often I have company. Of course, I have my cats. Anyway, you'll spend the night? I have a nice little guest room that's been waiting such a long time for a guest. In the morning you can walk to the highway and catch a ride into town, where you'll find a garage to fix your car. It's about five miles away."

I wondered aloud how she could live so isolatedly, without transportation or a telephone; she told me her good friend, the mailman, took care of all her shopping needs. "Albert. He's really so dear and faithful. But he's due to retire next year. After that I don't know what I'll do. But something will turn up. Perhaps a kindly new mailman. Tell me, just what sort of accident did you have?"

When I explained the truth of the matter, she responded indignantly: "You did exactly the right thing. I wouldn't set foot in a car with a man who had sniffed a glass of sherry. That's how I lost my husband. Married forty years, forty happy years, and I lost him because a drunken driver ran him down. If it wasn't for my cats . . ." She stroked an orange tabby purring in her lap.

We talked by the fire until my eyes grew heavy. We talked about Jane Austen ("Ah, Jane. My tragedy is that I've read all her books so often I have them memorized"), and other admired authors: Thoreau, Willa Cather, Dickens, Lewis Carroll, Agatha Christie, Raymond Chandler, Hawthorne, Chekhov, De Maupassant—she was a woman with a good and varied mind; intelligence illuminated her hazel eyes like the small lamp shining on the table beside her. We talked about the hard Connecticut winters, politicians, far places ("I've never been abroad, but if ever I'd had the chance, the place I would have gone is Africa. Sometimes I've dreamed of it, the green hills, the heat, the beautiful giraffes, the elephants walking about"), religion ("Of course,

I was raised a Catholic, but now, I'm almost sorry to say, I have an open mind. Too much reading, perhaps"), gardening ("I grow and can all my own vegetables; a necessity"). At last: "Forgive my babbling on. You have no idea how much pleasure it gives me. But it's way past your bedtime. I know it is mine."

She escorted me upstairs, and after I was comfortably arranged in a double bed under a blissful load of pretty scrapquilts, she returned to wish me goodnight, sweet dreams. I lay awake thinking about it. What an exceptional experience—to be an old woman living alone here in the wilderness and have a stranger knock on your door in the middle of the night and not only open it but warmly welcome him inside and offer him shelter. If our situations had been reversed, I doubt that I would have had the courage, to say nothing of the generosity.

The next morning she gave me breakfast in her kitchen. Coffee and hot oatmeal with sugar and tinned cream, but I was hungry and it tasted great. The kitchen was shabbier than the rest of the house; the stove, a rattling refrigerator, everything seemed on the edge of expiring. All except one large, somewhat modern object, a deep-freeze that fitted into a corner of the room.

She was chatting on: "I love birds. I feel so guilty about not tossing them crumbs during the winter. But I can't have them gathering around the house. Because of the cats. Do you care for cats?"

"Yes, I once had a Siamese named Toma. She lived to be twelve, and we traveled everywhere together. All over the world. And when she died I never had the heart to get another."

"Then maybe you will understand this," she said, leading me over to the deep-freeze, and opening it. Inside was nothing but cats: stacks of frozen, perfectly preserved cats—dozens of them. It gave me an odd sensation. "All my old friends. Gone to rest. It's just that I couldn't bear to lose them. *Completely.*" She laughed, and said: "I guess you think I'm a bit dotty."

A bit dotty. Yes, a bit dotty, I thought as I walked under grey skies in the direction of the highway she had pointed out to me. But radiant: a lamp in a window.

4
Mojave

At 5 P.M. that winter afternoon she had an appointment with Dr. Bentsen, formerly her psychoanalyst and currently her lover. When their relationship had changed from the analytical to the emotional, he insisted, on ethical grounds, that she cease to be his patient. Not that it mattered. He had not been of much help as an analyst, and as a lover—well, once she had watched him running to catch a bus, two hundred and twenty pounds of shortish, fiftyish, frizzly-haired, hip-heavy, myopic Manhattan Intellectual, and she had laughed: how was it possible that she could love a man so ill-humored, so ill-favored as Ezra Bentsen? The answer was she didn't; in fact, she disliked him. But at least she didn't associate him with resignation and despair. She feared her husband; she was not afraid of Dr. Bentsen. Still, it was her husband she loved.

She was rich; at any rate, had a substantial allowance from her husband, who was rich, and so could afford the studio-apartment hideaway where she met her lover perhaps once a week, sometimes twice, never more. She could also afford gifts he seemed to expect on these occasions. Not that he appreciated their quality: Verdura cuff links, classic Paul Flato cigarette cases, the obligatory Cartier watch, and (more to the point) occasional specific amounts of cash he asked to "borrow."

He had never given *her* a single present. Well, one: a mother-of-pearl Spanish dress comb that he claimed was an heirloom, a mother-treasure. Of course, it was nothing she could wear, for she wore her own hair, fluffy and tobacco-colored, like a childish aureole around her deceptively naïve and youthful face. Thanks to dieting, private exercises with Joseph Pilatos, and the dermatological attentions of Dr. Orentreich, she looked in her early twenties; she was thirty-six.

The Spanish comb. Her hair. That reminded her of Jaime Sanchez and something that had happened yesterday. Jaime Sanchez was her hairdresser, and though they had known each other scarcely a year, they were, in their own way, good friends. She confided in him somewhat; he confided in her considerably more. Until recently she had judged Jaime to be a happy, almost overly blessed young man. He shared an apartment with an attractive lover, a young dentist named Carlos. Jaime and Carlos had been schoolmates in San Juan; they had left Puerto Rico together, settling first in New Orleans, then New York, and it was Jaime, working as a beautician, a talented one, who had put Carlos through dental school. Now Carlos had his own office and a clientele of prosperous Puerto Ricans and blacks.

However, during her last several visits she had noticed that Jaime Sanchez's usually unclouded eyes were somber, yellowed, as though he had a hangover, and his expertly articulate hands, ordinarily so calm and capable, trembled a little.

Yesterday, while scissor-trimming her hair, he had stopped and stood gasping, gasping—not as though fighting for air, but as if struggling against a scream.

She had said: "What is it? Are you all right?"

"No."

He had stepped to a washbasin and splashed his face with cold water. While drying himself, he said: "I'm going to kill Carlos." He waited, as if expecting her to ask him why; when she merely stared, he continued: "There's no use talking any more. He understands nothing. My words mean nothing. The only way I can communicate with him is to kill him. Then he will understand."

"I'm not sure that I do, Jaime."

"Have I ever mentioned to you Angelita? My cousin Angelita? She came here six months ago. She has always been in love with Carlos. Since she was, oh, twelve years old. And now Carlos is in love with her. He wants to marry her and have a household of children."

She felt so awkward that all she could think to ask was: "Is she a nice girl?"

"Too nice." He had seized the scissors and resumed clipping. "No, I mean that. She is an excellent girl, very petite, like a pretty parrot, and much too nice; her kindness becomes cruel. Though she doesn't understand that she is being cruel. For example . . ." She glanced at Jaime's face moving in the mirror above the washbasin; it was not the merry face that had often beguiled her, but pain and perplexity exactly reflected. "Angelita and Carlos want me to live with them after they are married, all of us together in one apartment. It was her idea, but Carlos says yes! yes! we must all stay together and from now on he and I will live like brothers. That is the reason I have to kill him. He could never have loved me, not if he could ignore my enduring such hell. He says, 'Yes, I love you, Jaime; but Angelita—this is different.' There is no difference. You love or you do not. You destroy or you do not. But Carlos will never understand that. Nothing reaches him, nothing can—only a bullet or a razor."

She wanted to laugh; at the same time she couldn't because she realized he was serious and also because she well knew how true it was that certain persons could only be made to recognize the truth, be made to *understand,* by subjecting them to extreme punishment.

Nevertheless, she did laugh, but in a manner that Jaime would not interpret as genuine laughter. It was something comparable to a sympathetic shrug. "You could never kill anyone, Jaime."

He began to comb her hair; the tugs were not gentle, but she knew the anger implied was against himself, not her. "Shit!" Then: "No. And that's the reason for most suicides. Someone is torturing you. You want to kill them, but you can't. All that pain is because you love them, and you can't kill them because you love them. So you kill yourself instead."

Leaving, she considered kissing him on the cheek, but settled for shaking his hand. "I know how trite this is, Jaime. And for the moment certainly no help at all. But remember—there's always somebody else. Just don't look for the same person, that's all."

The rendezvous apartment was on East Sixty-fifth Street; today she walked to it from her home, a small town house on Beekman Place. It was windy, there was leftover snow on the sidewalk and a promise of more in the air, but she was snug enough in the coat her husband had given her for Christmas—a sable-colored suede coat that was lined with sable.

A cousin had rented the apartment for her in his own name. The cousin, who was married to a harridan and lived in Greenwich, sometimes visited the apartment with his secretary, a fat Japanese woman who drenched herself in nose-boggling amounts of Mitsouko. This afternoon the apartment reeked of the lady's perfume, from which she deduced that her cousin had lately been dallying here. That meant she would have to change the sheets.

She did so, then prepared herself. On a table beside the bed she placed a small box wrapped in shiny cerulean paper; it contained a gold toothpick she had bought at Tiffany, a gift for Dr. Bentsen, for one of his unpleasing habits was constantly picking his teeth, and, moreover, picking them with an endless series of paper matches. She had thought the gold pick might make the whole process a little less disagreeable. She put a stack of Lee Wiley and Fred Astaire records on a phonograph, poured herself a glass of cold white wine, undressed entirely, lubricated herself, and stretched out on the bed, humming, singing along with the divine Fred and listening for the scratch of her lover's key at the door.

To judge from appearances, orgasms were agonizing events in the life of

Ezra Bentsen: he grimaced, he ground his dentures, he whimpered like a frightened mutt. Of course, she was always relieved when she heard the whimper; it meant that soon his lathered carcass would roll off her, for he was not one to linger, whispering tender compliments: he just rolled right off. And today, having done so, he greedily reached for the blue box, knowing it was a present for him. After opening it, he grunted.

She explained: "It's a gold toothpick."

He chuckled, an unusual sound coming from him, for his sense of humor was meager. "That's kind of cute," he said, and began picking his teeth. "You know what happened last night? I slapped Thelma. But good. And I punched her in the stomach, too."

Thelma was his wife; she was a child psychiatrist, and by reputation a fine one.

"The trouble with Thelma is you can't talk to her. She doesn't understand. Sometimes that's the only way you can get the message across. Give her a fat lip."

She thought of Jaime Sanchez.

"Do you know a Mrs. Roger Rhinelander?" Dr. Bentsen said.

"Mary Rhinelander? Her father was my father's best friend. They owned a racing stable together. One of her horses won the Kentucky Derby. Poor Mary, though. She married a real bastard."

"So she tells me."

"Oh? Is Mrs. Rhinelander a new patient?"

"Brand-new. Funny thing. She came to me for more or less the particular reason that brought you; her situation is almost identical."

The particular reason? Actually, she had a number of problems that had contributed to her eventual seduction on Dr. Bentsen's couch, the principal one being that she had not been capable of having a sexual relationship with her husband since the birth of their second child. She had married when she was twenty-four; her husband was fifteen years her senior. Though they had fought a lot, and were jealous of each other, the first five years of their marriage remained in her memory as an unblemished vista. The difficulty started when he asked her to have a child; if she hadn't been so much in love with him, she would never have consented—she had been afraid of children when she herself was a child, and the company of a child still made her uneasy. But she had given him a son, and the experience of pregnancy had traumatized her: when she wasn't actually suffering, she imagined she was, and after the birth she descended into a depression that continued more than a year. Every day she slept fourteen hours of Seconal sleep; as for the other ten, she kept awake by fueling herself with amphetamines. The second child, another boy, had been a drunken accident—though she suspected that really her husband had tricked her. The instant she knew she was pregnant again she had insisted on having an abortion; he had told her that if she went ahead with it, he would divorce her. Well, he had lived to regret that. The child had been born two months prematurely, had nearly died, and because of massive internal hemorrhaging, so had she; they had both hovered above an abyss through months of intensive care. Since then, she had never shared a bed with her husband; she wanted to, but she couldn't, for the naked presence of him, the thought of his body inside hers, summoned intolerable terrors.

Dr. Bentsen wore thick black socks with garters, which he never removed while "making love"; now, as he was sliding his gartered legs into a pair of shiny-seated blue serge trousers, he said: "Let's see. Tomorrow is Tuesday. Wednesday is our anniversary . . ."

"Our anniversary?"

"Thelma's! Our twentieth. I want to take her to . . . Tell me the best restaurant around now?"

"What does it matter? It's very small and very smart and the owner would never give you a table."

His lack of humor asserted itself: "That's a damn strange thing to say. What do you mean, he wouldn't give me a table?"

"Just what I said. One look at you and he'd know you had hairy heels. There are *some* people who won't serve people with hairy heels. He's one of them."

Dr. Bentsen was familiar with her habit of introducing unfamiliar lingo, and he had learned to pretend he knew what it signified; he was as ignorant of her ambience as she was of his, but the shifting instability of his character would not allow him to admit it.

"Well, then," he said, "is Friday all right? Around five?"

She said: "No, thank you." He was tying his tie and stopped; she was still lying on the bed, uncovered, naked; Fred was singing "By Myself." "No, thank you, darling Dr. B. I don't think we'll be meeting here any more."

She could see he was startled. Of course he would miss her—she was beautiful, she was considerate, it never bothered her when he asked her for money. He knelt beside the bed and fondled her breast. She noticed an icy mustache of sweat on his upper lip. "What is this? Drugs? Drink?"

She laughed and said: "All I drink is white wine, and not much of that. No, my friend. It's simply that you have hairy heels."

Like many analysts, Dr. Bentsen was quite literal-minded; just for a second she thought he was going to strip off his socks and examine his feet. Churlishly, like a child, he said: "I *don't* have hairy heels."

"Oh, yes you do. Just like a horse. All ordinary horses have hairy heels. Thoroughbreds don't. The heels of a well-bred horse are flat and glistening. Give my love to Thelma."

"Smart-ass. Friday?"

The Astaire record ended. She swallowed the last of the wine.

"Maybe. I'll call you," she said.

As it happened, she never called, and she never saw him again—except once, a year later, when she sat on a banquette next to him at La Grenouille; he was lunching with Mary Rhinelander, and she was amused to see that Mrs. Rhinelander signed the check.

The promised snow had arrived by the time she returned, again on foot, to the house on Beekman Place. The front door was painted pale yellow and had a brass knocker shaped like a lion's claw. Anna, one of four Irishwomen who staffed the house, answered the door and reported that the children, exhausted from an afternoon of ice-skating at Rockefeller Center, had already had their supper and been put to bed.

Thank God. Now she wouldn't have to undergo the half-hour of playtime and tale-telling and kiss-goodnight that customarily concluded her children's day; she may not have been an affectionate mother, but she was a dutiful one —just as her own mother had been. It was seven o'clock, and her husband had phoned to say he would be home at seven-thirty; at eight they were supposed to go to a dinner party with the Sylvester Hales, friends from San Francisco. She bathed, scented herself to remove memories of Dr. Bentsen, remodeled her makeup, of which she wore the most modest quantity, and changed into a grey silk caftan and grey silk slippers with pearl buckles.

She was posing by the fireplace in the library on the second floor when she heard her husband's footsteps on the stairs. It was a graceful pose, inviting as the room itself, an unusual octagonal room with cinnamon lacquered walls, a yellow lacquered floor, brass bookshelves (a notion borrowed from Billy Baldwin), two huge bushes of brown orchids ensconced in yellow Chinese vases, a Marino Marini horse standing in a corner, a South Seas Gauguin over the mantel, and a delicate fire fluttering in the fireplace. French windows offered a view of a darkened garden, drifting snow, and lighted tugboats floating like lanterns on the East River. A voluptuous couch, upholstered in mocha velvet, faced the fireplace, and in front of it, on a table lacquered the yellow of the floor, rested an ice-filled silver bucket; embedded in the bucket was a carafe brimming with pepper-flavored red Russian vodka.

Her husband hesitated in the doorway, and nodded at her approvingly: he was one of those men who truly noticed a woman's appearance, gathered at a glance the total atmosphere. He was worth dressing for, and it was one of her lesser reasons for loving him. A more important reason was that he resembled her father, a man who had been, and forever would be, the man in her life; her father had shot himself, though no one ever knew why, for he was a gentleman of almost abnormal discretion. Before this happened, she had terminated three engagements, but two months after her father's death she met George, and married him because in both looks and manners he approximated her great lost love.

She moved across the room to meet her husband halfway. She kissed his cheek, and the flesh against her lips felt as cold as the snowflakes at the window. He was a large man, Irish, black-haired and green-eyed, handsome even though he had lately accumulated considerable poundage and had gotten a bit jowly, too. He projected a superficial vitality; both men and women were drawn to him by that alone. Closely observed, however, one sensed a secret fatigue, a lack of any real optimism. His wife was severely aware of it, and why not? She was its principal cause.

She said: "It's such a rotten night out, and you look so tired. Let's stay home and have supper by the fire."

"Really, darling—you wouldn't mind? It seems a mean thing to do to the Haleses. Even if she is a cunt."

"*George!* Don't use that word. You know I hate it."

"Sorry," he said; he was, too. He was always careful not to offend her, just as she took the same care with him: a consequence of the quiet that simultaneously kept them together and apart.

"I'll call and say you're coming down with a cold."

"Well, it won't be a lie. I think I am."

While she called the Haleses, and arranged with Anna for a soup and soufflé supper to be served in an hour's time, he chugalugged a dazzling dose of the scarlet vodka and felt it light a fire in his stomach; before his wife returned, he poured himself a respectable shot and stretched full length on the couch. She knelt on the floor and removed his shoes and began to massage his feet: God knows, *he* didn't have hairy heels.

He groaned. "Hmm. That feels good."

"I love you, George."

"I love you, too."

She thought of putting on a record, but no, the sound of the fire was all the room needed.

"George?"

"Yes, darling."

"What are you thinking about?"

"A woman named Ivory Hunter."

"You really know somebody named Ivory Hunter?"

"Well. That was her stage name. She'd been a burlesque dancer."

She laughed. "What is this, some part of your college adventures?"

"I never knew her. I only heard about her once. It was the summer after I left Yale."

He closed his eyes and drained his vodka. "The summer I hitchhiked out to New Mexico and California. Remember? That's how I got my nose broke. In a bar fight in Needles, California." She liked his broken nose, it offset the extreme gentleness of his face; he had once spoken of having it rebroken and reset, but she had talked him out of it. "It was early September, and that's always the hottest time of the year in Southern California; over a hundred almost every day. I ought to have treated myself to a bus ride, at least across the desert. But there I was like a fool, deep in the Mojave, hauling a fifty-pound knapsack and sweating until there was no sweat in me. I swear it was a hundred and fifty in the shade. Except there wasn't any shade. Nothing but sand and mesquite and this boiling blue sky. Once a big truck drove by, but it wouldn't stop for me. All it did was kill a rattlesnake that was crawling across the road.

"I kept thinking something was bound to turn up somewhere. A garage. Now and then cars passed, but I might as well have been invisible. I began to feel sorry for myself, to understand what it means to be helpless, and to understand why it's a good thing that Buddhists send out their young monks to beg. It's chastening. It rips off that last layer of baby fat.

"And then I met Mr. Schmidt. I thought maybe it was a mirage. An old white-haired man about a quarter mile up the highway. He was standing by the road with heat waves rippling around him. As I got closer I saw that he carried a cane and wore pitch-black glasses, and he was dressed as if headed for church—white suit, white shirt, black tie, black shoes.

"Without looking at me, and while some distance away, he called out: 'My name is George Schmidt.'

"I said: 'Yes. Good afternoon, sir.'

"He said: '*Is* it afternoon?'

" 'After three.'

" 'Then I must have been standing here two hours or more. Would you mind telling me where I am?'

" 'In the Mojave Desert. About eighteen miles west of Needles.'

" 'Imagine that,' he said. 'Leaving a seventy-year-old blind man stranded alone in the desert. Ten dollars in my pocket, and not another rag to my name. Women are like flies: they settle on sugar or shit. I'm not saying I'm sugar, but she's sure settled for shit now. My name is George Schmidt.'

"I said: 'Yes, sir, you told me. I'm George Whitelaw.' He wanted to know where I was going, what I was up to, and when I said I was hitchhiking, heading for New York, he asked if I would take his hand and help him along a bit, maybe until we could catch a ride. I forgot to mention that he had a German accent and was extremely stout, almost fat; he looked as if he'd been lying in a hammock all his life. But when I held his hand I felt the roughness, the immense strength of it. You wouldn't have wanted a pair of hands like that around your throat. He said: 'Yes, I have strong hands. I've worked as a masseur for fifty years, the last twelve in Palm Springs. You got any water?' I gave him my canteen, which was still half full. And he said: 'She left me here without even a drop of water. The whole thing took me by surprise. Though I can't say it should have, knowing Ivory good as I did. That's my wife. Ivory Hunter, she was. A stripper; she played the Chicago World's Fair, 1932, and she would have been a star if it hadn't been for that Sally Rand. Ivory invented this fan-dance thing and that Rand woman stole it off her. So Ivory said. Probably just more of her bullshit. Uh-oh, watch out for that rattler, he's over there someplace, I can hear him really singing. There's two things I'm scared of. Snakes and women. They have a lot in common. One thing they have in common is: the last thing that dies is their tail.'

"A couple of cars passed and I stuck out my thumb and the old man tried to flag them down with his stick, but we must have looked too peculiar—a dirty kid in dungarees and a blind fat man dressed in his city best. I guess we'd still be out there if it hadn't been for this truckdriver. A Mexican. He was parked by the road fixing a flat. He could speak about five words of Tex-Mex, all of them four-letter, but I still remembered a lot of Spanish from the summer with Uncle Alvin in Cuba. So the Mexican told me he was on his way to El Paso, and if that was our direction, we were welcome aboard.

"But Mr. Schmidt wasn't too keen. I had practically to drag him into the caboose. 'I hate Mexicans. Never met a Mexican I liked. If it wasn't for a Mexican . . . Him only nineteen and her I'd say from the touch of her skin, I'd say Ivory was a woman way past sixty. When I married her a couple of years ago, she said she was fifty-two. See, I was living in this trailer camp out on Route 111. One of those trailer camps halfway between Palm Springs and Cathedral City. Cathedral City! Some name for a dump that's nothing but honky-tonks and pool halls and fag bars. The only thing you can say about it is Bing Crosby lives there. If that's saying something. Anyway, living next to me in this other trailer is my friend Hulga. Ever since my wife died—she died the same day Hitler died—Hulga had been driving me to work; she works as a waitress at this Jew club where I'm the masseur. All the waiters and waitresses at the club are big blond Germans. The Jews like that; they really keep them stepping. So one day Hulga tells me she has a cousin coming to visit. Ivory Hunter. I forget her legal name, it was on the marriage certificate, but I forget. She had about three husbands before; she probably didn't remember the name she was born with. Anyway, Hulga tells me that this cousin of hers, Ivory, used to be a famous dancer, but now she's just come out of the hospital and she's lost her last husband on account of she's spent a year in the hospital with TB. That's why Hulga asked her out to Palm Springs. Because of the air. Also, she didn't have any place else to go. The first night she was there, Hulga invited me over, and I liked her cousin right away; we didn't talk much, we listened to the radio mostly, but I liked Ivory. She had a real nice voice, real slow and gentle, she sounded like nurses ought to sound; she said she didn't smoke or drink and she was a member of the Church of God, same as me. After that, I was over at Hulga's almost every night.' "

George lit a cigarette, and his wife tilted out a jigger more of the pepper vodka for him. To her surprise, she poured one for herself. A number of things about her husband's narrative had accelerated her ever-present but usually Librium-subdued anxiety; she couldn't imagine where his memoir was leading, but she knew there was some destination, for George seldom rambled. He had gradua-ted third in his class at Yale Law School, never practiced law but had gone on to top his class at Harvard Business School; within the past decade he had been offered a presidential Cabinet post, and an ambassadorship to England or France or wherever he wanted. However, what had made her feel the need for red vodka, a ruby bauble burning in the firelight, was the disquieting manner in which George Whitelaw had become Mr. Schmidt; her husband was an exceptional mimic. He could imitate certain of their friends with infuriating accuracy. But this was not casual mimicry; he seemed entranced, a man fixed in another man's mind.

" 'I had an old Chevy nobody had driven since my wife died. But Ivory got it tuned up, and pretty soon it wasn't Hulga driving me to work and bringing me home, but Ivory. Looking back, I can see it was all a plot between Hulga and Ivory, but I didn't put it together then. Everybody around the trailer park, and everybody that met her, all they said was what a lovely woman she was, big blue eyes and pretty legs. I figured it was just good-heartedness, the Church of God—I figured that was why she was spending her evenings cooking dinner and keeping house for an old blind man. One night we were listening to the *Hit Parade* on the radio, and she kissed me and rubbed her hand along my leg. Pretty soon we were doing it twice a day—once before breakfast and once after dinner, and me a man of sixty-nine. But it seemed like she was as crazy about my cock as I was about her cunt—' "

She tossed her vodka into the fireplace, a splash that made the flames hiss and flourish; but it was an idle protest: Mr. Schmidt would not be reproached.

" 'Yes, sir, Ivory was all cunt. Whatever way you want to use the word. It was exactly one month from the day I met her to the day I married her. She didn't change much, she fed me good, she was always interested to hear about the Jews at the club, and it was me that cut down on the sex—*way* down, what with my blood pressure and all. But she never complained. We read the Bible together, and night after night she would read aloud from magazines, good magazines like *Reader's Digest* and *The Saturday Evening Post,* until I fell asleep. She was always saying she hoped she died before I did because she would be heartbroken and destitute. It was true I didn't have much to leave. No insurance, just some bank-savings that I turned into a joint account, and I had the trailer put in her name. No, I can't say there was a harsh word between us until she had the big fight with Hulga.

" 'For a long time I didn't know what the fight was about. All I knew was that they didn't speak to each other any more, and when I asked Ivory what was going on, she said: "Nothing." As far as she was concerned, she hadn't had any falling-out with Hulga: "But you know how much she drinks." That was true. Well, like I told you, Hulga was a waitress at the club, and one day she comes barging into the massage room. I had a customer on the table, had him there spread out buck-naked, but a lot she cared—she smelled like a Four Roses factory. She could hardly stand up. She told me she had just got fired, and suddenly she started swearing and pissing. She was hollering at me and pissing all over the floor. She said everybody at the trailer park was laughing at me. She said Ivory was an old whore who had latched onto me because she was down and out and couldn't do any better. And she said what kind of a chowderhead was I? Didn't I know my wife was fucking the balls off Freddy Feo since God knows when?

" 'Now, see, Freddy Feo was an itinerant Tex-Mex kid—he was just out of jail somewhere, and the manager of the trailer park had picked him up in one of those fag bars in Cat City and put him to work as a handyman. I don't guess he could have been one-hundred-percent fag because he was giving plenty of the old girls around there a tickle for their money. One of them was Hulga. She was loop-de-do over him. On hot nights him and Hulga used to sit outside her trailer on her swing-seat drinking straight tequila, forget the lime, and he'd play the guitar and sing spic songs. Ivory described it to me as a green guitar with his name spelled out in rhinestone letters. I'll say this, the spic could sing. But Ivory always claimed she couldn't stand him; she said he was a cheap little greaser out to take Hulga for every nickel she had. Myself, I don't remember exchanging ten words with him, but I didn't like him because of the way he smelled. I have a nose like a bloodhound and I could smell him a hundred yards off, he wore so much brilliantine in his hair, and something else that Ivory said was called Evening in Paris.

" 'Ivory swore up and down it wasn't so. Her? *Her* let a Tex-Mex monkey like Freddy Feo put a finger on her? She said it was because Hulga had been dumped by this kid that she was crazy and jealous and thought he was humping everything from Cat City to Indio. She said she was insulted that I'd listen to such lies, even though Hulga was more to be pitied than reviled. And she took off the wedding ring I'd given her—it had belonged to my first wife, but she said that didn't make any difference because she knew I'd loved Hedda and that made it all the better—and she handed it to me and she said if I didn't believe her, then here was the ring and she'd take the next bus going anywhere. So I put it back on her finger and we knelt on the floor and prayed together.

" 'I did believe her; at least I thought I did; but in some way it was like a seesaw in my head—yes, no, yes, no. And Ivory had lost her looseness; before she had an easiness in her body that was like the easiness in her voice. But now it was all wire—tense, like those Jews at the club that keep whining and scolding because you can't rub away all their worries. Hulga got a job at the Miramar, but out at the trailer park I always turned away when I smelled her coming. Once she sort of whispered up beside me: "Did you know that sweet wife of yours gave the greaser a pair of gold earrings! But his boyfriend won't let him wear them." I don't know. Ivory prayed every night with me that the Lord would keep us together, healthy in spirit and body. But I noticed . . . Well, on those warm summer nights when Freddy Feo would be out there somewhere in the dark, singing and playing his guitar, she'd turn off the radio right in the middle of Bob Hope or Edgar Bergen or whatever, and go sit outside and listen. She said she was looking at the stars: "I bet there's no place in the world you can see the stars like here." But suddenly it turned out she hated Cat City and the Springs. The whole desert, the sandstorms, summers with temperatures up to a hundred thirty degrees, and nothing to do if you wasn't rich and belonged to the Racquet Club. She just announced this one morning. She said we should pick up the trailer and plant it down anywhere where the air was cool. Wisconsin. Michigan. I felt good about the idea; it set my mind to rest as to what might be going on between her and Freddy Feo.

" 'Well, I had a client there at the club, a fellow from Detroit, and he said he might be able to get me on as a masseur at the Detroit Athletic Club; nothing definite, only one of them maybe deals. But that was enough for Ivory. Twenty-three skidoo, and she's got the trailer uprooted, fifteen years of planting strewn all over the ground, the Chevy ready to roll, and all our savings turned into traveler's checks. Last night she scrubbed me top to bottom and shampooed my hair, and this morning we set off a little after daylight.

" 'I realized something was wrong, and I'd have known what it was if I hadn't dozed off soon as we hit the highway. She must have dumped sleeping pills in my coffee.

" 'But when I woke up I smelled him. The brilliantine and the dime-store perfume. He was hiding in the trailer. Coiled back there somewhere like a snake. What I thought was: Ivory and the kid are going to kill me and leave me for the buzzards. She said, "You're awake, George." The way she said it, the slight fear, I could tell she knew what was going on in my head. That I'd guessed it all. I told her, *Stop the car.* She wanted to know what for? Because I had to take a leak. She stopped the car, and I could hear she was crying. As I got out, she said: "You been good to me, George, but I didn't know nothing else to do. And you got a profession. There'll always be a place for you somewhere."

" 'I got out of the car, and I really did take a leak, and while I was standing there the motor started up and she drove away. I didn't know where I was until you came along, Mr. . . . ?'

" 'George Whitelaw.' And I told him: 'Jesus, that's just like murder. Leaving a blind man helpless in the middle of nowhere. When we get to El Paso we'll go to the police station.'

"He said: 'Hell, no. She's got enough trouble without the cops. She settled on shit—leave her to it. Ivory's the one out in nowhere. Besides, I love her. A woman can do you like that, and still you love her.' "

George refilled his vodka; she placed a small log on the fire, and the new rush of flame was only a little brighter than the furious red suddenly flushing her cheeks.

"That *women* do," she said, her tone aggressive, challenging. "Only a crazy person . . . Do you think I could do something like that?"

The expression in his eyes, a certain visual silence, shocked her and made her avert her eyes, withdrawing the question. "Well, what happened to him?"

"Mr. Schmidt?"

"Mr. Schmidt."

He shrugged. "The last I saw of him he was drinking a glass of milk in a diner, a truck stop outside El Paso. I was lucky; I got a ride with a trucker all the way to Newark. I sort of forgot about it. But for the last few months I find myself wondering about Ivory Hunter and George Schmidt. It must be age; I'm beginning to feel old myself."

She knelt beside him again; she held his hand, interweaving her fingers with his. "Fifty-two? And you feel *old*?"

He had retreated; when he spoke, it was the wondering murmur of a man addressing himself. "I always had such confidence. Just walking the street, I felt such a *swing*. I could feel people looking at me—on the street, in a restaurant, at a party—envying me, wondering who is that guy. Whenever I walked into a party, I knew I could have half the women in the room if I wanted them. But that's all over. Seems as though old George Whitelaw has become the invisible man. Not a head turns. I called Mimi Stewart twice last week, and she never returned the calls. I didn't tell you, but I stopped at Buddy Wilson's yesterday, he was having a little cocktail thing. There must have been twenty fairly attractive girls, and they all looked right through me; to them I was a tired old guy who smiled too much."

She said: "But I thought you were still seeing Christine."

"I'll tell you a secret. Christine is engaged to that Rutherford boy from Philadelphia. I haven't seen her since November. He's okay for her; she's happy and I'm happy for her."

"Christine! Which Rutherford boy? Kenyon or Paul?"

"The older one."

"That's Kenyon. You knew that and didn't tell me?"

"There's so much I haven't told you, my dear."

Yet that was not entirely true. For when they had stopped sleeping together, they had begun discussing together—indeed, collaborating on—each of his affairs. Alice Kent: five months; ended because she'd demanded he divorce and marry her. Sister Jones: terminated after one year when her husband found out about it. Pat Simpson: a *Vogue* model who'd gone to Hollywood, promised to return and never had. Adele O'Hara: beautiful, an alcoholic, a rambunctious scenemaker; he'd broken that one off himself. Mary Campbell, Mary Chester, Jane Vere-Jones. Others. And now Christine.

A few he had discovered himself; the majority were "romances" she herself had stage-managed, friends she'd introduced him to, confidantes she had trusted to provide him with an outlet but not to exceed the mark.

"Well," she sighed. "I suppose we can't blame Christine. Kenyon Rutherford's rather a catch." Still, her mind was running, searching like the flames shivering through the logs: a name to fill the void. Alice Combs: available, but too dull. Charlotte Finch: too rich, and George felt emasculated by women—or men, for that matter—richer than himself. Perhaps the Ellison woman? The soigné Mrs. Harold Ellison who was in Haiti getting a swift divorce . . .

He said: "Stop frowning."

"I'm not frowning."

"It just means more silicone, more bills from Orentreich. I'd rather see the human wrinkles. It doesn't matter whose fault it is. We all, sometimes, leave each other out there under the skies, and we never understand why."

An echo, caverns resounding: Jaime Sanchez and Carlos and Angelita; Hulga and Freddy Feo and Ivory Hunter and Mr. Schmidt; Dr. Bentsen and George, George and herself, Dr. Bentsen and Mary Rhinelander . . .

He gave a slight pressure to their interwoven fingers, and with his other hand, raised her chin and insisted on their eyes meeting. He moved her hand up to his lips and kissed its palm.

"I love you, Sarah."

"I love you, too."

But the touch of his lips, the insinuated threat, tautened her. Below stairs, she heard the rattle of silver on trays: Anna and Margaret were ascending with the fireside supper.

"I love you, too," she repeated with pretended sleepiness, and with a feigned languor moved to draw the window draperies. Drawn, the heavy silk concealed the night river and the lighted riverboats, so snow-misted that they were as muted as the design in a Japanese scroll of winter night.

"George?" An urgent plea before the supper-laden Irishwomen arrived, expertly balancing their offerings: "*Please,* darling. We'll think of somebody."

5
Hospitality

Once upon a time, in the rural South, there were farmhouses and farm wives who set tables where almost any passing stranger, a traveling preacher, a knife-grinder, an itinerant worker, was welcome to sit down to a hearty midday meal. Probably many such farm wives still exist. Certainly my aunt does, Mrs. Jennings Carter. Mary Ida Carter.

As a child I lived for long periods of time on the Carters' farm, small then, but today a considerable property. The house was lighted by oil lamps in those days; water was pumped from a well and carried, and the only warmth was provided by fireplaces and stoves, and the only entertainment was what we ourselves manufactured. In the evenings, after supper, likely as not my uncle Jennings, a handsome, virile man, would play the piano accompanied by his pretty wife, my mother's younger sister.

They were hard-working people, the Carters. Jennings, with the help of a few sharecropping field hands, cultivated his land with a horse-drawn plow. As for his wife, her chores were unlimited. I helped her with many of them: feeding the pigs, milking the cows, churning milk into butter, husking corn, shelling peas and pecans—it was fun, except for one assignment I sought to avoid, and when forced to perform, did so with my eyes shut: I just plain hated wringing the necks of chickens, though I certainly didn't object to eating them afterward.

This was during the Depression, but there was plenty to eat on Mary Ida's table for the principal meal of the day, which was served at noon and to which her sweating husband and his helpers were summoned by clanging a big bell. I loved to ring the bell; it made me feel powerful and beneficent.

It was to these midday meals, where the table was covered with hot biscuits and cornbread and honey-in-the-comb and chicken and catfish or fried squirrel and butter beans and black-eyed peas, that guests sometimes appeared, sometimes expected, sometimes not. "Well," Mary Ida would sigh, seeing a footsore Bible salesman approaching along the road, "we don't need another Bible. But I guess we'd better set another place."

Of all those we fed, there were three who will never slip my memory. First, the Presbyterian missionary, who was traveling around the countryside soliciting funds for his Christian duties in unholy lands. Mary Ida said she couldn't afford a cash contribution, but she would be pleased to have him take dinner with us. Poor man, he definitely looked as though he needed one. Arrayed in a rusty, dusty, shiny black suit, creaky black undertaker shoes, and a blackgreenish hat, he was thin as a stalk of sugar cane. He had a long red wrinkled neck with a bobbing Adam's apple the size of a goiter. I never saw a greedier fellow; he sucked up a quart of buttermilk in three swallows, devoured a whole platter of chicken single-handed (or rather, double-handedly, for he was eating with both hands), and so many biscuits, dripping with butter and molasses, that I lost count. However, for all his gobbling, he managed to give us hair-raising accounts of his exploits in perilous territories. "I'll tell you somethin'. I've seen cannibals roast black men and white men on a spit—just like you'd roast a pig—and eat every morsel, toes, brains, ears, and all. One of them cannibals told me the best eatin' is a roasted newborn baby; said it tasted just like lamb. I spec the reason they didn't eat me is 'cause I didn't have enough meat on my bones. I've seen men hung by their heels till blood gushed out their ears. Once I got bit by a green mamba, the deadliest snake in the world. I was kinda nauseated there for a spell, but I didn't die, so the black men figured I was a god and they gave me a coat made of leopard skins."

After the gluttonous preacher had departed, Mary Ida felt dizzy; she was sure she would have bad dreams for a month. But her husband, comforting her, said: "Oh, honey, you didn't believe any of that malarkey? That man's no more a missionary than I am. He's just a heathen liar."

Then there was the time we entertained a convict who had escaped from a chain gang at the Alabama State Prison in Atmore. Obviously, we didn't *know* he was a dangerous character serving a life sentence for umpteen armed robberies. He simply appeared at our door and told Mary Ida he was hungry and could she give him something to eat. "Well, sir," she said, "you've come to the right place. I'm just putting dinner on the table now."

Somehow, probably by raiding a washline, he had exchanged his convict stripes for overalls and a worn blue work shirt. I thought he was nice, we all did; he had a flower tattooed on his wrist, his eyes were gentle, he was gently spoken. He said his name was Bancroft (which, as it turned out, *was* his true name). My uncle Jennings asked him: "What's your line of work, Mr. Bancroft?"

"Well," he drawled, "I'm just lookin' for some. Like most everybody else. I'm pretty handy. Can do most anythin'. You wouldn't have somethin' for me?"

Jennings said: "I sure could use a man. But I can't afford him."

"I'd work for most nothin'."

"Yeah," said Jennings. "But nothing is what I've got."

Unpredictably, for it was a subject seldom alluded to in that household, crime came into the conversation. Mary Ida complained: "Pretty Boy Floyd. And that Dillinger man. Running around the country shooting people. Robbing banks."

"Oh, I don't know," said Mr. Bancroft. "I got no sympathy with them banks. And Dillinger, he's real smart, you got to hand him that. It kinda makes me laugh the way he knocks off them banks and gets clean away with it." Then he actually laughed, displaying tobacco-tinted teeth.

"Well," Mary Ida countered, "I'm slightly surprised to hear you say that, Mr. Bancroft."

Two days later Jennings drove his wagon into town and returned with a keg of nails, a sack of flour, and a copy of the *Mobile Register*. On the front page was a picture of Mr. Bancroft—"Two-Barrels" Bancroft, as he was colloquially known to the authorities. He had been captured in Evergreen, thirty miles away. When Mary Ida saw his photo, she rapidly fanned her face with a paper fan, as though to prevent a fainting fit. "Heaven help me," she cried. "He could have killed us all."

Jennings said sourly: "There was a reward. And we missed out on it. *That's* what gets my goat."

Next, there was a girl called Zilla Ryland. Mary Ida discovered her bathing a two-year-old baby, a red-haired boy, in a creek that ran through the woods back of the house. As Mary Ida described it: "I saw her before she saw me. She was standing naked in the water bathing this beautiful little boy. On the bank there was a calico dress and the child's clothes and an old suitcase tied together with a piece of rope. The boy was laughing, and so was she. Then she saw me, and she was startled. Scared. I said: 'Nice day. But hot. The water must feel good.' But she snatched up the baby and scampered out of the creek, and I said: 'You don't have to be frightened of me. I'm only Mrs. Carter that lives just over yonder. Come on up and rest a spell.' Then she commenced to cry; she was only a little thing, no more than a child herself. I asked what's the matter, honey? But she wouldn't answer. By now she had pulled on her dress and dressed the boy. I said maybe I could help you if you'd tell me what's wrong. But she shook her head, and said there was nothing wrong, and I said well, we don't cry over nothing, do we? Now you just follow me up to the house and we'll talk about it. And she did."

Indeed she did.

I was swinging in the porch swing reading an old *Saturday Evening Post* when I noticed them coming up the path, Mary Ida toting a broken-down suitcase and this barefooted girl carrying a child in her arms.

Mary Ida introduced me: "This is my nephew, Buddy. And—I'm sorry, honey, I didn't catch your name."

"Zilla," the girl whispered, eyes lowered.

"I'm sorry, honey. I can't hear you."

"Zilla," she again whispered.

"Well," said Mary Ida cheerfully, "that sure is an unusual name."

Zilla shrugged. "My mama give it to me. Was her name, too."

Two weeks later Zilla was still with us; she proved to be as unusual as her name. Her parents were dead, her husband had "run off with another woman. She was real fat, and he liked fat women, he said I was too skinny, so he run off with her and got a divorce and married her up in Athens, Georgia." Her only living kin was a brother: Jim James. "That's why I come down here to Alabama. The last I heard, he was located somewhere around here."

Uncle Jennings did everything in his power to trace Jim James. He had good reason, for, although he liked Zilla's little boy, Jed, he'd come to feel quite hostile toward Zilla—her thin voice aggravated him, and her habit of humming mysterious tuneless melodies.

Jennings to Mary Ida: "Just the hell how much longer is our boarder going to hang around?" Mary Ida: "Oh, Jennings. Shhh! Zilla might hear you. Poor soul. She's got nowhere to go." So Jennings intensified his labors. He brought the sheriff into the case; he even *paid* to place an ad in the local paper—and that was really going far. But nobody hereabouts had ever heard of Jim James.

At last Mary Ida, clever woman, had an idea. The idea was to invite a neighbor, Eldridge Smith, to evening supper, usually a light meal served at six. I don't know why she hadn't thought of it before. Mr. Smith was not much to look at, but he was a recently widowed farmer of about forty with two school-aged children.

After that first supper Mr. Smith got to stopping by almost every twilight. After dark we all left Zilla and Mr. Smith alone, where they swung together on the creaking porch swing and laughed and talked and whispered. It was driving Jennings out of his mind because he didn't like Mr. Smith any better than he liked Zilla; his wife's repeated requests to "Hush, honey. Wait and see" did little to soothe him.

We waited a month. Until finally one night Jennings took Mr. Smith aside and said: "Now look here, Eldridge. Man to man, what are your intentions toward this fine young lady?" The way Jennings said it, it was more like a threat than anything else.

Mary Ida made the wedding dress on her foot-pedaled Singer sewing machine. It was white cotton with puffed sleeves, and Zilla wore a white silk ribbon bow in her hair, especially curled for the occasion. She looked surprisingly pretty. The ceremony was held under the shade of a mulberry tree on a cool September afternoon, the Reverend Mr. L. B. Persons presiding. Afterward everybody was served cupcakes and fruit punch spiked with scuppernong wine. As the newlyweds rode away in Mr. Smith's mule-drawn wagon, Mary Ida lifted the hem of her skirt to dab at her eyes, but Jennings, eyes dry as a snake's skin, declared: "Thank you, dear Lord. And while You're doing favors, my crops could use some rain."

6
Dazzle

She fascinated me.

She fascinated everyone, but most people were ashamed of their fascination, especially the proud ladies who presided over some of the grander households of New Orleans' Garden District, the neighborhood where the big plantation owners lived, the shipowners and oil operators, the richest professional men. The only persons not secretive about their fascination with Mrs. Ferguson were the servants of these Garden District families. And, of course, some of the children, who were too young or guileless to conceal their interest.

I was one of those children, an eight-year-old boy temporarily living with Garden District relatives. However, as it happened, I did keep my fascination to myself, for I felt a certain guilt: I had a secret, something that was bothering me, something that was really worrying me very much, something I was afraid to tell anybody, *any*body—I couldn't imagine what their reaction would be, it was such an odd thing that was worrying me, that had been worrying me for almost two years. I had never heard of anyone with a problem like the one that was troubling me. On the one hand it seemed maybe silly; on the other . . .

I wanted to tell my secret to Mrs. Ferguson. Not *want* to, but felt I had to. Because Mrs. Ferguson was said to have magical powers. It was said, and believed by many serious-minded people, that she could tame errant husbands, force proposals from reluctant suitors, restore lost hair, recoup squandered fortunes. In short, she was a witch who could make wishes come true. I had a wish.

Mrs. Ferguson did not seem clever enough to be capable of magic. Not even card tricks. She was a plain woman who might have been forty but was perhaps thirty; it was hard to tell, for her round Irish face, with its round full-moon eyes, had few lines and little expression. She was a laundress, probably the only white laundress in New Orleans, and an artist at her trade: the great ladies of the town sent for her when their finest laces and linens and silks required attention. They sent for her for other reasons as well: to obtain desires—a new lover, a certain marriage for a daughter, the death of a husband's mistress, a codicil to a mother's will, an invitation to be Queen of Comus, grandest of the Mardi Gras galas. It was not merely as a laundress that Mrs. Ferguson was courted. The source of her success, and principal income, was her alleged abilities to sift the sands of daydreams until she produced the solid stuff, golden realities.

Now, about this wish of my own, the worry that was with me from first thing in the morning until last thing at night: it wasn't anything I could just straight out ask her. It required the right time, a carefully prepared moment. She seldom came to our house, but when she did I stayed close by, pretending to watch the delicate movements of her thick ugly fingers as they handled lace-trimmed napkins, but really attempting to catch her eye. We never talked; I was too nervous and she was too stupid. Yes, stupid. It was just something I sensed; powerful witch or not, Mrs. Ferguson was a stupid woman. But now and again our eyes did lock, and dumb as she was, the intensity, the *fascination* she saw in my gaze told her that I desired to be a client. She probably thought I wanted a bike, or a new air rifle; anyway, she wasn't about to concern herself with a kid like me. What could I give her? So she would turn her tiny lips down and roll her full-moon eyes elsewhere.

About this time, early December in 1932, my paternal grandmother arrived for a brief visit. New Orleans had cold winters; the chilly humid winds from the river drift deep into your bones. So my grandmother, who was living in Florida, where she taught school, had wisely brought with her a fur coat, one she had borrowed from a friend. It was made of black Persian lamb, the belonging of a rich woman, which my grandmother was not. Widowed young, and left with three sons to raise, she had not had an easy life, but she never complained. She was an admirable woman; she had a lively mind, and a sound, sane one as well. Due to family circumstances, we rarely met, but she wrote often and sent me small gifts. She loved me and I wanted to love her, but until she died, and she lived beyond ninety, I kept my distance, behaved indifferently. She felt it, but she never knew what caused my apparent coldness, nor did anyone else, for the reason was part of an intricate guilt, faceted as the dazzling yellow stone dangling from a slender gold-chain necklace that she often wore. Pearls would have suited her better, but she attached great value to this somewhat theatrical gewgaw, which I understood her own grandfather had won in a card game in Colorado.

Of course the necklace wasn't valuable; as my grandmother always scrupulously explained to anyone who inquired, the stone, which was the size of a cat's paw, was not a "gem" stone, not a canary diamond, nor even a topaz, but a chunk of rock-crystal deftly faceted and tinted dark yellow. Mrs. Ferguson, however, was unaware of the trinket's true worth, and when one afternoon, during the course of my grandmother's stay, the plump youngish witch arrived to stiffen some linen, she seemed spellbound by the brilliant bit of glass swinging from the thin chain around my grandmother's neck. Her ignorant moon eyes glowed, and that's a fact: they truly glowed. I now had no difficulty attracting her attention; she studied me with an interest absent heretofore.

As she departed, I followed her into the garden, where there was a century-old wisteria arbor, a mysterious place even in winter when the foliage had shriveled, stripping this leaf-tunnel of its concealing shadows. She walked under it and beckoned to me.

Softly, she said: "You got something on your mind?"

"Yes."

"Something you want done? A favor?"

I nodded; she nodded, but her eyes shifted nervously: she didn't want to be seen talking to me.

She said: "My boy will come. He will tell you."

"*When?*"

But she said hush, and hurried out of the garden. I watched her waddle off into the dusk. It dried my mouth to think of having all my hopes pinned on this stupid woman. I couldn't eat supper that night; I didn't sleep until dawn. Aside from the thing that was worrying me, now I had a whole lot of new worries. If Mrs. Ferguson did what I wanted her to do, then what about my clothes, what about my name, where would I go, who would I be? Holy smoke, it was enough to drive you crazy! Or was I already crazy? That was part of the problem: I must be crazy to want Mrs. Ferguson to do this thing I wanted her to do. That was one reason why I couldn't tell anybody: they would think I was crazy. Or something worse. I didn't know what that something worse could be, but instinctively I felt that people saying I was crazy, my family and their friends and the other kids, might be the least of it.

Because of fear and superstition combined with greed, the servants of the Garden District, some of the snobbiest mammies and haughtiest housemen who ever tread a parquet floor, spoke of Mrs. Ferguson with respect. They also spoke of her in quiet tones, and not only because of her peculiar gifts, but because of her equally peculiar private life, various details of which I had gradually collected by eavesdropping on the tattletale of these elegant blacks and mulattoes and Creoles, who considered themselves the real royalty of New Orleans, and certainly superior to any of their employers. As for Mrs. Ferguson—she was not a madame, merely a mamselle: an unmarried woman with a raft of children, at least six, who came from East Texas, one of those redneck hamlets across the border from Shreveport. At the age of fifteen she had been tied to a hitching post in front of the town post office and publicly flogged with a horsewhip by her own father. The reason for this terrible punishment was a child she had borne, a boy with green eyes but unmistakably the product of a black father. With the baby, who was called Skeeter and was now fourteen and said to be a devil himself, she came to New Orleans and found work as a housekeeper for an Irish Catholic priest, whom she seduced, had a second baby by, abandoned for another man, and went on from there, living with a succession of handsome lovers, men she could only have succeeded in acquiring through potions poured into their wine, for after all, without her particular powers, who was she? White trash from East Texas who carried on with black men, the mother of six bastards, a laundress, a servant herself. And yet they respected her; even Mme. Jouet, the head mammy of the Vaccaro family, who owned the United Fruit Company, always addressed her civilly.

Two days after my conversation with Mrs. Ferguson, a Sunday, I accompanied my grandmother to church, and as we were walking home, a matter of a few blocks, I noticed that someone was following us: a well-built boy with tobacco-colored skin and green eyes. I knew at once that it was the infamous Skeeter, the boy whose birth had caused his mother to be flogged, and I knew that he was bringing me a message. I felt nauseated, but also elated, almost tipsy, enough so to make me laugh.

Merrily, my grandmother asked: "Ah, you know a joke?"

I thought: No, but I know a secret. However, I only said: "It was just something the minister said."

"Really? I'm glad you found some humor. It struck me as a very dry sermon. But the choir was good."

I refrained from making the following comment: "Well, if they're just going to talk about sinners and hell, when they don't know what hell is, they ought to ask me to preach the sermon. I could tell them a thing or two."

"Are you happy here?" my grandmother asked, as if it were a question she had been considering ever since her arrival. "I know it's been difficult. The divorce. Living here, living there. I want to help; I don't know how."

"I'm fine. Everything's hunky-dory."

But I wished she'd shut up. She did, with a frown. So at least I'd got one wish. One down and one to go.

When we reached home my grandmother, saying she felt the start of a migraine and might try to ward it off with a pill and a nap, kissed me and went inside the house. I raced through the garden toward the old wisteria arbor and hid myself inside it, like a bandit in a bandit's cave waiting for a confederate.

Soon Mrs. Ferguson's son arrived. He was tall for his age, just shy of six feet, and muscular as a dockworker. He resembled his mother in no respect. It wasn't only his dark coloring; his features were nicely defined, the bone structure quite precise—his father must have been a handsome man. And unlike Mrs. Ferguson, his emerald eyes were not dumb comic-strip dots, but narrow and mean, weapons, bullets threateningly aimed and primed to explode. I wasn't surprised when, not many years later, I heard he'd committed a double murder in Houston and died in the electric chair at Texas State Prison.

He was natty, dressed like the adult sharp-guy hoodlums who lounged around the waterfront hangouts: Panama hat, two-toned shoes, a tight stained white linen suit that some much slighter man must have given him. An impressive cigar jutted from his handkerchief pocket: a Havana Castle Morro, the connoisseur's cigar Garden District gentlemen served along with their after-dinner absinthe and framboise. Skeeter Ferguson lit his cigar with movie-gangster showmanship, constructed an impeccable smoke ring, blew it straight into my face, and said: "I've come to get you."

"*Now?*"

"Just as soon as you bring me the old lady's necklace."

It was useless to stall, but I tried: "What necklace?"

"Save your breath. Go get it and then we'll head somewhere. Or else we won't. And you'll never have another chance."

"But she's wearing it!"

Another smoke ring, professionally manufactured, effortlessly projected. "How you get it ain't none of my beeswax. I'll just be right here. Waiting."

"But it may take a long time. And suppose I can't do it?"

"You will. I'll wait till you do."

The house sounded empty when I entered through the kitchen door, and except for my grandmother, it was; everyone else had driven off to visit a newly married cousin who lived across the river. After calling my grandmother's name, and hearing silence, I tiptoed upstairs and listened at her bedroom door. She must be asleep. Accepting the risk, I inched the door open.

The curtains were drawn and the room dark except for the hot shine of coal burning inside a porcelain stove. My grandmother was lying in bed with covers drawn up to her chin; she must have taken the headache pill, for her breathing was deep and even. Still, I drew back the quilt covering her with the meticulous stealth of a robber tumbling the dials of a bank safe. Her throat was naked; she was wearing only an undergarment, a pink slip. I found the necklace on a bureau; it was lying in front of a photograph of her three sons, one of them my father. I hadn't seen him for so long that I'd forgotten what he looked like —and after today, I'd probably never see him again. Or if I did, he wouldn't know who I was. But I had no time to think about that. Skeeter Ferguson was waiting for me, standing inside the wisteria arbor tapping his foot and sucking on his millionaire's cigar. Nevertheless, I hesitated.

I had never stolen anything before; well, some Hershey bars from the candy counter at the movies, and a few books I'd not returned to the public library. But this was so important. My grandmother would forgive me if she knew why I had to steal the necklace. No, she wouldn't forgive me; nobody would forgive me if they knew *exactly* why. But I had no choice. It was like Skeeter said: if I didn't do it now, his mother would never give me another chance. And the thing that was worrying me would go on and on, maybe forever and forever. So I took it. I stuffed it in my pocket and fled the room without even closing the door. When I rejoined Skeeter, I didn't show him the necklace, I just told him I had it, and his green eyes grew greener, turned nastier, as he issued one of his big-shot smoke rings and said: "Sure you do. You're just a born rascal. Like me."

First we walked, then we took a trolley car down Canal Street, usually so crowded and cheerful but spooky now with the stores closed and a Sabbath stillness hovering over it like a funeral cloud. At Canal and Royal we changed trolleys and rode all the way across the French Quarter, a familiar neighborhood where many of the longer-established families lived, some with purer lineage than any names the Garden District could offer. Eventually we started walking again; we walked miles. The stiff churchgoing shoes I was still wearing hurt, and now I didn't know where we were, but wherever it was I didn't like it. It was no use questioning Skeeter Ferguson, for if you did, he smiled and whistled, or spit and smiled and whistled. I wonder if he whistled on his way to the electric chair.

I really had no idea where we were; it was a section of the city I'd not seen before. And yet there was nothing unusual about it, except that there were fewer white faces around than one was accustomed to, and the farther we walked the scarcer they became: an occasional white resident surrounded by blacks and Creoles. Otherwise it was an ordinary collection of humble wooden structures, rooming houses with peeling paint, modest family homes, mostly poorly kept but with some exceptions. Mrs. Ferguson's house, when at last we reached it, was one of the exceptions.

It was an old house but a *real* house, with seven or eight rooms; it didn't look as though the first strong breeze from the Gulf would blow it away. It was painted an ugly brown, but at least the paint was not sun-blistered and flaking. And it stood inside a well-tended yard that contained a big shade tree —a chinaberry tree with old rubber tires, several of them, suspended on ropes from its branches: swings for children. And there were other playthings scattered around the yard: a tricycle, buckets, and little shovels for making mud pies—evidence of Mrs. Ferguson's fatherless brood. A mongrel puppy held captive by a chain attached to a stake began bouncing about and yapping the second he glimpsed Skeeter.

Skeeter said: "Here we are. Just open the door and walk in."

"Alone?"

"She's expectin' you. Do what I tell you. Walk right in. And if you catch her in the middle of a hump, keep your eyes open: that's how I got to be a champion humper."

The last remark, meaningless to me, ended with a chuckle, but I followed his instructions, and as I started toward the front door, glanced back at him. It didn't seem possible, but he was already gone, and I never saw him again —or if I did, I don't remember it.

The door opened directly into Mrs. Ferguson's parlor. At least it was furnished as a parlor (a couch, easy chairs, two wicker rocking chairs, maplewood side tables), though the floor was covered with a brown kitchen linoleum that perhaps was meant to match the color of the house. When I came into the room Mrs. Ferguson was tilting to and fro in one of the rocking chairs, while a good-looking young man, a Creole not many years older than Skeeter, rocked away in the other. A bottle of rum rested on a table between them, and they were both drinking from glasses filled with the stuff. The young man, who was not introduced to me, was wearing only an undershirt and somewhat unbuttoned bell-bottom sailor's trousers. Without a word he stopped rocking, stood up, and swaggered down a hall, taking the rum bottle with him. Mrs. Ferguson listened until she heard a door close.

Then all she said was: "Where is it?"

I was sweating. My heart was acting funny. I felt as though I had run a hundred miles and lived a thousand years in just the last few hours.

Mrs. Ferguson stilled her chair, and repeated herself: "Where is it?"

"Here. In my pocket."

She held out a thick red hand, palm up, and I dropped the necklace into it. Rum had already done something to alter the usual dullness of her eyes; the dazzling yellow stone did more. She turned it this way and that, staring at it; I tried not to, I tried to think of other things, and found myself wondering if she had scars on her back, lash marks.

"Am I expected to guess?" she asked, never removing her gaze from the bijou dangling from its fragile gold chain. "Well? Am I supposed to tell you why you are here? What it is you want?"

She didn't know, she couldn't, and suddenly I didn't want her to. I said: "I like to tap-dance."

For an instant her attention was diverted from the sparkling new toy.

"I want to be a tap dancer. I want to run away. I want to go to Hollywood and be in the movies." There was some truth in this; running away to Hollywood was high on my list of escape-fantasies. But that wasn't what I'd decided not to tell her, after all.

"Well," she drawled. "You sure are pretty enough to be in picture shows. Prettier than any boy ought to be."

So she *did* know. I heard myself shouting: "Yes! Yes! That's it!"

"That's what? And stop hollering. I'm not deaf."

"I don't want to be a boy. I want to be a girl."

It began as a peculiar noise, a strangled gurgling far back in her throat that bubbled into laughter. Her tiny lips stretched and widened; drunken laughter spilled out of her mouth like vomit, and it seemed to be spurting all over me —laughter that sounded like vomit smells.

"Please, please. Mrs. Ferguson, you don't understand. I'm very worried. I'm worried all the time. There's something wrong. Please. You've got to understand."

She went on rocking with laughter and her rocking chair rocked with her.

Then I said: "You *are* stupid. Dumb and stupid." And I tried to grab the necklace away from her.

The laughter stopped as though she had been struck by lightning; a storm overtook her face, total fury. Yet when she spoke her voice was soft and hissing and serpentine: "You don't know what you want, boy. I'll show you what you want. Look at me, boy. Look here. I'll show you what you want."

"Please. I don't want anything."

"Open your eyes, boy."

Somewhere in the house a baby was crying.

"Look at me, boy. Look here."

What she wanted me to look at was the yellow stone. She was holding it above her head, and slightly swinging it. It seemed to have gathered up all the light in the room, accumulated a devastating brilliance that plunged everything else into blackness. Swing, spin, dazzle, dazzle.

"I hear a baby crying."

"That's you you hear."

"Stupid woman. Stupid. Stupid."

"Look here, boy."

Spindazzlespinspindazzledazzledazzle.

It was still daylight, and it was still Sunday, and here I was back in the Garden District, standing in front of my house. I don't know how I got there. Someone must have brought me, but I don't know who; my last memory was the noise of Mrs. Ferguson's laughter returning.

Of course, a huge commotion was made over the missing necklace. The police were not called, but the whole household was upside down for days; not an inch was left unsearched. My grandmother was very upset. But even if the necklace had been of high value, a jewel that could have been sold and assured her of comfort the rest of her life, I still would not have accused Mrs. Ferguson. For if I did, she might reveal what I'd told her, the thing I never told anyone again, not ever. Finally it was decided that a thief had stolen into the house and taken the necklace while my grandmother slept. Well, that was the truth. Everyone was relieved when my grandmother concluded her visit and returned to Florida. It was hoped that the whole sad affair of the missing jewel would soon be forgotten.

But it was not forgotten. Forty-four years evaporated, and it was not forgotten. I became a middle-aged man, riddled with quirks and quaint notions. My grandmother died, still sane and sound of mind despite her great age.

A cousin called to inform me of her death, and to ask when I would be arriving for the funeral; I said I'd let her know. I was ill with grief, inconsolable; and it was absurd, out of all proportion. My grandmother was not someone I had loved. Yet how I grieved! But I did not travel to the funeral, nor even send flowers. I stayed home and drank a quart of vodka. I was very drunk, but I can remember answering the telephone and hearing my father identify himself. His old man's voice trembled with more than the weight of years; he vented the pent-up wrath of a lifetime, and when I remained silent, he said: "You sonofabitch. She died with your picture in her hand." I said "I'm sorry," and hung up. What was there to say? How could I explain that all through the years any mention of my grandmother, any letter from her or thought of her, evoked Mrs. Ferguson? Her laughter, her fury, the swinging, spinning yellow stone: spindazzledazzle.

II
Handcarved
Coffins

Handcarved Coffins:

A Nonfiction Account of an
American Crime

March, 1975.

A town in a small Western state. A focus for the many large farms and cattle-raising ranches surrounding it, the town, with a population of less than ten thousand, supports twelve churches and two restaurants. A movie house, though it has not shown a movie in ten years, still stands stark and cheerless on Main Street. There once was a hotel, too; but that also had been closed, and nowadays the only place a traveler can find shelter is the Prairie Motel.

The motel is clean, the rooms are well heated; that's about all you can say for it. A man named Jake Pepper has been living there for almost five years. He is fifty-eight, a widower with four grown sons. He is five-foot-ten, in top condition, and looks fifteen years younger than his age. He has a handsome-homely face with periwinkle blue eyes and a thin mouth that twitches into quirky shapes that are sometimes smiles and sometimes not. The secret of his boyish appearance is not his lanky trimness, not his chunky ripe-apple cheeks, nor his naughty mysterious grins; it's because of his hair that looks like somebody's kid brother: dark blond, clipped short, and so afflicted with cow-licks that he cannot really comb it; he sort of wets it down.

Jake Pepper is a detective employed by the State Bureau of Investigation. We had first met each other through a close mutual friend, another detective in a different state. In 1972 he wrote a letter saying he was working on a murder case, something that he thought might interest me. I telephoned him and we talked for three hours. I was very interested in what he had to tell me, but he became alarmed when I suggested that I travel out there and survey the situation myself; he said that would be premature and might endanger his investigation, but he promised to keep me informed. For the next three years we exchanged telephone calls every few months. The case, developing along lines intricate as a rat's maze, seemed to have reached an impasse. Finally I said: Just let me come there and look around.

And so it was that I found myself one cold March night sitting with Jake Pepper in his motel room on the wintry, windblown outskirts of this forlorn little Western town. Actually, the room was pleasant, cozy; after all, off and on, it had been Jake's home for almost five years, and he had built shelves to display pictures of his family, his sons and grandchildren, and to hold hundreds of books, many of them concerning the Civil War and all of them the selections of an intelligent man: he was partial to Dickens, Melville, Trollope, Mark Twain.

Jake sat crosslegged on the floor, a glass of bourbon beside him. He had a chessboard spread before him; absently he shifted the chessmen about.

TC: The amazing thing is, nobody seems to know anything about this case. It's had almost no publicity.
JAKE: There are reasons.
TC: I've never been able to put it into proper sequence. It's like a jigsaw puzzle with half the pieces missing.
JAKE: Where shall we begin?
TC: From the beginning.
JAKE: Go over to the bureau. Look in the bottom drawer. See that little cardboard box? Take a look at what's inside it.

(What I found inside the box was a miniature coffin. It was a beautifully made object, carved from light balsam wood. It was undecorated; but when one opened the hinged lid one discovered the coffin was not empty. It contained a photograph—a casual, candid snapshot of two middle-aged people, a man and a woman, crossing a street. It was not a posed picture; one sensed that the subjects were unaware that they were being photographed.)

That little coffin. I guess that's what you might call the beginning.
TC: And the picture?
JAKE: George Roberts and his wife. George and Amelia Roberts.
TC: Mr. and Mrs. Roberts. Of course. The first victims. He was a lawyer?
JAKE: He was a lawyer, and one morning (to be exact: the tenth of August 1970) he got a present in the mail. That little coffin. With the picture inside it. Roberts was a happy-go-lucky guy; he showed it to some people around the courthouse and acted like it was a joke. One month later George and Amelia were two very dead people.
TC: How soon did you come on the case?

JAKE: Immediately. An hour after they found them I was on my way here with two other agents from the Bureau. When we got here the bodies were still in the car. And so were the snakes. That's something I'll never forget. Never.

TC: Go back. Describe it exactly.

JAKE: The Robertses had no children. Nor enemies, either. Everybody liked them. Amelia worked for her husband; she was his secretary. They had only one car, and they always drove to work together. The morning it happened was hot. A sizzler. So I guess they must have been surprised when they went out to get in their car and found all the windows rolled up. Anyway, they each entered the car through separate doors, and as soon as they were inside—*wam!* A tangle of rattlesnakes hit them like lightning. We found nine big rattlers inside that car. All of them had been injected with amphetamine; they were crazy, they bit the Robertses everywhere: neck, arms, ears, cheeks, hands. Poor people. Their heads were huge and swollen like Halloween pumpkins painted green. They must have died almost instantly. I hope so. That's one hope I really hope.

TC: Rattlesnakes aren't that prevalent in these regions. Not rattlesnakes of that caliber. They must have been brought here.

JAKE: They were. From a snake farm in Nogales, Texas. But now's not the time to tell you how I know that.

(Outside, crusts of snow laced the ground; spring was a long way off— a hard wind whipping the window announced that winter was still with us. But the sound of the wind was only a murmur in my head underneath the racket of rattling rattlesnakes, hissing tongues. I saw the car dark under a hot sun, the swirling serpents, the human heads growing green, expanding with poison. I listened to the wind, letting it wipe the scene away.)

JAKE: 'Course, we don't know if the Baxters ever got a coffin. I'm sure they did; it wouldn't fit the pattern if they hadn't. But they never mentioned receiving a coffin, and we never found a trace of it.

TC: Perhaps it got lost in the fire. But wasn't there someone with them, another couple?

JAKE: The Hogans. From Tulsa. They were just friends of the Baxters who were passing through. The killer never meant to kill them. It was an accident.

See, what happened was: the Baxters were building a fancy new house, but the only part of it that was really finished was the basement. All the rest was still under construction. Roy Baxter was a well-to-do man; he could've afforded to rent this whole motel while his house was being built. But he chose to live in this underground basement, and the only entrance to it was through a trap door.

It was December—three months after the rattlesnake murders. All we know for certain is: the Baxters invited this couple from Tulsa to spend the night with them in their basement. And sometime just before dawn one humdinger of a fire broke out in that basement, and the four people were incinerated. I mean that literally: burned to ashes.

TC: But couldn't they have escaped through the trap door?

JAKE (twisting his lips, snorting): Hell, no. The arsonist, the murderer, had piled cement blocks on top of it. King Kong couldn't have budged it.

TC: But obviously there had to be some connection between the fire and the rattlesnakes.

JAKE: That's easy to say now. But damned if I could make any connection. We had five guys working this case; we knew more about George and Amelia Roberts, about the Baxters and the Hogans, than they ever knew about themselves. I'll bet George Roberts never knew his wife had had a baby when she was fifteen and had given it away for adoption.

'Course, in a place this size, everybody more or less knows everybody else, at least by sight. But we could find nothing that linked the victims. Or any motivations. There was no reason, none that we could find, why anybody would want to kill any of those people. (He studied his chessboard; he lit a pipe and sipped his bourbon) The victims, all of them were strangers to me. I'd never heard of them till they were dead. But the next fellow was a friend of mine. Clem Anderson. Second-generation Norwegian; he'd inherited a ranch here from his father, a pretty nice spread. We'd gone to college together, though he was a freshman when I was a senior. He married an old girl friend of mine, wonderful girl, the only girl I've ever seen with lavender eyes. Like amethyst. Sometimes, when I'd had a snootful, I used to talk about Amy and her amethyst eyes, and my wife didn't think it was one bit funny. Anyway, Clem and Amy got married and settled out here and had seven children. I had dinner at their house the night before he got killed, and Amy said the only regret she had in life was that she hadn't had more children.

But I'd been seeing a lot of Clem right along. Ever since I came out here on the case. He had a wild streak, he drank too much; but he was shrewd, he taught me a lot about this town.

One night he called me here at the motel. He sounded funny. He said he had to see me right away. So I said come on over. I thought he was drunk, but it wasn't that—he was scared. Know why?

TC: Santa Claus had sent him a present.

JAKE: Uh-huh. But you see, he didn't know what it was. What it meant. The coffin, and its possible connection to the rattlesnake murders, had never been made public. We were keeping that a secret. I had never mentioned the matter to Clem.

So when he arrived in this very room, and showed me a coffin that was an exact replica of the one the Robertses had received, I knew my friend was in great danger. It had been mailed to him in a box wrapped in brown paper; his name and address were printed in an anonymous style. Black ink.

TC: And was there a picture of him?

JAKE: Yes. And I'll describe it carefully because it is very relevant to the manner of Clem's death. Actually, I think the murderer meant it as a little joke, a sly hint as to how Clem was going to die.

In the picture, Clem is seated in a kind of jeep. An eccentric vehicle of his own invention. It had no top and it had no windshield, nothing to protect the driver at all. It was just an engine with four wheels. He said he'd never seen the picture before, and had no idea who had taken it or when.

Now I had a difficult decision. Should I confide in him, admit that the Roberts family had received a similar coffin before their deaths, and that the Baxters probably had as well? In some ways it might be better not to inform him: that way, if we kept close surveillance, he might lead us to the killer, and do it more easily by not being aware of his danger.

TC: But you decided to tell him.

JAKE: I did. Because, with this second coffin in hand, I was certain the murders were connected. And I felt that Clem must know the answer. He *must*.

But after I explained the significance of the coffin, he went into shock. I had to slap his face. And then he was like a child; he lay down on the bed and began to cry: "Somebody's going to kill me. Why? Why?" I told him: "Nobody's going to kill you. I can promise you that. But *think*, Clem! What do you have in common with these people who *did* die? There must be something. Maybe something very trivial." But all he could say was: "I don't know. I don't know." I forced him to drink until he was drunk enough to fall asleep. He spent the night here. In the morning he was calmer. But he still could not think of anything that connected him with the crimes, see how he in any way fitted into a pattern. I told him not to discuss the coffin with anyone, not even his wife; and I told him not to worry—I was importing an extra two agents just to keep an eye on him.

TC: And how long was it before the coffin-maker kept his promise?

JAKE: Oh, I think he must have been enjoying it. He teased it along like a fisherman with a trout trapped in a bowl. The Bureau recalled the extra agents, and finally even Clem seemed to shrug it off. Six months went by. Amy called and invited me out to dinner. A warm summer night. The air was full of fireflies. Some of the children chased about catching them and putting them into jars.

As I was leaving, Clem walked me out to my car. A narrow river ran along the path where it was parked, and Clem said: "About that connection business. The other day I suddenly thought of something. The river." I said what river; and he said that river, the one flowing past us. "It's kind of a complicated story. And probably silly. But I'll tell you the next time I see you."

Of course I never saw him again. At least, not alive.

TC: It's almost as though he must have overheard you.

JAKE: Who?

TC: Santa Claus. I mean, isn't it curious that after all those months Clem Anderson mentions the river, and the very next day, before he can tell you why he suddenly remembered the river, the murderer kept his promise?

JAKE: How's your stomach?

TC: Okay.

JAKE: I'll show you some photographs. But better pour yourself a stiff one. You'll need it.

(The pictures, three of them, were glossy black-and-whites made at night with a flash camera. The first was of Clem Anderson's homemade jeep on a narrow ranch road, where it had overturned and was lying on its side, headlights still shining. The second photograph was of a headless torso sprawled across the same road: a headless man wearing boots and Levis and a sheepskin jacket. The last picture was of the victim's head. It could not have been more cleanly severed by a guillotine or a master surgeon. It lay alone among some leaves, as though a prankster had tossed it there. Clem Anderson's eyes were open, but they did not look dead, merely serene, and except for a jagged gash along the forehead, his face seemed as calm, as unmarked by violence as his innocent, pale Norwegian eyes. As I examined the photographs, Jake leaned over my shoulder, looking at them with me.)

JAKE: It was around dusk. Amy was expecting Clem home for supper. She sent one of their boys down to the main road to meet him. It was the boy who found him.

First he saw the overturned car. Then, a hundred yards farther on, he found the body. He ran back home, and his mother called me. I cursed myself up one row and down the other. But when we drove out there, it was one of my agents who discovered the head. It was quite a distance from the body. In fact, it was still lying where the wire had hit him.

TC: The wire, yes. I never have understood about the wire. It's so—

JAKE: Clever?

TC: More than clever. Preposterous.

JAKE: Nothing preposterous about it. Our friend had simply figured out a nice neat way to decapitate Clem Anderson. Kill him without any possibility of witnesses.

TC: I suppose it's the mathematical element. I'm always bewildered by anything involving mathematics.

JAKE: Well, the gentleman responsible for this certainly has a mathematical mind. At least he had a lot of very accurate measuring to do.

TC: He strung a wire between two trees?

JAKE: A tree and a telephone pole. A strong steel wire sharpened thin as a razor. Virtually invisible, even in broad daylight. But at dusk, when Clem turned off the highway and was driving in that crazy little wagon along that narrow road, he couldn't possibly have glimpsed it. It caught him exactly where it was supposed to: just under the chin. And, as you can see, sliced off his head as easily as a girl picking petals off a daisy.

TC: So many things could have gone *wrong*.

JAKE: What if they had? What's one failure? He would have tried again. And continued till he succeeded.

TC: *That's* what's so preposterous. He always does succeed.

JAKE: Yes and no. But we'll come back to that later.

(Jake slipped the pictures in a manila envelope. He sucked on his pipe and combed his fingers through his cowlicked hair. I was silent, for I felt a sadness had overtaken him. Finally I asked if he was tired, would he rather I left him? He said no, it was only nine o'clock, he never went to bed before midnight.)

TC: Are you here all alone now?

JAKE: No, Christ, I'd go crazy. I take turns with two other agents. But I'm still the principal guy on the case. And I want it that way. I've got a real investment here. And I'm going to nail our chum if it's the last thing I ever do. He'll make a mistake. In fact, he's already made some. Though I can't say that the manner in which he disposed of Dr. Parsons was one of them.

TC: The coroner?

JAKE: The coroner. The skinny itsy-bitsy hunchbacked little coroner.

TC: Let's see, now. At first you thought that was a suicide?

JAKE: If you'd known Dr. Parsons, you'd have thought it was a suicide, too. There was a man who had every reason to kill himself. Or get himself killed. His wife's a beautiful woman, and he had her hooked on morphine; that's how he got her to marry him. He was a loan shark. An abortionist. At least a dozen dotty old women left him everything in their wills. A true-blue scoundrel, Dr. Parsons.

TC: So you didn't like him?

JAKE: Nobody did. But what I said before was wrong. I said Parsons was a guy who had every reason to kill himself. Actually, he had no reason at all. God was in His heaven, and the sun was shining on Ed Parsons right around the clock. The only thing bothering him was he had ulcers. And a kind of permanent indigestion. He always carried around these big bottles of Maalox. Polished off a couple of those a day.

TC: All the same, everyone was surprised when they heard Dr. Parsons had killed himself?

JAKE: Well, no. Because nobody thought he had killed himself. Not at first.

TC: Sorry, Jake. But I'm getting confused again.

(Jake's pipe had gone out; he dumped it in an ashtray and unwrapped a cigar, which he did not light; it was an object to chew on, not to smoke. A dog with a bone.)

To begin with, how long was it between funerals? Between Clem Anderson's funeral and Dr. Parsons'?

JAKE: Four months. Just about.

TC: And did Santa send the doctor a gift?

JAKE: Wait. Wait. You're going too fast. The day Parsons died—well, we just thought he had died. Plain and simple. His nurse found him lying on the floor of his office. Alfred Skinner, another doctor here in town, said he'd probably had a heart attack; it would take an autopsy to find out for sure.

That same night I got a call from Parsons' nurse. She said Mrs. Parsons would like to talk to me, and I said fine, I'll drive out there now.

Mrs. Parsons received me in her bedroom, a room I gather she seldom leaves; confined there, I suppose, by the pleasures of morphine. Certainly she isn't an invalid, not in any ordinary sense. She's a lovely woman, and a quite healthy-looking one. Good color in her cheeks, though her skin is smooth and pale as pearls. But her eyes were too bright, the pupils dilated.

She was lying in bed, propped up by a pile of lace-covered pillows. I noticed her fingernails—so long and carefully varnished; and her hands were very elegant, too. But what she was holding in her hands wasn't very elegant.

TC: A gift?

JAKE: Exactly the same as the others.

TC: What did she say?

JAKE: She said "I think my husband was murdered." But she was very calm; she didn't seem upset, under any stress at all.

TC: Morphine.

JAKE: But it was more than that. She's a woman who has already left life. She's looking back through a door—without regret.

TC: Did she realize the significance of the coffin?

JAKE: Not really, no. And neither would her husband. Even though he was the county coroner, and in theory was part of our team, we never confided in him. He knew nothing about the coffins.

TC: Then why did she think her husband had been murdered?

JAKE (chewing his cigar, frowning): *Because* of the coffin. She said her husband had shown it to her a few weeks ago. He hadn't taken it seriously; he thought it was just a spiteful gesture, something sent to him by one of his enemies. But *she* said—she said the moment she saw the coffin and saw the picture of him inside it—she felt "a shadow" had fallen. Strange, but I think she loved him. That beautiful woman. That bristling little hunchback.

When we said goodnight I took the coffin with me and impressed on her the importance of not mentioning it to anyone. After that, all we could do was wait for the autopsy report. Which was: Death by poisoning, probably self-administered.

TC: But *you* knew it was a murder.

JAKE: I knew. And Mrs. Parsons knew. But everybody else thought it was a suicide. Most of them still think so.

TC: And what brand of poison did our friend choose?

JAKE: Liquid nicotine. A very pure poison, fast and powerful, colorless, odorless. We don't know exactly how it was administered, but I suspect it was mixed together with some of the doctor's beloved Maalox. One good gulp, and down you go.

TC: Liquid nicotine. I've never heard of it.

JAKE: Well, it's not exactly a name brand—like arsenic. Speaking of our friend, I came across something the other day, something by Mark Twain, that struck me as very appropriate. (After searching his bookshelves, and finding the volume he wanted, Jake paced the room, reading aloud in a voice unlike his own: a hoarse, angry voice) "Of all the creatures that were made, man is the most *detestable*. Of the entire brood he is the only one, the solitary one, that possesses malice. That is the basest of all instincts, passions, vices—the most hateful. He is the only creature that inflicts pain for sport, knowing it to *be* pain. Also in all the list, he is the only creature that has a nasty mind." (Jake banged the book shut and threw it on the bed) Detestable. Malicious. A nasty mind. Yessir, that describes Mr. Quinn perfectly. Not the whole of him. Mr. Quinn is a man of varied talents.

TC: You never told me his name before.

JAKE: I've only known it myself the last six months. But that's it. Quinn.

> (Again and again Jake slammed a hard fist into a cupped hand, like an angry prisoner too long confined, frustrated. Well, he had now been imprisoned by this case for many years; great fury, like great whiskey, requires long fermentation.)

Robert Hawley Quinn, Esquire. A most esteemed gentleman.

TC: But a gentleman who makes mistakes. Otherwise, you wouldn't know his name. Or rather, you wouldn't know he *was* our friend.

JAKE: (Silence; he's not listening.)

TC: Was it the snakes? You said they came from a Texas snake farm. If you know that, then you must know who bought them.

JAKE (anger gone; yawning): What?

TC: Incidentally, why were the snakes injected with amphetamine?

JAKE: Why do you think? To stimulate them. Increase their ferocity. It was like throwing a lighted match into a gasoline tank.

TC: I wonder, though. I wonder how he managed to inject the snakes, and install them in that car, all without getting bitten himself.

JAKE: He was taught how to do it.

TC: By whom?

JAKE: By the woman who sold him the snakes.

TC: A *woman*?

JAKE: The snake farm in Nogales, it's owned by a woman. You think that's funny? My oldest boy married a girl who works for the Miami police department; she's a professional deep-sea diver. The best car mechanic I know is a woman—

> (The telephone interrupted; Jake glanced at his wristwatch and smiled, and his smile, so real and relaxed, told me not only that he knew who the caller was, but that it was someone whose voice he'd been happily expecting to hear.)

Hello, Addie. Yeah, he's here. He says it's spring in New York; I said he should've stayed there. Naw, nothin'. Just knocking off some drinks and discussing you-know-what. Is tomorrow Sunday? I thought it was Thursday. Maybe I'm losing my marbles. Sure, we'd love to come to dinner. Addie— don't *worry* about it. He'll like anything you cook. You're the greatest cook either side of the Rockies, east or west. So don't make a big deal out of it. Yeah, well, maybe that raisin pie with the apple crust. Lock your doors. Sleep tight. Yes, I do. You know I do. *Buenas noches.*

(After he'd hung up, his smile remained, broadened. At last he lit the cigar, puffed on it with pleasure. He pointed at the phone, chuckled.)

That was the mistake Mr. Quinn made. Adelaide Mason. She invited us to dinner tomorrow.

TC: And who is Mrs. Mason?

JAKE: *Miss* Mason. She's a terrific cook.

TC: But other than that?

JAKE: Addie Mason was what I had been waiting for. My big break.

You know, my wife's dad was a Methodist minister. She was very serious about the whole family going to church. I used to get out of it as much as I could, and after she died I never went at all. But about six months ago the Bureau was ready to close shop on this case. We'd spent a lot of time and a lot of money. And we had nothing to show for it; no case at all. Eight murders, and not a single clue that would link the victims together to produce some semblance of a motive. Nothing. Except those three little handcarved coffins.

I said to myself: No! No, it can't be! There's a *mind* behind all this, a reason. I started going to church. There's nothing to do here on Sunday anyway. Not even a golf course. And I prayed: Please, God, don't let this sonofabitch get away with it!

Over on Main Street there's a place called the Okay Café. Everybody knows you can find me there just about any morning between eight and ten. I have my breakfast in the corner booth, and then just hang around reading the papers and talking to the different guys, local businessmen, that stop by for a cup of coffee.

Last Thanksgiving Day, I was having breakfast there as usual. I had the place pretty much to myself, it being a holiday and all; and I was in low spirits anyway—the Bureau was putting the final pressure on me to close this case and clear out. Christ, it wasn't that I didn't want to dust off this damn town! I sure as hell did. But the idea of quitting, of leaving that devil to dance on all those graves, made me sick to my guts. One time, thinking about it, I did vomit. I actually did.

Well, suddenly Adelaide Mason walked into the café. She came straight to my table. I'd met her many times, but I'd never really talked to her. She's a schoolteacher, teaches first grade. She lives here with her sister, Marylee, a widow. Addie Mason said: "Mr. Pepper, surely you're not going to spend Thanksgiving in the Okay Café? If you haven't other plans, why don't you take dinner at our house? It's just my sister and myself." Addie isn't a nervous woman, but despite her smiles and cordiality, she seemed, hmnn, distracted. I thought: Maybe she considers it not quite proper for an unmarried lady to invite an unmarried man, a mere acquaintance, to her home. But before I could say yes or no, she said: "To be truthful, Mr. Pepper, I have a problem.

Something I need to discuss with you. This will give us the chance. Shall we say noon?"

I've never eaten better food—and instead of turkey they served squabs with wild rice and a good champagne. All during the meal Addie kept the conversation moving in a very amusing manner. She didn't appear nervous at all, but her sister did.

After dinner we sat down in the living room with coffee and brandy. Addie excused herself from the room, and when she came back she was carrying—

TC: Two guesses?

JAKE: She handed it to me, and said: "This is what I wanted to discuss with you."

(Jake's thin lips manufactured a smoke ring, then another. Until he sighed, the only sound in the room was the meowing wind clawing at the window.)

You've had a long trip. Maybe we ought to call it a night.

TC: You mean you're going to leave me hanging out here?

JAKE (seriously, but with one of his mischievously ambiguous grins): Just until tomorrow. I think you should hear Addie's story from Addie herself. Come along; I'll walk you to your room.

(Oddly, sleep struck me as though I'd been hit by a thief's blackjack; it *had* been a long journey, my sinus was troubling me, I was tired. But within minutes I was awake; or, rather, I entered some sphere between sleep and wakefulness, my mind like a crystal lozenge, a suspended instrument that caught the reflections of spiraling images: a man's head among leaves, the windows of a car streaked with venom, the eyes of serpents sliding through heat-mist, fire flowing from the earth, scorched fists pounding at a cellar door, taut wire gleaming in the twilight, a torso on a roadway, a head among leaves, fire, fire, fire flowing like a river, river, river. Then a telephone rings.)

MAN'S VOICE: How about it? Are you going to sleep all day?

TC (the curtains are drawn, the room is dark, I don't know where I am, who I am): Hello?

MAN'S VOICE: Jake Pepper speaking. Remember him? Mean guy? With mean blue eyes?

TC: Jake! What time is it?

JAKE: A little after eleven. Addie Mason's expecting us in about an hour. So jump under the shower. And wear something warm. It's snowing outside.

(It was a heavy snow, thick flakes too heavy to float; it fell to the ground and covered it. As we drove away from the motel in Jake's car, he turned on his windshield wipers. Main Street was grey and white and empty, lifeless except for a solitary traffic light winking its colors. Everything was closed, even the Okay Café. The somberness, the gloomy snow-silence, infected us; neither of us spoke. But I sensed that Jake was in a good mood, as though he was anticipating pleasant events. His healthy face was shiny, and he smelled, a bit too sharply, of after-shave lotion. Though his hair was rumpled as ever, he was carefully dressed—but not as though he was headed for church. The red tie he wore was appropriate for a more festive occasion. A suitor en route to a rendezvous? The possibility had occurred to me last night when I'd heard him talking to Miss Mason; there was a tone, a timbre, an intimacy.

But the instant I met Adelaide Mason, I crossed the thought right out of my mind. It didn't matter how bored and lonely Jake might be, the woman was simply too plain. That, at least, was my initial impression. She was somewhat younger than her sister, Marylee Connor, who was a woman in her late forties; her face was a nice face, amiable, but too strong, masculine—cosmetics would only have underlined this quality, and very wisely she wore none. Cleanliness was her most attractive physical feature —her brown bobbed hair, her fingernails, her skin: it was as though she bathed in some special spring rain. She and her sister were fourth-genera-tion natives of the town, and she had been teaching school there since she left college; one wondered why—with her intelligence, her character and general sophistication, it was surprising that she hadn't sought a vaster auditorium for her abilities than a schoolroom full of six-year-olds. "No," she told me, "I'm very happy. I'm doing what I enjoy. Teaching first grade. To be there at the beginning, that's what I like. And with first-graders, you see, I get to teach all subjects. That includes manners. Manners are very important. So few of my children ever learn any at home."

The rambling old house that the sisters shared, a family inheritance, reflected, in its warm soothing comfort, its civilized solid colors and atmospheric "touches," the personality of the younger woman, for Mrs. Connor, agreeable as she was, lacked Adelaide Mason's selective eye, imagination.

The living room, mostly blue and white, was filled with flowering plants, and contained an immense Victorian birdcage, the residence of a half-dozen musical canaries. The dining room was yellow and white and green, with pine-plank floors, bare and polished mirror-bright; logs blazed in a big fireplace. Miss Mason's culinary gifts were even greater than Jake had claimed. She served an extraordinary Irish stew, an amazing apple and raisin pie; and there was red wine, white wine, champagne. Mrs. Connor's husband had left her well-off.

It was during dinner that my original impression of our younger hostess began to change. Yes, very definitely an understanding existed between Jake and this lady. They were lovers. And watching her more attentively, seeing her, as it were, through Jake's eyes, I began to appreciate his unmistakable sensual interest. True, her face was flawed, but her figure, displayed in a close-fitting grey jersey dress, was adequate, not bad really; and she *acted* as though it was *sensational*: a rival to the sexiest film star imaginable. The sway of her hips, the loose movements of her fruity breasts, her contralto voice, the fragility of her hand-gestures: all ultra seductive, ultra feminine without being effeminate. Her power resided in her attitude: she behaved as though she believed she was irresistible; and whatever her opportunities may have been, the style of the woman implied an erotic history complete with footnotes.

As dinner ended, Jake looked at her as if he'd like to march her straight into the bedroom: the tension between them was as taut as the steel wire that had severed Clem Anderson's head. However, he unwrapped a cigar, which Miss Mason proceeded to light for him. I laughed.)

JAKE: Eh?

TC: It's like an Edith Wharton novel. *The House of Mirth*—where ladies are forever lighting gentlemen's cigars.

MRS. CONNOR (defensively): That's quite the custom here. My mother always lighted our father's cigars. Even though she disliked the aroma. Isn't that so, Addie?

ADDIE: Yes, Marylee. Jake, would you like more coffee?

JAKE: Sit still, Addie. I don't want anything. It was a wonderful dinner, and it's time for you to quiet down. Addie? How do you feel about the aroma?

ADDIE (*almost* blushing): I'm very partial to the smell of a good cigar. If I smoked, I'd smoke cigars myself.

JAKE: Addie, let's go back to last Thanksgiving. When we were sitting around like we are now.

ADDIE: And I showed you the coffin?

JAKE: I want you to tell my friend your story. Just as you told it to me.

MRS. CONNOR (pushing back her chair): Oh, please! Must we talk about that? Always! Always! I have nightmares.

ADDIE (rising, placing an arm around her sister's shoulder): That's all right, Marylee. We won't talk about it. We'll move to the living room, and you can play the piano for us.

MRS. CONNOR: It's so *vile.* (Then, looking at me) I'm sure you think I'm a dreadful sissy. No doubt I am. In any event, I've had too much wine.

ADDIE: Darling, what you need is a nap.

MRS. CONNOR: A nap? Addie, how many times have I told you? *I* have *night-mares.* (Now, recovering) Of course. A nap. If you'll excuse me.

(As her sister departed, Addie poured herself a glass of red wine, lifted it, letting the glow from the fireplace enhance its scarlet sparkle. Her eyes drifted from the fire to the wine to me. Her eyes were brown, but the various illuminations—firelight, candles on the table—colored them, made them cat-yellow. In the distance the caged canaries sang, and snow, fluttering at the windows like torn lace curtains, emphasized the comforts of the room, the warmth of the fire, the redness of the wine.)

ADDIE: My story. Ho-hum.

I'm forty-four, I've never married, I've been around the world twice, I try to go to Europe every other summer; but it's fair to say that except for a drunken sailor who went berserk and tried to rape me on a Swedish tramp steamer, nothing of a bizarre nature has ever happened to me until this year —the week before Thanksgiving.

My sister and I have a box at the post office; what they call a "drawer"— it's not that we have such a lot of correspondence, but we subscribe to so many magazines. Anyway, on my way home from school I stopped to pick up the mail, and in our drawer there was a package, rather large but very light. It was wrapped in old wrinkled brown paper that looked as if it had been used before, and it was tied with old twine. The postmark was local and it was addressed to me. My name was precisely printed in thick black ink. Even before I opened it I thought: What kind of rubbish is this? Of course, you know all about the coffins?

TC: I've seen one, yes.

ADDIE: Well, I knew nothing about them. No one did. That was a secret between Jake and his agents.

> (She winked at Jake, and tilting her head back, swallowed all her wine in one swoop; she did this with astonishing grace, an agility that revealed a lovely throat. Jake, winking back, directed a smoke ring toward her, and the empty oval, floating through the air, seemed to carry with it an erotic message.)

Actually, I didn't open the package until quite late that night. Because when I got home I found my sister at the bottom of the stairs; she'd fallen and sprained an ankle. The doctor came. There was so much commotion. I forgot about the package until after I'd gone to bed. I decided: Oh well, it can wait until tomorrow. I wish I'd abided by that decision; at least I wouldn't have lost a night's sleep.

Because. Because it was *shocking.* I once received an anonymous letter, a truly atrocious one—especially upsetting because, just between us, a good deal of what the writer wrote happened to be true. (Laughing, she replenished her glass) It wasn't really the coffin that shocked me. It was the snapshot inside —a quite recent picture of me, taken on the steps outside the post office. It seemed such an intrusion, a theft—having one's picture made when one is unaware of it. I can sympathize with those Africans who run away from cameras, fearing the photographer intends to steal their spirit. I was shocked, but not frightened. It was my sister who was frightened. When I showed her my little gift, she said: "You don't suppose it has anything to do with that other business?" By "other business" she meant what's been happening here the past five years—murders, accidents, suicides, whatever: it depends on who you're talking to.

I shrugged it off, put it in a category with the anonymous letter; but the more I thought about it—perhaps my sister had stumbled on to something. That package had not been sent to me by some jealous woman, a mere mischief-making ill-wisher. This was the work of a man. A man had whittled that coffin.

A man with strong fingers had printed my name on that package. And the whole thing was meant as a threat. But why? I thought: Maybe Mr. Pepper will know.

I'd met Mr. Pepper. Jake. Actually, I had a crush on him.

JAKE: Stick to the story.

ADDIE: I am. I only used the story to lure you into my lair.

JAKE: That's not true.

ADDIE (sadly, her voice in dull counterpoint to the canaries' chirping serenades): No, it isn't true. Because by the time I decided to speak to Jake, I had concluded that someone did indeed intend to kill me; and I had a fair notion who it was, even though the motive was so improbable. Trivial.

JAKE: It's neither improbable nor trivial. Not after you've studied the style of the beast.

ADDIE (ignoring him; and impersonally, as if she were reciting the multiplication table to her students): Everybody knows everybody else. That's what they say about small-town people. But it isn't true. I've never met the parents of some of my pupils. I pass people every day who are virtual strangers. I'm a Baptist, our congregation isn't all that large; but we have some members—well, I couldn't tell you their names if you held a revolver to my head.

The point is: when I began to think about the people who had died, I realized I had known them all. Except the couple from Tulsa who were staying with Ed Baxter and his wife—

JAKE: The Hogans.

ADDIE: Yes. Well, they're not part of this anyway. Bystanders—who got caught in an inferno. Literally.

Not that any of the victims were close friends—except, perhaps, Clem and Amy Anderson. I'd taught all their children in school.

But I knew the others: George and Amelia Roberts, the Baxters, Dr. Parsons. I knew them rather well. And for only one reason. (She gazed into her wine, observed its ruby flickerings, like a gypsy consulting clouded crystal, ghostly glass) The river. (She raised the wineglass to her lips, and again drained it in one long luxuriously effortless gulp) Have you seen the river? Not yet? Well, now is not the time of year. But in the summer it is very nice. By far the prettiest thing around here. We call it Blue River; it is blue—not Caribbean blue, but very clear all the same and with a sandy bottom and deep quiet pools for swimming. It originates in those mountains to the north and flows through the plains and ranches; it's our main source of irrigation, and it has two tributaries—much smaller rivers, one called Big Brother and the other Little Brother.

The trouble started because of these tributaries. Many ranchers, who were dependent on them, felt that a diversion should be created in Blue River to enlarge Big Brother and Little Brother. Naturally, the ranchers whose property was nourished by the main river were against this proposition. None more so than Bob Quinn, owner of the B.Q. Ranch, through which the widest and deepest stretches of Blue River travels.

JAKE (spitting into the fire): Robert Hawley Quinn, Esquire.

ADDIE: It was a quarrel that had been simmering for decades. Everyone knew that strengthening the two tributaries, even at the expense of Blue River (in terms of power and sheer beauty), was the fair and logical thing to do. But the Quinn family, and others among the rich Blue River ranchers, had always, through various tricks, prevented any action from being taken.

Then we had two years of drought, and that brought the situation to a head. The ranchers whose survival depended upon Big Brother and Little Brother were raising holy hell. The drought had hit them hard; they'd lost a lot of cattle, and now they were out full-force demanding their share of Blue River.

Finally the town council voted to appoint a special committee to settle the matter. I have no idea how the members of the committee were chosen. Certainly I had no particular qualification; I remember old Judge Hatfield— he's retired now, living in Arizona—phoned me and asked if I would serve; that's all there was to it. We had our first meeting in the Council Room at the courthouse, January 1970. The other members of the committee were Clem Anderson, George and Amelia Roberts, Dr. Parsons, the Baxters, Tom Henry, and Oliver Jaeger—

JAKE (to me): Jaeger. He's the postmaster. A crazy sonofabitch.

ADDIE: He's not really crazy. You only say that because—

JAKE: Because he's really crazy.

> (Addie was disconcerted. She contemplated her wineglass, moved to refill it, found the bottle empty, and then produced from a small purse, conveniently nestling in her lap, a pretty little silver box filled with blue pills: Valiums; she swallowed one with a sip of water. And Jake had said that Addie was not a nervous woman?)

TC: Who's Tom Henry?

JAKE: Another nut. Nuttier than Oliver Jaeger. He owns a filling station.

ADDIE: Yes, there were nine of us. We met once a week for about two months. Both sides, those for and those against, sent in experts to testify. Many of the ranchers appeared themselves—to talk to us, to present their own case.

But not Mr. Quinn. Not Bob Quinn—we never heard a word from him, even though, as the owner of the B.Q. Ranch, he stood to lose the most if we voted to divert "his" river. I figured: He's too high and mighty to bother with us and our silly little committee; Bob Quinn, he's been busy talking to the governor, the congressmen, the senators; he thinks he's got all those boys in his hip pocket. So whatever we might decide didn't matter. His big-shot buddies would veto it.

But that's not how it turned out. We voted to divert Blue River at exactly the point where it entered Quinn's property; of course, that didn't leave him without a river—he just wouldn't have the hog's share he'd always had before.

The decision would have been unanimous if Tom Henry hadn't gone against us. You're right, Jake. Tom Henry *is* a nut. So the vote stood eight to one.

And it proved such a popular decision, a verdict that really harmed no one and benefited many, there wasn't much Quinn's political cronies could do about it, not if they wanted to stay in office.

A few days after the vote I ran into Bob Quinn at the post office. He made a tremendous point of tipping his hat, smiling, asking after my welfare. Not that I expected him to spit on me; still, I'd never met with so much courtesy from him before. One would never have supposed he was resentful. Resentful? Insane!

TC: What does he look like—Mr. Quinn?

JAKE: *Don't tell him!*

ADDIE: Why not?

JAKE: Just because.

> (Standing, he walked over to the fireplace and offered what remained of his cigar to the flames. He stood with his back to the fire, legs slightly apart, arms folded: I'd never thought of Jake as vain, but clearly he was posing a bit—trying, successfully, to look attractive. I laughed.)

Eh?

TC: Now it's a Jane Austen novel. In her novels, sexy gentlemen are always warming their fannies at fireplaces.

ADDIE (laughing): Oh, Jake, it's true! It's true!

JAKE: I never read female literature. Never have. Never will.

ADDIE: Just for that, I'm going to open another bottle of wine, and drink it all myself.

> (Jake returned to the table and sat down next to Addie; he took one of her hands in one of his and entwined their fingers. The effect upon her was embarrassingly visible—her face flushed, splashes of red blotched her neck. As for him, he seemed unaware of her, unaware of what he was doing. Rather, he was looking at me; it was as if we were alone together.)

JAKE: Yes, I know. Having heard what you have, you're thinking: Well, now the case is solved. Mr. Quinn did it.

That's what I thought. Last year, after Addie told me what she told you, I lit out of here like a bear with a bumblebee up his ass. I drove straight to the city. Thanksgiving or no Thanksgiving, that very night we had a meeting of the whole Bureau. I laid it on the line: this is the motive, this is the guy. Nobody said boo!—except the chief, and he said: "Slow down, Pepper. The man you're accusing is no flyweight. And where's your case? This is all speculation. Guesswork." Everybody agreed with him. Said: "Where's the evidence?"

I was so mad I was shouting; I said: "What the hell do you think I'm here for? We've all got to pull together and build the evidence. I know Quinn did it." The chief said: "Well, I'd be careful who you said that to. Christ, you could get us all fired."

ADDIE: That next day, when he came back here, I wish I'd taken Jake's picture. In the line of duty I've had to paddle many boys, but none of them ever looked as sad as you, Jake.

JAKE: I wasn't too happy. That's the fact of that.

The Bureau backed me; we began checking out the life of Robert Hawley Quinn from the year one. But we had to move on tiptoe—the chief was jittery as a killer on Death Row. I wanted a warrant to search the B.Q. Ranch, the houses, the whole property. Denied. He wouldn't even let me question the man—

TC: Did Quinn know you suspected him?

JAKE (snorting): Right off the bat. Someone in the governor's office tipped him off. Probably the governor himself. And guys in our own Bureau—they probably told him, too. I don't trust nobody. Nobody connected with this case.

ADDIE: The whole town knew before you could say Rumpelstiltskin.

JAKE: Thanks to Oliver Jaeger. *And* Tom Henry. That's my fault. Since they had both been on the River Committee, I felt I had to take them into my confidence, discuss Quinn, warn them about the coffins. They both promised me they would keep it confidential. Well, telling them, I might as well have had a town meeting and made a speech.

ADDIE: At school, one of my little boys raised his hand and said: "My daddy told my mama somebody sent you a coffin, like for the graveyard. Said Mr. Quinn done it." And I said: "Oh, Bobby, your daddy was just teasing your mama, telling her fairy tales."

JAKE: One of Oliver Jaeger's fairy tales! That bastard called everybody in Christendom. And you say he isn't crazy?

ADDIE: You think he's crazy because he thinks *you're* crazy. He sincerely believes that you're mistaken. That you're persecuting an innocent man. (Still looking at Jake, but addressing me) Oliver would never win any contest, neither for charm nor brains. But he's a rational man—a gossip, but good-hearted. He's related to the Quinn family; Bob Quinn is his second cousin. That may be relevant to the violence of his opinions. It's Oliver's contention, and one that is shared by most people, that even if some connection exists between the decision of the Blue River Committee and the deaths that have occurred here, why point the finger at Bob Quinn? He's not the only Blue River rancher that might bear a grievance. What about Walter Forbes? Jim Johanssen? The Throby family. The Millers. The Rileys. Why pick on Bob Quinn? What are the special circumstances that single him out?

JAKE: He did it.

ADDIE: Yes, he did. We know that. But you can't even prove he bought the rattlesnakes. And even if you could—

JAKE: I'd like a whiskey.

ADDIE: You shall have it, sir. Anybody else?

JAKE (after Addie left on her errand): She's right. We can't prove he bought the snakes, even though we know he did. See, I always figured those snakes came from a professional source; breeders who breed for the venom—they sell it to medical laboratories. The major suppliers are Florida and Texas, but there are snake farms all across the country. Over the last few years we sent inquiries to most of them—and never received a single reply.

But in my heart I knew those rattlers came from the Lone Star State. It was only logical—why would a man go all the way to Florida when he could find what he wanted more or less next door? Well, as soon as Quinn entered the picture, I decided to zero in on the snake angle—an angle we'd never concentrated on to the degree we should have, mainly because it required personal investigation and traveling expenses. When it comes to getting the chief to spend money—hell, it's easier to crack walnuts with store-bought teeth. But I know this fellow, an old-time investigator with the Texas Bureau; he owed me a favor. So I sent him some material: pictures of Quinn I'd managed to collect, and photographs of the rattlers themselves—nine of them hanging on a washline after we'd killed them.

TC: How did you kill them?

JAKE: Shotguns. Blasted their heads off.

TC: I killed a rattler once. With a garden hoe.

JAKE: I don't think you could've killed these bastards with any hoe. Even put a dent in them. The smallest one was seven feet long.

TC: There were nine snakes. And nine members of the Blue River Committee. Nice quaint coincidence.

JAKE: Bill, my Texas friend, he's a determined guy; he covered Texas from border to border, spent most of his vacation visiting snake farms, talking to the breeders. Now, about a month ago, he called and said he thought he had located my party: a Mrs. Garcia, a Tex-Mex lady who owned a snake farm near Nogales. That's about a ten-hour drive from here. If you're driving a State car and doing ninety miles an hour. Bill promised to meet me there.

Addie went with me. We drove overnight, and had breakfast with Bill at a Holiday Inn. Then we visited Mrs. Garcia. Some of these snake farms are tourist attractions; but her place was nothing like that—it was way off the highway, and quite a small operation. But she sure had some impressive specimens. All the time we were there she kept hauling out these huge rattlers, wrapping them around her neck, her arms: laughing; she had almost solid gold-teeth. At first I thought she was a man; she was built like Pancho Villa, and she was wearing cowboy britches with a zipper fly.

She had a cataract in one eye; and the other didn't look too sharp. But she wasn't hesitant about identifying Quinn's picture. She said he had visited her place in either June or July 1970 (the Robertses died 5 September 1970), and that he had been accompanied by a young Mexican; they arrived in a small truck with a Mexican license plate. She said she never spoke to Quinn; according to her, he never said a word—simply listened while she dealt with the Mexican. She said it was not her policy to question a customer as to his reasons for purchasing her merchandise; but, she told us, the Mexican volunteered the information—he wanted a dozen adult rattlers to use in a religious ceremony. That didn't surprise her; she said people often bought snakes for ritualistic usage. But the Mexican wanted her to guarantee that the snakes he bought would attack and kill a bull weighing a thousand pounds. She said yes, that was possible—provided the snakes had been injected with a drug, an amphetamine stimulant, before being put in contact with the bull.

She showed him how to do it, with Quinn observing. She showed us, too. She used a pole, about twice the length of a riding crop and limber as a willow wand; it had a leather loop attached to the end of it. She caught the head of the snake in the loop, dangled him in the air, and jabbed a syringe into the belly. She let the Mexican run a few practice sessions; he did just fine.

TC: Had she ever seen the Mexican before?

JAKE: No. I asked her to describe him, and she described any border-town Mexicali Rose between twenty and thirty. He paid her; she packed the snakes in individual containers, and away they went.

Mrs. Garcia was a very obliging lady. Very cooperative. Until we asked her the important question: would she give us a sworn affidavit that Robert Hawley Quinn was one of two men who had bought a dozen rattlesnakes from her on a certain summer day in 1970? She sure turned sour then. Said she wouldn't sign nothing.

I told her those snakes had been used to murder two people. You should have seen her face then. She walked in the house and locked the doors and pulled down the shades.

TC: An affidavit from her. That wouldn't have carried much legal weight.

JAKE: It would have been something to confront him with: an opening gambit. More than likely, it was the Mexican who put the snakes into Roberts' car; of course, Quinn hired him to do it. Know what? I'll bet that Mexican is dead, buried out there on the lone prairie. Courtesy of Mr. Quinn.

TC: But surely, somewhere in Quinn's history, there must be something to indicate that he was capable of psychotic violence?

(Jake nodded, nodded, nodded.)

JAKE: The gentleman was well acquainted with homicide.

(Addie returned with the whiskey. He thanked her, and kissed her on the cheek. She sat down next to him, and again their hands met, their fingers mingled.)

The Quinns are one of the oldest families here. Bob Quinn is the eldest of three brothers. They all own a share of the B.Q. Ranch, but he's the boss.

ADDIE: No, his wife's the boss. He married his first cousin, Juanita Quinn. Her mother was Spanish, and she has the temper of a hot tamale. Their first child died in childbirth, and she refused to ever have another. It's generally known, though, that Bob Quinn does have children. By another woman in another town.

JAKE: He was a war hero. A colonel in the marines during the Second World War. He never refers to it himself, but to hear other people tell it, Bob Quinn single-handedly slaughtered more Japanese than the Hiroshima bomb.

But right after the war he did a little killing that wasn't quite so patriotic. Late one night he called the sheriff to come out to the B.Q. Ranch and collect a couple of corpses. He claimed he'd caught two men rustling cattle and had shot them dead. That was his tale, and nobody challenged it, at least not publicly. But the truth is those two guys weren't cattle rustlers; they were gamblers from Denver and Quinn owed them a stack of money. They'd traveled down to B.Q. for a promised payoff. What they got was a load of buckshot.

TC: Have you ever questioned him about that?

JAKE: Questioned who?

TC: Quinn.

JAKE: Strictly speaking, I've never *questioned* him at all.

> (His quirky cynical smile bent his mouth; he tinkled the ice in his whiskey, drank some, and chuckled—a deep rough chuckle, like a man trying to bring up phlegm.)

Just lately, I've talked to him plenty. But during the five years I'd been on the case, I'd never met the man. I'd seen him. Knew who he was.

ADDIE: But now they're like two peas in a pod. Real buddies.

JAKE: Addie!

ADDIE: Oh, Jake. I'm only teasing.

JAKE: That's nothing to tease about. It's been pure torture for me.

ADDIE (squeezing his hand): I know. I'm sorry.

> (Jake drained his glass, banged it on the table.)

JAKE: Looking at him. Listening to him. Laughing at his dirty jokes. I hate him. He hates me. We both know that.

ADDIE: Let me sweeten you up with another whiskey.

JAKE: Sit still.

ADDIE: Perhaps I ought to peek in on Marylee. See if she's all right.

JAKE: Sit still.

> (But Addie wanted to escape the room, for she was uncomfortable with Jake's anger, the numb fury inhabiting his face.)

ADDIE (glancing out the window): It's stopped snowing.

JAKE: The Okay Café is always crowded Monday mornings. After the weekend everybody has to stop by to catch up on the news. Ranchers, businessmen, the sheriff and his gang, people from the courthouse. But on this particular Monday—the Monday after Thanksgiving—the place was packed; guys were squatting on each other's laps, and everybody was yakking like a bunch of sissy old women.

You can guess what they were yakking about. Thanks to Tom Henry and Oliver Jaeger, who'd spent the weekend spreading the word, saying that guy from the Bureau, that Jake Pepper fella, was accusing Bob Quinn of murder. I sat in my booth pretending not to notice. But I couldn't help but notice when Bob Quinn himself walked in; you could hear the whole café hold its breath.

He squeezed into a booth next to the sheriff; the sheriff hugged him, and laughed, and let out a cowboy holler. Most of the crowd mimicked him, yelled wahoo, Bob! hiya, Bob! Yessir, the Okay Café was one hundred percent behind Bob Quinn. I had the feeling—a feeling that even if I could prove dead-certain this man was a murderer many times over, they'd lynch me before I could arrest him.

ADDIE (pressing a hand to her forehead, as though she had a headache): He's right. Bob Quinn has the whole town on his side. That's one reason my sister doesn't like to hear us talk about it. She says Jake's wrong, Mr. Quinn's a fine fellow. It's her theory that Dr. Parsons was responsible for these crimes, and that's why he committed suicide.

TC: But Dr. Parsons was dead long before you received the coffin.

JAKE: Marylee's sweet but not too bright. Sorry, Addie, but that's how it is.

> (Addie removed her hand from Jake's: an admonishing gesture, but not
> a severe one. Anyway, it left Jake free to stand up and pace the floor,
> which he did. His footsteps echoed on the polished pine planks.)

So back to the Okay Café. As I was leaving, the sheriff reached out and grabbed my arm. He's a fresh Irish bastard. And crooked as the devil's toes. He said: "Hey, Jake. I wantcha to meet Bob Quinn. Bob, this is Jake Pepper. From the Bureau." I shook Quinn's hand. Quinn said: "I heard plenty about you. I hear you're a chess player. I don't find too many games. How about us getting together?" I said sure, and he said: "Tomorrow okay? Come by around five. We'll have a drink and play a couple of games."

That's how I started. I went to the B.Q. Ranch the next afternoon. We played for two hours. He's a better player than I am, but I won often enough to make it interesting. He's garrulous, he'll talk about anything: politics, women, sex, trout fishing, bowel movements, his trip to Russia, cattle versus wheat, gin versus vodka, Johnny Carson, his safari in Africa, religion, the Bible, Shakespeare, the genius of General MacArthur, bear hunting, Reno whores versus Las Vegas whores, the stock market, venereal diseases, corn-flakes versus Shredded Wheat, gold versus diamonds, capital punishment (he's all for it), football, baseball, basketball—*anything*. Anything except why I'm stuck in this town.

TC: You mean he won't discuss the case?

JAKE (halting in his pacing): It's not that he won't discuss the case. He simply behaves as though it doesn't exist. I discuss it, but he never reacts. I showed him the Clem Anderson photographs: I hoped I could shock him into some response. *Some* comment. But he only looked back at the chessboard, made a move, and told me a dirty joke.

So Mr. Quinn and I have been playing our games within a game several afternoons a week for the last few months. In fact, I'm going there later today. And you—(Cocking a finger in my direction) are going with me.

TC: Am I welcome?

JAKE: I called him this morning. All he asked was: Does he play chess?

TC: I do. But I'd rather watch.

> (A log collapsed, and its crackling drew my attention to the fireplace. I
> stared into the purring flames, and wondered why he had forbidden Addie
> to describe Quinn, tell me what he looked like. I tried to imagine him; I

couldn't. Rather, I remembered the passage from Mark Twain that Jake had read aloud: "Of all the creatures that were made, man is the most detestable . . . the only one, the solitary one, that possesses malice . . . he is the only creature that has a nasty mind." Addie's voice rescued me from my queasy reverie.)

ADDIE: Oh, dear. It's snowing again. But lightly. Just floating. (Then, as though the resumption of the snow had prompted thoughts of mortality, the evaporation of time) You know, it's been almost five months. That's quite long for him. He usually doesn't wait that long.

JAKE (vexed): Addie, what is it now?

ADDIE: My coffin. It's been almost five months. And as I say, he doesn't usually wait that long.

JAKE: Addie! I'm here. Nothing is going to happen to you.

ADDIE: Of course, Jake. I wonder about Oliver Jaeger. I wonder when he'll receive his coffin. Just think, Oliver is the postmaster. He'll be sorting the mail and—(Her voice was suddenly, startlingly quavery, vulnerable—wistful in a way that accentuated the canaries' carefree songfest) Well, it won't be very soon.

TC: Why not?

ADDIE: Because Quinn has to fill my coffin first.

It was after five when we left, the air was still, free of snow, and shimmering with the embers of a sunset and the first pale radiance of a moonrise: a full moon rolling on the horizon like a round white wheel, or a mask, a white featureless menacing mask peering at us through our car windows. At the end of Main Street, just before the town turns into prairie, Jake pointed at a filling station: "That's Tom Henry's place. Tom Henry, Addie, Oliver Jaeger; out of the original River Committee, they're the only three left. I said Tom Henry was a nut. And he is. But he's a lucky nut. He voted against the others. That leaves him in the clear. No coffin for Tom Henry."

TC: *A Coffin for Dimitrios.*

JAKE: What say?

TC: A book by Eric Ambler. A thriller.

JAKE: Fiction? (I nodded; he grimaced) You really read that junk?

TC: Graham Greene was a first-class writer. Until the Vatican grabbed him. After that, he never wrote anything as good as *Brighton Rock.* I like Agatha Christie, love her. And Raymond Chandler is a great stylist, a poet. Even if his plots are a mess.

JAKE: Junk. Those guys are just daydreamers—squat at a typewriter and jerk themselves off, that's all they do.

TC: So no coffin for Tom Henry. How about Oliver Jaeger?

JAKE: He'll get his. One morning he'll be shuffling around the post office, emptying out the incoming mail sacks, and there it will be, a brown box with his very own name printed on it. Forget the cousin stuff; forget that he's been hanging halos over Bob Quinn's head. Saint Bob isn't going to let him off with a few Hail Marys. Not if I know Saint Bob. Chances are, he's already used his whittling knife, made a little something, and popped Oliver Jaeger's picture inside it—

> (Jake's voice jolted to a stop, and as though it were a correlated action, his foot hit the brake pedal: the car skidded, swerved, straightened; we drove on. I knew what had happened. He had remembered, as I was remembering, Addie's pathetic complaint: ". . . Quinn will have to fill my coffin first." I tried to hold my tongue; it rebelled.)

TC: But that means—

JAKE: Better turn on my headlights.

TC: That means Addie is going to die.

JAKE: Hell, no! I just knew you were going to say that! (He slapped a flattened palm against the steering wheel) I've built a wall around Addie. I gave her a .38 Detective Special, and taught her how to use it. She can put a bullet between a man's eyes at a hundred yards. She's learned enough karate to split a plank with one hand-chop. Addie's smart; she won't be tricked. And I'm here. I'm watching her. I'm watching Quinn, too. So are other people.

> (Strong emotion, fears edging toward terror, can demolish the logic of even so logical a man as Jake Pepper—whose precautions had not saved Clem Anderson. I wasn't prepared to argue the point with him, not in his present irrational humor; but why, since he assumed Oliver Jaeger was doomed, was he so certain Addie was not? That she would be spared? For if Quinn stayed true to his design, then absolutely he would have to dispatch Addie, remove her from the scene before he could start the last step of his task by addressing a package to his second cousin and staunch defender, the local postmaster.)

TC: I know Addie's been around the world. But I think it's time she went again.

JAKE (truculently): She can't leave here. Not now.

TC: Oh? She doesn't strike me as suicidal.

JAKE: Well, for one thing, school. School's not out till June.

TC: Jake! My God! How can you talk about *school*?

> (Dim though the light was, I could discern his ashamed expression; at the same time, he jutted his jaw.)

JAKE: We've discussed it. Talked about her and Marylee taking a long cruise. But she doesn't want to go anywhere. She said: "The shark needs bait. If we're going to hook the shark, then the bait has to be available."

TC: So Addie is a stakeout? A goat waiting for the tiger to pounce?

JAKE: Hold on. I'm not sure I like the way you put that.

TC: Then how would you put it?

JAKE: (Silence)

TC: (Silence)

JAKE: Quinn has Addie in his thoughts, he does indeed. He means to keep his promise. And that's when we'll nail him: in the attempt. Catch him when the curtain is up and all the lights are on. There's some risk, sure; but we have to take it. Because—well, to be goddamned honest, it's probably the only damn chance we're gonna get.

> (I leaned my head against the window: saw Addie's pretty throat as she threw back her head and drank the dazzling red wine in one delicious swallow. I felt weak, feeble; and disgusted with Jake.)

TC: I like Addie. She's real; and yet there's mystery. I wonder why she never married.

JAKE: Keep this under your hat. Addie's going to marry me.

TC (my mental-eye was still elsewhere; still, in fact, watching Addie drink her wine): When?

JAKE: Next summer. When I get my vacation. We haven't told anybody. Except Marylee. So now do you understand? Addie's *safe*; I won't let anything happen to her; I love her; I'm going to marry her.

> (Next summer: a lifetime away. The full moon, higher, whiter now, and celebrated by coyotes, rolled across the snow-gleaming prairies. Clumps of cattle stood in the cold snowy fields, bunched together for warmth. Some stood in pairs. I noticed two spotted calves huddled side by side, lending each other comfort, protection: like Jake, like Addie.)

TC: Well, congratulations. That's wonderful. I know you'll both be very happy.

Soon an impressive barbed-wire fence, like the high fences of a concentration camp, bordered both sides of the highway; it marked the beginnings of the B.Q. Ranch: ten thousand acres, or thereabouts. I lowered the window, and accepted a rush of icy air, sharp with the scent of new snow and old sweet hay. "Here we go," said Jake as we left the highway and drove through wooden swung-open gates. At the entrance, our headlights caught a handsomely lettered sign: *B.Q./Ranch R. H. Quinn/Proprietor.* A pair of crossed tomahawks was painted underneath the proprietor's name; one wondered whether it was the ranch's logo or the family crest. Either way, an ominous set of tomahawks seemed suitable.

The road was narrow, and lined with leafless trees, dark except for a rare glitter of animal-eyes among the silhouetted branches. We crossed a wooden bridge that rumbled under our weight, and I heard the sound of water, deep-toned liquid tumblings, and I knew it must be Blue River, but I couldn't see it, for it was hidden by trees and snowdrifts; as we continued along the road, the sound followed, for the river was running beside us, occasionally eerily quiet, then abruptly bubbling with the broken music of waterfalls, cascades.

The road widened. Sprinklings of electric light pierced the trees. A beautiful boy, a child with bouncing yellow hair and riding a horse bareback, waved at us. We passed a row of bungalows, lamplit and vibrating with the racket of television voices: the homes of ranch hands. Ahead, standing in distinguished isolation, was the main house, Mr. Quinn's house. It was a large white clapboard two-storied structure with a covered veranda running its full length; it seemed abandoned, for all the windows were dark.

Jake honked the car horn. At once, like a fanfare of welcoming trumpets, a blaze of floodlights swept the veranda; lamps bloomed in downstairs windows. The front door opened; a man stepped out and waited to greet us.

My first introduction to the owner of the B.Q. Ranch failed to resolve the question of why Jake had not wanted Addie to describe him to me. Although he wasn't a man who would pass unnoticed, his appearance was not excessively unusual; and yet the sight of him startled me: *I knew Mr. Quinn.* I was positive, I would have sworn on my own heartbeat that somehow, and undoubtedly long ago, I had encountered Robert Hawley Quinn, and that together we had, in fact, shared an alarming experience, an adventure so disturbing, memory had kindly submerged it.

He sported expensive high-heel boots, but even without them the man measured over six feet, and if he had stood straight, instead of assuming a stooped, slope-shouldered posture, he would have presented a fine tall figure. He had long simianlike arms; the hands dangled to his knees, and the fingers were long, capable, oddly aristocratic. I recalled a Rachmaninoff concert; Rachmaninoff's hands were like Quinn's. Quinn's face was broad but gaunt, hollow-cheeked, weather-coarsened—the face of a medieval peasant, the man behind the plow with all the woes of the world lashed to his back. But Quinn was no dumb, sadly burdened peasant. He wore thin wire-rimmed glasses, and these professorial spectacles, and the grey eyes looming behind their thick lenses, betrayed him: his eyes were alert, suspicious, intelligent, merry with malice, complacently superior. He had a hospitable, fraudulently genial laugh and voice. But he was not a fraud. He was an idealist, an achiever; he set himself tasks, and his tasks were his cross, his religion, his identity; no, not a fraud—a fanatic; and presently, while we were still gathered on the veranda, my sunken memory surfaced: I remembered where and in what form I had met Mr. Quinn before.

He extended one of his long hands toward Jake; his other hand plowed through a rough white-and-grey mane worn pioneer-style—a length not popular with his fellow ranchers: men who looked as though they visited the barber every Saturday for a close clip and a talcum shampoo. Tufts of grey hair sprouted from his nostrils and his ears. I noticed his belt buckle; it was decorated with two crossed tomahawks made of gold and red enamel.

QUINN: Hey, Jake. I told Juanita, I said honey, that rascal's gonna chicken out. Account of the snow.
JAKE: You call this *snow*?

QUINN: Just pullin' your leg, Jake. (To me) You oughta see the snow we do get! Back in 1952 we had a whole week when the only way I could get out of the house was to climb through the attic window. Lost seven hundred head of cattle, all my Santa Gertrudis. Ha ha! Oh, I tell you that was a time. Well, sir, you play chess?

TC: Rather the way I speak French. *Un peu.*

QUINN (cackling, slapping his thighs with spurious mirth): Yeah, I know. You're the city slicker come to skin us country boys. I'll bet you could play me and Jake at the same time and beat us blindfolded.

(We followed him down a wide high hallway into an immense room, a cathedral stuffed with huge heavy Spanish furniture, armoires and chairs and tables and baroque mirrors commensurate with their spacious surroundings. The floor was covered with brick-red Mexican tiles and dotted with Navajo rugs. An entire wall had been composed from blocks of irregularly cut granite, and this granite cavelike wall housed a fireplace big enough to roast a brace of oxen; in consequence, the dainty fire ensconced there seemed as insignificant as a twig in a forest.

But the person seated near the hearth was not insignificant. Quinn introduced me to her: "My wife, Juanita." She nodded, but was not to be distracted from the television screen confronting her: the set was working with the sound turned off—she was watching the zany ditherings of muted images, some visually boisterous game show. The chair in which she sat may well have once decorated the throne room of an Iberian castle; she shared it with a shivering little Chihuahua dog and a yellow guitar, which lay across her lap.

Jake and our host settled themselves at a table furnished with a splendid ebony-and-ivory chess set. I observed the start of a game, listened to their easygoing badinage, and it was strange: Addie was right, they seemed real buddies, two peas in a pod. But eventually I wandered back to the fireplace, determined to further explore the quiet Juanita. I sat near her on the hearth and searched for some topic to start a conversation. The guitar? The quivering Chihuahua, now jealously yapping at me?)

JUANITA QUINN: Pepe! You stupid mosquito!

TC: Don't bother. I like dogs.

(She looked at me. Her hair, center-parted and too black to be true, was slicked to her narrow skull. Her face was like a fist: tiny features tightly bunched together. Her head was too big for her body—she wasn't fat, but she weighed more than she should, and most of the overweight was distributed between her bosom and her belly. But she had slender, nicely shaped legs, and she was wearing a pair of very prettily beaded Indian moccasins. The mosquito yap-yapped, but now she ignored him. The television regained her attention.)

I was just wondering: why do you watch without the sound?

(Her bored onyx eyes returned to me. I repeated the question.)

JUANITA QUINN: Do you drink tequila?

TC: Well, there's a little dump in Palm Springs where they make fantastic Margaritas.

JUANITA QUINN: A man drinks tequila straight. No lime. No salt. Straight. Would you like some?

TC: Sure.

JUANITA QUINN: So would I. Alas, we have none. We can't keep it in the house. If we did, I would drink it; my liver would dry up . . .

> (She snapped her fingers, signifying disaster. Then she touched the yellow guitar, strummed the strings, developed a tune, a tricky, unfamiliar melody that for a moment she happily hummed and played. When she stopped, her face retied itself into a knot.)

I used to drink every night. Every night I drank a bottle of tequila and went to bed and slept like a baby. I was never sick a day; I looked good, I felt good, I slept well. No more. Now I have one cold after the other, headaches, arthritis; and I can't sleep a wink. All because the doctor said I had to stop drinking tequila. But don't jump to conclusions. I'm not a drunk. You can take all the wine and whiskey in the world and dump it down the Grand Canyon. It's only that I like tequila. The dark yellow kind. I like that best. (She pointed at the television set) You asked why I have the sound off. The only time I have the sound on is to hear the weather report. Otherwise, I just watch and imagine what's being said. If I actually listen, it puts me right to sleep. But just imagining keeps me awake. And I have to stay awake—at least till midnight. Otherwise, I'd never get any sleep at all. Where do you live?

TC: New York, mostly.

JUANITA QUINN: We used to go to New York every year or two. The Rainbow Room: now there's a view. But it wouldn't be any fun now. Nothing is. My husband says you're an old friend of Jake Pepper's.

TC: I've known him ten years.

JUANITA QUINN: Why does he suppose my husband has any connection with this thing?

TC: Thing?

JUANITA QUINN (amazed): You *must* have heard about it. Well, why does Jake Pepper think my husband's involved?

TC: *Does* Jake think your husband's involved?

JUANITA QUINN: That's what some people say. My sister told me—

TC: But what do you think?

JUANITA QUINN (lifting her Chihuahua and cuddling him against her bosom): I feel sorry for Jake. He must be lonely. And he's mistaken; there's nothing here. It all ought to be forgotten. He ought to go home. (Eyes closed; utterly weary) Ah well, who knows? *Or* cares? Not I. Not I, said the Spider to the Fly. Not I.

.   .   .

Beyond us, there was a commotion at the chess table. Quinn, celebrating a victory over Jake, vociferously congratulated himself: "Sonofagun! Thought you had me trapped there. But the moment you moved your queen—it's hot beer and horse piss for the Great Pepper!" His hoarse baritone rang through the vaulted room with the *brio* of an opera star. "Now you, young man," he shouted at me. "I need a game. A bona-fide challenge. Old Pepper here ain't fit to lick my boots." I started to excuse myself, for the prospect of a chess game with Quinn was both intimidating and tiresome; I might have felt differently if I'd thought I could beat him, triumphantly invade that citadel of conceit. I had once won a prep-school chess championship, but that was eons ago; my knowledge of the game had long been stored in a mental attic. However, when Jake beckoned, stood up, and offered me his chair, I acquiesced, and leaving Juanita Quinn to the silent flickerings of her television screen, seated myself opposite her husband; Jake stood behind my chair, an encouraging presence. But Quinn, assessing my faltering manner, the indecision of my first moves, dismissed me as a walkover, and resumed a conversation he'd been having with Jake, apparently concerning cameras and photography.

QUINN: The Krauts are good. I've always used Kraut cameras. Leica. Rolliflex. But the Japs are whippin' their ass. I bought a new Jap number, no bigger than a deck of cards, that will take five hundred pictures on a single roll of film.
TC: I know that camera. I've worked with a lot of photographers and I've seen some of them use it. Richard Avedon has one. He says it's no good.
QUINN: To tell the truth, I haven't tried mine yet. I hope your friend's wrong. I could've bought a prize bull for what that doodad set me back.
    (I suddenly felt Jake's fingers urgently squeezing my shoulder, which I interpreted as a message that he wished me to pursue the subject.)
TC: Is that your hobby—photography?
QUINN: Oh, it comes and goes. Fits and starts. How I started was, I got tired of paying so-called professionals to take pictures of my prize cattle. Pictures I need to send round to different breeders and buyers. I figured I could do just as good, and save myself a nickel to boot.
    (Jake's fingers goaded me again.)
TC: Do you make many portraits?
QUINN: Portraits?
TC: Of people.
QUINN (scoffingly): I wouldn't call them *portraits*. Snapshots, maybe. Aside from cattle, mostly I do nature pictures. Landscapes. Thunderstorms. The seasons here on the ranch. The wheat when it's green and then when it's gold. My river—I've got some dandy pictures of my river in full flood.
    (The river. I tensed as I heard Jake clear his throat, as though he were about to speak; instead, his fingers prodded me even more firmly. I toyed with a pawn, stalling.)

TC: Then you must shoot a lot of color.

QUINN (nodding): That's why I do my own developing. When you send your stuff off to those laboratories, you never know what the hell you're gonna get back.

TC: Oh, you have a darkroom?

QUINN: If you want to call it that. Nothing fancy.

(Once more Jake's throat rumbled, this time with serious intent.)

JAKE: Bob? You remember the pictures I told you about? The coffin pictures. They were made with a fast-action camera.

QUINN: (Silence)

JAKE: A Leica.

QUINN: Well, it wasn't mine. My old Leica got lost in darkest Africa. Some nigger stole it. (Staring at the chessboard, his face suffused with a look of amused dismay) Why, you little rascal! Damn your hide. Look here, Jake. Your friend almost has me checkmated. *Almost* . . .

It was true; with a skill subconsciously resurrected, I had been marching my ebony army with considerable, though unwitting, competence, and had indeed managed to maneuver Quinn's king into a perilous position. In one sense I regretted my success, for Quinn was using it to divert the angle of Jake's inquiry, to revert from the suddenly sensitive topic of photography back to chess; on the other hand, I was elated—by playing flawlessly, I might now very well win. Quinn scratched his chin, his grey eyes dedicated to the religious task of rescuing his king. But for me the chessboard had blurred; my mind was snared in a time warp, numbed by memories dormant almost half a century.

It was summer, and I was five years old, living with relatives in a small Alabama town. There was a river attached to this town, too; a sluggish muddy river that repelled me, for it was full of water moccasins and whiskered catfish. However, much as I disliked their ferocious snouts, I was fond of captured catfish, fried and dripping with ketchup; we had a cook who served them often. Her name was Lucy Joy, though I've seldom known a less joyous human. She was a hefty black woman, reserved, very serious; she seemed to live from Sunday to Sunday, when she sang in the choir of some pineywoods church. But one day a remarkable change came over Lucy Joy. While I was alone with her in the kitchen she began talking to me about a certain Reverend Bobby Joe Snow, describing him with an excitement that kindled my own imagination: he was a miracle-maker, a famous evangelist, and he was traveling soon to this very town; the Reverend Snow was due here next week, come to preach, to baptize and save souls! I pleaded with Lucy to take me to see him, and she smiled and promised she would. The fact was, it was necessary that I accompany her. For the Reverend Snow was a white man, his audiences were segregated, and Lucy had figured it out that the only way she would be welcome was if she brought along a little white boy to be baptized. Naturally, Lucy did not let on that such an event was in store for me. The following week, when we set off to attend the Reverend's camp meeting, I only envisioned the drama of watching a holy man sent from heaven to help the blind see and the lame walk. But I began to feel uneasy when I realized we were headed toward the river; when we got there and I saw hundreds of people gathered along the bank, country people, backwoods white trash stomping and hollering, I hesitated. Lucy was furious—she pulled me into the sweltering mob. Jingling bells, cavorting bodies; I could hear one voice above the others, a chanting booming baritone. Lucy chanted, too; moaned, shook. Magically, a stranger hoisted me onto his shoulder and I got a quick view of the man with the dominant voice. He was planted in the river with water up to his white-robed waist; his hair was grey and white, a drenched tangled mass, and his long hands, stretched skyward, implored the humid noon sun. I tried to see his face, for I knew this must be the Reverend Bobby Joe Snow, but before I could, my benefactor dropped me back into the disgusting confusion of ecstatic feet, undulating arms, trembling tambourines. I begged to go home; but Lucy, drunk with glory, held me close. The sun churned; I tasted vomit in my throat. But I didn't throw up; instead, I started to yell and punch and scream: Lucy was pulling me toward the river, and the crowd parted to create a path for us. I struggled until we reached the river's bank; then stopped, silenced by the scene. The white-robed man standing in the river was holding a reclining young girl; he recited biblical scripture before rapidly immersing her underwater, then swooping her up again: shrieking, weeping, she stumbled to shore. Now the Reverend's simian arms reached for me. I bit Lucy's hand, fought free of her grip. But a redneck boy grabbed me and dragged me into the water. I shut my eyes; I smelled the Jesus hair, felt the Reverend's arms carrying me downward into drowning blackness, then hours later lifting me into sunlight. My eyes, opening, looked into his grey, manic eyes. His face, broad but gaunt, moved closer, and he kissed my lips. I heard a loud laugh, an eruption like gunfire: "Checkmate!"

QUINN: Checkmate!

JAKE: Hell, Bob. He was just being polite. He let you win.

(The kiss dissolved; the Reverend's face, receding, was replaced by a face virtually identical. So it was in Alabama, some fifty years earlier, that I had first seen Mr. Quinn. At any rate, his counterpart: Bobby Joe Snow, evangelist.)

QUINN: How about it, Jake? You ready to lose another dollar?

JAKE: Not tonight. We're driving to Denver in the morning. My friend here has to catch a plane.

QUINN (to me): Shucks. That wasn't much of a visit. Come again soon. Come in the summer and I'll take you trout fishing. Not that it's like what it was. Used to be I could count on landing a six-pound rainbow with the first cast. Back before they ruined my river.

(We departed without saying goodnight to Juanita Quinn; she was sound asleep, snoring. Quinn walked with us to the car: "Be careful!" he warned, as he waved and waited until our taillights vanished.)

JAKE: Well, I learned one thing, thanks to you. Now I *know* he developed those pictures himself.

TC: So—why wouldn't you let Addie tell me what he looked like?

JAKE: It might have influenced your first impression. I wanted you to see him with a clear eye, and tell me what you saw.

TC: I saw a man I'd seen before.

JAKE: *Quinn?*

TC: No, not Quinn. But someone like him. His twin.

JAKE: Speak English.

(I described that summer day, my baptism—it was so clear to me, the similarities between Quinn and the Reverend Snow, the linking fibers; but I spoke too emotionally, metaphysically, to communicate what I felt, and I could sense Jake's disappointment: he had expected from me a series of sensible perceptions, pristine, pragmatic insights that would help clarify his own concept of Quinn's character, the man's motivations.

I fell silent, chagrined to have failed Jake. But as we arrived at the highway, and steered toward town, Jake let me know that, garbled, confused as my memoir must have seemed, he had partially deciphered what I had so poorly expressed.)

Well, Bob Quinn *does* think he's the Lord Almighty.

TC: Not think. Knows.

JAKE: Any doubts?

TC: No, no doubts. Quinn's the man who whittles coffins.

JAKE: And some day soon he'll whittle his own. Or my name ain't Jake Pepper.

Over the next few months I called Jake at least once a week, usually on Sundays when he was at Addie's house, which gave me a chance to talk with them both. Jake usually opened our conversations by saying: "Sorry, pardner. Nothing new to report." But one Sunday, Jake told me that he and Addie had settled on a wedding date: August 10. And Addie said: "We hope you can come." I promised I would, though the day conflicted with a planned three-week trip to Europe; well, I'd juggle my dates. However, in the end it was the bride and groom who had to alter schedules, for the Bureau agent who was supposed to replace Jake while he was on his honeymoon ("We're going to Honolulu!") had a hepatitis attack, and the wedding was postponed until the first of September. "That's rotten luck," I told Addie. "But I'll be back by then; I'll be there."

So, early in August, I flew Swissair to Switzerland, and lolled away several weeks in an Alpine village, sunbathing among the eternal snows. I slept, I ate, I reread the whole of Proust, which is rather like plunging into a tidal wave, destination unknown. But my thoughts too often revolved around Mr. Quinn; occasionally, while I slept, he knocked at the door and entered my dreams, sometimes as himself, his grey eyes glittering behind the wire-framed spectacles, but now and then he appeared guised as the white-robed Reverend Snow.

A brief whiff of Alpine air is exhilarating, but extended holidays in the mountains can become claustrophobic, arouse inexplicable depressions. Anyway, one day when one of these black moods descended, I hired a car and drove via the Grand St. Bernard pass into Italy and on to Venice. In Venice one is always in costume and wearing a mask; that is, you are not yourself, and not responsible for your behavior. It wasn't the real me who arrived in Venice at five in the afternoon and before midnight boarded a train bound for Istanbul. It all began in Harry's Bar, as so many Venetian escapades do. I had just ordered a martini when who should slam through the swinging doors but Gianni Paoli, an energetic journalist whom I had known in Moscow when he had been a correspondent for an Italian newspaper: together, aided by vodka, we had enlivened many a morose Russian restaurant. Gianni was in Venice en route to Istanbul; he was catching the Orient Express at midnight. Six martinis later he had talked me into going with him. It was a journey of two days and two nights; the train meandered through Jugoslavia and Bulgaria, but our impressions of those countries were confined to what we glimpsed out the window of our wagon-lit compartment, which we never left except to renew our supply of wine and vodka.

The room spun. Stopped. Spun. I stepped out of bed. My brain, a hunk of shattered glass, painfully clinked inside my head. But I could stand; I could walk; I even remembered where I was: the Hilton Hotel in Istanbul. Gingerly, I made my way toward a balcony overlooking the Bosphorus. Gianni Paoli was basking there in the sunshine, eating breakfast and reading the Paris *Herald Tribune*. Blinking, I glanced at the newspaper's date. It was the first of September. Now, why should that cause such severe sensations? Nausea; guilt; remorse. Holy smoke, I'd missed the wedding! Gianni couldn't fathom why I was so upset (Italians are always upset; but they never understand why anybody else should be); he poured vodka into his orange juice, offered it to me, and said drink, get drunk: "But first, send them a telegram." I took his advice, all of it. The telegram said: *Unavoidably detained but wish you every happiness on this wonderful day.* Later, when rest and abstinence had steadied my hand, I wrote them a short letter; I didn't lie, I simply didn't explain why I had been "unavoidably detained"; I said I was flying to New York in a few days, and would telephone them as soon as they returned from their honeymoon. I addressed the letter to Mr. and Mrs. Jake Pepper, and when I left it at the desk to be mailed I felt relieved, exonerated; I thought of Addie with a flower in her hair, of Addie and Jake walking at dusk along Waikiki beach, the sea beside them, stars above them; I wondered if Addie was too old to have children.

But I didn't go home; things happened. I encountered an old friend in

Istanbul, an archeologist who was working on a "dig" on the Anatolia coast in southern Turkey; he invited me to join him, he said I would enjoy it, and he was right, I did. I swam every day, learned to dance Turkish folk dances, drank ouzo and danced outdoors all night every night at the local bistro; I stayed two weeks. Afterward I traveled by boat to Athens, and from there took a plane to London, where I had a suit fitted. It was October, almost autumn, before I turned the key that opened the door of my New York apartment.

A friend, who had been visiting the apartment to water the plants, had arranged my mail in orderly stacks on the library table. There were a number of telegrams, and I leafed through those before taking off my coat. I opened one; it was an invitation to a Halloween party. I opened another; it was signed Jake: *Call me urgent.* It was dated August 29, six weeks ago. Hurriedly, not allowing myself to believe what I was thinking, I found Addie's telephone number and dialed it; no answer. Then I placed a person-to-person call to the Prairie Motel: No, Mr. Pepper was not at present registered there; yes, the operator thought he could be contacted through the State Bureau of Investigation. I called it; a man—an ornery bastard—informed me that Detective Pepper was on a leave of absence, and no, he couldn't tell me his whereabouts ("That's against the rules"); and when I gave him my name and told him I was calling from New York he said oh yeah and when I said listen, please, this is very important the sonofabitch hung up.

I needed to take a leak; but the desire, which had been insistent all during the ride from Kennedy airport, subsided, disappeared as I stared at the letters piled on the library table. Intuition attracted me to them. I flipped through the stacks with the professional speed of a mail sorter, seeking a sample of Jake's handwriting. I found it. The envelope was postmarked September 10; it was on the official stationery of the Investigation Bureau, and had been sent from the state capital. It was a brief letter, but the firm masculine style of the penmanship disguised the author's anguish:

Your letter from Istanbul arrived today. When I read it I was sober. I'm not so sober now. Last August, the day Addie died, I sent a telegram asking you to call me. But I guess you were overseas. But that is what I had to tell you—Addie is gone. I still don't believe it, and I never will, not until I know what really happened. Two days before our wedding she and Marylee were swimming in Blue River. Addie drowned; but Marylee didn't see her drown. I can't write about it. I've got to get away. I don't trust myself. Wherever I go, Marylee Connor will know how to locate me. Sincerely . . .

MARYLEE CONNOR: Why, hello! Why, sure, I recognized your voice right off.
TC: I've been calling you every half-hour all afternoon.
MARYLEE: Where are you?
TC: New York.
MARYLEE: How's the weather?

TC: It's raining.

MARYLEE: Raining here, too. But we can use it. We've had such a dry summer. Can't get the dust out of your hair. You say you've been calling me?

TC: All afternoon.

MARYLEE: Well, I was home. But I'm afraid my hearing's not too good. And I've been down in the cellar and up in the attic. Packing. Now that I'm alone, this house is too much for me. We have a cousin—she's a widow, too—she bought a place in Florida, a condominium, and I'm going to live with her. Well, how are you? Have you spoken to Jake lately?

(I explained that I'd just returned from Europe, and had not been able to contact Jake; she said he was staying with one of his sons in Oregon, and gave me the telephone number.)

Poor Jake. He's taken it all so hard. Somehow he seems to blame himself. Oh? Oh, you didn't *know*?

TC: Jake wrote me, but I didn't get the letter until today. I can't tell you how sorry . . .

MARYLEE (a catch in her voice): You didn't know about Addie?

TC: Not until today . . .

MARYLEE (suspiciously): What did Jake say?

TC: He said she drowned.

MARYLEE (defensively, as though we were arguing): Well, she did. And I don't care what Jake thinks. Bob Quinn was nowhere in sight. He *couldn't* have had anything to do with it.

(I heard her take a deep breath, followed by a long pause—as if, attempting to control her temper, she was counting to ten.)

If anybody's to blame, it's me. It was my idea to drive out to Sandy Cove for a swim. Sandy Cove doesn't even belong to Quinn. It's on the Miller ranch. Addie and I always used to go there; it's shady and you can hide from the sun. It's the safest part of Blue River; it has a natural pool, and it's where we learned to swim when we were little girls. That day we had Sandy Cove all to ourselves; we went into the water together, and Addie remarked how this time next week she'd be swimming in the Pacific Ocean. Addie was a strong swimmer, but I tire easily. So after I'd cooled off, I spread a towel under a tree and started reading through some of the magazines we'd brought along. Addie stayed in the water; I heard her say: "I'm going to swim around the bend and sit on the waterfall." The river flows out of Sandy Cove and sweeps around a bend; beyond the bend a rocky ridge runs across the river, creating a small waterfall —a short drop, not more than two feet. When we were children it was fun to sit on the ridge and feel the water rushing between our legs.

I was reading, not noticing the time until I felt a shiver and saw the sun was slanting toward the mountains; I wasn't worried—I imagined Addie was still enjoying the waterfall. But after a while I walked down to the river and shouted Addie! Addie! I thought: Maybe she's trying to tease me. So I climbed the embankment to the top of Sandy Cove; from there I could see the waterfall and the whole river moving north. There was no one there; no Addie. Then, just below the fall, I saw a white lily pad floating on the water, bobbing. But then I realized it wasn't a lily; it was a hand—with a diamond twinkling: Addie's engagement ring, the little diamond Jake gave her. I slid down the embankment and waded into the river and crawled along the waterfall ridge. The water was very clear and not too deep: I could see Addie's face under the surface and her hair tangled in the twigs of a tree branch, a sunken tree. It was hopeless—I grabbed her hand and pulled and pulled with all my strength but I couldn't budge her. Somehow, we'll never know how, she'd fallen off the ridge and the tree had caught her hair, held her down. *Accidental death by drowning.* That was the coroner's verdict. Hello?

TC: Yes, I'm here.

MARYLEE: My grandmother Mason never used the word "death." When someone died, especially someone she cared about, she always said that they had been "called back." She meant that they had not been buried, lost forever; but, rather, that the person had been "called back" to a happy childhood place, a world of living things. And that's how I feel about my sister. Addie was called back to live among the things she loves. Children. Children and flowers. Birds. The wild plants she found in the mountains.

TC: I'm so very sorry, Mrs. Connor. I . . .

MARYLEE: That's all right, dear.

TC: I wish there was something . . .

MARYLEE: Well, it was good to hear from you. And when you speak to Jake, remember to give him my love.

I showered, set a bottle of brandy beside my bed, climbed under the covers, took the telephone off the night table, nestled it on my stomach, and dialed the Oregon number that I had been given. Jake's son answered; he said his father was out, he wasn't sure where and didn't know when to expect him. I left a message for Jake to call as soon as he came home, no matter the hour. I filled my mouth with all the brandy it could hold, and rinsed it around like a mouthwash, a medicine to stop my teeth from chattering. I let the brandy trickle down my throat. Sleep, in the curving shape of a murmuring river, flowed through my head; in the end, it was always the river; everything returned to it. Quinn may have provided the rattlesnakes, the fire, the nicotine, the steel wire; but the river had inspired those deeds, and now it had claimed Addie, too. Addie: her hair, tangled in watery undergrowths, drifted, in my dream, across her wavering drowned face like a bridal veil.

An earthquake erupted; the earthquake was the telephone, rumbling on my stomach where it had still been resting when I dozed off. I knew it was Jake. I let it ring while I poured myself a guaranteed eye-opener.

. . .

TC: Jake?

JAKE: So you finally made it back stateside?

TC: This morning.

JAKE: Well, you didn't miss the wedding, after all.

TC: I got your letter. Jake—

JAKE: No. You don't have to make a speech.

TC: I called Mrs. Connor. Marylee. We had a long talk—

JAKE (alertly): Yeah?

TC: She told me everything that happened—

JAKE: Oh, no she didn't! Damned if she did!

TC (jolted by the harshness of his response): But, Jake, she said—

JAKE: *Yeah.* What did she say?

TC: She said it was an accident.

JAKE: You believed that?

(The tone of his voice, grimly mocking, suggested Jake's expression: his eyes hard, his thin quirky lips twitching.)

TC: From what she told me, it seems the only explanation.

JAKE: She doesn't know what happened. She wasn't *there.* She was sitting on her butt reading magazines.

TC: Well, if it was Quinn—

JAKE: I'm listening.

TC: Then he must be a magician.

JAKE: Not necessarily. But I can't discuss it just now. Soon, maybe. A little something happened that might hasten matters. Santa Claus came early this year.

TC: Are we talking about Jaeger?

JAKE: Yessir, the postmaster got his package.

TC: When?

JAKE: Yesterday. (He laughed, not with pleasure but excitement, released energy) Bad news for Jaeger but good news for me. My plan was to stay up here till after Thanksgiving. But boy, I was going nuts. All I could hear was slamming doors. All I could think was: Suppose he doesn't go after Jaeger? Suppose he doesn't give me that one last chance? Well, you can call me at the Prairie Motel tomorrow night. Because that's where I'll be.

TC: Jake, wait a minute. It has to have been an accident. Addie, I mean.

JAKE (unctuously patient, as though instructing a retarded aborigine): Now I'll leave you with something to sleep on.

Sandy Cove, where this "accident" occurred, is the property of a man named A. J. Miller. There are two ways to reach it. The shortest way is to take a back road that cuts across Quinn's place and leads straight to Miller's ranch. Which is what the ladies did.

Adios, amigo.

· · ·

Naturally, the something he had left me to sleep on kept me sleepless until daybreak. Images formed, faded; it was as though I were mentally editing a motion picture.

Addie and her sister are in their car driving along the highway. They turn off the highway and onto a dirt road that is part of the B.Q. Ranch. Quinn is standing on the veranda of his house; or perhaps watching from a window: whenever, however, at some point he spies the trespassing car, recognizes its occupants, and guesses that they are headed for a swim at Sandy Cove. He decides to follow them. By car? or horseback? afoot? Anyway, he approaches the area where the women are bathing by a roundabout route. Once there, he conceals himself among the shady trees above Sandy Cove. Marylee is resting on a towel reading magazines. Addie is in the water. He hears Addie tell her sister: "I'm going to swim around the bend and sit on the waterfall." Ideal; now Addie will be unprotected, alone, out of her sister's view. Quinn waits until he is certain she is playfully absorbed at the waterfall. Presently, he slides down the embankment (the same embankment the searching Marylee later used). Addie doesn't hear him; the splashing waterfall covers the sound of his movements. But how can he avoid her eyes? For surely, the instant she sees him, she will acknowledge her danger, protest, scream. No, he obtains her silence with a gun. Addie hears something, looks up, sees Quinn swiftly striding across the ridge, revolver aimed—he shoves her off the waterfall, plunges after her, pulls her under, holds her there: a final baptism.

It was possible.

But daybreak, and the beginning noise of New York traffic, lessened my enthusiasm for fevered fantasizing, briskly dropped me deep into that discouraging abyss—reality. Jake was without choice: like Quinn, he had set himself a passionate task, and his task, his human duty, was to prove that Quinn was responsible for ten indecent deaths, particularly the death of a warm, companionable woman he had wanted to marry. But unless Jake had evolved a theory more convincing than my own imagination had managed, then I preferred to forget it; I was satisfied to fall asleep remembering the coroner's common-sense verdict: *Accidental death by drowning.*

An hour later I was wide awake, a victim of jet lag. Awake but weary, fretful; and hungry, starved. Of course, due to my prolonged absence, the refrigerator contained nothing edible. Soured milk, stale bread, black bananas, rotten eggs, shriveled oranges, withered apples, putrid tomatoes, a chocolate cake iced with fungus. I made a cup of coffee, added brandy to it, and with that to fortify me, examined my accumulated mail. My birthday had fallen on September 30, and a few well-wishers had sent cards. One of them was from Fred Wilson, the retired detective and mutual friend who had first introduced me to Jake Pepper. I knew he was familiar with Jake's case, that Jake often consulted him, but for some reason we had never discussed it, an omission I now rectified by calling him.

. . .

TC: Hello? May I speak to Mr. Wilson, please?

FRED WILSON: Speaking.

TC: Fred? You sound like you have a helluva cold.

FRED: You bet. It's a real granddaddy.

TC: Thanks for the birthday card.

FRED: Aw, hell. You didn't have to spend your money just for that.

TC: Well, I wanted to talk to you about Jake Pepper.

FRED: Say, there must be something to this telepathy stuff. I was thinking about Jake when the phone rang. You know, his Bureau has him on leave. They're trying to force him off that case.

TC: He's back on it now.

> (After I recounted the conversation I'd had with Jake the previous evening, Fred asked several questions, mostly about Addie Mason's death and Jake's opinions pertaining to it.)

FRED: I'm damned surprised the Bureau would let him go back there. Jake's the fairest-minded man I've ever met. There's nobody in our business I respect more than Pepper. But he's lost all judgment. He's been banging his head against a wall so long he's knocked all the sense out of it. Sure, it was terrible what happened to his girl friend. But it was an accident. She drowned. But Jake can't accept that. He's standing on rooftops shouting murder. Accusing this man Quinn.

TC (resentfully): Jake could be right. It's possible.

FRED: And it's also possible the man is one-hundred-percent innocent. In fact, that seems to be the general consensus. I've talked with guys in Jake's own Bureau, and they say you couldn't swat a fly with the evidence they've got. Said it was downright embarrassing. And Jake's own chief told me, said so far as he knew Quinn had never killed anybody.

TC: He killed two cattle rustlers.

FRED (chuckles, followed by a coughing fit): Well, sir. We don't exactly call that killin'. Not around these parts.

TC: Except they weren't cattle rustlers. They were two gamblers from Denver; Quinn owed them money. And what's more, I don't think Addie's death was an accident.

> (Defiantly, with astounding authority, I related the "murder" as I had imagined it; the surmises I had rejected at dawn now seemed not only plausible but vividly convincing: Quinn *had* trailed the sisters to Sandy Cove, hidden among the trees, slid down the embankment, threatened Addie with a gun, trapped her, drowned her.)

FRED: That's Jake's story.

TC: No.

FRED: It's just something you worked out by yourself?

TC: More or less.

FRED: All the same, that *is* Jake's story. Hang on, I gotta blow my honker.

TC: What do you mean—"that *is* Jake's story"?

FRED: Like I said, there must be something to this telepathy stuff. Give or take a lotta little details, and that *is* Jake's story. He filed a report, and sent me a copy. And in the report that's how he reconstructed events: Quinn saw the car, he followed them . . .

> (Fred continued. A hot wave of shame hit me; I felt like a schoolboy caught cheating in an exam. Irrationally, instead of blaming myself, I blamed Jake; I was angry at him for not having produced a solid solution, crestfallen that his conjectures were no better than mine. I trusted Jake, the professional man, and was miserable when I felt that trust seesawing. But it was such a haphazard concoction—Quinn and Addie and the waterfall. Even so, regardless of Fred Wilson's destructive comments, I knew that the basic faith I had in Jake was justified.)

The Bureau's in a tough spot. They have to take Jake off this case. He's disqualified himself. Oh, he'll fight them! But it's for the sake of his own reputation. Safety, too. One night here, it was after he lost his girl friend, he rang me up around four in the morning. Drunker than a hundred Indians dancing in a cornfield. The gist of it was: he was gonna challenge Quinn to a duel. I checked on him the next day. Bastard, he didn't even remember calling me.

Anxiety, as any expensive psychiatrist will tell you, is caused by depression; but depression, as the same psychiatrist will inform you on a second visit and for an additional fee, is caused by anxiety. I rotated around in that humdrum circle all afternoon. By nightfall the two demons had combined; while anxiety copulated with depression, I sat staring at Mr. Bell's controversial invention, fearing the moment when I would have to dial the Prairie Motel and hear Jake admit that the Bureau was taking him off the case. Of course, a good meal might have helped; but I had already abolished my hunger by eating the chocolate cake with the fungus icing. Or I could have gone to a movie and smoked some grass. But when you're in that kind of sweat, the only lasting remedy is to ride with it: accept the anxiety, be depressed, relax, and let the current carry you where it will.

OPERATOR: Good evening. Prairie Motel. Mr. Pepper? Hey, Ralph, you seen Jake Pepper? In the bar? Hello, sir—your party's in the bar. I'm ringing.

TC: Thank you.

> (I remembered the Prairie Bar; unlike the motel, it had a certain comic-strip charm. Cowboy customers, rawhide walls decorated with girlie posters and Mexican sombreros, a rest room for BULLS, another for BELLES, and a jukebox devoted to the twangs of Country & Western music. A jukebox blast announced that the bartender had answered.)

BARTENDER: Jake Pepper! Somebody for you. Hello, mister. He wants to know who is it?

TC: A friend from New York.

JAKE'S VOICE (distantly; rising in volume as he approaches the phone): Sure I have friends in New York. Tokyo. Bombay. Hello, my friend from New York!

TC: You sound jolly.

JAKE: About as jolly as a beggar's monkey.

TC: Can you talk? Or should I call later?

JAKE: This is okay. It's so noisy nobody can hear me.

TC (tentative; wary of opening wounds): So. How's it going?

JAKE: Not so hotsy-totsy.

TC: Is it the Bureau?

JAKE (puzzled): The Bureau?

TC: Well, I thought they might be giving you trouble.

JAKE: They ain't giving *me* no trouble. But I'm giving them plenty. Buncha nitwits. No, it's that knucklehead Jaeger. Our beloved postmaster. He's chicken. He wants to skip the coop. And I don't know how to stop him. But I've got to.

TC: Why?

JAKE: "The shark needs bait."

TC: Have you talked to Jaeger?

JAKE: For hours. He's with me now. Sitting over there in the corner like a little white rabbit ready to jump down a hole.

TC: Well, I can sympathize with that.

JAKE: I can't afford to. I've got to hold on to this old sissy. But how? He's sixty-four; he's got a bundle of dough and a pension coming. He's a bachelor; his closest living relative is Bob Quinn! For Christ's sake. And get this: he still doesn't believe Quinn did it. He says yes, maybe somebody means to harm me, but it can't be Bob Quinn; he's my own flesh and blood. There's just one thing that gives him pause.

TC: Something to do with the package?

JAKE: Uh-huh.

TC: The handwriting? No, it can't be that. It must be the picture.

JAKE: Nice shot. This picture's different. It's not like the others. For one thing, it's about twenty years old. It was made at the State Fair; Jaeger is marching in a Kiwanis parade—he's wearing a Kiwanis hat. *Quinn took the picture.* Jaeger says he saw him take it; the reason he remembers is because he asked Quinn to give him a copy, and Quinn never did.

TC: That ought to make the postmaster think twice. I doubt that it would do much to a jury.

JAKE: Actually, it doesn't do much to the postmaster.

TC: But he's frightened enough to leave town?

JAKE: He's scared, sure. But even if he wasn't, there's nothing to keep him here. He says he always planned to spend the last years of his life traveling. My job is to delay the journey. Indefinitely. Listen, I'd better not leave my little rabbit alone too long. So wish me luck. And keep in touch.

I wished him luck, but he was not lucky; within a week, both the postmaster and the detective had gone their separate ways: the former packed for global wanderings, the latter because the Bureau had removed him from the case.

The following notes are excerpted from my personal journals: 1975 through 1979.

20 October 1975: Spoke to Jake. Very bitter; spewing venom in all directions. He said "for two pins and a Confederate dollar" he'd quit, write in his resignation, go to Oregon and work on his son's farm. "But as long as I'm here with the Bureau, I've still got a whip to crack." Also, if he quit now, he could forfeit his retirement pension, a *beau geste* I'm sure he can't afford.

6 November 1975: Spoke to Jake. He said they were having a cattle-rustling epidemic in the northeast part of the state. Rustlers steal the cattle at night, load them into trucks, and drive them down into the Dakotas. He said that he and some other agents had spent the last few nights out on the open range, hiding among the cattle herds, waiting for rustlers who never showed up: "Man, it's cold out there! I'm too old for this tough-guy stuff." He mentioned that Marylee Connor had moved to Sarasota.

25 November 1975: Thanksgiving. Awoke this morning, and thought of Jake, and remembered it was just a year ago that he had got his "big break": that he had gone to Addie's for dinner and she had told him about Quinn and Blue River. I decided against calling him; it might aggravate, rather than alleviate, the painful ironies attached to this particular anniversary. Did call Fred Wilson and his wife, Alice, to wish them *"bon appétit."* Fred asked about Jake; I said the last I heard he was busy chasing cattle rustlers. Fred said: "Yeah, they're workin' his ass off. Trying to keep his mind off that other deal, what the Bureau guys call 'The Rattlesnake Baby.' They've assigned a young fellow named Nelson to it; but that's just for appearance sake. Legally, the case is open; but for all practical purposes the Bureau has drawn a line through it."

5 December 1975: Spoke to Jake. The first thing he said was: "You'll be pleased to hear the postmaster is safe and sound in Honolulu. He's been mailing postcards to everybody. I'm sure he sent one to Quinn. Well, he got to go to Honolulu, and I didn't. Yessir, life is strange." He said he was still in the "cattle-rustling business. And damned sick of it. I ought to join the rustlers. They make a hundred times the money I do."

20 December 1975: Received a Christmas card from Marylee Connor. She wrote: "Sarasota is lovely! This is my first winter in a warm climate, and I can honestly say I don't miss home. Did you know that Sarasota is famous as a winter quarter for the Ringling Bros. Circus? My cousin and I often drive over to watch the performers practice. It's the best fun! We've become friendly with a Russian woman who trains acrobats. May God see you through the New

Year, and please find enclosed a small gift." The gift was an amateurish family-album snapshot of Addie as a young girl, perhaps sixteen, standing in a flower garden, wearing a white summer dress with a matching hair ribbon, and cradling in her arms, as though it were as fragile as the surrounding foliage, a white kitten; the kitten is yawning. On the back of the picture, Marylee had written: *Adelaide Minerva Mason. Born 14 June 1939. Called Back 29 August 1975.*

1 January 1976: Jake called—"Happy New Year!" He sounded like a grave-digger digging his own grave. He said he'd spent New Year's Eve in bed reading *David Copperfield.* "The Bureau had a big party. But I didn't go. I knew if I did I'd get drunk and knock some heads together. Maybe a lotta heads. Drunk or sober, whenever I'm around the chief it's all I can do not to throw a punch bang into his fat gut." I told him I'd received a card from Marylee at Christmas and described the picture of Addie accompanying it, and he said yes, Marylee had sent him a very similar picture: "But what does it mean? What she wrote—'Called Back'?" When I tried to interpret the phrase as I understood it, he stopped me with a grunt: it was too fanciful for him; and he remarked: "I love Marylee. I've always said she's a sweet woman. But simple. Just a mite simple."

5 February 1976: Last week I bought a frame for Addie's snapshot. I put it on a table in my bedroom. Yesterday I removed it to a drawer. It was too disturbing, alive—especially the kitten's yawn.

14 February 1976: Three valentines—one from an old schoolteacher, Miss Wood; another from my tax accountant; and a third signed Love, Bob Quinn. A joke, of course. Jake's idea of black comedy?

15 February 1976: Called Jake, and he confessed yes, he'd sent the valentine. I said well, you must have been drunk. He said: "I was."

20 April 1976: A short letter from Jake scribbled on Prairie Motel stationery: "Have been here two days collecting gossip, mostly at the Okay Café. The postmaster is still in Honolulu. Juanita Quinn had a pretty bad stroke. I like Juanita, so I was sorry to hear it. But her husband is fit as a fiddle. Which is the way I prefer it. I don't want anything to happen to Quinn until I have a final crack at him. The Bureau may have forgotten this matter, but not me. I'll never give up. Sincerely . . ."

10 July 1976: Called Jake last night, not having heard from him for more than two months. The man I spoke to was a new Jake Pepper; or rather, the old Jake Pepper, vigorous, optimistic—it was as though he had at last emerged from an inebriated slumber, his rested muscles primed to prowl. I quickly learned what had roused him: "I've got a devil by the tail. A humdinger." The humdinger, though it contained one intriguing element, turned out to be a very ordinary murder; or so it struck me. A young man, aged twenty-two, lived alone on a modest farm with an elderly grandfather. Earlier in the spring the grandson killed the old man in order to inherit his property and steal money the victim had misered away under a mattress. Neighbors noticed the farmer's

disappearance and saw that the young man was driving a flashy new car. The police were notified, and they soon discovered that the grandson, who had no explanation for his relative's sudden and complete absence, had bought the new car with old cash. The suspect would neither admit nor deny that he had murdered his grandfather, though the authorities were certain he had. The difficulty was: no corpse. Without a body they couldn't make an arrest. But search as they might, the victim remained invisible. The local constabulary requested aid from the State Bureau of Investigation, and Jake was assigned to the case. "It's fascinating. This kid is smart as hell. Whatever he did to that old man is diabolical. And if we can't find the body, he'll go scotfree. But I'm sure it's somewhere on that farm. Every instinct tells me he chopped Grandpa into mincemeat and buried the parts in different spots. All I need is the head. I'll find it if I have to plow the place up acre by acre. Inch by inch." After we'd hung up, I felt a surge of anger; and jealousy: not just a twinge, but a mean jab, as though I'd recently learned of a lover's betrayal. In truth, I don't want Jake to be interested in any case other than the case that interests me.

20 July 1976: A telegram from Jake. *Have Head One Hand Two Feet Stop Gone Fishing Jake.* I wonder why he sent a telegram instead of calling? Can he imagine that I resent this success? I'm pleased, for I know his pride has been at least partially restored. I only hope that wherever he has "gone fishing," it is somewhere in the neighborhood of Blue River.

22 July 1976: Wrote Jake a congratulatory letter, and told him I was going abroad for three months.

20 December 1976: A Christmas card from Sarasota. "If you ever come this way, please stop by. God bless you. Marylee Connor."

22 February 1977: A note from Marylee: "I still subscribe to the hometown paper, and thought the enclosed clipping might interest you. I've written her husband. He sent me such a lovely letter at the time of Addie's accident." The clipping was Juanita Quinn's obituary; she had died in her sleep. Surprisingly, there was to be no service or burial, for the deceased had requested that she be cremated and her ashes scattered over Blue River.

23 February 1977: Called Jake. He said, rather sheepishly: "Hiya, pardner! You've been quite the stranger." In fact, I'd mailed him a letter from Switzerland, to which he had not replied; and though I'd failed to reach him, had twice phoned during the Christmas holidays. "Oh yeah, I was in Oregon." Then I came to the point: Juanita Quinn's obituary. Predictably, he said: "I'm suspicious"; and when I asked why, answered: "Cremations always make me suspicious." We talked another quarter-hour, but it was a self-conscious conversation, an effort on his part. Perhaps I remind him of matters that, for all his moral strength, he is beginning to want to forget.

10 July 1977: Jake called, elated. Without preamble, he announced: "Like I told you, cremations always make me suspicious. Bob Quinn's a bridegroom! Well, everybody knew he had another family, a woman with four children fathered by Squire Quinn. He kept them hidden over in Appleton, a place

about a hundred miles southwest. Last week he married the lady. Brought his bride and brood back to the ranch, proud as a rooster. Juanita would spin in her grave. If she *had* a grave." Stupidly, dazed by the speed of Jake's narrative, I asked: "How old are the children?" He said: "The youngest is ten and the oldest seventeen. All girls. I tell you, the town is in an uproar. Sure, they can handle murder, a couple of homicides don't faze them; but to have their shining knight, their big War Hero, show up with this brazen trollop and her four little bastards is too much for their Presbyterian eyebrows." I said: "I feel sorry for the children. The woman, too." Jake said: "I'll save my sorrow for Juanita. If there was a body to exhume, I'll bet the coroner would find a nice dose of nicotine inside it." I said: "I doubt that. He wouldn't hurt Juanita. She was an alcoholic. He was her savior. He loved her." Quietly, Jake said: "And I gather you don't think he had anything to do with Addie's 'accident'?" I said: "He meant to kill her. He would have, eventually. But then she drowned." Jake said: "Saving him the trouble! Okay. Explain Clem Anderson, the Baxters." I said: "Yes, that was all Quinn's work. He had to do it. He's a messiah with a task." Jake said: "Then why did he let the postmaster glide through his fingers?" I said: "Has he? My guess is that old Mr. Jaeger has an appointment in Samarra. Quinn will cross his path one day. Quinn can't rest until that happens. He's not sane, you know." Jake hung up, but not before acrimoniously asking: "Are you?"

15 December 1977: Saw a black alligator wallet in a pawnshop window. It was in fine condition, and initialed J.P. I bought it, and because our last conversation had ended angrily (he was angry, I wasn't), I sent it to Jake as both a Christmas present and a peace offering.

22 December 1977: A Christmas card from the faithful Mrs. Connor: "I'm working for the circus! No, I'm not an acrobat. I'm a receptionist. It beats shuffleboard! All wishes for the New Year."

17 January 1978: A four-line scrawl from Jake thanking me for the wallet— curtly, inadequately. I'm receptive to hints. I won't write or call again.

20 December 1978: A Christmas card from Marylee Connor, just her signature; nothing from Jake.

12 September 1979: Fred Wilson and his wife were in New York last week, en route to Europe (their first trip), happy as honeymooners. I took them to dinner; all talk was limited to the excitements of their impending tour until, while selecting desserts, Fred said: "I notice you haven't mentioned Jake." I pretended surprise, and casually remarked that I hadn't heard from Jake in well over a year. Shrewdly, Fred asked: "You fellows have a falling out?" I shrugged: "Nothing quite so clean-cut. But we haven't always seen eye to eye." Then Fred said: "Jake's had bad health problems lately. Emphysema. He's retiring the end of this month. Now, it's none of my business, but I think it would be a nice gesture if you called him. Just now he needs a pat on the back."

14 September 1979: I shall always be grateful to Fred Wilson; he had made it easy for me to swallow my pride and call Jake. We spoke this morning; it

was as if we had talked yesterday, and the day before. One wouldn't believe that there had ever been an interruption in our friendship. He confirmed the news of his retirement: "Just sixteen days to go!"—and said that he planned to live with his son in Oregon. "But before that, I'm going to spend a day or two at the Prairie Motel. I've some unfinished chores in that town. There's some records in the courthouse I want to steal for my files. Hey, listen! Why don't we go together? Have a real reunion. I could meet you at Denver and drive you down." Jake did not have to pressure me; if he hadn't offered the invitation, I would have suggested it myself: I had often dreamed, while awake or asleep, of returning to that melancholy village, for I wanted to see Quinn again—meet and talk with him, just the two of us alone.

It was the second day of October.

Jake, declining an offer to accompany me, had lent me his car, and after lunch I left the Prairie Motel to keep an appointment at the B.Q. Ranch. I remembered the last time I had traveled this territory: the full moon, the fields of snow, the cutting cold, the cattle banded together, gathered in groups, their warm breath smoking the arctic air. Now, in October, the landscape was gloriously different: the macadam highway was like a skinny black sea dividing a golden continent; on either side, the sun-bleached stubble of threshed wheat flamed, rippled with yellow colors, sable shadows under a cloudless sky. Bulls pranced about these pastures; and cows, among them mothers with new calves, grazed, dozed.

At the entrance to the ranch, a young girl was leaning against a sign, the one with the crossed tomahawks. She smiled, and waved for me to stop.

YOUNG GIRL: Afternoon! I'm Nancy Quinn. My dad sent me to meet you.

TC: Well, thanks.

NANCY QUINN (opening the car door, climbing in): He's fishing. I'll have to show you where he is.

> (She was a cheerful twelve-year-old snaggle-toothed tomboy. Her tawny hair was chopped short, and she was splashed with freckles from top to bottom. She was wearing only an old bathing suit. One of her knees was wrapped in a dirty bandage.)

TC (referring to the bandage): Hurt yourself?

NANCY QUINN: Naw. Well, I got throwed.

TC: Throwed?

NANCY QUINN: Bad Boy throwed me. He's one mean horse. That's how come they call him Bad Boy. He's throwed every kid on the ranch. Most of the guys, too. I said well, I bet I can ride him. And I did. For 'bout two seconds flat. You been here before?

TC: Once; years ago. But it was at night. I remember a wooden bridge—

NANCY QUINN: That's it yonder!

(We crossed the bridge: finally I saw Blue River; but it was a glimpse as swift and flurried as a hummingbird's flight, for overhanging trees, leafless when last seen, blazed with obscuring autumn-trimmed foliage.)

You ever been to Appleton?

TC: No.

NANCY QUINN: *Never?* That's funny. I never met nobody that's never been to Appleton.

TC: Have I missed something?

NANCY QUINN: Oh, it's okay. We used to live there. But I like it here better. It's easier to get off by yourself and do the kinda stuff I like. Fish. Shoot coyotes. My dad said he'd give me a dollar for every coyote I shot down; but after he'd give me more'n two hundred dollars, he cut me down to a dime. Well, I don't need money. I'm not like my sisters. Always got their face stuck in a mirror.

I got three sisters, and I'll tell you they're not too happy here. They don't like horses; they hate most everything. Boys. That's all they've got on their mind. When we lived in Appleton, we didn't see so much of my dad. Maybe like once a week. So they put on perfume and lipstick and had plenty of boyfriends. That was okay with my mom. She's a lot like them, someways. She likes to fuss with herself and look pretty. But my dad is real strict. He won't let my sisters have any boyfriends. Or wear lipstick. One time some of their old boyfriends drove over from Appleton, and my dad met them at the door with a shotgun; he told them, said the next time he saw them on his property he'd blow their heads off. Wow, did those guys scoot! The girls cried them-selves sick. But the whole thing gives me the biggest laugh.

See that fork in the road? Stop there.

(I stopped the car; we both got out. She pointed to an opening in the trees: a dark, leafy, downward-sloping path.)

Just follow that.

TC (suddenly afraid to be alone): You're not coming with me?

NANCY QUINN: My dad don't like anybody around when he talks business.

TC: Well, thanks again.

NANCY QUINN: My pleasure!

She walked away whistling.

Parts of the path were so overgrown that I had to bend branches, shield my face against brushing leaves. Briars, strange thorns caught at my trousers; high in the trees, crows cawed, screamed. I saw an owl; it's odd to see an owl in daylight; he blinked, but did not stir. Once, I almost stumbled into a beehive —an old hollow tree-stump swarming with wild black bees. Always I could hear the river, a slow soft churning roar; then, at a curve in the path, I saw it; and saw Quinn, too.

He was wearing a rubber suit, and holding aloft, as though it were a conductor's baton, a supple fishing rod. He stood waist-deep, his hatless head in profile; his hair was no longer flecked with grey—it was white as the waterfoam circling his hips. I wanted to turn and run, for the scene was so strongly reminiscent of that other day, that long-ago time when Quinn's look-alike, the Reverend Billy Joe Snow, had waited for me in waist-high water. Suddenly I heard my name; Quinn was calling it, and beckoning to me as he waded toward shore.

I thought of the young bulls I had seen parading in the golden pastures; Quinn, glistening in his rubber suit, reminded me of them—vital, powerful, dangerous; except for his white hair, he hadn't aged an iota; indeed, he seemed years younger, a man of fifty in perfect health.

Smiling, he squatted on a rock, and motioned for me to join him. He displayed some trout he'd caught. "Kinda puny. But they'll eat good."

I mentioned Nancy. He grinned and said: "Nancy. Oh, yeah. She's a good kid." He left it at that. He didn't refer to his wife's death, or the fact that he had remarried: he assumed I was aware of his recent history.

He said: "I was surprised when you called me."

"Oh?"

"I don't know. Just surprised. Where you staying?"

"At the Prairie Motel. Where else?"

After a silence, and almost shyly, he asked: "Jake Pepper with you?"

I nodded.

"Somebody told me he was leaving the Bureau."

"Yes. He's going to live in Oregon."

"Well, I don't guess I'll ever see the old bastard again. Too bad. We could've been real friends. If he hadn't had all those suspicions. Damn his soul, he even thought I drowned poor Addie Mason!" He laughed; then scowled. "The way I look at it is: it was the hand of God." He raised his own hand, and the river, viewed between his spread fingers, seemed to weave between them like a dark ribbon. "God's work. His will."

III
Conversational Portraits

1

A Day's Work

Scene: A rainy April morning, 1979. I am walking along Second Avenue in New York City, carrying an oilcloth shopping satchel bulging with house-cleaning materials that belong to Mary Sanchez, who is beside me trying to keep an umbrella above the pair of us, which is not difficult as she is much taller than I am, a six-footer.

Mary Sanchez is a professional cleaning woman who works by the hour, at five dollars an hour, six days a week. She works approximately nine hours a day, and visits on the average twenty-four different domiciles between Monday and Saturday: generally her customers require her services just once a week.

Mary is fifty-seven years old, a native of a small South Carolina town who has "lived North" the past forty years. Her husband, a Puerto Rican, died last summer. She has a married daughter who lives in San Diego, and three sons, one of whom is a dentist, one who is serving a ten-year sentence for armed robbery, a third who is "just gone, God knows where. He called me last Christmas, he sounded far away. I asked where are you, Pete, but he wouldn't say, so I told him his daddy was dead, and he said good, said that was the best Christmas present I could've given him, so I hung up the phone, slam, and I hope he never calls again. Spitting on Dad's grave that way. Well, sure, Pedro was never good to the kids. Or me. Just boozed and rolled dice. Ran around with bad women. They found him dead on a bench in Central Park. Had a mostly empty bottle of Jack Daniel's in a paper sack propped between his legs; never drank nothing but the best, that man. Still, Pete was way out of line, saying he was *glad* his father was dead. He owed him the gift of life, didn't he? And I owed Pedro something too. If it wasn't for him, I'd still be an ignorant Baptist, lost to the Lord. But when I got married, I married in the Catholic church, and the Catholic church brought a *shine* to my life that has never gone out, and never will, not even when I die. I raised my children in the Faith; two of them turned out fine, and I give the church credit for that more than me."

Mary Sanchez is muscular, but she has a pale round smooth pleasant face with a tiny upturned nose and a beauty mole high on her left cheek. She dislikes the term "black," racially applied. "I'm not black. I'm brown. A light-brown colored woman. And I'll tell you something else. I don't know many other colored people that like being called blacks. Maybe some of the young people. And those radicals. But not folks my age, or even half as old. Even people who really are black, they don't like it. What's wrong with Negroes? I'm a Negro, and a Catholic, and proud to say it."

I've known Mary Sanchez since 1968, and she has worked for me, periodically, all these years. She is conscientious, and takes far more than a casual interest in her clients, many of whom she has scarcely met, or not met at all, for many of them are unmarried working men and women who are not at home when she arrives to clean their apartments; she communicates with them, and they with her, via notes: "Mary, please water the geraniums and feed the cat. Hope this finds you well. Gloria Scotto."

Once I suggested to her that I would like to follow her around during the course of a day's work, and she said well, she didn't see anything wrong with that, and in fact, would enjoy the company: "This can be kind of lonely work sometimes."

Which is how we happen to be walking along together on this showery April morning. We're off to her first job: a Mr. Andrew Trask, who lives on East Seventy-third Street.

TC: What the hell have you got in this sack?

MARY: Here, give it to me. I can't have you cursing.

TC: No. Sorry. But it's heavy.

MARY: Maybe it's the iron.

TC: You iron their clothes? You never iron any of mine.

MARY: Some of these people just have no equipment. That's why I have to carry so much. I leave notes: get this, get that. But they forget. Seems like all my people are bound up in their troubles. Like this Mr. Trask, where we're going. I've had him seven, eight months, and I've never seen him yet. But he drinks too much, and his wife left him on account of it, and he owes bills everywhere, and if ever I answered his phone, it's somebody trying to collect. Only now they've turned off his phone.

(We arrive at the address, and she produces from a shoulder-satchel a massive metal ring jangling with dozens of keys. The building is a four-story brownstone with a midget elevator.)

TC (after entering and glancing around the Trask establishment—one fair-sized room with greenish arsenic-colored walls, a kitchenette, and a bathroom with a broken, constantly flowing toilet): Hmm. I see what you mean. This guy has problems.

MARY (opening a closet crammed and clammy with sweat-sour laundry): Not a clean sheet in the house! And look at that bed! Mayonnaise! Chocolate! Crumbs, crumbs, chewing gum, cigarette butts. Lipstick! What kind of woman would subject herself to a bed like that? I haven't been able to change the sheets for weeks. Months.

(She turns on several lamps with awry shades; and while she labors to organize the surrounding disorder, I take more careful note of the premises. Really, it looks as though a burglar had been plundering there, one who had left some drawers of a bureau open, others closed. There's a leather-framed photograph on the bureau of a stocky swarthy macho man and a blond hoity-toity Junior League woman and three tow-headed grinning snaggle-toothed suntanned boys, the eldest about fourteen. There is another unframed picture stuck in a blurry mirror: another blonde, but definitely not Junior League—perhaps a pickup from Maxwell's Plum; I imagine it is her lipstick on the bed sheets. A copy of the December issue of *True Detective* magazine is lying on the floor, and in the bathroom, stacked by the ceaselessly churning toilet, stands a pile of girlie literature—*Penthouse, Hustler, Oui*; otherwise, there seems to be a total absence of cultural possessions. But there are hundreds of empty vodka bottles everywhere—the miniature kind served by airlines.)

TC: Why do you suppose he drinks only these miniatures?

MARY: Maybe he can't afford nothing bigger. Just buys what he can. He has a good job, if he can hold on to it, but I guess his family keeps him broke.

TC: What does he do?

MARY: Airplanes.

TC: That explains it. He gets these little bottles free.

MARY: Yeah? How come? He's not a steward. He's a pilot.

TC: Oh, my God.

(A telephone rings, a subdued noise, for the instrument is submerged under a rumpled blanket. Scowling, her hands soapy with dishwater, Mary unearths it with the finesse of an archeologist.)

MARY: He must have got connected again. Hello? (Silence) Hello?

A WOMAN'S VOICE: Who *is* this?

MARY: This is Mr. Trask's residence.

WOMAN'S VOICE: Mr. Trask's *residence*? (Laughter; then, hoity-toity) To whom am I speaking?

MARY: This is Mr. Trask's maid.

WOMAN'S VOICE: So Mr. Trask has a maid, has he? Well, that's more than

Mrs. Trask has. Will Mr. Trask's maid please tell Mr. Trask that Mrs. Trask would like to speak to him?

MARY: He's not home.

MRS. TRASK: Don't give me that. Put him on.

MARY: I'm sorry, Mrs. Trask. I guess he's out flying.

MRS. TRASK (bitter mirth): Out flying? He's always flying, dear. Always.

MARY: What I mean is, he's at work.

MRS. TRASK: Tell him to call me at my sister's in New Jersey. Call the instant he comes in, if he knows what's good for him.

MARY: Yes, ma'am. I'll leave that message. (She hangs up) Mean woman. No wonder he's in the condition he's in. And now he's out of a job. I wonder if he left me my money. Uh-huh. That's it. On top of the fridge.

> (Amazingly, an hour or so afterward she has managed to somewhat camouflage the chaos and has the room looking not altogether shipshape but reasonably respectable. With a pencil, she scribbles a note and props it against the bureau mirror: "Dear Mr. Trask yr. wive want you fone her at her sistar place sinsirly Mary Sanchez." Then she sighs and perches on the edge of the bed and from her satchel takes out a small tin box containing an assortment of roaches; selecting one, she fits it into a roach-holder and lights up, dragging deeply, holding the smoke down in her lungs and closing her eyes. She offers me a toke.)

TC: Thanks. It's too early.

MARY: It's never too early. Anyway, you ought to try this stuff. *Mucho cojones.* I get it from a customer, a real fine Catholic lady; she's married to a fellow from Peru. His family sends it to them. Sends it right through the mail. I never use it so's to get high. Just enough to lift the uglies a little. That heaviness. (She sucks on the roach until it all but burns her lips) Andrew Trask. Poor scared devil. He could end up like Pedro. Dead on a park bench, nobody caring. Not that I didn't care none for that man. Lately, I find myself remembering the good times with Pedro, and I guess that's what happens to most people if ever they've once loved somebody and lose them; the bad slips away, and you linger on the nice things about them, what made you like them in the first place. Pedro, the young man I fell in love with, he was a beautiful dancer, oh he could tango, oh he could rumba, he taught me to dance and danced me off my feet. We were regulars at the old Savoy Ballroom. He was clean, neat —even when the drink got to him his fingernails were always trimmed and polished. And he could cook up a storm. That's how he made a living, as a short-order cook. I said he never did anything good for the children; well, he fixed their lunchboxes to take to school. All kinds of sandwiches wrapped in wax paper. Ham, peanut butter and jelly, egg salad, tuna fish, and fruit, apples, bananas, pears, and a thermos filled with warm milk mixed with honey. It hurts now to think of him there in the park, and how I didn't cry when the police came to tell me about it; how I never did cry. I ought to have. I owed him that. I owed him a sock in the jaw, too.

I'm going to leave the lights on for Mr. Trask. No sense letting him come home to a dark room.

(When we emerged from the brownstone the rain had stopped, but the sky was sloppy and a wind had risen that whipped trash along the gutters and caused passers-by to clutch their hats. Our destination was four blocks away, a modest but modern apartment house with a uniformed doorman, the address of Miss Edith Shaw, a young woman in her mid-twenties who was on the editorial staff of a magazine. "Some kind of news magazine. She must have a thousand books. But she doesn't look like no bookworm. She's a very healthy kind of girl, and she has lots of boy-friends. Too many—just can't seem to stay very long with one fellow. We got to be close because . . . Well, one time I came to her place and she was sick as a cat. She'd come from having a baby murdered. Normally I don't hold with that; it's against my beliefs. And I said why didn't you marry this man? The truth was, she didn't know who to marry; she didn't know who the dad was. And anyway, the last thing she wanted was a husband or a baby.")

MARY (surveying the scene from the opened front door of Miss Shaw's two-room apartment): Nothing much to do here. A little dusting. She takes good care of it herself. Look at all those books. Ceiling to floor, nothing but library.

(Except for the burdened bookshelves, the apartment was attractively spare, Scandinavianly white and gleaming. There was one antique: an old roll-top desk with a typewriter on it; a sheet of paper was rolled into the machine; and I glanced at what was written on it:

"Zsa Zsa Gabor is
305 years old
I know
Because I counted
Her Rings"

And triple-spaced below that, was typed:

"Sylvia Plath, I hate you
And your damn daddy.
I'm glad, do you hear,
Glad you stuck your head
In a gas-hot oven!"

TC: Is Miss Shaw a poet?

MARY: She's always writing something. I don't know what it is. Stuff I see, sounds like she's on dope to me. Come here, I want to show you something.

(She leads me into the bathroom, a surprisingly large and sparkling chamber. She opens a cabinet door and points at an object on a shelf: a pink plastic vibrator molded in the shape of an average-sized penis.)

Know what that is?

TC: Don't you?

MARY: I'm the one asking.

TC: It's a dildo vibrator.

MARY: I know what a vibrator is. But I never saw one like that. It says "Made in Japan."

TC: Ah, Well. The Oriental mind.

MARY: Heathens. She's sure got some lovely perfumes. If you like perfume. Me, I only put a little vanilla behind my ears.

> (Now Mary began to work, mopping the waxed carpetless floors, flicking the bookshelves with a feather duster; and while she worked she kept her roach-box open and her roach-holder filled. I don't know how much "heaviness" she had to lift, but the aroma alone was lofting me.)

MARY: You sure you don't want to try a couple of tokes? You're missing something.

TC: You twisted my arm.

> (Man and boy, I've dragged some powerful grass, never enough to have acquired a habit, but enough to judge quality and know the difference between ordinary Mexican weed and luxurious contraband like Thai-sticks and the supreme Maui-Wowee. But after smoking the whole of one of Mary's roaches, and while halfway through another, I felt as though seized by a delicious demon, embraced by a mad marvelous merriment: the demon tickled my toes, scratched my itchy head, kissed me hotly with his red sugary lips, shoved his fiery tongue down my throat. Everything sparkled; my eyes were like zoom lenses; I could read the titles of books on the highest shelves: *The Neurotic Personality of Our Time* by Karen Horney; *Eimi* by e.e. cummings; *Four Quartets; The Collected Poems of Robert Frost.*)

TC: I despise Robert Frost. He was an evil, selfish bastard.

MARY: Now, if we're going to curse—

TC: Him with his halo of shaggy hair. An egomaniacal double-crossing sadist. He wrecked his whole family. Some of them. Mary, have you ever discussed this with your confessor?

MARY: Father McHale? Discussed what?

TC: The precious nectar we're so divinely devouring, my adorable chickadee. Have you informed Father McHale of this delectable enterprise?

MARY: What he don't know won't hurt him. Here, have a Life Saver. Peppermint. It makes that stuff taste better.

> (Odd, she didn't seem high, not a bit. I'd just passed Venus, and Jupiter, jolly old Jupiter, beckoned beyond in the lilac star-dazzled planetary distance. Mary marched over to the telephone and dialed a number; she let it ring a long while before hanging up.)

MARY: Not home. That's one thing to be grateful for. Mr. and Mrs. Berkowitz. If they'd been home, I couldn't have took you over there. On account of they're these real stuffy Jewish people. And you know how stuffy *they* are!

TC: Jewish people? Gosh, yes. Very stuffy. They all ought to be in the Museum of Natural History. All of them.

MARY: I've been thinking about giving Mrs. Berkowitz notice. The trouble is, Mr. Berkowitz, he was in garments, he's retired, and the two of them are always home. Underfoot. Unless they drive up to Greenwich, where they got some property. That's where they must have gone today. Another reason I'd like to quit them. They've got an old parrot—makes a mess everywhere. And stupid! All that dumb parrot can say is two things: "Holy cow!" and "*Oy vey!*" Every time you walk in the house it starts shouting "*Oy vey!*" Gets on my nerves something terrible. How about it? Let's toke another roach and blow this joint.

(The rain had returned and the wind increased, a mixture that made the air look like a shattering mirror. The Berkowitzes lived on Park Avenue in the upper Eighties, and I suggested we take a taxi, but Mary said no, what kind of sissy was I, we can walk it, so I realized that despite appearances, she, too, was traveling stellar paths. We walked along slowly, as though it were a warm tranquil day with turquoise skies, and the hard slippery streets ribbons of pearl-colored Caribbean beach. Park Avenue is not my favorite boulevard; it is rich with lack of charm; if Mrs. Lasker were to plant it with tulips all the way from Grand Central to Spanish Harlem, it would be of no avail. Still, there are certain buildings that prompt memories. We passed a building where Willa Cather, the American woman writer I've most admired, lived the last years of her life with her companion, Edith Lewis; I often sat in front of their fireplace and drank Bristol Cream and observed the firelight enflame the pale prairie-blue of Miss Cather's serene genius-eyes. At Eighty-fourth Street I recognized an apartment house where I had once attended a small black-tie dinner given by Senator and Mrs. John F. Kennedy, then so young and insouciant. But despite the agreeable efforts of our hosts, the evening was not as enlightening as I had anticipated, because after the ladies had been dismissed and the men left in the dining room to savor their cordials and Havana cigars, one of the guests, a rather slope-chinned dressmaker named Oleg Cassini, overwhelmed the conversation with a travelogue account of Las Vegas and the myriad showgirls he'd recently auditioned there: their measurements, erotic accomplishments, financial requirements—a recital that hypnotized its auditors, none of whom was more chucklingly attentive than the future President.

When we reach Eighty-seventh Street, I point out a window on the fourth floor at 1060 Park Avenue, and inform Mary: "My mother lived there. That was her bedroom. She was beautiful and very intelligent, but she didn't want to live. She had many reasons—at least she thought she did. But in the end it was just her husband, my stepfather. He was a self-made man, fairly successful—she worshipped him, and he really was a nice guy, but he gambled, got into trouble and embezzled a lot of money, and lost his business and was headed for Sing Sing."

Mary shakes her head: "Just like my boy. Same as him."

We're both standing staring at the window, the downpour drenching us. "So one night she got all dressed up and gave a dinner party; everybody said she looked lovely. But after the party, before she went to bed, she took thirty Seconals and she never woke up."

Mary is angry; she strides rapidly away through the rain: "She had no right to do that. I don't hold with that. It's against my beliefs.")

SQUAWKING PARROT: Holy cow!

MARY: Hear that? What did I tell you?

PARROT: *Oy vey! Oy vey!*

(The parrot, a surrealist collage of green and yellow and orange moulting feathers, is esconced on a mahogany perch in the relentlessly formal parlor of Mr. and Mrs. Berkowitz, a room suggesting that it had been entirely made of mahogany: the parquet floors, the wall paneling, and the furniture, all of its costly reproductions of grandiose period-piece furniture—though God knows what period, perhaps early Grand Concourse. Straight-back chairs; settees that would have tested the endurance of a posture professor. Mulberry velvet draperies swathed the windows, which were incongruously covered with mustard-brown venetian blinds. Above a carved mahogany mantelpiece a mahogany-framed portrait of a jowly, sallow-skinned Mr. Berkowitz depicted him as a country squire outfitted for a fox hunt: scarlet coat, silk cravat, a bugle tucked under one arm, a riding crop under the other. I don't know what the remainder of this rambling abode looked like, for I never saw any of it except the kitchen.)

MARY: What's so funny? What you laughing at?

TC: Nothing. It's just this Peruvian tobacco, my cherub. I take it Mr. Berkowitz is an equestrian?

PARROT: *Oy vey! Oy vey!*

MARY: Shut up! Before I wring your damn neck.

TC: Now, if we're going to curse . . . (Mary mumbles; crosses herself) Does the critter have a name?

MARY: Uh-huh. Try and guess.

TC: Polly.

MARY (truly surprised): How'd you know that?

TC: So she's a female.

MARY: That's a girl's name, so she must be a girl. Whatever she is, she's a bitch. Just look at all that crap on the floor. All for me to clean it up.

TC: Language, language.

POLLY: Holy cow!

MARY: My nerves. Maybe we better have a little lift. (Out comes the tin box, the roaches, the roach-holder, matches) And let's see what we can locate in the kitchen. I'm feeling real munchie.

(The interior of the Berkowitz refrigerator is a glutton's fantasy, a cornu-copia of fattening goodies. Small wonder the master of the house has such jowls. "Oh yes," confirms Mary, "they're both hogs. Her stomach. She looks like she's about to drop the Dionne quintuplets. And all his suits are tailor-made: nothing store-bought could fit him. Hmm, yummy, I sure do feel munchie. Those coconut cupcakes look desirable. And that mocha cake, I wouldn't mind a hunk of that. We could dump some ice cream on it." Huge soup bowls are found, and Mary masses them with cupcakes and mocha cake and fist-sized scoops of pistachio ice cream. We return to the parlor with this banquet and fall upon it like abused orphans. There's nothing like grass to grow an appetite. After finishing off the first helping, and fueling ourselves with more roaches, Mary refills the bowls with even heftier portions.)

MARY: How you feel?

TC: I feel good.

MARY: How good?

TC: Real good.

MARY: Tell me exactly how you feel.

TC: I'm in Australia.

MARY: Ever been to Austria?

TC: Not Austria. Australia. No, but that's where I am now. And everybody always said what a dull place it is. Shows what they know! Greatest surfing in the world. I'm out in the ocean on a surfboard riding a wave high as a, as a—

MARY: High as you. Ha-ha.

TC: It's made of melting emeralds. The wave. The sun is hot on my back, and the spray is salting my face, and there are hungry sharks all around me. *Blue Water, White Death.* Wasn't that a terrific movie? Hungry white man-eaters everywhere, but they don't worry me—frankly, I don't give a fuck . . .

MARY (eyes wide with fear): Watch for the sharks! They got killer teeth. You'll be crippled for life. You'll be begging on street corners.

TC: Music!

MARY: Music! That's the ticket.

(She weaves like a groggy wrestler toward a gargoyle object that had heretofore happily escaped my attention: a mahogany console combining television, phonograph, and a radio. She fiddles with the radio until she finds a station booming music with a Latin beat.

Her hips maneuver, her fingers snap, she is elegant yet smoothly aban-doned, as if recalling a sensuous youthful night, and dancing with a phantom partner some remembered choreography. And it is magic, how her now-ageless body responds to the drums and guitars, contours itself to the subtlest rhythm: she is in a trance, the state of grace saints sup-posedly achieve when experiencing visions. And I am hearing the music, too; it is speeding through me like amphetamine—each note ringing with the separate clarity of cathedral chimings on a silent winter Sunday. I move toward her, and into her arms, and we match each other step for step, laughing, undulating, and even when the music is interrupted by an announcer speaking Spanish as rapid as the rattle of castanets, we continue dancing, for the guitars are locked in our heads now, as we are locked in our laughter, our embrace: louder and louder, so loud that we are unaware of a key clicking, a door opening and shutting. But the parrot hears it.)

POLLY: Holy cow!

WOMAN'S VOICE: What is this? What's happening here?

POLLY: *Oy vey! Oy vey!*

MARY: Why, hello there, Mrs. Berkowitz. Mr. Berkowitz. How ya doin'?
(And there they are, hovering in view like the Mickey and Minnie Mouse balloons in a Macy's Thanksgiving Day parade. Not that there's anything mousey about this twosome. Their infuriated eyes, hers hot behind harlequin spectacles with sequined frames, absorb the scene: our naughty ice-cream mustaches, the pungent roach smoke polluting the premises. Mr. Berkowitz stalks over and stops the radio.)

MRS. BERKOWITZ: Who is this man?

MARY: I din't think you was home.

MRS. BERKOWITZ: Obviously. I asked you: Who is this man?

MARY: He's just a friend of mine. Helping me out. I got so much work today.

MR. BERKOWITZ: You're drunk, woman.

MARY (deceptively sweet): How's that you say?

MRS. BERKOWITZ: He said you're drunk. I'm shocked. Truly.

MARY: Since we're speaking truly, what I have truly to say to you is: today is my last day of playing nigger around here—I'm giving you notice.

MRS. BERKOWITZ: You are giving *me* notice?

MR. BERKOWITZ: Get out of here! Before we call the police.
(Without ado, we gather our belongings. Mary waves at the parrot: "So long, Polly. You're okay. You're good girl. I was only kidding." And at the front door, where her former employers have sternly stationed themselves, she announces: "Just for the record, I've never touched a drop in my life."
Downstairs, the rain is still going. We trudge along Park Avenue, then cut across to Lexington.)

MARY: Didn't I tell you they were stuffy.

TC: Belong in a museum.
(But most of our buoyancy has departed; the power of the Peruvian foliage recedes, a letdown has set in, my surfboard is sinking, and any sharks sighted now would scare the piss out of me.)

MARY: I still got Mrs. Kronkite to do. But she's nice; she'll forgive me if I don't come till tomorrow. Maybe I'll head on home.

TC: Let me catch you a cab.

MARY: I hate to give them my business. Those taxi people don't like coloreds. Even when they're colored themselves. No, I can get the subway down here at Lex and Eighty-sixth.

(Mary lives in a rent-controlled apartment near Yankee Stadium; she says it was cramped when she had a family living with her, but now that she's by herself, it seems immense and dangerous: "I've got three locks on every door, and all the windows nailed down. I'd buy me a police dog if it didn't mean leaving him by himself so much. I know what it is to be alone, and I wouldn't wish it on a dog.")

TC: Please, Mary, let me treat you to a taxi.

MARY: The subway's a lot quicker. But there's someplace I want to stop. It's just down here a ways.

(The place is a narrow church pinched between broad buildings on a side street. Inside, there are two brief rows of pews, and a small altar with a plaster figure of a crucified Jesus suspended above it. An odor of incense and candle wax dominates the gloom. At the altar a woman is lighting a candle, its light fluttering like the sleep of a fitful spirit; otherwise, we are the only supplicants present. We kneel together in the last pew, and from the satchel Mary produces a pair of rosary beads—"I always carry a couple extra"—one for herself, the other for me, though I don't know quite how to handle it, never having used one before. Mary's lips move whisperingly.)

MARY: Dear Lord, in your mercy. Please, Lord, help Mr. Trask to stop boozing and get his job back. Please, Lord, don't leave Miss Shaw a bookworm and an old maid; she ought to bring your children into this world. And, Lord, I beg you to remember my sons and daughter and my grandchildren, each and every one. And please don't let Mr. Smith's family send him to that retirement home; he don't want to go, he cries all the time . . .

(Her list of names is more numerous than the beads on her rosary, and her requests in their behalf have the earnest shine of the altar's candle-flame. She pauses to glance at me.)

MARY: Are you praying?

TC: Yes.

MARY: I can't hear you.

TC: I'm praying for you, Mary. I want you to live forever.

MARY: Don't pray for me. I'm already saved. (She takes my hand and holds it) Pray for your mother. Pray for all those souls lost out there in the dark. Pedro. Pedro.

2
Hello, Stranger

Time: December 1977.

Place: A New York restaurant, The Four Seasons.

The man who had invited me to lunch, George Claxton, had suggested we meet at noon, and made no excuse for setting such an early hour. I soon discovered the reason, however; in the year or more since I had lást seen him, George Claxton, heretofore a man moderately abstemious, had become a two-fisted drinker. As soon as we were seated he ordered a double Wild Turkey ("Just straight, please; no ice"), and within fifteen minutes requested an encore.

I was surprised, and not just by the urgency of his thirst. He had gained at least thirty pounds; the buttons of his pinstripe vest seemed on the verge of popping loose, and his skin color, usually ruddy from jogging or tennis, had an alien pallor, as though he had just emerged from a penitentiary. Also, he was sporting dark glasses, and I thought: How theatrical! Imagine good old plain George Claxton, solidly entrenched Wall Street fellow living in Greenwich or Westport or wherever it was with a wife named Gertrude or Alice or whatever it was, with three or four or five children, imagine this guy chugging double Wild Turkeys and wearing dark glasses!

It was all I could do not to ask straight out: Well, what the hell happened to you? But I said: "How are you, George?"

. . .

GEORGE: Fine. Fine. Christmas. Jesus. Just can't keep up with it. Don't expect a card from me this year. I'm not sending any.

TC: Really? Your cards seemed such a tradition. Those family things, with dogs. And how is your family?

GEORGE: Growing. My oldest daughter just had her second baby. A girl.

TC: Congratulations.

GEORGE: Well, we wanted a boy. If it had been a boy, she would have named him after me.

TC (thinking: Why am I here? Why am I having lunch with this jerk? He bores me, he's always bored me): And Alice? How is Alice?

GEORGE: Alice?

TC: I mean Gertrude.

GEORGE (frowning, peevish): She's painting. You know our house is right there on the Sound. Have our own little beach. She stays locked in her room all day painting what she sees from the window. Boats.

TC: That's nice.

GEORGE: I'm not so sure. She was a Smith girl; majored in art. She did a little painting before we were married. Then she forgot about it. Seemed to. Now she paints all the time. *All the time.* Stays locked in her room. Waiter, could you send the maître d' over with a menu? And bring me another of these things. No ice.

TC: That's very British, isn't it? Neat whiskey without ice.

GEORGE: I'm having root-canal. Anything cold hurts my teeth. You know who I got a Christmas card from? Mickey Manolo. The rich kid from Caracas? He was in our class.

(Of course, I didn't remember Mickey Manolo, but I nodded and pretended yes, yes. Nor would I have remembered George Claxton if he hadn't kept careful track of me for forty-odd years, ever since we had been students together at an especially abysmal prep school. He was a straight-arrow athletic kid from an upper-middle-class Pennsylvania family; we had nothing in common, but we stumbled into an alliance because in exchange for my writing all his book reports and English compositions, he did my algebra homework and during examinations slipped me the answers. As a result, I had been stuck for four decades with a "friendship" that demanded a duty lunch every year or two.)

TC: You very seldom see women in this restaurant.

GEORGE: That's what I like about it. Not a lot of gibbering broads. It has a nice masculine look. You know, I don't think I'll have anything to eat. My teeth. It hurts too much to chew.

TC: Poached eggs?

GEORGE: There's something I'd like to tell you. Maybe you could give me a little advice.

TC: People who take my advice usually regret it. However . . .

GEORGE: This started last June. Just after Jeffrey's graduation—he's my youngest boy. It was a Saturday and Jeff and I were down on our little beach painting a boat. Jeff went up to the house to get us some beer and sandwiches, and while he was gone I suddenly stripped down and went for a swim. The water was still too cold. You can't really swim in the Sound much before July. But I just felt like it.

I swam out quite a ways and was lying there floating on my back and looking at my house. It's really a great house—six-car garage, swimming pool, tennis courts; too bad we've never been able to get you out there. Anyway, I was floating on my back feeling pretty good about life when I noticed this bottle bobbing in the water.

It was a clear-glass bottle that had contained some kind of soda pop. Someone had stoppered it with a cork and sealed it with adhesive tape. But I could see there was a piece of paper inside, a note. It made me laugh; I used to do that when I was a kid—stuff messages in bottles and throw them in the water: *Help! Man Lost at Sea!*

So I grabbed the bottle and swam ashore. I was curious to see what was inside it. Well, it was a note dated a month earlier, and it was written by a girl who lived in Larchmont. It said: *Hello, stranger. My name is Linda Reilly and I am twelve years old. If you find this letter please write and let me know when and where you found it. If you do I will send you a box of homemade fudge.*

The thing is, when Jeff came back with our sandwiches I didn't mention the bottle. I don't know why, but I didn't. Now I wish I had. Maybe then nothing would have happened. But it was like a little secret I wanted to keep to myself. A joke.

TC: Are you sure you aren't hungry? I'm only having an omelette.

GEORGE: Okay. An omelette, very soft.

TC: And so you wrote this young lady, Miss Reilly?

GEORGE (hesitantly): Yes. Yes, I did.

TC: What did you say?

GEORGE: On Monday, when I was back in my office, I was checking through my briefcase and I found the note. I say "found" because I don't remember putting it there. It had vaguely crossed my mind I'd drop the kid a card—just a nice gesture, you know. But that day I had lunch with a client who likes martinis. Now, I never used to drink at lunch—nor much any other time, either. But I had two martinis, and I went back to the office feeling swivel-headed. So I wrote this little girl quite a long letter; I didn't dictate it, I wrote it in longhand and told her where I lived and how I'd found her bottle and wished her luck and said some dumb thing like that though I was a stranger, I sent her the affectionate wishes of a friend.

TC: A two-martini missive. Still, where's the harm?

GEORGE: Silver Bullets. That's what they call martinis. Silver Bullets.

TC: How about that omelette? Aren't you even going to touch it?

GEORGE: Jesus Christ! My teeth *hurt*.

TC: It's really quite good. For a restaurant omelette.

GEORGE: About a week later a big box of fudge arrived. Sent to my office. Chocolate fudge with pecans. I passed it around the office and told everybody my daughter had made it. One of the guys said: "Oh, yeah! I'll bet old George has a secret girl friend."

TC: And did she send a letter with the fudge?

GEORGE: No. But I wrote a thank-you note. Very brief. Have you got a cigarette?

TC: I stopped smoking years ago.

GEORGE: Well, I just started. I still don't buy them, though. Just bum one now and then. Waiter, could you bring me a pack of cigarettes? Doesn't matter what brand, as long as it isn't menthol. And another Wild Turkey, please?

TC: I'd like some coffee.

GEORGE: But I got an answer to my thank-you note. A long letter. It really threw me. She enclosed a picture of herself. A color Polaroid. She was wearing a bathing suit and standing on a beach. She may have been twelve, but she looked sixteen. A lovely kid with short curly black hair and the bluest eyes.

TC: Shades of Humbert Humbert.

GEORGE: Who?

TC: Nothing. A character in a novel.

GEORGE: I never read novels. I hate to read.

TC: Yes, I know. After all, I used to do all your book reports. So what did Miss Linda Reilly have to say?

GEORGE (after pausing a full five seconds): It was very sad. Touching. She said she hadn't been living in Larchmont very long, and that she had no friends, and that she had tossed dozens of bottles into the water, but that I was the only person who had found one and answered. She said she was from Wisconsin, but that her father had died and her mother had married a man who had three daughters of his own and that none of them liked her. It was a ten-page letter, no misspellings. She said a lot of intelligent things. But she sounded really miserable. She said she hoped I'd write again, and maybe I could drive over to Larchmont and we could meet someplace. Do you mind listening to all this? If you do . . .

TC: Please. Go ahead.

GEORGE: I kept the picture. In fact, I put it in my wallet. Along with snaps of my other kids. See, because of the letter, I started to think of her as one of my own children. I couldn't get the letter out of my mind. And that night, when I took the train home, I did something I'd done only a very few times. I went into the club car and ordered myself a couple of stiff drinks and read the letter over and over. Memorized it, practically. Then when I got home I told my wife I had some office work to do. I shut myself in my den and started a letter to Linda. I wrote until midnight.

TC: Were you drinking all this time?

GEORGE (surprised): Why?

TC: It might have some bearing on what you wrote.

GEORGE: Yes, I was drinking, and I guess maybe it was a pretty emotional letter. But I felt so upset about this kid. I really wanted to help her. I wrote her about some of the troubles my own kids had had. About Harriet's acne and how she never had a single boyfriend. Not till she had her skin-peel. I told her about the hard times I'd had when I was growing up.

TC: Oh? I thought you'd enjoyed the ideal life of an ideal American youth.

GEORGE: I let people see what I wanted them to see. Inside was a different story.

TC: Had me fooled.

GEORGE: Around midnight my wife knocked on the door. She wanted to know if anything was wrong, and I told her to go back to bed, I had an urgent business letter to finish, and when it was finished I was going to drive down to the post office. She said why couldn't it wait until morning, it's after twelve. I lost my temper. Married thirty years, and I could count on ten fingers the times I've lost my temper with her. Gertrude is a wonderful, wonderful woman. I love her heart and soul. I do, goddamnit! But I shouted at her: No, it can't wait. It has to go tonight. It's very important.

> (A waiter handed George a pack of cigarettes already opened. He stuck one in his mouth, and the waiter lit it for him, which was just as well, for his fingers were too agitated to hold a match without endangering himself.)

And Jesus Christ, it *was* important. Because I felt if I didn't mail the letter that night, I never would. Maybe, sober, I'd think it was too personal or something. And here was this lonely unhappy kid who'd shown me her heart: how would she feel if she never heard one word from me? No. I got in my car and drove down to the post office and as soon as I'd mailed the letter, dropped it into the slot, I felt too tired to drive home. I fell asleep in the car. It was dawn when I woke up, but my wife was asleep and she didn't notice when I came in.

I just about had time to shave and change my clothes before rushing off to catch the train. While I was shaving, Gertrude came into the bathroom. She was smiling; she hadn't mentioned my little temper tantrum. But she had my wallet in her hand, and she said, "George, I'm going to have Jeff's graduation picture enlarged for your mother," and with that she started shuffling through all the pictures in my wallet. I didn't think anything about it until suddenly she said: "Who is this girl?"

TC: And it was the young lady from Larchmont.

GEORGE: I should have told her the whole story right then. But I . . . Anyway, I said it was the daughter of one of my commuter friends. I said he'd been showing it to some of the guys on the train, and he'd forgot and left it on the bar. So I'd put it in my wallet to return the next time I saw him.

Garçon, un autre de Wild Turkey, s'il vous plaît.

TC (to the waiter): Make that a single.

GEORGE (in a tone unpleasantly pleasant): Are you telling me I've had too much to drink?

TC: If you have to go back to the office, yes.

GEORGE: But I'm not going back to my office. I haven't been there since early November. I'm supposed to have had a nervous breakdown. Overwork. Exhaustion. I'm supposed to be resting quietly at home, tenderly cared for by my adoring wife. Who is locked in her room painting pictures of boats. A boat. The same damn boat over and over.

TC: George, I've got to take a leak.

GEORGE: Not running out on me? Not running out on your old school buddy that sneaked you all the algebra answers?

TC: And even so, I flunked! Be back in a jiffy.

(I didn't need to take a leak; I needed to collect my thoughts. I didn't have the nerve to steal out of there and hide in a quiet movie somewhere, but I sure as hell didn't want to go back to that table. I washed my hands and combed my hair. Two men came in and stationed themselves at urinals. One said: "That guy that's so loaded. For a moment I thought it was somebody I know." His friend said: "Well, he's not a complete stranger. That's George Claxton." "You're kidding!" "I ought to know. He used to be my boss." "But my God! What happened?" "There are different stories." Then both men fell silent, perhaps out of deference to my presence. I returned to the dining room.)

GEORGE: So you *didn't* cut out?

(Actually, he seemed more subdued, less intoxicated. He was able to strike a match and light a cigarette with reasonable competence.)

Are you ready to hear the rest of this?

TC: (Silent, but with an encouraging nod.)

GEORGE: My wife didn't say anything, just tucked the picture back in my wallet. I went on shaving, but cut myself twice. It had been so long since I'd had a real hangover, I'd forgotten what it was like. The sweat; my stomach —it felt like I was trying to shit razor blades. I stuffed a bottle of bourbon in my briefcase, and as soon as I got on the train I headed straight for the john. The first thing I did was to tear up the picture and drop it in the toilet. Then I sat down on the toilet and opened up that bottle. At first it made me gag. And it was hot as hell in there. Like Hades. But after a while I began to calm down, and to wonder: Well, what am I in such a stew about? I haven't done anything wrong. But when I stood up I saw that the torn-up Polaroid was still floating in the toilet bowl. I flushed it, and the pieces of the picture, her head and legs and arms, started churning around, and it made me dizzy: I felt like a killer who had taken a knife and cut her up.

By the time we got to Grand Central, I knew I was in no state to handle the office, so I walked over to the Yale Club and took a room. I called my secretary and said I had to go to Washington and wouldn't be in till the next day. Then I called home and told my wife that something had come up, a business thing, and I'd be staying overnight at the club. Then I got into bed, and thought: I'll sleep all day; I'll have one good long drink to relax me, stop the jitters, and go to sleep. But I couldn't—not until I'd downed the whole bottle. Boy, did I sleep then! Until around ten the next morning.

TC: About twenty hours.

GEORGE: About that. But I was feeling fairly okay when I woke up. They have a great masseur at the Yale Club, a German, hands strong as a gorilla's. That guy can really fix you up. So I had some sauna, a real storm-trooper massage, and fifteen minutes under a freezing shower. I stayed on and ate lunch at the club. No drinks, but boy, did I wolf it down. Four lamb chops, two baked potatoes, creamed spinach, corn-on-the-cob, a quart of milk, two deep-dish blueberry pies . . .

TC: I wish you'd eat something now.

GEORGE (a sharp bark, startlingly rude): Shut up!

TC: (Silence)

GEORGE: I'm sorry. I mean, it was like I was talking to myself. Like I'd forgotten you were here. And your voice . . .

TC: I understand. Anyway, you had a hearty lunch and you were feeling good.

GEORGE: Indeed. Indeed. The condemned man had a hearty lunch. Cigarette?

TC: I don't smoke.

GEORGE: That's right. Don't smoke. Haven't smoked for years.

TC: Here, I'll light that for you.

GEORGE: I'm perfectly capable of coping with a match without blowing up the place, thank you.

Well now, where were we? Oh yes, the condemned man was on his way to his office, subdued and shining.

It was Wednesday, the second week in July, a scorcher. I was alone in my office when my secretary rang through and said a Miss Reilly was on the phone. I didn't make the connection right off, and said: Who? What does she want? And my secretary said she says it's personal. The penny dropped. I said: Oh yes, put her on.

And I heard: "Mr. Claxton, this is Linda Reilly. I got your letter. It's the nicest letter I've ever had. I feel you really are a friend, and that's why I decided to take a chance on calling you. I was hoping you could help me. Because something has happened, and I don't know what I'll do if you can't help me." She had a sweet young-girl's voice, but was so breathless, so excited, that I had to ask her to speak more slowly. "I don't have much time, Mr. Claxton. I'm calling from upstairs and my mother might pick up the phone downstairs any minute. The thing is, I have a dog. Jimmy. He's six years old but frisky as can be. I've had him since I was a little girl, and he's the only thing I have. He's a real gent, just the cutest little dog you ever saw. But my mother is going to have him put to sleep. I'll die! I'll just die. Mr. Claxton, please, can you come to Larchmont and meet me in front of the Safeway? I'll have Jimmy with me, and you can take him away with you. Hide him until we can figure out what to do. I can't talk any more. My mother's coming up the stairs. I'll call you first chance I get tomorrow and we can make a date—"

TC: What did *you* say?

GEORGE: Nothing. She'd hung up.

TC: But what *would* you have said?

GEORGE: Well, as soon as she hung up, I decided that when she called back I'd say yes. Yes, I'd help the poor kid save her dog. That didn't mean I had to take it home with me. I could have put it in a kennel, or something. And if matters had turned out differently, that's what I would have done.

TC: I see. But she never called back.

GEORGE: Waiter, I'll have another one of these dark things. And a glass of Perrier, please. Yes, she called. And what she had to say was very brief. "Mr. Claxton, I'm sorry; I sneaked into a neighbor's house to phone, and I've got to hurry. My mother found your letters last night, the letters you wrote me. She's crazy, and her husband's crazy, too. They think all kinds of terrible things, and she took Jimmy away first thing this morning, but I can't talk any more; I'll try to call later."

But I didn't hear from her again—at least, not personally. My wife phoned a few hours later; I'd say it was about three in the afternoon. She said: "Darling, please come home as soon as you can," and her voice was so calm that I knew she was in extreme distress; I even half-knew why, although I acted surprised when she told me: "There are two policemen here. One from Larchmont and one from the village. They want to talk to you. They won't tell me why."

I didn't bother with the train. I hired a limousine. One of those limousines with a bar installed. It's not much of a drive, just over an hour, but I managed to knock down quite a few Silver Bullets. It didn't help much; I was really scared.

TC: Why, for Christ's sake? What had you done? Play Mr. Good Guy, Mr. Pen Pal.

GEORGE: If only it were that neat. That tidy. Anyway, when I got home the cops were sitting in the living room watching television. My wife was serving them coffee. When she offered to leave the room, I said no, I want you to stay and hear this, whatever it is. Both the cops were very young and embarrassed. After all, I was a rich man, a prominent citizen, a churchgoer, the father of five children. I wasn't frightened of them. It was Gertrude.

The Larchmont cop outlined the situation. His office had received a complaint from a Mr. and Mrs. Henry Wilson that their twelve-year-old daughter, Linda Reilly, had been receiving letters of a "suspicious nature" from a fifty-two-year-old man, namely, me, and the Wilsons intended to bring charges if I couldn't explain myself satisfactorily.

I laughed. Oh, I was just as jovial as Santa Claus. I told the whole story. About finding the bottle. Said I'd only answered it because I liked chocolate fudge. I had them grinning, apologizing, shuffling their big feet, and saying well, you know how parents get nutty ideas nowadays. The only one not taking it all as a dumb joke was Gertrude. In fact, without my realizing it, she'd left the room before I'd finished talking.

After the cops left, I knew where I'd find her. In that room, the one where she does her painting. It was dark and she was sitting there in a straight-back chair staring out at the darkness. She said: "The picture in your wallet. That was the girl." I denied it, and she said: "Please, George. You don't have to lie. You'll never have to lie again."

And she slept in that room that night, and every night ever since. Keeps herself locked in there painting boats. A boat.

TC: Perhaps you did behave a bit recklessly. But I can't see why she should be so unforgiving.

GEORGE: I'll tell you why. That wasn't our first visit from the police.

Seven years ago we had a sudden heavy snowstorm. I was driving my car, and even though I wasn't far from home, I lost my way several times. I asked directions from a number of people. One was a child, a young girl. A few days later the police came to the house. I wasn't there, but they talked to Gertrude. They told her that during the recent snowstorm a man answering my description and driving a Buick with my license plate had got out of his car and exposed himself to a young girl. Spoken lewdly to her. The girl said she had copied down the license number in the snow under a tree, and when the storm had stopped, it was still decipherable. There was no denying that it was my license number, but the story was untrue. I convinced Gertrude, and I convinced the police, that the girl was either lying or that she had made a mistake concerning the number.

But now the police have come a second time. About another young girl.

And so my wife stays in her room. Painting. Because she doesn't believe me. She believes that the girl who wrote the number in the snow told the truth. I'm innocent. Before God, on the heads of my children, I am innocent. But my wife locks her door and looks out the window. She doesn't believe me. Do you?

(George removed his dark glasses and polished them with a napkin. Now I understood why he wore them. It wasn't because of the yellowed whites engraved with swollen red veins. It was because his eyes were like a pair of shattered prisms. I have never seen pain, a suffering, so permanently implanted, as if the slip of a surgeon's knife had left him forever disfigured. It was unbearable, and as he stared at me my own eyes flinched away.)

Do *you* believe me?

TC (reaching across the table and taking his hand, holding it for dear life): Of course, George. Of course I believe you.

3
Hidden Gardens

Scene: Jackson Square, named after Andrew Jackson—a three-hundred-year-old oasis complacently centered inside New Orleans' old quarter: a moderate-sized park dominated by the grey towers of St. Louis Cathedral, and the oldest, in some ways most somberly elegant, apartment houses in America, the Pontalba Buildings.

Time: 26 March 1979, an exuberant spring day. Bougainvillaea descends, azaleas thrust, hawkers hawk (peanuts, roses, horse-drawn carriage rides, fried shrimp in paper scoops), the horns of drifting ships hoot on the closeby Mississippi, and happy balloons, attached to giggling skipping children, bounce high in the blue silvery air.

"Well, I do declare, a boy sure do get around"—as my Uncle Bud, who was a traveling salesman when he could pry himself away from his porch swing and gin fizzes long enough to travel, used to complain. Yes, indeed, a boy sure do get around; in just the last several months I've been in Denver, Cheyenne, Butte, Salt Lake City, Vancouver, Seattle, Portland, Los Angeles, Boston, Toronto, Washington, Miami. But if somebody asked, I'd probably say, and really think: Why, I haven't been anywhere, I've just been in New York all winter.

Still, a boy do get around. And now here I am back in New Orleans, my birthplace, my old hometown. Sunning myself on a park bench in Jackson Square, always, since schoolboy days, a favorite place to stretch my legs and look and listen, to yawn and scratch and dream and talk to myself. Maybe you're one of those people who never talk to themselves. Aloud, I mean. Maybe you think only crazies do that. Personally, I consider it's a healthy thing. To keep yourself company that way: nobody to argue back, free to rant along, getting a lot of stuff out of your system.

For instance, take those Pontalba Buildings over there. Pretty fancy places, with their grillwork façades and tall dark French-shuttered windows. The first apartment houses ever built in the U.S.A.; relatives of the original occupants of those high airy aristocratic rooms are still living in them. For a long time I had a grudge against the Pontalba. Here's why. Once, when I was nineteen or so, I had an apartment a few blocks away on Royal Street, an insignificant, decrepit, roach-heaven apartment that erupted into earthquake shivers every time a streetcar clickety-clacked by on the narrow street outside. It was un-heated; in the winter one dreaded getting out of bed, and during the swampy summers it was like swimming inside a bowl of tepid consommé. My constant fantasy was that one excellent day I would move out of that dump and into the celestial confines of the Pontalba. But even if I had been able to afford it, it could never have happened. The usual way of acquiring a place there is if a tenant dies and wills it to you; or, if an apartment should become vacant, generally it is the custom of the city of New Orleans to offer it to a distin-guished local citizen for a very nominal fee.

A lot of fey folk have strolled about this square. Pirates. Lafitte himself. Bonnie Parker and Clyde Barrow. Huey Long. Or, moseying under the shade of a scarlet parasol, the Countess Willie Piazza, the proprietress of one of the ritzier *maisons de plaisir* in the red-light neighborhood: her house was famous for an exotic refreshment it offered—fresh cherries boiled in cream sweetened with absinthe and served stuffed inside the vagina of a reclining quadroon beauty. Or another lady, so unlike the Countess Willie: Annie Christmas, a female keelboat operator who was seven feet tall and was often observed toting a hundred-pound barrel of flour under either arm. And Jim Bowie. And Mr. Neddie Flanders, a dapper gentleman in his eighties, maybe nineties, who, until recent years, appeared in the square each evening, and accompanying himself on a harmonica, tap-danced from midnight until dawn in the most delicate, limber-puppet way. The *characters*. I could list hundreds.

Uh-oh. What's this I hear across the way? Trouble. A ruckus. A man and a woman, both black: the man is heavyset, bull-necked, smartly coiffed but withal weak-mannered; she is thin, lemon-colored, shrill, but almost pretty.

HER: Sombitch. What you mean—hold out bread?! I ain't hold out no bread. Sombitch.

HIM: Hush, woman. I seen you. I counted. Three guys. Makes sixty bucks. You onna gimme thirty.

HER: Damn you, nigger. I oughta take a razor on your ear. I oughta cut out your liver and feed the cats. I oughta fry your eyes in turpentine. Listen, nigger. Let me hear you call me a liar again.

HIM (placating): Sugar—

HER: *Sugar.* I'll sugar you.

HIM: Miss Myrtle, now I knows what I seen.

HER (slowly: a serpentine drawl): Bastard. Nigger bastard. Fact is, you never had no mother. You was born out of a dog's ass.

> (She slaps him. Hard. Turns and walks off, head high. He doesn't follow, but stands with a hand rubbing his cheek.)

For a while I watch the prancing spring-spry balloon children and see them greedily gather around a pushcart salesman selling a concoction known as Sweetmouth: scoops of flaked ice flavored with a rainbow-variety of colored syrups. Suddenly I recognize that I am hungry, too, and thirsty. I consider walking over to the French Market and filling up on deep-fried doughnuts and that bitter delicious chicory-flavored coffee peculiar to New Orleans. It's better than anything on the menu at Antoine's—which, by the way, is a lousy restaurant. So are most of the city's famous eateries. Gallatoire's isn't bad, but it's too crowded; they don't accept reservations, you always have to wait in long lines, and it's not worth it, at least not to me. Just as I've decided to amble off to the Market, an interruption occurs.

Now, if there is one thing I hate, it's people who sneak up behind you and say—

VOICE (whiskey-husky, virile, but female): Two guesses. (Silence) Come on, Jockey. You know it's me. (Silence; then, removing her blindfolding hands, somewhat petulantly) Jockey, you mean you didn't know it was *me*? Junebug?

TC: As I breathe—Big Junebug Johnson! *Comment ça va?*

BIG JUNEBUG JOHNSON (giggling with merriment): Oh, don't let me *commence.* Stand up, boy. Give old Junebug a hug. My, you're skinny. Like the first time I saw you. How much you weigh, Jockey?

TC: One twenty-five. Twenty-six.

> (It is difficult to get my arms around her, for she weighs double that; more. I've known her going on forty years—ever since I lived alone at the gloomy Royal Street address and used to frequent a raucous waterfront bar she owned, and still does. If she had pink eyes, one might call her an albino, for her skin is white as calla lilies; so is her curly, skimpy hair. [Once she told me her hair had turned white overnight, before she was sixteen, and when I said *"Overnight?"* she said: "It was the roller-coaster ride and Ed Jenkins' peter. The two things coming so close together. See, one night I was riding on a roller-coaster out at the lake, and we were in the last car. Well, it came uncoupled, the car ran wild, we damn near fell off the track, and the next morning my hair had grey freckles. About a week later I had this experience with Ed Jenkins, a kid I knew. One of

my girl friends told me that her brother had told her Ed Jenkins had the biggest peter anybody ever saw. He was nice-looking, but a scrawny fellow, not much taller than you, and I didn't believe it, so one day, joking him, I said, 'Ed Jenkins, I hear you have one helluva peter,' and he said, 'Yeah, I'll show you,' and he did, and I screamed; he said, 'And now I'm gonna put it in you,' and I said, 'Oh no you ain't!'—it was big as a baby's arm holding an apple. Lord's mercy! But he did. Put it in me. After a terrific tussle. And I was a virgin. Just about. Kind of. So you can imagine. Well, it wasn't long after that my hair went white like a witch."]

B.J.J. dresses stevedore-style: overalls, men's blue shirts rolled up to the elbow, ankle-high lace-up workman's boots, and no makeup to relieve her pallor. But she is womanly, a dignified figure for all her down-to-earth ways. And she wears expensive perfumes, Parisian smells bought at the Maison Blanche on Canal Street. Also, she has a glorious gold-toothed smile; it's like a heartening sunburst after a cold rainfall. You'd probably like her; most people do. Those who don't are mainly the proprietors of rival waterfront bars, for Big Junebug's is a popular hangout, if little known beyond the waterfront and that area's denizens. It contains three rooms—the big barroom itself with its mammoth zinc-topped bar, a second chamber furnished with three busy pool tables, and an alcove with a jukebox for dancing. It's open right around the clock, and is as crowded at dawn as it is at twilight. Of course, sailors and dockworkers go there, and the truck farmers who bring their produce to the French Market from outlying parishes, cops and firemen and hard-eyed gamblers and harder-eyed floozies, and around sunrise the place overflows with entertainers from the Bourbon Street tourist traps. Topless dancers, strippers, drag queens, B-girls, waiters, bartenders, and the hoarse-voiced doormen-barkers who so stridently labor to lure yokels into *vieux carré* sucker dives.

As for this "Jockey" business, it was a nickname I owed to Ginger Brennan. Forty-some years ago Ginger was the chief counterman at the old original all-night doughnuts-and-coffee café in the Market; that particular café is gone now, and Ginger was long ago killed by a bolt of lightning while fishing off a pier at Lake Pontchartrain. Anyway, one night I overheard another customer ask Ginger who the "little punk" was in the corner, and Ginger, who was a pathological liar, bless his heart, told him I was a professional jockey: "He's pretty hot stuff out at the race track." It was plausible enough; I was short and featherweight and could easily have posed as a jockey; as it happened, it was a fantasy I cottoned to: I liked the idea of people mistaking me for a wise-guy race-track character. I started reading *Racing Form* and learned the lingo. Word spread, and before you could say Boo! everybody was calling me "The Jockey" and soliciting tips on the horses.)

BIG JUNEBUG JOHNSON: I lost weight myself. Maybe fifty pounds. Ever since

I got married, I been losing weight. Most ladies, they get the ring, then start swelling up. But after I snagged Jim, I was so happy I stopped cleaning out my icebox. The blues, that's what makes you fat.

TC: Big Junebug Johnson married? Nobody wrote me that. I thought you were a devout bachelor.

BIG JUNEBUG JOHNSON: Can't a gal change her mind? Once I got over the Ed Jenkins incident, once I got that view out of my noggin, I was partial as the next lady for men. 'Course, that took years.

TC: Jim? That's his name?

BIG JUNEBUG JOHNSON: Jim O'Reilly. Ain't Irish, though. He comes from Plaquemine, and they're mostly Cajun, his people. I don't even know if that's his right name. I don't know a whole lot about him. He's kind of quiet.

TC: But some lover. To catch you.

BIG JUNEBUG JOHNSON (eyes rotating): Oh, honey, don't let me *commence*.

TC (laughs): That's one of the things I remember best about you. No matter what anybody said, whether it was the weather or whatever, you always said: "Oh, honey, don't let me *commence*."

BIG JUNEBUG JOHNSON: Well. That kind of covers it all, wouldn't you say?
    (Something I ought to have mentioned: she has a Brooklyn accent. If this
    sounds odd, it's not. Half the people in New Orleans don't sound South-
    ern at all; close your eyes, and you would imagine you were listening to
    a taxi driver from Bensonhurst, a phenomenon that supposedly stems
    from the speech patterns idiosyncratic to a sector of the city known as the
    Irish Channel, a quarter predominantly populated by the descendants of
    Emerald Isle immigrants.)

TC: Just how long have you been Mrs. O'Reilly?

BIG JUNEBUG JOHNSON: Three years next July. Actually, I didn't have much choice. I was real confused. He's a lot younger than me, maybe twenty years. And good-looking, my goodness. Catnip to the ladies. But he was plain crazy about me, followed my every footstep, every minute begging me to hitch up, said he'd jump off the levee if I didn't. And presents every day. One time a pair of pearl earrings. Natural-born pearls: I bit them and they didn't crack. And a whole litter of kittens. He didn't know cats make me sneeze; make my eyes swell up, too. Everybody warned me he was only after my money. Why else would a cutie like him want an old hag like me? But that didn't altogether figure 'cause he has a real good job with the Streckfus Steamship Company. But they said he was broke, and in a lot of trouble with Red Tibeaux and Ambrose Butterfield and all those gamblers. I asked him, and he said it was a lie, but it could've been true, there was a lot I didn't know about him, and still don't. All I do know is he never asked me for a dime. I was so confused. So I went to Augustine Genet. You recall Madame Genet? Who could read the spirits? I heard she was on her deathbed, so I rushed right over there, and sure enough she was sinking. A hundred if she was a day, and blind as a mole; couldn't hardly whisper, but she told me: Marry that man, he's a good man, and he'll make you happy—marry him, promise me you will. So I promised. So that's why I had no choice. I couldn't ignore a promise made to a lady on her deathbed. And I'm soooo glad I didn't. *I am happy.* I am a happy woman. Even if those cats do make me sneeze. And you, Jockey. You feel good about yourself?

TC: So-so.

BIG JUNEBUG JOHNSON: When was the last time you got to Mardi Gras?

TC (reluctant to reply, not desiring to evoke Mardi Gras memories: they were not amusing events to me, the streets swirling with drunken, squalling, shrouded figures wearing bad-dream masks; I always had nightmares after childhood excursions into Mardi Gras melees): Not since I was a kid. I was always getting lost in the crowds. The last time I got lost they took me to the police station. I was crying there all night before my mother found me.

BIG JUNEBUG JOHNSON: The damn police! You know we didn't have any Mardi Gras this year 'cause the police went on strike. Imagine, going on strike at a time like that. Cost this town millions. Blackmail is all it was. I've got some good police friends, good customers. But they're all a bunch of crooks, the entire shebang. I've never had no respect for the law around here, and how they treated Mr. Shaw finished me off for good. That so-called District Attorney *Jim* Garrison. What a sorry sonofagun. I hope the devil turns him on a slooow spit. And he will. Too bad Mr. Shaw won't be there to see it. From up high in *heaven,* where I know he is, Mr. Shaw won't be able to see old Garrison rotting in hell.

(B.J.J. is referring to Clay Shaw, a gentle, cultivated architect who was responsible for much of the finer-grade historical restoration in New Orleans. At one time Shaw was accused by James Garrison, the city's abrasive, publicity-deranged D.A., of being the key figure in a purported plot to assassinate President Kennedy. Shaw stood trial twice on this contrived charge, and though fully acquitted both times, he was left more or less bankrupt. His health failed, and he died several years ago.)

TC: After his last trial, Clay wrote me and said: "I've always thought I was a little paranoid, but having survived this, I know I never was, and know now I never will be."

BIG JUNEBUG JOHNSON: What is it—paranoid?

TC: Well. Oh, nothing. Paranoia's nothing. As long as you don't take it seriously.

BIG JUNEBUG JOHNSON: I sure do miss Mr. Shaw. All during his trouble, there was one way you could tell who was and who wasn't a gentleman in this town. A gentleman, when he passed Mr. Shaw on the street, tipped his hat; the bastards looked straight ahead. (Chuckling) Mr. Shaw, he was a card. Every time he come in my bar, he kept me laughing. Ever hear his Jesse James story? Seems one day Jesse James was robbing a train out West. Him and his gang barged into a car with their pistols drawn, and Jesse James shouts: "Hands up! We're gonna rob all the women and rape all the men." So this one fellow says:

"Haven't you got that wrong, sir? Don't you mean you're gonna rob all the men and rape all the women?" But there was this sweet little fairy on the train, and he pipes up: "Mind your own business! Mr. James knows how to rob a train."

(Two and three and four: the hour-bells of St. Louis Cathedral toll: . . . five . . . six . . . The toll is grave, like a gilded baritone voice reciting, echoing ancient episodes, a sound that drifts across the park as solemnly as the oncoming dusk: music that mingles with the laughing chatter, the optimistic farewells of the departing, sugar-mouthed, balloon-toting kids, mingles with the solitary grieving howl of a far-off shiphorn, and the jangling springtime bells of the syrup-ice peddler's cart. Redundantly, Big Junebug Johnson consults her big ugly Rolex wristwatch.)

BIG JUNEBUG JOHNSON: Lord save us. I ought to be halfway home. Jim has to have his supper on the table seven sharp, and he won't let anybody fix it for him 'cept me. Don't ask why. I can't cook worth an owl's ass, never could. Only thing I could ever do real good was draw beer. And . . . Oh hell, that reminds me: I'm on duty at the bar tonight. Usually now I just work days, and Irma's there the rest of the time. But one of Irma's little boys took sick, and she wants to be home with him. See, I forgot to tell you, but I got a partner now, a widow gal with a real sense of fun, and hard-working, too. Irma was married to a chicken farmer, and he up and died, leaving her with five little boys, two of them twins, and her not thirty yet. So she was scratching out a living on that farm—raising chickens and wringing their necks and trucking them into the market here. All by herself. And her just a mite of a thing, but with a scrumptious figure, and natural strawberry hair, curly like mine. She could go up to Atlantic City and win a beauty contest if she wasn't cockeyed: Irma, she's so cockeyed you can't tell what she's looking at or who. She started coming into the bar with some of the other gal truckers. First off I reckoned she was a dyke, same as most of those gal truckers. But I was wrong. She likes men, and they dote on her, cockeyes and all. Truth is, I think my guy's got a sneaker for her; I tease him about it, and it makes him *soooo* mad. But if you want to know, I have more than a slight notion that Irma gets a real tingle when Jim's around. You can tell who she's looking at *then*. Well, I won't live forever, and after I'm gone, if they want to get together, that's fine by me. I'll have had my happiness. And I know Irma will take good care of Jim. She's a wonderful kid. That's why I talked her into coming into business with me. Say now, it's great to see you again, Jockey. Stop by later. We've got a lot to catch up on. But I've got to get my old bones rattling now.

Six . . . six . . . six . . .: the voice of the hour-bell tarries in the greening air, shivering as it subsides into the sleep of history.

Some cities, like wrapped boxes under Christmas trees, conceal unexpected gifts, secret delights. Some cities will always remain wrapped boxes, containers of riddles never to be solved, nor even to be seen by vacationing visitors, or, for that matter, the most inquisitive, persistent travelers. To know such cities, to unwrap them, as it were, one has to have been born there. Venice is like that. After October, when Adriatic winds sweep away the last American, even the last German, carry them off and send their luggage flying after them, another Venice develops: a clique of Venetian *élégants,* fragile dukes sporting embroidered waistcoats, spindly contessas supporting themselves on the arms of pale, elongated nephews; Jamesian creations, D'Annunzio romantics who would never consider emerging from the mauve shadows of their palazzos on a summer's day when the foreigners are abroad, emerge to feed the pigeons and stroll under the Piazza San Marco's arcades, sally forth to take tea in the lobby of the Danieli (the Gritti having closed until spring), and most amusing, to swill martinis and chew grilled-cheese sandwiches within the cozy confines of Harry's American Bar, so lately and exclusively the watering hole of loud-mouthed hordes from across the Alps and the seas.

Fez is another enigmatic city leading a double life, and Boston still another —we all understand that intriguing tribal rites are acted out beyond the groomed exteriors and purple-tinged bow windows of Louisburg Square, but except for what some literary, chosen-few Bostonians have divulged, we don't know what these coded rituals are, and never will. However, of all secret cities, New Orleans, so it seems to me, is the most secretive, the most unlike, in reality, what an outsider is permitted to observe. The prevalence of steep walls, of obscuring foliage, of tall thick locked iron gates, of shuttered windows, of dark tunnels leading to overgrown gardens where mimosa and camellias contrast colors, and lazing lizards, flicking their forked tongues, race along palm fronds—all this is not accidental décor, but architecture deliberately concocted to camouflage, to mask, as at a Mardi Gras Ball, the lives of those born to live among these protective edifices: two cousins, who between them have a hundred other cousins spread throughout the city's entangling, intertangling familial relationships, whispering together as they sit under a fig tree beside the softly spilling fountain that cools their hidden garden.

A piano is playing. I can't decide where it's coming from: strong fingers playing a striding, riding-it-on-out piano: "I want, I want . . ." That's a black man singing; he's good—"I want, I want a mama, a big fat mama, I want a big fat mama with the meat shakin' on her, yeah!"

Footfalls. High-heeled feminine footsteps that approach and stop in front of me. It is the thin, almost pretty, high-yeller who earlier in the afternoon I'd overheard having a fuss with her "manager." She smiles, then winks at me, just one eye, then the other, and her voice is no longer angry. She sounds the way bananas taste.

HER: How you doin'?
TC: Just taking it easy.

HER: How you doin' for time?

TC: Let's see. I think it's six, a little after.

HER (laughs): I mean how you doin' for *time*? I got a place just around the corner here.

TC: I don't think so. Not today.

HER: You're cute.

TC: Everybody's entitled to their opinion.

HER: I'm not playing you. I mean it. You're cute.

TC: Well, thanks.

HER: But you don't look like you're having any fun. Come on. I'll show you a good time. We'll have fun.

TC: I don't think so.

HER: What's the matter? You don't like me?

TC: No. I like you.

HER: Then what's wrong? Give me a reason.

TC: There's a lot of reasons.

HER: Okay. Give me one, just one.

TC: Oh, honey, don't let me *commence*.

4
Derring-do

Time: November, 1970.
Place: Los Angeles International Airport.

I am sitting inside a telephone booth. It is a little after eleven in the morning, and I've been sitting here half an hour, pretending to make a call. From the booth I have a good view of Gate 38, from which TWA's nonstop noon flight to New York is scheduled to depart. I have a seat booked on that flight, a ticket bought under an assumed name, but there is every reason to doubt that I will ever board the plane. For one thing, there are two tall men standing at the gate, tough guys with snap-brim hats, and I know both of them. They're detectives from the San Diego Sheriff's Office, and they have a warrant for my arrest. That's why I'm hiding in the phone booth. The fact is, I'm in a real predicament.

The cause of my predicament had its roots in a series of conversations I'd conducted a year earlier with Robert M., a slender, slight, harmless-looking young man who was then a prisoner on Death Row at San Quentin, where he was awaiting execution, having been convicted of three slayings: his mother, a sister, both of whom he had beaten to death, and a fellow prisoner, a man he had strangled while he was in jail awaiting trial for the two original homicides. Robert M. was an intelligent psychopath; I got to know him fairly well, and he discussed his life and crimes with me freely—with the understanding that I would not write about or repeat anything that he told me. I was doing research on the subject of multiple murderers, and Robert M. became another case history that went into my files. As far as I was concerned, that was the end of it.

Then, two months prior to my incarceration in a sweltering telephone booth at Los Angeles airport, I received a call from a detective in the San Diego Sheriff's Office. He had called me in Palm Springs, where I had a house. He was courteous and pleasant-voiced; he said he knew about the many interviews I'd conducted with convicted murderers, and that he'd like to ask me a few questions. So I invited him to drive down to the Springs and have lunch with me the following day.

The gentleman did not arrive alone, but with three other San Diego detectives. And though Palm Springs lies deep in the desert, there was a strong smell of fish in the air. However, I pretended there was nothing odd about suddenly having four guests instead of one. But they were not interested in my hospitality; indeed, they declined lunch. All they wanted to talk about was Robert M. How well did I know him? Had he ever admitted to me any of his killings? Did I have any records of our conversations? I let them ask their questions, and avoided answering them until I asked my own question: Why were they so interested in my acquaintance with Robert M.?

The reason was this: due to a legal technicality, a federal court had overruled Robert M.'s conviction and ordered the state of California to grant him a new trial. The starting date for the retrial had been set for late November—in other words, approximately two months hence. Then, having delivered these facts, one of the detectives handed me a slim but exceedingly legal-looking document. It was a subpoena ordering me to appear at Robert M.'s trial, presumably as a witness for the prosecution. Okay, they'd tricked me, and I was mad as hell, but I smiled and nodded, and they smiled and said what a good guy I was and how grateful they were that my testimony would help send Robert M. straight to the gas chamber. That homicidal lunatic! They laughed, and said goodbye: "See ya in court."

I had no intention of honoring the subpoena, though I was aware of the consequences of not doing so: I would be arrested for contempt of court, fined, and sent to jail. I had no high opinion of Robert M., or any desire to protect him; I knew he was guilty of the three murders with which he was charged, and that he was a dangerous psychotic who ought never to be allowed his freedom. But I also knew that the state had more than enough hard evidence to reconvict him without my testimony. But the main point was that Robert M. had confided in me on my sworn word that I would not use or repeat what he told me. To betray him under these circumstances would have been morally despicable, and would have proven to Robert M., and the many men like him whom I'd interviewed, that they had placed their trust in a police informer, a stool pigeon plain and simple.

I consulted several lawyers. They all gave the same advice: honor the subpoena or expect the worst. Everyone sympathized with my quandary, but no one could see any solution—*unless I left California.* Contempt of court was not an extraditable offense, and once I was out of the state, there was nothing the authorities could do to punish me. Yes, there was one thing: I could never *return* to California. That didn't strike me as a severe hardship, although, because of various property matters and professional commitments, it was difficult to depart on such short notice.

I lost track of time, and was still tarrying in Palm Springs the day the trial began. That morning my housekeeper, a devoted friend named Myrtle Bennett, rushed into the house hollering: "Hurry up! It's all on the radio. They've got a warrant out for your arrest. They'll be here any minute."

Actually, it was twenty minutes before the Palm Springs police arrived full-force and with handcuffs at the ready (an overkill scene, but believe me, California law enforcement is not an institution one toys with lightly). However, though they dismantled the garden and searched the house stem to stern, all they found was my car in the garage and the loyal Mrs. Bennett in the living room. She told them I'd left for New York the previous day. They didn't believe her, but Mrs. Bennett was a formidable figure in Palm Springs, a black woman who had been a distinguished and politically influential member of the community for forty years, so they didn't question her further. They simply sent out an all-points alarm for my arrest.

And where *was* I? Well, I was tooling along the highway in Mrs. Bennett's old powder-blue Chevrolet, a car that couldn't do fifty miles an hour the day she bought it. But we figured I'd be safer in her car than my own. Not that I was safe anywhere; I was jumpy as a catfish with a hook in its mouth. When I got to Palm Desert, which is about thirty minutes out of Palm Springs, I turned off the highway and onto the lonely curving careening little road that leads away from the desert and up into the San Jacinto mountains. It had been hot in the desert, over a hundred, but as I climbed higher in the desolate mountains the air became cool, then cold, then colder. Which was okay, except that the old Chevy's heater wouldn't work, and all I had to wear were the clothes I had on when Mrs. Bennett had rushed into the house with her panic-stricken warnings: sandals, white linen slacks, and a light polo sweater. I'd left with just that and my wallet, which contained credit cards and about three hundred dollars.

Still, I had a destination in mind, and a plan. High in the San Jacinto mountains, midway between Palm Springs and San Diego, there's a grim little village named Idylwyld. In the summer, people from the desert travel there to escape the heat; in the winter it's a ski resort, though the quality of both the snow and the runs is threadbare. But now, out of season, this grim collection of mediocre motels and fake chalets would be a good place to lie low, at least until I could catch my breath.

It was snowing when the old car grunted up the last hill into Idylwyld: one of those young snows that suffuses the air but dissolves as it falls. The village was deserted, and most of the motels closed. The one I finally stopped at was called Eskimo Cabins. God knows, the accommodations were icy as igloos. It had one advantage: the proprietor, and apparently the only human on the premises, was a semi-deaf octogenarian far more interested in the game of solitaire he was playing than he was in me.

I called Mrs. Bennett, who was very excited: "Oh, honey, they're looking for you everywhere! It's all on the TV!" I decided it was better not to let her know where I was, but assured her I was all right and would call again tomorrow. Then I telephoned a close friend in Los Angeles; he was excited, too: "Your picture is in the *Examiner!*" After calming him down, I gave specific instructions: buy a ticket for a "George Thomas" on a nonstop flight to New York, and expect me at his house by ten o'clock the next morning.

I was too cold and hungry to sleep; I left at daybreak, and reached Los Angeles around nine. My friend was waiting for me. We left the Chevrolet at his house, and after wolfing down some sandwiches and as much brandy as I could safely contain, we drove in his car to the airport, where we said goodbye and he gave me the ticket for the noon flight he had booked for me on TWA.

So that's how I happen now to be huddled in this forsaken telephone booth, sitting here contemplating my predicament. A clock above the departure gate announces the hour: 11:35. The passenger area is crowded; soon the plane will be ready for boarding. And there, standing on either side of the gate through which I must pass, are two of the gentlemen who had visited me in Palm Springs, two tall watchful detectives from San Diego.

I considered calling my friend, asking him to return to the airport and pick me up somewhere in the parking lot. But he'd already done enough, and if we were caught, he could be accused of harboring a fugitive. That held true for all the many friends who might be willing to assist me. Perhaps it would be wisest to surrender myself to the guardians at the gate. Otherwise, what? Only a miracle, to coin a phrase, was going to save me. And we don't believe in miracles, do we?

Suddenly a miracle occurs.

There, striding past my tiny glass-doored prison, is a haughty, beautiful black Amazon wearing a zillion dollars' worth of diamonds and golden sable, a star surrounded by a giddy, chattering entourage of gaudily dressed chorus boys. And who is this dazzling apparition whose plumage and presence are creating such a commotion among the passers-by? A friend! An old, old friend!

TC (opening the booth's door; shouting): *Pearl!* Pearl Bailey! (A miracle! She *hears* me. All of them do, her whole entourage) Pearl! Please come here . . .

PEARL (squinting at me, then erupting into a radiant grin): Why, baby! What you doing hiding in there?

TC (beckoning her to come closer; whispering): Pearl, listen. I'm in a terrific jam.

PEARL (immediatley serious, for she is a very intelligent woman, and at once understood that whatever this was, it wasn't funny): Tell it to me.

TC: Are you on that plane to New York?

PEARL: Yeah, we all are.

TC: I've got to get on it, Pearl. I have a ticket. But there're two guys waiting at the gate to stop me.

PEARL: Which guys? (I pointed them out) How can they stop you?

TC: They're detectives. Pearl, I haven't got time to explain all this . . .

PEARL: You don't have to explain nothing.

(She surveyed her troupe of handsome young black chorus boys; she had a half-dozen—Pearl, I remembered, always liked to travel with a lot of company. She motioned to one of them to join us; he was a sleek number sporting a yellow cowboy hat, a sweatshirt that said SUCK DAMMIT, DONT BLOW, a white leather windbreaker with an ermine lining, yellow jitterbug pants [circa 1940], and yellow wedgies.)

This is Jimmy. He's a little bigger than you, but I think it'll all fit. Jimmy, take my friend here to the men's room and change clothes with him. Jimmy, don't flap your yap, just do like Pearlie-Mae say. We'll wait right here for you. Now hurry up! Ten more minutes and we'll miss that plane.

(The distance between the telephone booth and the men's room was a ten-yard dash. We locked ourselves into a pay toilet and started our wardrobe exchange. Jimmy thought it was a riot: he was giggling like a schoolgirl who's just puffed her first joint. I said: "Pearl! That really was a miracle. I've never been so happy to see someone. Never." Jimmy said: "Oh, Miss Bailey's got spirit. She's all heart, know what I mean? All heart."

There was a time when I would have disagreed with him, a time when I would have described Pearl Bailey as a heartless bitch. That was when she was playing the part of Madame Fleur, the principal role in *House of Flowers,* a musical play for which I had written the book and, with Harold Arlen, co-authored the lyrics. There were many gifted men attached to that endeavor: the director was Peter Brook; the choreographer, George Balanchine; Oliver Messel was responsible for the legendarily enchanting décor and costumes. But Pearl Bailey was so strong, so determined to have her way, that she dominated the entire production, much to its ultimate detriment. However, live and learn, forgive and forget, and by the time the play ended its Broadway run, Pearl and I were friends again. Aside from her skill as a performer, I'd come to respect her character; it might occasionally be unpleasant to deal with, but certainly she had it: she was a woman of character—one knew who she was and where she stood.

As Jimmy was squeezing into my trousers, which were embarrassingly too tight for him, and as I was slipping on his white leather ermine-lined windbreaker, there was an agitated knock at the door.)

MAN'S VOICE: Hey! What's goin' on in there?

JIMMY: And just *who* are *you*, pray tell?

MAN'S VOICE: I'm the attendant. And don't sass me. What's goin' on in there is against the law.

JIMMY: No shit?

ATTENDANT: I see four feet in there. I see clothes comin' off. You think I'm too stupid I don't know what's goin' on? It's against the law. It's against the law for two men to lock themselves in the same toilet at the same time.

JIMMY: Aw, shove it up your ass.

ATTENDANT: I'll get the cops. They'll hand you an L and L.

JIMMY: What the hell's an L and L?

ATTENDANT: Lewd and lascivious conduct. Yessir. I'll get the cops.

TC: Jesus, Joseph, and Mary—

ATTENDANT: Open that door!

TC: You've got it all wrong.

ATTENDANT: I know what I see. I see four feet.

TC: We're changing our costumes for the next scene.

ATTENDANT: Next scene what?

TC: The movie. We're getting ready to shoot the next scene.

ATTENDANT (curious and impressed): They're making a movie out there?

JIMMY (catching on): With Pearl Bailey. She's the star. Marlon Brando, he's in it, too.

TC: Kirk Douglas.

JIMMY (biting his knuckles to keep from laughing): And Shirley Temple. She's making her comeback.

ATTENDANT (believing, yet not believing): Yeah, well, who are you?

TC: We're just extras. That's why we don't have a dressing room.

ATTENDANT: I don't care. Two men, four feet. It's against the law.

JIMMY: Look outside. You'll see Pearl Bailey in person. Marlon Brando. Kirk Douglas. Shirley Temple. Mahatma Gandhi—she's in it, too. Just a cameo.

ATTENDANT: Who?

JIMMY: Mamie Eisenhower.

TC (opening the door, having completed the transference of clothing; my stuff doesn't look too bad on Jimmy, but I suspect that his outfit, as worn by me, will produce a galvanizing effect, and the expression on the attendant's face, a bristling short black man, confirms this expectation): Sorry. We didn't realize we were doing anything against the rules.

JIMMY (regally sweeping past the attendant, who seems too befuddled to budge): Follow us, sweetheart. We'll introduce you to the gang. You can get some autographs.

(At last we were in the corridor, and an unsmiling Pearl wrapped her sable-soft arms around me; her companions closed about us in a concealing circle. There were no jokes or jesting. My nerves sizzled like a cat just hit by lightning, and as for Pearl, the qualities about her that had once alarmed me—that strength, that self-will—were flowing through her like power from a waterfall.)

PEARL: From now on keep quiet. Whatever I say, don't you say anything. Tuck the hat more over your face. Lean on me like you're weak and sick. Lean your face against my shoulder. Close your eyes. Let me lead you.

All right. We're moving now toward the counter. Jimmy has all the tickets. They've already announced the last boarding call, so there aren't too many people around. Those gumshoes haven't moved an inch, but they seem tired and kind of disgusted. They're looking at us now. Both of them. When we pass between them the boys will distract them and start jabbering. Here comes somebody. Lean closer, groan a little—it's one of those VIP guys from TWA. Watch Mama go into her act . . . (Changing voice, impersonating her theatrical self, simultaneously droll and drawling and slightly flaky) Mr. Calloway? Like in Cab? Well, aren't you just an angel to help us out. And we surely could use some help. We need to get on that plane just as fast as possible. My friend here —he's one of my musicians—he's feeling something terrible. Can't hardly walk. We've been playing Vegas, and maybe he got too much sun. Sun can addle your brain and your stomach both. Or maybe it's his diet. Musicians eat funny. Piano players in particular. He won't eat hardly anything but hot dogs. Last night he ate ten hot dogs. Now, that's just not healthy. I'm not surprised he feels poisoned. Are you surprised, Mr. Calloway? Well, I don't suppose very much surprises you, being in the airplane business. All this hijacking that's going on. Criminals afoot all over the place. Soon as we get to New York, I'm taking my friend straight to the doctor. I'm going to tell the doctor to tell him to stay out of the sun and stop eating hot dogs. Oh, thank you, Mr. Calloway. No, I'll take the aisle. We'll put my friend in the window seat. He'll be better off by the window. All that fresh air.

Okay, Buster. You can open your eyes now.

TC: I think I'll keep them closed. It makes it seem more like a dream.

PEARL (relaxed, chuckling): Anyway, we made it. Your friends never even saw you. As we went by, Jimmy goosed one, and Billy stomped on the other guy's toes.

TC: Where is Jimmy?

PEARL: All the kids go economy. Jimmy's duds do something for you. Pep you up. I like the wedgies especially—just love 'em.

STEWARDESS: Good morning, Miss Bailey. Would you care for a glass of champagne?

PEARL: No, honey. But maybe my friend could use something.

TC: Brandy.

STEWARDESS: I'm sorry, sir, but we only serve champagne until after takeoff.

PEARL: The man wants brandy.

STEWARDESS: I'm sorry, Miss Bailey. It's not permitted.

PEARL (in a smooth yet metallic tone familiar to me from *House of Flowers* rehearsals): Bring the man his brandy. The whole bottle. Now.

(The stewardess brought the brandy, and I poured myself a hefty dose with an unsteady hand: hunger, fatigue, anxiety, the dizzying events of the last twenty-four hours were presenting their bill. I treated myself to another drink and began to feel a bit lighter.)

TC: I suppose I ought to tell you what this is all about.

PEARL: Not necessarily.

TC: Then I won't. That way you'll have a free conscience. I'll just say that I haven't done anything a sensible person would classify as criminal.

PEARL (consulting a diamond wristwatch): We should be over Palm Springs by now. I heard the door close ages ago. Stewardess!

STEWARDESS: Yes, Miss Bailey?

PEARL: What's going on?

STEWARDESS: Oh, there's the captain now—

CAPTAIN'S VOICE (over loudspeaker): Ladies and gentlemen, we regret the delay. We should be departing shortly. Thank you for your patience.

TC: Jesus, Joseph, and Mary.

PEARL: Have another slug. You're shaking. You'd think it was a first night. I mean, it can't be *that* bad.

TC: It's worse. And I can't stop shaking—not till we're in the air. Maybe not till we land in New York.

PEARL: You still living in New York?

TC: Thank God.

PEARL: You remember Louis? My husband?

TC: Louis Bellson. Sure. The greatest drummer in the world. Better than Gene Krupa.

PEARL: We both work Vegas so much, it made sense to buy a house there. I've become a real homebody. I do a lot of cooking. I'm writing a cookbook. Living in Vegas is just like living anywhere else, as long as you stay away from the undesirables. *Gamblers.* Unemployeds. Any time a man says to me he'd work if he could find a job, I always tell him to look in the phone book under G. G for gigolo. He'll find work. In Vegas, anyways. That's a town of desperate women. I'm lucky; I found the right man and had the sense to know it.

TC: Are you going to work in New York?

PEARL: Persian Room.

CAPTAIN'S VOICE: I'm sorry, ladies and gentlemen, but we'll be delayed a few minutes longer. Please remain seated. Those who care to smoke may do so.

PEARL (suddenly stiffening): I don't like this. They're opening the door.

TC: What?

PEARL: *They're opening the door.*

TC: Jesus, Joseph—

PEARL: I don't like this.

TC: Jesus, Joseph—

PEARL: Slump down in the seat. Pull the hat over your face.

TC: I'm scared.

PEARL (gripping my hand, squeezing it): Snore.

TC: Snore?

PEARL: Snore!

TC: I'm strangling. I *can't* snore.

PEARL: You'd better start trying, 'cause our friends are coming through that door. Looks like they're gonna roust the joint. Clean-tooth it.

TC: Jesus, Joseph—

PEARL: Snore, you rascal, snore.

> (I snored, and she increased the pressure of her hold on my hand; at the same time she began to hum a low sweet lullaby, like a mother soothing a fretful child. All the while another kind of humming surrounded us: human voices concerned with what was happening on the plane, the purpose of the two mysterious men who were pacing up and down the aisles, pausing now and again to scrutinize a passenger. Minutes elapsed. I counted them off: six, seven. Tickticktick. Eventually Pearl stopped crooning her maternal melody, and withdrew her hand from mine. Then I heard the plane's big round door slam shut.)

TC: Have they gone?

PEARL: Uh-huh. But whoever it is they're looking for, they sure must want him bad.

They did indeed. Even though Robert M.'s retrial ended exactly as I had predicted, and the jury brought in a verdict of guilty on three counts of first-degree murder, the California courts continued to take a harsh view of my refusal to cooperate with them. I was not aware of this; I thought that in due time the matter would be forgotten. So I did not hesitate to return to California when a year later something came up that required at least a brief visit there. Well, sir, I had no sooner registered at the Bel Air Hotel than I was arrested, summoned before a hard-nosed judge who fined me five thousand dollars and gave me an indefinite sentence in the Orange County jail, which meant they could keep me locked up for weeks or months or years. However, I was soon released because the summons for my arrest contained a small but significant error: it listed me as a legal resident of California, when in fact I was a resident of New York, a fact which made my conviction and confinement invalid.

But all that was still far off, unthought of, undreamed of when the silver vessel containing Pearl and her outlaw friend swept off into an ethereal November heaven. I watched the plane's shadow ripple over the desert and drift across the Grand Canyon. We talked and laughed and ate and sang. Stars and the lilac of twilight filled the air, and the Rocky Mountains, shrouded in blue snow, loomed ahead, a lemony slice of new moon hovering above them.

.   .   .

TC: Look, Pearl. A new moon. Let's make a wish.

PEARL: What are you going to wish?

TC: I wish I could always be as happy as I am at this very moment.

PEARL: Oh, honey, that's like asking miracles. Wish for something real.

TC: But I believe in miracles.

PEARL: Then all I can say is: don't ever take up gambling.

5

Then It All
Came Down

Scene: A cell in a maximum-security cell block at San Quentin prison in California. The cell is furnished with a single cot, and its permanent occupant, Robert Beausoleil, and his visitor are required to sit on it in rather cramped positions. The cell is neat, uncluttered; a well-waxed guitar stands in one corner. But it is late on a winter afternoon, and in the air lingers a chill, even a hint of mist, as though fog from San Francisco Bay had infiltrated the prison itself.

Despite the chill, Beausoleil is shirtless, wearing only a pair of prison-issue denim trousers, and it is clear that he is satisfied with his appearance, his body particularly, which is lithe, feline, in well-toned shape considering that he has been incarcerated more than a decade. His chest and arms are a panorama of tattooed emblems: feisty dragons, coiled chrysanthemums, uncoiled serpents. He is thought by some to be exceptionally good-looking; he is, but in a rather hustlerish camp-macho style. Not surprisingly, he worked as an actor as a child and appeared in several Hollywood films; later, as a very young man, he was for a while the protégé of Kenneth Anger, the experimental film-maker *(Scorpio Rising)* and author *(Hollywood Babylon)*; indeed, Anger cast him in the title role of *Lucifer Rising,* an unfinished film.

Robert Beausoleil, who is now thirty-one, is the real mystery figure of the Charles Manson cult; more to the point—and it's a point that has never been clearly brought forth in accounts of that tribe—he is the key to the mystery of the homicidal escapades of the so-called Manson family, notably the Sharon Tate–Lo Bianco murders.

It all began with the murder of Gary Hinman, a middle-aged professional musician who had befriended various members of the Manson brethren and who, unfortunately for him, lived alone in a small isolated house in Topanga Canyon, Los Angeles County. Hinman had been tied up and tortured for several days (among other indignities, one of his ears had been severed) before his throat had been mercifully and lastingly slashed. When Hinman's body, bloated and abuzz with August flies, was discovered, police found bloody graffiti on the walls of his modest house ("Death to Pigs!")—graffiti similar to the sort soon to be found in the households of Miss Tate and Mr. and Mrs. Lo Bianco.

However, just a few days prior to the Tate–Lo Bianco slayings, Robert Beausoleil, caught driving a car that had been the property of the victim, was under arrest and in jail, accused of having murdered the helpless Mr. Hinman. It was then that Manson and his chums, in the hopes of freeing Beausoleil, conceived the notion of committing a series of homicides similar to the Hinman affair; if Beausoleil was still incarcerated at the time of these killings, then how could he be guilty of the Hinman atrocity? Or so the Manson brood reasoned. That is to say, it was out of devotion to "Bobby" Beausoleil that Tex Watson and those cutthroat young ladies, Susan Atkins, Patricia Krenwinkel, Leslie Van Hooten, sallied forth on their satanic errands.

RB: Strange. Beausoleil. That's French. My name is French. It means Beautiful Sun. Fuck. Nobody sees much sun inside this resort. Listen to the foghorns. Like train whistles. Moan, moan. And they're worse in the summer. Maybe it must be there's more fog in summer than in winter. Weather. Fuck it, I'm not going anywhere. But just listen. Moan, moan. So what've you been up to today?

TC: Just around. Had a little talk with Sirhan.

RB (laughs): Sirhan *B.* Sirhan. I knew him when they had me up on the Row. He's a sick guy. He don't belong here. He ought to be in Atascadero. Want some gum? Yeah, well, you seem to know your way around here pretty good. I was watching you out on the yard. I was surprised the warden lets you walk around the yard by yourself. Somebody might cut you.

TC: Why?

RB: For the hell of it. But you've been here a lot, huh? Some of the guys were telling me.

TC: Maybe half a dozen times on different research projects.

RB: There's just one thing here I've never seen. But I'd like to see that little apple-green room. When they railroaded me on that Hinman deal and I got the death sentence, well, they had me up on the Row a good spell. Right up to when the court abolished the death penalty. So I used to wonder about the little green room.

TC: Actually, it's more like three rooms.

RB: I thought it was a little round room with a sort of glass-sealed igloo hut set in the center. With windows in the igloo so the witnesses standing outside can see the guys choking to death on that peach perfume.

TC: Yes, that's the gas-chamber room. But when the prisoner is brought down from Death Row he steps from the elevator directly into a "holding" room that adjoins the witness room. There are two cells in this "holding" room, two, in case it's a double execution. They're ordinary cells, just like this one, and the prisoner spends his last night there before his execution in the morning, reading, listening to the radio, playing cards with the guards. But the interesting thing I discovered was that there's a *third* room in this little suite. It's behind a closed door right next to the "holding" cell. I just opened the door and walked in and none of the guards that were with me tried to stop me. And it was the most haunting room I've ever seen. Because you know what's in it? All the leftovers, all the paraphernalia that the different condemned men had had with them in the "holding" cells. Books. Bibles and Western paperbacks and Erle Stanley Gardner, James Bond. Old brown newspapers. Some of them twenty years old. Unfinished crossword puzzles. Unfinished letters. Sweetheart snapshots. Dim, crumbling little Kodak children. Pathetic.

RB: You ever seen a guy gassed?

TC: Once. But he made it look like a lark. He was happy to go, he wanted to get it over with; he sat down in that chair like he was going to the dentist to have his teeth cleaned. But in Kansas, I saw two men hanged.

RB: Perry Smith? And what's his name—Dick Hickock? Well, once they hit the end of the rope, I guess they don't feel anything.

TC: So we're told. But after the drop, they go on living—fifteen, twenty minutes. Struggling. Gasping for breath, the body still battling for life. I couldn't help it, I vomited.

RB: Maybe you're not so cool, huh? You seem cool. So, did Sirhan beef about being kept in Special Security?

TC: Sort of. He's lonesome. He wants to mix with the other prisoners, join the general population.

RB: He don't know what's good for him. Outside, somebody'd snuff him for sure.

TC: Why?

RB: For the same reason he snuffed Kennedy. Recognition. Half the people who snuff people, that's what they want: recognition. Get their picture in the paper.

TC: That's not why you killed Gary Hinman.

RB: (Silence)

TC: That was because you and Manson wanted Hinman to give you money and his car, and when he wouldn't—well . . .

RB: (Silence)

TC: I was thinking. I know Sirhan, and I knew Robert Kennedy. I knew Lee Harvey Oswald, and I knew Jack Kennedy. The odds against that—one person knowing all four of those men—must be astounding.

RB: Oswald? You knew Oswald? Really?

TC: I met him in Moscow just after he defected. One night I was having dinner with a friend, an Italian newspaper correspondent, and when he came by to pick me up he asked me if I'd mind going with him first to talk to a young American defector, one Lee Harvey Oswald. Oswald was staying at the Metropole, an old Czarist hotel just off Kremlin Square. The Metropole has a big gloomy lobby full of shadows and dead palm trees. And there he was, sitting in the dark under a dead palm tree. Thin and pale, thin-lipped, starved-looking. He was wearing chinos and tennis shoes and a lumberjack shirt. And right away he was angry—he was grinding his teeth, and his eyes were jumping every which way. He was boiling over about everything: the American ambassador; the Russians—he was mad at them because they wouldn't let him stay in Moscow. We talked to him for about half an hour, and my Italian friend didn't think the guy was worth filing a story about. Just another paranoid hysteric; the Moscow woods were rampant with those. I never thought about him again, not until many years later. Not until after the assassination when I saw his picture flashed on television.

RB: Does that make you the only one that knew both of them, Oswald and Kennedy?

TC: No. There was an American girl, Priscilla Johnson. She worked for U.P. in Moscow. She knew Kennedy, and she met Oswald around the same time I did. But I can tell you something else almost as curious. About some of those people your friends murdered.

RB: (Silence)

TC: I knew them. At least, out of the five people killed in the Tate house that night, I knew four of them. I'd met Sharon Tate at the Cannes Film Festival. Jay Sebring cut my hair a couple of times. I'd had lunch once in San Francisco with Abigail Folger and her boyfriend, Frykowski. In other words, I'd known them independently of each other. And yet one night there they were, all gathered together in the same house waiting for your friends to arrive. Quite a coincidence.

RB (lights a cigarette; smiles): Know what I'd say? I'd say you're not such a lucky guy to know. Shit. Listen to that. Moan, moan. I'm cold. You cold?

TC: Why don't you put on your shirt?

RB: (Silence)

TC: It's odd about tattoos. I've talked to several hundred men convicted of homicide—multiple homicide, in most cases. The only common denominator I could find among them was tattoos. A good eighty percent of them were heavily tattooed. Richard Speck. York and Latham. Smith and Hickock.

RB: I'll put on my sweater.

TC: If you weren't here, if you could be anywhere you wanted to be, doing anything you wanted to do, where would you be and what would you be doing?

RB: Tripping. Out on my Honda chugging along the Coast road, the fast curves, the waves and the water, plenty of sun. Out of San Fran, headed

Mendocino way, riding through the redwoods. I'd be making love. I'd be on the beach by a bonfire making love. I'd be making music and balling and sucking some great Acapulco weed and watching the sun go down. Throw some driftwood on the fire. Good gash, good hash, just tripping right along.

TC: You can get hash in here.

RB: And everything else. Any kind of dope—for a price. There are dudes in here on everything but roller skates.

TC: Is that what your life was like before you were arrested? Just tripping? Didn't you ever have a job?

RB: Once in a while. I played guitar in a couple of bars.

TC: I understand you were quite a cocksman. The ruler of a virtual seraglio. How many children have you fathered?

RB: (Silence—but shrugs, grins, smokes)

TC: I'm surprised you have a guitar. Some prisons don't allow it because the strings can be detached and used as weapons. A garrote. How long have you been playing?

RB: Oh, since I was a kid. I was one of those Hollywood kids. I was in a couple of movies. But my folks were against it. They're real straight people. Anyway, I never cared about the acting part. I just wanted to write music and play it and sing.

TC: But what about the film you made with Kenneth Anger—*Lucifer Rising*?

RB: Yeah.

TC: How did you get along with Anger?

RB: Okay.

TC: Then why does Kenneth Anger wear a picture locket on a chain around his neck? On one side of the locket there is a picture of you; on the other there is an image of a frog with an inscription: "Bobby Beausoleil changed into a frog by Kenneth Anger." A voodoo amulet, so to say. A curse he put on you because you're supposed to have ripped him off. Left in the middle of the night with his car—and a few other things.

RB (narrowed eyes): Did he tell you that?

TC: No, I've never met him. But I was told it by a number of other people.

RB (reaches for guitar, tunes it, strums it, sings): "This is my song, this is my song, this is my dark song, my dark song . . ." Everybody always wants to know how I got together with Manson. It was through our music. He plays some, too. One night I was driving around with a bunch of my ladies. Well, we came to this old roadhouse, beer place, with a lot of cars outside. So we went inside, and there was Charlie with some of his ladies. We all got to talking, played some together; the next day Charlie came to see me in my van, and we all, his people and my people, ended up camping out together. Brothers and sisters. A family.

TC: Did you see Manson as a leader? Did you feel influenced by him right away?

RB: Hell, no. He had his people, I had mine. If anybody was influenced, it was him. By me.

TC: Yes, he was attracted to you. Infatuated. Or so he says. You seem to have had that effect on a lot of people, men and women.

RB: Whatever happens, happens. It's all good.

TC: Do you consider killing innocent people a good thing?

RB: Who said they were innocent?

TC: Well, we'll return to that. But for now: What is your own sense of morality? How do you differentiate between good and bad?

RB: Good and bad? It's *all* good. If it happens, it's got to be good. Otherwise, it wouldn't be *happening*. It's just the way life flows. Moves together. I move with it. I don't question it.

TC: In other words, you don't question the act of murder. You consider it "good" because it "happens." Justifiable.

RB: I have my own justice. I live by my own law, you know. I don't respect the laws of this society. Because society doesn't respect its own laws. I make my own laws and live by them. I have my own sense of justice.

TC: And what is your sense of justice?

RB: I believe that what goes around comes around. What goes up comes down. That's how life flows, and I flow with it.

TC: You're not making much sense—at least to me. And I don't think you're stupid. Let's try again. In your opinion, it's all right that Manson sent Tex Watson and those girls into that house to slaughter total strangers, innocent people—

RB: I said: Who says they were innocent? They burned people on dope deals. Sharon Tate and that gang. They picked up kids on the Strip and took them home and whipped them. Made movies of it. Ask the cops; they found the movies. Not that they'd tell you the truth.

TC: The truth is, the Lo Biancos and Sharon Tate and her friends were killed to protect you. Their deaths were directly linked to the Gary Hinman murder.

RB: I hear you. I hear where you're coming from.

TC: Those were all imitations of the Hinman murder—to prove that you couldn't have killed Hinman. And thereby get you out of jail.

RB: To get me out of jail. (He nods, smiles, sighs—complimented) None of that came out at any of the trials. The girls got on the stand and tried to really tell how it all came down, but nobody would listen. People couldn't believe anything except what the media said. The media had them programmed to believe it all happened because we were out to start a race war. That it was mean niggers going around hurting all these good white folk. Only—it was like you say. The media, they called us a "family." And it was the only true thing they said. We *were* a family. We were mother, father, brother, sister, daughter, son. If a member of our family was in jeopardy, we didn't abandon that person. And so for the love of a brother, a brother who was in jail on a murder rap, all those killings came down.

TC: And you don't regret that?

RB: No. If my brothers and sisters did it, then it's good. Everything in life is good. It all flows. It's all good. It's all music.

TC: When you were up on Death Row, if you'd been forced to flow down to the gas chamber and whiff the peaches, would you have given that your stamp of approval?

RB: If that's how it came down. Everything that happens is good.

TC: War. Starving children. Pain. Cruelty. Blindness. Prisons. Desperation. Indifference. All good?

RB: What's that look you're giving me?

TC: Nothing. I was noticing how your face changes. One moment, with just the slightest shift of angle, you look so boyish, entirely innocent, a charmer. And then—well, one can see you as a sort of Forty-second Street Lucifer. Have you ever seen *Night Must Fall*? An old movie with Robert Montgomery? No? Well, it's about an impish, innocent-looking delightful young man who travels about the English countryside charming old ladies, then cutting off their heads and carrying the heads around with him in leather hat-boxes.

RB: So what's that got to do with me?

TC: I was thinking—if it was ever remade, if someone Americanized it, turned the Montgomery character into a young drifter with hazel eyes and a smoky voice, you'd be very good in the part.

RB: Are you trying to say I'm a psychopath? I'm not a nut. If I have to use violence, I'll use it, but I don't believe in killing.

TC: Then I must be deaf. Am I mistaken, or didn't you just tell me that it didn't matter what atrocity one person committed against another, it was good, all good?

RB: (Silence)

TC: Tell me, Bobby, how do you view yourself?

RB: As a convict.

TC: But beyond that.

RB: As a man. A *white* man. And everything a white man stands for.

TC: Yes, one of the guards told me you were the ringleader of the Aryan Brotherhood.

RB (hostile): What do *you* know about the Brotherhood?

TC: That it's composed of a bunch of hard-nosed white guys. That it's a somewhat fascist-minded fraternity. That it started in California, and has spread throughout the American prison system, north, south, east, and west. That the prison authorities consider it a dangerous, troublemaking cult.

RB: A man has to defend himself. We're outnumbered. You got no idea how rough it is. We're all more scared of each other than we are of the pigs in here. You got to be on your toes every second if you don't want a shiv in your back. The blacks and Chicanos, they got their own gangs. The Indians, too; or I should say the "Native Americans"—that's how these redskins call themselves: what a laugh! Yessir, *rough*. With all the racial tensions, politics, dope,

gambling, and sex. The blacks really go for the young white kids. They like
to shove those big black dicks up those tight white asses.

TC: Have you ever thought what you would do with your life if and when you
were paroled out of here?

RB: That's a tunnel I don't see no end to. They'll never let Charlie go.

TC: I hope you're right, and I think you are. But it's very likely that you'll be
paroled some day. Perhaps sooner than you imagine. Then what?

RB (strums guitar): I'd like to record some of my music. Get it played on the
air.

TC: That was Perry Smith's dream. And Charlie Manson's, too. Maybe you
fellows have more in common than mere tattoos.

RB: Just between us, Charlie doesn't have a whole lot of talent. (Strumming
chords) "This is my song, my dark song, my dark song." I got my first guitar
when I was eleven; I found it in my grandma's attic and taught myself to play
it, and I've been nuts about music ever since. My grandma was a sweet woman,
and her attic was my favorite place. I liked to lie up there and listen to the
rain. Or hide up there when my dad came looking for me with his belt. Shit.
You hear that? Moan, moan. It's enough to drive you crazy.

TC: Listen to me, Bobby. And answer carefully. Suppose, when you get out of
here, somebody came to you—let's say Charlie—and asked you to commit an
act of violence, kill a man, would you do it?

RB (after lighting another cigarette, after smoking it half through): I might. It
depends. I never meant to . . . to . . . hurt Gary Hinman. But one thing
happened. And another. And then it all came down.

TC: And it was all good.

RB: It was all good.

6

A Beautiful Child

Time: 28 April 1955.
Scene: The chapel of the Universal Funeral Home at Lexington Avenue and
Fifty-second Street, New York City. An interesting galaxy packs the pews:
celebrities, for the most part, from an international arena of theatre, films,
literature, all present in tribute to Constance Collier, the English-born actress
who had died the previous day at the age of seventy-five.

Born in 1880, Miss Collier had begun her career as a music-hall Gaiety Girl,
graduated from that to become one of England's principal Shakespearean
actresses (and the long-time fiancée of Sir Max Beerbohm, whom she never
married, and perhaps for that reason was the inspiration for the mischievously
unobtainable heroine in Sir Max's novel *Zuleika Dobson*). Eventually she
emigrated to the United States, where she established herself as a considerable
figure on the New York stage as well as in Hollywood films. During the last
decades of her life she lived in New York, where she practiced as a drama
coach of unique caliber; she accepted only professionals as students, and
usually only professionals who were already "stars"—Katharine Hepburn was
a permanent pupil; another Hepburn, Audrey, was also a Collier protégée, as
were Vivien Leigh and, for a few months prior to her death, a neophyte Miss
Collier referred to as "my special problem," Marilyn Monroe.

Marilyn Monroe, whom I'd met through John Huston when he was directing her in her first speaking role in *The Asphalt Jungle,* had come under Miss
Collier's wing at my suggestion. I had known Miss Collier perhaps a half-

dozen years, and admired her as a woman of true stature, physically, emotionally, creatively; and, for all her commanding manner, her grand cathedral voice, as an adorable person, mildly wicked but exceedingly warm, dignified yet *Gemütlich*. I loved to go to the frequent small lunch parties she gave in her dark Victorian studio in mid-Manhattan; she had a barrel of yarns to tell about her adventures as a leading lady opposite Sir Beerbohm Tree and the great French actor Coquelin, her involvements with Oscar Wilde, the youthful Chaplin, and Garbo in the silent Swede's formative days. Indeed she was a delight, as was her devoted secretary and companion, Phyllis Wilbourn, a quietly twinkling maiden lady who, after her employer's demise, became, and has remained, the companion of Katharine Hepburn. Miss Collier introduced me to many people who became friends: the Lunts, the Oliviers, and especially Aldous Huxley. But it was I who introduced her to Marilyn Monroe, and at first it was not an acquaintance she was too keen to acquire: her eyesight was faulty, she had seen none of Marilyn's movies, and really knew nothing about her except that she was some sort of platinum sex-explosion who had achieved global notoriety; in short, she seemed hardly suitable clay for Miss Collier's stern classic shaping. But I thought they might make a stimulating combination.

They did. "Oh yes," Miss Collier reported to me, "there is something there. She is a beautiful child. I don't mean that in the obvious way—the perhaps too obvious way. I don't think she's an actress at all, not in any traditional sense. What she has—this presence, this luminosity, this flickering intelligence —could never surface on the stage. It's so fragile and subtle, it can only be caught by the camera. It's like a hummingbird in flight: only a camera can freeze the poetry of it. But anyone who thinks this girl is simply another Harlow or harlot or whatever is *mad*. Speaking of mad, that's what we've been working on together: Ophelia. I suppose people would chuckle at the notion, but really, she could be the most exquisite Ophelia. I was talking to Greta last week, and I told her about Marilyn's Ophelia, and Greta said yes, she could believe that because she had seen two of her films, very bad and vulgar stuff, but nevertheless she had glimpsed Marilyn's possibilities. Actually, Greta has an amusing idea. You know that she wants to make a film of *Dorian Gray*? With her playing Dorian, of course. Well, she said she would like to have Marilyn opposite her as one of the girls Dorian seduces and destroys. Greta! So unused! Such a gift—and rather like Marilyn's, if you consider it. Of course, Greta is a consummate artist, an artist of the utmost control. This beautiful child is without any concept of discipline or sacrifice. Somehow I don't think she'll make old bones. Absurd of me to say, but somehow I feel she'll go young. I hope, I really pray, that she survives long enough to free the strange lovely talent that's wandering through her like a jailed spirit."

But now Miss Collier had died, and here I was loitering in the vestibule of the Universal Chapel waiting for Marilyn; we had talked on the telephone the evening before, and agreed to sit together at the services, which were scheduled to start at noon. She was now a half-hour late; she was *always* late, but I'd thought just for once! For God's sake, goddamnit! Then suddenly there she was, and I didn't recognize her until she said . . .

MARILYN: Oh, baby, I'm so sorry. But see, I got all made up, and then I decided maybe I shouldn't wear eyelashes or lipstick or anything, so then I had to wash all that off, and I couldn't imagine what to wear . . .

(What she had imagined to wear would have been appropriate for the abbess of a nunnery in private audience with the Pope. Her hair was entirely concealed by a black chiffon scarf; her black dress was loose and long and looked somehow borrowed; black silk stockings dulled the blond sheen of her slender legs. An abbess, one can be certain, would not have donned the vaguely erotic black high-heeled shoes she had chosen, or the owlish black sunglasses that dramatized the vanilla-pallor of her dairy-fresh skin.)

TC: You look fine.

MARILYN (gnawing an already chewed-to-the-nub thumbnail): Are you sure? I mean, I'm so jumpy. Where's the john? If I could just pop in there for a minute—

TC: And pop a pill? No! Shhh. That's Cyril Ritchard's voice: he's started the eulogy.

(Tiptoeing, we entered the crowded chapel and wedged ourselves into a narrow space in the last row. Cyril Ritchard finished; he was followed by Cathleen Nesbitt, a lifelong colleague of Miss Collier's, and finally Brian Aherne addressed the mourners. Through it all, my date periodically removed her spectacles to scoop up tears bubbling from her blue-grey eyes. I'd sometimes seen her without makeup, but today she presented a new visual experience, a face I'd not observed before, and at first I couldn't perceive why this should be. Ah! It was because of the obscuring head scarf. With her tresses invisible, and her complexion cleared of all cosmetics, she looked twelve years old, a pubescent virgin who has just been admitted to an orphanage and is grieving over her plight. At last the ceremony ended, and the congregation began to disperse.)

MARILYN: Please, let's sit here. Let's wait till everyone's left.

TC: Why?

MARILYN: I don't want to have to talk to anybody. I never know what to say.

TC: Then you sit here, and I'll wait outside. I've got to have a cigarette.

MARILYN: You can't leave me alone! My God! Smoke here.

TC: *Here?* In the chapel?

MARILYN: Why not? What do you want to smoke? A reefer?

TC: Very funny. Come on, let's go.

MARILYN: Please. There's a lot of shutterbugs downstairs. And I certainly don't want them taking my picture looking like this.

TC: I can't blame you for that.

MARILYN: You said I looked fine.

TC: You do. Just perfect—if you were playing the Bride of Frankenstein.

MARILYN: Now you're laughing at me.

TC: Do I look like I'm laughing?

MARILYN: You're laughing inside. And that's the worst kind of laugh. (Frowning; nibbling thumbnail) Actually, I could've worn makeup. I see all these other people are wearing makeup.

TC: I am. Globs.

MARILYN: Seriously, though. It's my hair. I need color. And I didn't have time to get any. It was all so unexpected, Miss Collier dying and all. See?

(She lifted her kerchief slightly to display a fringe of darkness where her hair parted.)

TC: Poor innocent me. And all this time I thought you were a bona-fide blonde.

MARILYN: I am. But nobody's *that* natural. And incidentally, fuck you.

TC: Okay, everybody's cleared out. So up, up.

MARILYN: Those photographers are still down there. I know it.

TC: If they didn't recognize you coming in, they won't recognize you going out.

MARILYN: One of them did. But I'd slipped through the door before he started yelling.

TC: I'm sure there's a back entrance. We can go that way.

MARILYN: I don't want to see any corpses.

TC: Why would we?

MARILYN: This is a funeral parlor. They must keep them somewhere. That's all I need today, to wander into a room full of corpses. Be patient. I'll take us somewhere and treat us to a bottle of bubbly.

(So we sat and talked and Marilyn said: "I hate funerals. I'm glad I won't have to go to my own. Only, I don't want a funeral—just my ashes cast on waves by one of my kids, if I ever have any. I wouldn't have come today except Miss Collier cared about me, my welfare, and she was just like a granny, a tough old granny, but she taught me a lot. She taught me how to breathe. I've put it to good use, too, and I don't mean just acting. There *are* other times when breathing is a problem. But when I first heard about it, Miss Collier cooling, the first thing I thought was: Oh, gosh, what's going to happen to Phyllis?! Her whole life was Miss Collier. But I hear she's going to live with Miss Hepburn. Lucky Phyllis; she's going to have fun now. I'd change places with her pronto. Miss Hepburn is a terrific lady, no shit. I wish she was my friend. So I could call her up sometimes and . . . well, I don't know, just call her up."

We talked about how much we liked New York and loathed Los Angeles ("Even though I was born there, I still can't think of one good thing to say about it. If I close my eyes, and picture L.A., all I see is one big varicose vein"); we talked about actors and acting ("Everybody says I can't act. They said the same thing about Elizabeth Taylor. And they were wrong. She was great in *A Place in the Sun.* I'll never get the right part, anything I really want. My looks are against me. They're too specific"); we talked some more about Elizabeth Taylor, and she wanted to know if I knew her, and I said yes, and she said well, what is she like, what is she *really* like, and I said well, she's a little bit like you, she wears her heart on her sleeve and talks salty, and Marilyn said fuck you and said well, if somebody asked me what Marilyn Monroe was like, what was Marilyn Monroe *really* like, what would I say, and I said I'd have to think about that.)

TC: Now do you think we can get the hell out of here? You promised me champagne, remember?

MARILYN: I remember. But I don't have any money.

TC: You're always late and you never have any money. By any chance are you under the delusion that you're Queen Elizabeth?

MARILYN: Who?

TC: Queen Elizabeth. The Queen of England.

MARILYN (frowning): What's that cunt got to do with it?

TC: Queen Elizabeth never carries money either. She's not allowed to. Filthy lucre must not stain the royal palm. It's a law or something.

MARILYN: I wish they'd pass a law like that for me.

TC: Keep going the way you are and maybe they will.

MARILYN: Well, gosh. How does she pay for anything? Like when she goes shopping.

TC: Her lady-in-waiting trots along with a bag full of farthings.

MARILYN: You know what? I'll bet she gets everything free. In return for endorsements.

TC: Very possible. I wouldn't be a bit surprised. By Appointment to Her Majesty. Corgi dogs. All those Fortnum & Mason goodies. Pot. Condoms.

MARILYN: What would she want with condoms?

TC: Not her, dopey. For that chump who walks two steps behind. Prince Philip.

MARILYN: Him. Oh, yeah. He's cute. He looks like he might have a nice prick. Did I ever tell you about the time I saw Errol Flynn whip out his prick and play the piano with it? Oh well, it was a hundred years ago, I'd just got into modeling, and I went to this half-ass party, and Errol Flynn, so pleased with himself, he was there and he took out his prick and played the piano with it. Thumped the keys. He played *You Are My Sunshine.* Christ! Everybody says Milton Berle has the biggest schlong in Hollywood. But who *cares*? Look, don't you have *any* money?

TC: Maybe about fifty bucks.

MARILYN: Well, that ought to buy us some bubbly.

(Outside, Lexington Avenue was empty of all but harmless pedestrians. It was around two, and as nice an April afternoon as one could wish: ideal strolling weather. So we moseyed toward Third Avenue. A few gawkers spun their heads, not because they recognized Marilyn as *the* Marilyn, but because of her funereal finery; she giggled her special little giggle, a sound as tempting as the jingling bells on a Good Humor wagon, and said: "Maybe I should always dress this way. Real anonymous."

As we neared P.J. Clarke's saloon, I suggested P.J.'s might be a good place to refresh ourselves, but she vetoed that: "It's full of those advertising creeps. And that bitch Dorothy Kilgallen, she's always in there getting bombed. What is it with these micks? The way they booze, they're worse than Indians."

I felt called upon to defend Kilgallen, who was a friend, somewhat, and I allowed as to how she could upon occasion be a clever funny woman. She said: "Be that as it may, she's written some bitchy stuff about me. But all those cunts hate me. Hedda. Louella. I know you're supposed to get used to it, but I just can't. It really hurts. What did I ever do to those hags? The only one who writes a decent word about me is Sidney Skolsky. But he's a guy. The guys treat me okay. Just like maybe I was a human person. At least they give me the benefit of the doubt. And Bob Thomas is a gentleman. And Jack O'Brian."

We looked in the windows of antique shops; one contained a tray of old rings, and Marilyn said: "That's pretty. The garnet with the seed pearls. I wish I could wear rings, but I hate people to notice my hands. They're too fat. Elizabeth Taylor has fat hands. But with those eyes, who's looking at her hands? I like to dance naked in front of mirrors and watch my titties jump around. There's nothing wrong with them. But I wish my hands weren't so fat."

Another window displayed a handsome grandfather clock, which prompted her to observe: "I've never had a home. Not a real one with all my own furniture. But if I ever get married again, and make a lot of money, I'm going to hire a couple of trucks and ride down Third Avenue buying every damn kind of crazy thing. I'm going to get a dozen grandfather clocks and line them all up in one room and have them all ticking away at the same time. That would be real homey, don't you think?")

MARILYN: Hey! Across the street!
TC: What?
MARILYN: See the sign with the palm? That must be a fortunetelling parlor.
TC: Are you in the mood for that?
MARILYN: Well, let's take a look.

(It was not an inviting establishment. Through a smeared window we could discern a barren room with a skinny, hairy gypsy lady seated in a canvas chair under a hellfire-red ceiling lamp that shed a torturous glow; she was knitting a pair of baby-booties, and did not return our stares. Nevertheless, Marilyn started to go in, then changed her mind.)

MARILYN: Sometimes I want to know what's going to happen. Then I think it's better not to. There's two things I'd like to know, though. One is whether I'm going to lose weight.
TC: And the other?

MARILYN: That's a secret.

TC: Now, now. We can't have secrets today. Today is a day of sorrow, and sorrowers share their innermost thoughts.

MARILYN: Well, it's a man. There's something I'd like to know. But that's all I'm going to tell. It really *is* a secret.

(And I thought: That's what you think; I'll get it out of you.)

TC: I'm ready to buy that champagne.

(We wound up on Second Avenue in a gaudily decorated deserted Chinese restaurant. But it did have a well-stocked bar, and we ordered a bottle of Mumm's; it arrived unchilled, and without a bucket, so we drank it out of tall glasses with ice cubes.)

MARILYN: This is fun. Kind of like being on location—if you like location. Which I most certainly don't. *Niagara.* That stinker. Yuk.

TC: So let's hear about your secret lover.

MARILYN: (Silence)

TC: (Silence)

MARILYN: (Giggles)

TC: (Silence)

MARILYN: You know so many women. Who's the most attractive woman you know?

TC: No contest. Barbara Paley. Hands down.

MARILYN (frowning): Is that the one they call "Babe"? She sure doesn't look like any Babe to me. I've seen her in *Vogue* and all. She's so elegant. Lovely. Just looking at her pictures makes me feel like pig-slop.

TC: She might be amused to hear that. She's very jealous of you.

MARILYN: Jealous of *me*? Now there you go again, laughing.

TC: Not at all. She *is* jealous.

MARILYN: But why?

TC: Because one of the columnists, Kilgallen I think, ran a blind item that said something like: "Rumor hath it that Mrs. DiMaggio rendezvoused with television's toppest tycoon and it wasn't to discuss business." Well, she read the item and she believes it.

MARILYN: Believes *what*?

TC: That her husband is having an affair with you. William S. Paley. TV's toppest tycoon. He's partial to shapely blondes. Brunettes, too.

MARILYN: But that's batty. I've never met the guy.

TC: Ah, come on. You can level with me. This secret lover of yours—it's William S. Paley, *n'est-ce pas*?

MARILYN: No! It's a writer. He's a writer.

TC: That's more like it. Now we're getting somewhere. So your lover is a writer. Must be a real hack, or you wouldn't be ashamed to tell me his name.

MARILYN (furious, frantic): What does the "S" stand for?

TC: "S." What "S"?

MARILYN: The "S" in William S. Paley.

TC: Oh, *that* "S." It doesn't stand for anything. He sort of tossed it in there for appearance sake.

MARILYN: It's just an initial with no name behind it? My goodness. Mr. Paley must be a little insecure.

TC: He twitches a lot. But let's get back to our mysterious scribe.

MARILYN: Stop it! You don't understand. I have so much to lose.

TC: Waiter, we'll have another Mumm's, please.

MARILYN: Are you trying to loosen my tongue?

TC: Yes. Tell you what. We'll make an exchange. I'll tell you a story, and if you think it's interesting, then perhaps we can discuss your writer friend.

MARILYN (tempted, but reluctant): What's your story about?

TC: Errol Flynn.

MARILYN: (Silence)

TC: (Silence)

MARILYN (hating herself): Well, go on.

TC: Remember what you were saying about Errol? How pleased he was with his prick? I can vouch for that. We once spent a cozy evening together. If you follow me.

MARILYN: You're making this up. You're trying to trick me.

TC: Scout's honor. I'm dealing from a clean deck. (Silence; but I can see that she's hooked, so after lighting a cigarette . . .) Well, this happened when I was eighteen. Nineteen. It was during the war. The winter of 1943. That night Carol Marcus or maybe she was already Carol Saroyan, was giving a party for her best friend, Gloria Vanderbilt. She gave it in her mother's apartment on Park Avenue. Big party. About fifty people. Around midnight Errol Flynn rolls in with his alter ego, a swashbuckling playboy named Freddie McEvoy. They were both pretty loaded. Anyway, Errol started yakking with me, and he was bright, we were making each other laugh, and suddenly he said he wanted to go to El Morocco, and did I want to go with him and his buddy McEvoy. I said okay, but then McEvoy didn't want to leave the party and all those debutantes, so in the end Errol and I left alone. Only we didn't go to El Morocco. We took a taxi down to Gramercy Park, where I had a little one-room apartment. He stayed until noon the next day.

MARILYN: And how would you rate it? On a scale of one to ten.

TC: Frankly, if it hadn't been Errol Flynn, I don't think I would have remembered it.

MARILYN: That's not much of a story. Not worth mine—not by a long shot.

TC: Waiter, where is our champagne? You've got two thirsty people here.

MARILYN: And it's not as if you'd told me anything new. I've always known Errol zigzagged. I have a masseur, he's practically my sister, and he was Tyrone Power's masseur, and he told me all about the thing Errol and Ty Power had going. No, you'll have to do better than that.

TC: You drive a hard bargain.

MARILYN: I'm listening. So let's hear your best experience. Along those lines.

TC: The best? The most memorable? Suppose you answer the question first.

MARILYN: And *I* drive hard bargains! Ha! (Swallowing champagne) Joe's not bad. He can hit home runs. If that's all it takes, we'd still be married. I still love him, though. He's genuine.

TC: Husbands don't count. Not in this game.

MARILYN (nibbling nail; really thinking): Well, I met a man, he's related to Gary Cooper somehow. A stockbroker, and nothing much to look at—sixty-five, and he wears those very thick glasses. Thick as jellyfish. I can't say what it was, but—

TC: You can stop right there. I've heard all about him from other girls. That old swordsman really scoots around. His name is Paul Shields. He's Rocky Cooper's stepfather. He's supposed to be sensational.

MARILYN: He is. Okay, smart-ass. Your turn.

TC: Forget it. I don't have to tell you damn nothing. Because I know who your masked marvel is: Arthur Miller. (She lowered her black glasses: Oh boy, if looks could kill, wow!) I guessed as soon as you said he was a writer.

MARILYN (stammering): But how? I mean, nobody . . . I mean, hardly anybody—

TC: At least three, maybe four years ago Irving Drutman—

MARILYN: Irving *who*?

TC: Drutman. He's a writer on the *Herald Tribune*. He told me you were fooling around with Arthur Miller. Had a hangup on him. I was too much of a gentleman to mention it before.

MARILYN: Gentleman! You bastard. (Stammering again, but dark glasses in place) You don't understand. That was long ago. That ended. But this is new. It's all different now, and—

TC: Just don't forget to invite me to the wedding.

MARILYN: If you talk about this, I'll murder you. I'll have you bumped off. I know a couple of men who'd gladly do me the favor.

TC: I don't question that for an instant.

(At last the waiter returned with the second bottle.)

MARILYN: Tell him to take it back. I don't want any. I want to get the hell out of here.

TC: Sorry if I've upset you.

MARILYN: I'm not upset.

(But she was. While I paid the check, she left for the powder room, and I wished I had a book to read: her visits to powder rooms sometimes lasted as long as an elephant's pregnancy. Idly, as time ticked by, I wondered if she was popping uppers or downers. Downers, no doubt. There was a newspaper on the bar, and I picked it up; it was written in Chinese. After twenty minutes had passed, I decided to investigate. Maybe she'd popped a lethal dose, or even cut her wrists. I found the ladies' room, and knocked on the door. She said: "Come in." Inside, she was confronting a dimly lit mirror. I said: "What are you doing?" She said: "Looking at Her." In fact, she was coloring her lips with ruby lipstick. Also, she had removed the somber head scarf and combed out her glossy fine-as-cotton-candy hair.)

MARILYN: I hope you have enough money left.

TC: That depends. Not enough to buy pearls, if that's your idea of making amends.

MARILYN (giggling, returned to good spirits. I decided I wouldn't mention Arthur Miller again): No. Only enough for a long taxi ride.

TC: Where are we going—Hollywood?

MARILYN: Hell, no. A place I like. You'll find out when we get there.

(I didn't have to wait that long, for as soon as we had flagged a taxi, I heard her instruct the cabby to drive to the South Street Pier, and I thought: Isn't that where one takes the ferry to Staten Island? And my next conjecture was: She's swallowed pills on top of the champagne and now she's off her rocker.)

TC: I hope we're not going on any boat rides. I didn't pack my Dramamine.

MARILYN (happy, giggling): Just the pier.

TC: May I ask why?

MARILYN: I like it there. It smells foreign, and I can feed the seagulls.

TC: With what? You haven't anything to feed them.

MARILYN: Yes, I do. My purse is full of fortune cookies. I swiped them from that restaurant.

TC (kidding her): Uh-huh. While you were in the john I cracked one open. The slip inside was a dirty joke.

MARILYN: Gosh. Dirty fortune cookies?

TC: I'm sure the gulls won't mind.

(Our route carried us through the Bowery. Tiny pawnshops and blood-donor stations and dormitories with fifty-cent cots and tiny grim hotels with dollar beds and bars for whites, bars for blacks, everywhere bums, bums, young, far from young, ancient, bums squatting curbside, squatting amid shattered glass and pukey debris, bums slanting in doorways and huddled like penguins at street corners. Once, when we paused for a red light, a purple-nosed scarecrow weaved toward us and began swabbing the taxi's windshield with a wet rag clutched in a shaking hand. Our protesting driver shouted Italian obscenities.)

MARILYN: What is it? What's happening?

TC: He wants a tip for cleaning the window.

MARILYN (shielding her face with her purse): How horrible! I can't stand it. Give him something. Hurry. Please!

(But the taxi had already zoomed ahead, damn near knocking down the old lush. Marilyn was crying.)

I'm sick.

TC: You want to go home?

MARILYN: Everything's ruined.

TC: I'll take you home.

MARILYN: Give me a minute. I'll be okay.

(Thus we traveled on to South Street, and indeed the sight of a ferry moored there, with the Brooklyn skyline across the water and careening, cavorting seagulls white against a marine horizon streaked with thin fleecy clouds fragile as lace—this tableau soon soothed her soul.

As we got out of the taxi we saw a man with a chow on a leash, a prospective passenger, walking toward the ferry, and as we passed them, my companion stopped to pat the dog's head.)

THE MAN (firm, but not unfriendly): You shouldn't touch strange dogs. Especially chows. They might bite you.

MARILYN: Dogs never bite me. Just humans. What's his name?

THE MAN: Fu Manchu.

MARILYN (giggling): Oh, just like the movie. That's cute.

THE MAN: What's yours?

MARILYN: My name? Marilyn.

THE MAN: That's what I thought. My wife will never believe me. Can I have your autograph?

(He produced a business card and a pen; using her purse to write on, she wrote: *God Bless You—Marilyn Monroe*.)

MARILYN: Thank you.

THE MAN: Thank *you*. Wait'll I show this back at the office.

(We continued to the edge of the pier, and listened to the water sloshing against it.)

MARILYN: I used to ask for autographs. Sometimes I still do. Last year Clark Gable was sitting next to me in Chasen's, and I asked him to sign my napkin.

(Leaning against a mooring stanchion, she presented a profile: Galatea surveying unconquered distances. Breezes fluffed her hair, and her head turned toward me with an ethereal ease, as though a breeze had swiveled it.)

TC: So when do we feed the birds? I'm hungry, too. It's late, and we never had lunch.

MARILYN: Remember, I said if anybody ever asked you what I was like, what Marilyn Monroe was *really* like—well, how would you answer them? (Her tone was teaseful, mocking, yet earnest, too: she wanted an honest reply) I bet you'd tell them I was a slob. A banana split.

TC: Of course. But I'd also say . . .

(The light was leaving. She seemed to fade with it, blend with the sky and clouds, recede beyond them. I wanted to lift my voice louder than the seagulls' cries and call her back: Marilyn! Marilyn, why did everything have to turn out the way it did? Why does life have to be so fucking rotten?)

TC: I'd say . . .

MARILYN: I can't hear you.

TC: I'd say you are a beautiful child.

7

Nocturnal Turnings, or How Siamese Twins Have Sex

TC: Shucks! Wide awake! Lawsamercy, we ain't been dozed off a minute. How long we been dozed off, honey?

TC: It's two now. We tried to go to sleep around midnight, but we were too tense. So you said why don't we jack off, and I said yes, that ought to relax us, it usually does, so we jacked off and went right to sleep. Sometimes I wonder: Whatever would we do without Mother Fist and her Five Daughters? They've certainly been a friendly bunch to us through the years. Real pals.

TC: A lousy two hours. Lawd knows when we'll shut our eyes agin. An' cain't do nothin' 'bout it. Cain't haf a lil old sip of sompin 'cause dats a naw-naw. Nor none of dem snoozy pills, dat bein' also a naw-naw.

TC: Come on. Knock off the Amos 'n' Andy stuff. I'm not in the mood tonight.

TC: You're never in the mood. You didn't even want to jack off.

TC: Be fair. Have I ever denied you that? When you want to jack off, I always lie back and let you.

TC: Y'all ain't got de choice, dat's why.

TC: I much prefer solitary satisfaction to some of the duds you've forced me to endure.

TC: 'Twas up to you, we'd never have sex with anybody except each other.

TC: Yes, and think of all the misery *that* would have saved us.

TC: But then, we would never have been in love with people other than each other.

TC: Ha ha ha ha ha. Ho ho ho ho ho. "Is it an earthquake, or only a shock?

Is it the real turtle soup, or merely the mock? Is it the Lido I see, or Asbury Park?" Or is it at long last shit?

TC: You never could sing. Not even in the bathtub.

TC: You really are bitchy tonight. Maybe we could pass some time by working on your Bitch List.

TC: I wouldn't call it a *Bitch* List. It's more sort of what you might say is a Strong Dislike List.

TC: Well, who are we strongly disliking tonight? Alive. It's not interesting if they're not alive.

TC: Billy Graham
    Princess Margaret
    Billy Graham
    Princess Anne
    The Reverend Ike
    Ralph Nader
    Supreme Court Justice Byron "Whizzer" White
    Princess Z
    Werner Erhard
    The Princess Royal
    Billy Graham
    Madame Gandhi
    Masters and Johnson
    Princess Z
    Billy Graham
    CBSABCNBCNET
    Sammy Davis, Jr.
    Jerry Brown, Esq.
    Billy Graham
    Princess Z
    J. Edgar Hoover
    Werner Erhard

TC: One minute! J. Edgar Hoover is dead.

TC: No, he's not. They cloned old Johnny, and he's everywhere. They cloned Clyde Tolson, too, just so they could go on goin' steady. Cardinal Spellman, cloned version, occasionally joins them for a partouze.

TC: Why harp on Billy Graham?

TC: Billy Graham, Werner Erhard, Masters and Johnson, Princess Z—they're all full of horse manure. But the Reverend Billy is just *so* full of it.

TC: The fullest of anybody thus far?

TC: No, Princess Z is more fully packed.

TC: How so?

TC: Well, after all, she *is* a horse. It's only natural that a horse can hold more horse manure than a human, however great his capacity. Don't you remember Princess Z, that filly that ran in the fifth at Belmont? We bet on her and lost a bundle, practically our last dollar. And you said: "It's just like Uncle Bud used to say—'Never put your money on a horse named Princess.' "

TC: Uncle Bud was smart. Not like our old cousin Sook, but smart. Anyway, who do we Strongly Like? Tonight, at least.

TC: Nobody. They're all dead. Some recently, some for centuries. Lots of them are in *Père-Lachaise.* Rimbaud isn't there; but it's amazing who is. Gertrude and Alice. Proust. Sarah Bernhardt. Oscar Wilde. I wonder where Agatha Christie is buried—

TC: Sorry to interrupt, but surely there is someone alive we Strongly Like?

TC: Very difficult. A real toughie. Okay. Mrs. Richard Nixon. The Empress of Iran. Mr. William "Billy" Carter. Three victims, three saints. If Billy Graham was Billy Carter, then Billy Graham would be Billy Graham.

TC: That reminds me of a woman I sat next to at dinner the other night. She said: "Los Angeles is the perfect place to live—if you're Mexican."

TC: Heard any other good jokes lately?

TC: That wasn't a joke. That was an accurate social observation. The Mexicans in Los Angeles have their own culture, and a genuine one; the rest have zero. A city of suntanned Uriah Heeps.

However, I *was* told something that made me chuckle. Something D. D. Ryan said to Greta Garbo.

TC: Oh, yes. They live in the same building.

TC: And have for more than twenty years. Too bad they're not good friends, they'd like each other. They both have humor and conviction, but only *en passant* pleasantries have been exchanged, nothing more. A few weeks ago D.D. stepped into the elevator and found herself alone with Garbo. D.D. was costumed in her usual striking manner, and Garbo, as though she'd never truly noticed her before, said: "Why, Mrs. Ryan, you're *beautiful.*" And D.D., amused but really touched, said: "Look who's talkin'."

TC: That's all?

TC: *C'est tout.*

TC: It seems sort of pointless to me.

TC: Look, forget it. It's not important. Let's turn on the lights and get out the pens and paper. Start that magazine article. No use lying here gabbing with an oaf like you. May as well try to make a nickel.

TC: You mean that Self-Interview article where you're supposed to interview yourself? Ask your own questions and answer them?

TC: Uh-huh. But why don't you just lie there quiet while I do this? I need a rest from your evil frivolity.

TC: Okay, scumbag.

TC: Well, here goes.

Q: What frightens you?
A: Real toads in imaginary gardens.
Q: No, but in real life—

A: I'm talking about real life.

Q: Let me put it another way. What, of your own experiences, have been the most frightening?

A: Betrayals. Abandonments.

But you want something more specific? Well, my very earliest childhood memory was on the scary side. I was probably three years old, perhaps a little younger, and I was on a visit to the St. Louis Zoo, accompanied by a large black woman my mother had hired to take me there. Suddenly there was pandemonium. Children, women, grown-up men were shouting and hurrying in every direction. Two lions had escaped from their cages! Two bloodthirsty beasts were on the prowl in the park. My nurse panicked. She simply turned and ran, leaving me alone on the path. That's all I remember about it.

When I was nine years old I was bitten by a cottonmouth water moccasin. Together with some cousins, I'd gone exploring in a lonesome forest about six miles from the rural Alabama town where we lived. There was a narrow, shallow crystal river that ran through this forest. There was a huge fallen log that lay across it from bank to bank like a bridge. My cousins, balancing themselves, ran across the log, but I decided to wade the little river. Just as I was about to reach the farther bank, I saw an enormous cottonmouth moccasin swimming, slithering on the water's shadowy surface. My own mouth went dry as cotton; I was paralyzed, numb, as though my whole body had been needled with Novocaine. The snake kept sliding, winding toward me. When it was within inches of me, I spun around, and slipped on a bed of slippery creek pebbles. The cottonmouth bit me on the knee.

Turmoil. My cousins took turns carrying me piggyback until we reached a farmhouse. While the farmer hitched up his mule-drawn wagon, his only vehicle, his wife caught a number of chickens, ripped them apart alive, and applied the hot bleeding birds to my knee. "It draws out the poison," she said, and indeed the flesh of the chickens turned green. All the way into town, my cousins kept killing chickens and applying them to the wound. Once we were home, my family telephoned a hospital in Montgomery, a hundred miles away, and five hours later a doctor arrived with a snake serum. I was one sick boy, and the only good thing about it was I missed two months of school.

Once, on my way to Japan, I stayed overnight in Hawaii with Doris Duke in the extraordinary, somewhat Persian palace she had built on a cliff at Diamond Head. It was scarcely daylight when I woke up and decided to go exploring. The room in which I slept had French doors leading into a garden overlooking the ocean. I'd been strolling in the garden perhaps half a minute when a terrifying herd of Dobermans appeared, seemingly out of nowhere; they surrounded and kept me captive within the snarling circle they made. No one had warned me that each night after Miss Duke and her guests had retired, this crowd of homicidal canines was let loose to deter, and possibly punish, unwelcome intruders.

The dogs did not attempt to touch me; they just stood there, coldly staring at me and quivering in controlled rage. I was afraid to breathe; I felt if I moved my foot one scintilla, the beasts would spring forward to rip me apart. My hands were trembling; my legs, too. My hair was as wet as if I'd just stepped out of the ocean. There is nothing more exhausting than standing perfectly still, yet I managed to do it for over an hour. Rescue arrived in the form of a gardener, who, when he saw what was happening, merely whistled and clapped his hands, and all the demon dogs rushed to greet him with friendly wagging tails.

Those are instances of specific terror. Still, our real fears are the sounds of footsteps walking in the corridors of our minds, and the anxieties, the phantom floatings, they create.

Q: What are some of the things you can do?

A: I can ice-skate. I can ski. I can read upside down. I can ride a skateboard. I can hit a tossed can with a .38 revolver. I have driven a Maserati (at dawn, on a flat, lonely Texas road) at 170 mph. I can make a soufflé Furstenberg (quite a stunt: it's a cheese-and-spinach concoction that involves sinking six poached eggs into the batter before cooking; the trick is to have the egg yolks remain soft and runny when the soufflé is served). I can tap-dance. I can type sixty words a minute.

Q: And what are some of the things you can't do?

A: I can't recite the alphabet, at least not correctly or all the way through (not even under hypnosis; it's an impediment that has fascinated several psychotherapists). I am a mathematical imbecile—I can add, more or less, but I can't subtract, and I failed first-year algebra three times, even with the help of a private tutor. I can read without glasses, but I can't drive without them. I can't speak Italian, even though I lived in Italy a total of nine years. I can't make a prepared speech—it has to be spontaneous, "on the wing."

Q: Do you have a "motto"?

A: Sort of. I jotted it down in a schoolboy dairy: *I Aspire.* I don't know why I chose those particular words; they're odd, and I like the ambiguity —do I aspire to heaven or hell? Whatever the case, they have an undeniably noble ring.

Last winter I was wandering in a seacoast cemetery near Mendocino —a New England village in far Northern California, a rough place where the water is too cold to swim and where the whales go piping past. It was a lovely little cemetery, and the dates on the sea-grey-green tombstones were mostly nineteenth century; almost all of them had an inscription of some sort, something that revealed the tenant's philosophy. One read: NO COMMENT.

So I began to think what I would have inscribed on my tombstone—

except that I shall never have one, because two very gifted fortunetellers, one Haitian, the other an Indian revolutionary who lives in Moscow, have told me I will be lost at sea, though I don't know whether by accident or by choice (*comme ça,* Hart Crane). Anyway, the first inscription I thought of was: AGAINST MY BETTER JUDGMENT. Then I thought of something far more characteristic. An excuse, a phrase I use about almost any commitment: I TRIED TO GET OUT OF IT, BUT I COULDN'T.

Q: Some time ago you made your debut as a film actor (in *Murder by Death*). And?

A: I'm not an actor; I have no desire to be one. I did it as a lark; I thought it would be amusing, and it was fun, more or less, but it was also hard work: up at six and never out of the studio before seven or eight. For the most part, the critics gave me a bouquet of garlic. But I expected that; everyone did—it was what you might call an obligatory reaction. Actually, I was adequate.

Q: How do you handle the "recognition factor"?

A: It doesn't bother me a bit, and it's very useful when you want to cash a check in some strange locale. Also, it can occasionally have amusing consequences. For instance, one night I was sitting with friends at a table in a crowded Key West bar. At a nearby table, there was a mildly drunk woman with a very drunk husband. Presently, the woman approached me and asked me to sign a paper napkin. All this seemed to anger her husband; he staggered over to the table, and after unzipping his trousers and hauling out his equipment, said: "Since you're autographing things, why don't you autograph this?" The tables surrounding us had grown silent, so a great many people heard my reply, which was: "I don't know if I can autograph it, but perhaps I can *initial* it."

Ordinarily, I don't mind giving autographs. But there *is* one thing that gets my goat: without exception, every grown man who has ever asked me for an autograph in a restaurant or on an airplane has always been careful to say that he wanted it for his wife or his daughter or his girl friend, but never, *never* just for himself.

I have a friend with whom I often take long walks on city streets. Frequently, some fellow stroller will pass us, hesitate, produce a sort of is-it-or-isn't-it frown, then stop me and ask, "Are you Truman Capote?" And I'll say, "Yes, I'm Truman Capote." Whereupon my friend will scowl and shake me and shout, "For Christ's sake, George—when are you going to stop this? Some day you're going to get into serious trouble!"

Q: Do you consider conversation an art?

A: A dying one, yes. Most of the renowned conversationalists—Samuel Johnson, Oscar Wilde, Whistler, Jean Cocteau, Lady Astor, Lady Cunard, Alice Roosevelt Longworth—are monologists, not conversationalists. A conversation is a dialogue, not a monologue. That's why there are so few good conversations: due to scarcity, two intelligent talkers seldom meet. Of the list just provided, the only two I've known personally are Cocteau and Mrs. Longworth. (As for her, I take it back—she is not a solo performer; she lets you share the air.)

Among the best conversationalists I've talked with are Gore Vidal (if you're not the victim of his couth, sometimes uncouth, wit), Cecil Beaton (who, not surprisingly, expresses himself almost entirely in visual images —some very beautiful and *some* sublimely wicked). The late Danish genius, the Baroness Blixen, who wrote under the pseudonym Isak Dinesen, was, despite her withered though distinguished appearance, a true seductress, a *conversational* seductress. Ah, how fascinating she was, sitting by the fire in her beautiful house in a Danish seaside village, chain-smoking black cigarettes with silver tips, cooling her lively tongue with draughts of champagne, and luring one from this topic to that—her years as a farmer in Africa (be certain to read, if you haven't already, her autobiographical *Out of Africa,* one of this century's finest books), life under the Nazis in occupied Denmark ("They adored me. We argued, but they didn't care what I said; they didn't care what *any* woman said—it was a completely masculine society. Besides, they had no idea I was hiding Jews in my cellar, along with winter apples and cases of champagne").

Just skimming off the top of my head, other conversationalists I'd rate highly are Christopher Isherwood (no one surpasses him for total but lightly expressed candor) and the felinelike Colette. Marilyn Monroe was very amusing when she felt sufficiently relaxed and had had enough to drink. The same might be said of the lamented screen-scenarist Harry Kurnitz, an exceedingly homely gentleman who conquered men, women, and children of all classes with his verbal flights. Diana Vreeland, the eccentric Abbess of High Fashion and one-time, longtime editor of *Vogue,* is a charmer of a talker, a snake charmer.

When I was eighteen I met the person whose conversation has impressed me the most, perhaps because the person in question is the one who has most impressed me. It happened as follows:

In New York, on East Seventy-ninth Street, there is a very pleasant shelter known as the New York Society Library, and during 1942 I spent many afternoons there researching a book I intended writing but never did. Occasionally, I saw a woman there whose appearance rather mesmerized me—her eyes especially: blue, the pale brilliant cloudless blue of prairie skies. But even without this singular feature, her face was interesting—firm-jawed, handsome, a bit androgynous. Pepper-salt hair parted in the middle. Sixty-five, thereabouts. A lesbian? Well, yes.

One January day I emerged from the library into the twilight to find a heavy snowfall in progress. The lady with the blue eyes, wearing a nicely cut black coat with a sable collar, was waiting at the curb. A gloved, taxi-summoning hand was poised in the air, but there were no taxis. She looked at me and smiled and said: "Do you think a cup of hot chocolate would help? There's a Longchamps around the corner."

She ordered hot chocolate; I asked for a "very" dry martini. Half seriously, she said, "Are you old enough?"

"I've been drinking since I was fourteen. Smoking, too."

"You don't look more than fourteen now."

"I'll be nineteen next September." Then I told her a few things: that I was from New Orleans, that I'd published several short stories, that I wanted to be a writer and was working on a novel. And she wanted to know what American writers I liked. "Hawthorne, Henry James, Emily Dickinson . . ." "No, living." Ah, well, hmm, let's see: how difficult, the rivalry factor being what it is, for one contemporary author, or would-be author, to confess admiration for another. At last I said, "Not Heming-way—a really dishonest man, the closet-everything. Not Thomas Wolfe —all that purple upchuck; of course, he isn't living. Faulkner, sometimes: *Light in August.* Fitzgerald, sometimes: *Diamond as Big as the Ritz, Tender Is the Night.* I really like Willa Cather. Have you read *My Mortal Enemy*?"

With no particular expression, she said, "Actually, I wrote it."

I had seen photographs of Willa Cather—long-ago ones, made perhaps in the early twenties. Softer, homelier, less elegant than my companion. Yet I knew instantly that she *was* Willa Cather, and it was one of the *frissons* of my life. I began to babble about her books like a schoolboy— my favorites: *A Lost Lady, The Professor's House, My Ántonia.* It wasn't that I had anything in common with her as a writer. I would never have chosen for myself her sort of subject matter, or tried to emulate her style. It was just that I considered her a great artist. As good as Flaubert.

We became friends; she read my work and was always a fair and helpful judge. She was full of surprises. For one thing, she and her lifelong friend, Miss Lewis, lived in a spacious, charmingly furnished Park Avenue apart-ment—somehow, the notion of Miss Cather living in an apartment on Park Avenue seemed incongruous with her Nebraska upbringing, with the simple, rather elegiac nature of her novels. Secondly, her principal interest was not literature, but music. She went to concerts constantly, and almost all her closest friends were musical personalities, particularly Yehudi Menuhin and his sister Hepzibah.

Like all authentic conversationalists, she was an excellent listener, and when it was her turn to talk, she was never garrulous, but crisply pointed. Once she told me I was overly sensitive to criticism. The truth was that she was more sensitive to critical slights than I; any disparaging reference to her work caused a decline in spirits. When I pointed this out to her, she said: "Yes, but aren't we always seeking out our own vices in others and reprimanding them for such possessions? I'm alive. I have clay feet. Very definitely."

Q: Do you have any favorite spectator sport?

A: Fireworks. Myriad-colored sprays of evanescent designs glittering the night skies. The very best I've seen were in Japan—these Japanese masters can create fiery creatures in the air: slithering dragons, exploding cats, faces of pagan deities. Italians, Venetians especially, can explode master-works above the Grand Canal.

Q: Do you have many sexual fantasies?

A: When I do have a sexual fantasy, usually I try to transfer it into reality —sometimes successfully. However, I do often find myself drifting into erotic daydreams that remain just that: daydreams.

I remember once having a conversation on this subject with the late E. M. Forster, to my mind the finest English novelist of this century. He said that as a schoolboy sexual thoughts dominated his mind. He said: "I felt as I grew older this fever would lessen, even leave me. But that was not the case; it raged on through my twenties, and I thought: Well, surely by the time I'm forty, I will receive some release from this torment, this constant search for the perfect love object. But it was not to be; all through my forties, lust was always lurking inside my head. And then I was fifty, and then I was sixty, and nothing changed: sexual images continued to spin around my brain like figures on a carrousel. Now here I am in my *seventies,* and I'm still a prisoner of my sexual imagination. I'm stuck with it, just at an age when I can no longer do anything about it."

Q: Have you ever considered suicide?

A: Certainly. And so has everyone else, except possibly the village idiot. Soon after the suicide of the esteemed Japanese writer Yukio Mishima, whom I knew well, a biography about him was published, and to my dismay, the author quotes him as saying: "Oh yes, I think of suicide a great deal. And I know a number of people I'm certain will kill them-selves. Truman Capote, for instance." I couldn't imagine what had brought him to this conclusion. My visits with Mishima had always been jolly, very cordial. But Mishima was a sensitive, extremely intuitive man, not someone to be taken lightly. But in this matter, I think his intuition failed him; I would never have the courage to do what he did (he had a friend decapitate him with a sword). Anyway, as I've said somewhere before, most people who take their own lives do so because they really want to kill someone else—a philandering husband, an unfaithful lover, a treacherous friend—but they haven't the guts to do it, so they kill themselves instead. Not me; anyone who had worked me into that kind of a position would find himself looking down the barrel of a shotgun.

Q: Do you believe in God, or at any rate, some higher power?

A: I believe in an afterlife. That is to say, I'm sympathetic to the notion of reincarnation.

Q: In your own afterlife, how would you like to be reincarnated?

A: As a bird—preferably a buzzard. A buzzard doesn't have to bother about his appearance or ability to beguile and please; he doesn't have to put on airs. Nobody's going to like him anyway; he is ugly, unwanted, unwelcome everywhere. There's a lot to be said for the sort of freedom that allows. On the other hand, I wouldn't mind being a sea turtle. They can roam the land, and they know the secrets of the ocean's depths. Also, they're long-lived, and their hooded eyes accumulate much wisdom.

Q: If you could be granted one wish, what would it be?

A: To wake up one morning and feel that I was at last a grown-up person, emptied of resentment, vengeful thoughts, and other wasteful, childish emotions. To find myself, in other words, an adult.

TC: Are you still awake?

TC: Somewhat bored, but still awake. How can I sleep when you're not asleep?

TC: And what do you think of what I've written here? So far?

TC: Wellll . . . since you *ask.* I'd say Billy Grahamcrackers isn't the only one familiar with horse manure.

TC: Bitch, bitch, bitch. Moan and bitch. That's all you ever do. Never a kind word.

TC: Oh, I didn't mean there's anything *very* wrong. Just a few things here and there. Trifles. I mean, perhaps you're not as honest as you pretend to me.

TC: I don't pretend to be honest. I *am* honest.

TC: Sorry. I didn't mean to fart. It wasn't a comment, just an accident.

TC: It was a diversionary tactic. You call me dishonest, compare me to Billy Graham, for Christ's sake, and now you're trying to weasel out of it. Speak up. What have I written here that's dishonest?

TC: Nothing. Trifles. Like that business about the movie. Did it for a lark, eh? You did it for the moola—and to satisfy that clown side of you that's so exasperating. Get rid of that guy. He's a jerk.

TC: Oh, I don't know. He's unpredictable, but I've got a soft spot for him. He's part of me—same as you. And what are some of these other trifles?

TC: The next thing—well, it's not a trifle. It's how you answered the question: Do you believe in God? And you skipped right by it. Said something about an afterlife, reincarnation, coming back as a buzzard. I've got news for you, buddy, you won't have to wait for reincarnation to be treated like a buzzard; plenty of folks are doing it already. Multitudes. But that's not what's so phony about your answer. It's the fact that you don't come right out and say that you *do* believe in God. I've heard you, cool as a cucumber, confess things that would make a baboon blush blue, and yet you won't admit that you believe in God. What is it? Are you afraid of being called a Reborn Christian, a Jesus Freak?

TC: It's not that simple. I did believe in God. And then I didn't. Remember when we were very little and used to go way out in the woods with our dog

Queenie and old Cousin Sook? We hunted for wildflowers, wild asparagus. We caught butterflies and let them loose. We caught perch and threw them back in the creek. Sometimes we found giant toadstools, and Sook told us that was where the elves lived, under the beautiful toadstools. She told us the Lord had arranged for them to live there just as He had arranged for everything we saw. The good and the bad. The ants and the mosquitoes and the rattlesnakes, every leaf, the sun in the sky, the old moon and the new moon, rainy days. And we believed her.

But then things happened to spoil that faith. First it was church and itching all over listening to some ignorant redneck preacher shoot his mouth off; then it was all those boarding schools and going to chapel every damn morning. And the Bible itself—nobody with any sense could believe what it asked you to believe. Where were the toadstools? Where were the moons? And at last life, plain living, took away the memories of whatever faith still lingered. I'm not the worst person that's crossed my path, not by a considerable distance, but I've committed some serious sins, deliberate cruelty among them; and it didn't bother me one whit, I never gave it a thought. Until I had to. When the rain started to fall, it was a hard black rain, and it just kept on falling. So I started to think about God again.

I thought about St. Julian. About Flaubert's story *St. Julien, L'Hospitalier*. It had been so long since I'd read that story, and where I was, in a sanitarium far distant from libraries, I couldn't get a copy. But I remembered (at least I thought this was more or less the way it went) that as a child Julian loved to wander in the forests and loved all animals and living things. He lived on a great estate, and his parents worshipped him; they wanted him to have everything in the world. His father bought him the finest horses, bows and arrows, and taught him to hunt. To kill the very animals he had loved so much. And that was too bad, because Julian discovered that he liked to kill. He was only happy after a day of the bloodiest slaughter. The murdering of beasts and birds became a mania, and after first admiring his skill, his neighbors loathed and feared him for his bloodlust.

Now there's a part of the story that was pretty vague in my head. Anyway, somehow or other Julian killed his mother and father. A hunting accident? Something like that, something terrible. He became a pariah and a penitent. He wandered the world barefoot and in rags, seeking forgiveness. He grew old and ill. One cold night he was waiting by a river for a boatman to row him across. Maybe it was the River Styx? Because Julian was dying. While he waited, a hideous old man appeared. He was a leper, and his eyes were running sores, his mouth rotting and foul. Julian didn't know it, but this repulsive evil-looking old man was God. And God tested him to see if all his sufferings had truly changed Julian's savage heart. He told Julian He was cold, and asked to share his blanket, and Julian did; then the leper wanted Julian to embrace Him, and Julian did; then He made a final request—He asked Julian to kiss His diseased and rotting lips. Julian did. Whereupon Julian and the old leper, who was suddenly transformed into a radiant shining vision, ascended together to heaven. And so it was that Julian became St. Julian.

So there I was in the rain, and the harder it fell the more I thought about Julian. I prayed that I would have the luck to hold a leper in my arms. And that's when I began to believe in God again, and understand that Sook was right: that everything was His design, the old moon and the new moon, the hard rain falling, and if only I would ask Him to help me, He would.

TC: And has He?

TC: Yes. More and more. But I'm not a saint yet. I'm an alcoholic. I'm a drug addict. I'm homosexual. I'm a genius. Of course, I could be all four of these dubious things and still be a saint. But I shonuf ain't no saint yet, nawsuh.

TC: Well, Rome wasn't built in a day. Now let's knock it off and try for some shut-eye.

TC: But first let's say a prayer. Let's say our *old* prayer. The one we used to say when we were real little and slept in the same bed with Sook and Queenie, with the quilts piled on top of us because the house was so big and cold.

TC: Our old prayer? Okay.

TC and TC: Now I lay me down to sleep, I pray the Lord my soul to keep. And if I should die before I wake, I pray the Lord my soul to take. Amen.

TC: Goodnight.

TC: Goodnight.

TC: I love you.

TC: I love you, too.

TC: You'd better. Because when you get right down to it, all we've got is each other. Alone. To the grave. And that's the tragedy, isn't it?

TC: You forget. We have God, too.

TC: Yes. We have God.

TC: Zzzzzzz

TC: Zzzzzzzzz

TC and TC: Zzzzzzzzzzz